S

‖‖‖ ‖‖‖‖‖ ‖ ‖‖‖ ‖‖‖‖‖‖‖‖ ‖ ‖‖
W9-CBM-906

THESE NAMELESS THINGS

Center Point
Large Print

Also by Shawn Smucker and available from Center Point Large Print:

Light from Distant Stars

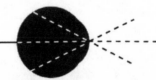

This Large Print Book carries the Seal of Approval of N.A.V.H.

THESE NAMELESS THINGS

SHAWN SMUCKER

CENTER POINT LARGE PRINT
THORNDIKE, MAINE

This Center Point Large Print edition
is published in the year 2020 by arrangement with
Revell, a division of Baker Publishing Group.

The text of this Large Print edition is unabridged.
In other aspects, this book may vary
from the original edition.
Printed in the United States of America
on permanent paper.
Set in 16-point Times New Roman type.

ISBN: 978-1-64358-735-6

The Library of Congress has cataloged this record
under Library of Congress Control Number: 2020943866

To Priscilla

"The undiscovered country,
        from whose bourn
No traveler returns, puzzles the will."
                        Shakespeare, *Hamlet*

"Why do we let our guilt consume us so?"
        Dante Alighieri, *The Divine Comedy*

"Be grateful for whoever comes,
because each has been sent as a guide
        from beyond."
                        Rumi

THESE
NAMELESS
THINGS

PROLOGUE

A Confession

We move in a loose group, winding through the trees. We are more people than you can even imagine, yet there is hardly a word spoken. We smell like exhaustion, like miles piled on top of miles, like time when it has already run out. Yet somehow we also sound like hope, like fresh water washing through the reeds. We discreetly share food with each other, nearly all of us strangers, nodding politely, and in spite of our condition, we cannot keep the inexplicable hope from showing in our eyes.

This is our first day out from under the shadow of the mountain. Which sounds exactly like something he would have said in that deep, rich voice of his, if he was here with us. And he would have smiled—how happy he would have been, saying those words!

Then he would have laughed, and the thought of him laughing is too much for me right now. It brings up an ache that makes it hard to breathe. I shake my head and try to laugh it off, but my grin falters, and any kind of sound I might make lodges somewhere in my throat.

It's my fault he's not with us. There's no way around it.

How could I let him go back on his own?

It's more an accusation than a question, and now the aching wells up behind my eyes. I squeeze them shut. I stop walking and think about turning around. It's the guilt that threatens to consume me.

The path goes up and up and up, and everyone is so tired, but the old fears are fresh enough to keep us walking, to keep us moving through this heavy weariness. I reluctantly rejoin the movement up the mountain. Nearly everyone stares at the ground in front of their feet. Maybe that's all that matters right now. One step after the other. Moving farther up. Moving farther in, away from her. Hoping she won't find us, won't convince us to go back.

Up ahead and to the left, I notice that the trees clear along the edge of the cliff, and I find myself walking faster, faster, stumbling over my own feet, pushing between this person and that person, mumbling my apologies, my voice strange in the voiceless woods. I get to the clearing and it is what I hoped it would be: an overlook. A cold wind blows up from the valley, rushes through that open space, agitating the leaves behind me into the wild rustling sound of secrets. I climb a kind of stone platform, and the rock is gritty under my fingers. There's no snow up here, but the rock is cold. Everything feels present and real.

Have you ever, for a flash of time, understood the significance of being? The miracle of existing? That's what I feel now, climbing up onto the ledge: the particular roughness of the rocks under my knees, the chill of the wind on my face. The unique expression of my existence, here, as I stand.

I look out over that huge expanse of miles that all of us walked through, and I scan the valley. I hold one hand up, shield my eyes from the glare of those bright clouds, and hope to see nothing out there except empty plains.

At first I'm relieved and my shoulders relax because all I see is the undulating ground stretching to the west, as far as the horizon. The wind continues to whip up around me, and I draw my arms closer to my chest, duck my chin down, and try to find warmth in my body. It is there somewhere inside of me, that warmth, that fire. I can sense the rustling of all the people hiking, moving up the mountain behind me. I can feel them glancing at my back as they pass, taking in my silhouette on the overlook, probably wondering why I would stop, why I would look back. This makes me angry. I want to turn and answer them, answer all of their unasked questions.

I knew him.

I loved him.

Do you have any idea what our freedom cost?

But I keep looking out over the plains, and finally I see something like two ants wandering along a dusty pile. I sigh. All the way down there in the valley, where we began the climb up this mountain, through the trees, those two small specks walk away, walk west. Their progress is barely visible, but there is nothing to stop them, not as far as the eye can see. We will soon be separated by this great chasm. Everything has fallen into a stark, dazzling white, the light glaring off endless miles of glittering frost. I can smell snow, but none is falling.

He is going with her.

I hoped that he might be among the last of the crowd, that he could possibly be tagging along at the back, that he would come up and surprise me. We would hug and I would laugh out loud— my first real laugh in a long time—and he would explain how he got out of going back and that all the wrong I had done was magically undone.

But he couldn't do it. He couldn't reverse my mistakes, couldn't easily untie my deceptions, and the only option was for someone to go back. He is doing it. I strain my eyes toward the horizon, but even from that height, I can't see the mountain we came from, the one whose shadow we have finally escaped. I don't think I'd want to see it, but I search that far-off horizon anyway.

"Do you see him?" she asks, walking up behind me. Not long ago, she would have wrapped her arms around my body, moved in close and held me. I would have felt her warmth against my back. But not now. Not after everything that has happened.

I close my eyes, imagining. I shiver and nod. "I can't believe he has to go back." Unspoken are the words, *It's my fault.*

We stand there in those words, the wind whipping them around us, catching on them, sailing away with them. She doesn't offer any kind of consolation.

"It was here all along," she says, a lining of amazement in her voice. "This mountain was here, waiting for us."

"Are you . . ." I begin, then start over. My voice is hoarse, and I clear it against the dry, cold air. "Do you . . . remember?"

"Everything. It's all coming back to me."

"Even before?"

"Even before."

"Me too," I whisper.

How is it that a mind can contain so many memories? Where does it all fit? Into what nooks and crannies do we place these recollections of love and sadness, horror and joy? Into what tiny space of our minds do we put a person we met long ago, or a disappointment, or a lie? And where do memories go when we forget, and how

15

is it that they can come rushing back, unbidden?

I am embarrassed by what I did, the choices I made. There are things I would rather forget, but because I can think of nothing else to say, a confession emerges: "I'm such a liar. You know that by now, right? How many things I said that weren't true?"

She is still as a fence post. It almost seems like she's holding her breath.

"You know, I would lie for the fun of it," I whisper, "even when there was nothing in it. Just because. I don't even know why. What's wrong with a person who lies for no reason?"

I don't realize she is crying until I hear her try to stifle a sob, like a hiccup. She moves closer but we're still not touching, and we remain there for a time, watching the two people down on the plain. We cry together. She sighs a trembling sigh, and when she speaks I can tell she is trying to lift our spirits.

"The rumor coming back from the front is that the higher you go, the warmer it gets."

"Then we should keep walking," I say, but I don't move. A great silence falls on us as the last people pass by behind us. He is not among them. I knew he wouldn't be, was positive of this after seeing the two far-off figures walking away, but I had still allowed myself to hope.

"There they go." She steps away, as if she can't stay too close or she'll give in to old impulses like hugging me or pulling me close. "He saved all of us," she says, and I can hear the tears in her voice. "And now he's going back."

I nod again, the tears flowing. I wipe them away hastily with the back of my hand. They're embarrassing, those tears. They make me feel small.

"Dan," she says. "It's time. He'll find her, and he'll follow us over."

I look over at her for the first time since she came up behind me. "Will he? Will he find her? Will he find us?"

She doesn't answer.

"Will he find me?" I ask, my voice tiny and quivering.

Wordlessly, we climb down the rock and turn toward the top of this new mountain, this fresh start, this beginning. We can see the tail end of the procession of people moving up the trail. We will soon be back among them, or maybe we'll stay back a bit, find our own pace.

"I wonder," I say quietly.

"Wonder?" she asks, falling into step beside me. I want to take her hand again, but those days are long gone. "Wonder what?"

My response is a whisper. I can't imagine she even hears me. "Can he really cross from there to us? Or is he lost? Forever?"

The breeze snatches my words and throws them out into the void, but she hears them. And she smiles. "He'll find us."

So childlike. So trusting. I want to question her. I want to raise my flag of doubt, but before I can, she says it again.

"He'll find us."

PART ONE

1 The Lie

Months before I stood on that overlook and searched for any sight of him, on the opposite side of the endless plains and under the shadow of the western mountain, the three of us laughed together—Miho and Abe and me. Miho was nearly crying, she was laughing so hard, shaking her head and trying to stop but then starting right up again, her body bobbing up and down. She waved a weak hand at us: *Stop it!* Abe and I grinned at each other, huge, sappy grins. We didn't know what to do in the face of such laughter. When she did that, when she leaned back and laughed like that, I could sit and watch her for days. I felt lighter in that moment than I had in a long time, released, like a balloon untied and rising.

Miho caught her breath and sighed, and I was filled with something close to pure joy. What were we laughing about? I don't know. I can't remember, because there was a pause, and Abe said those three words, and everything we were laughing about melted away. They stared at me to see how I would handle the news, Abe with his steady gaze trained on my face, and Miho, her eyes dancing nervously from me to the sky to the plains and back to me again. I realized that's why they had come up to my house: to share this news, to see how I would take it, and to talk me off the ledge if needed.

Mary is leaving.

We ended up sitting against the back wall of my house. I went from joyful to exhausted. We looked out over the plains, absorbing the gentle breeze, not saying a word. There was the smell of fresh green grass and wet earth coming toward us from off in the distance, and rain on the way. The breeze was cool and weightless, but I felt the heaviness of nameless things.

The horizon seemed impossibly far off, the clouds low, and I experienced a kind of dizziness, a spinning, an inability to determine what was up and what was down, and then a low-grade panic. Air was suddenly in short supply, and I wondered if this was what it was like to hyperventilate. I rested my head against the wall and stared into the slits of blue sky peeking through. But that didn't help, so I closed my eyes completely.

"Are you sure, Abe?" I asked, and even though my question was aimed at him, I hoped Miho would chime in and tell me it wasn't true, it was all just a joke. I watched a small speck drift across the red horizon inside my eyelids.

Please, Miho, I thought. *Tell me it's not true.*

"She'd like to leave tonight," Abe admitted.

The deep, quiet sound of his voice stayed with me even when he stopped talking. His voice was like the earth, solid beneath the long, soft grass. If Mary left, would everyone else leave too? Even Miho? Even Abe? The thought of living there in town alone made me sick. I couldn't keep waiting, not by myself.

"We haven't lost anyone for years," I said. "Why is she leaving now?"

"We're not losing her, Dan," Miho said, the tiniest exasperation in her voice. "Everyone will leave sooner or later. You know that. There's nothing lost. Everyone will leave, eventually."

She paused, and I could tell she was trying to decide if she should keep talking.

"Even you," she added.

I opened my eyes and looked at her, took in her short, black-rooted, dyed-blonde hair rustling in the wind. Her eyes softened when our gazes met, and she surrendered a small smile that showed only at the corners of her mouth and the slopes of her temples. It was an expression as far removed from the minutes-ago mirth as I could imagine, but it was full of compassion. She had a triangle tattoo below the corner of one eye, like a tear. Another, much larger swirling tattoo filled with lines and shapes and blocks made its way up her neck, touched her jaw below her ear, extended up along her temple, and edged her hairline like a kind of border.

I remembered when she had received those tattoos, and why—she had been so sad, trying to cover up the marks of what had happened to her in the mountain. We had all tried to cover up our scars, most of us through distraction or busyness or work or fun. Some of us used tattoos. Some of us, eventually, tried to escape the horror by simply leaving, walking east. I had held her hand while Lou filled in the dark lines. How tightly she had squeezed my fingers, until the tattoo was hurting both of us. Lou had left town soon after that, headed east over the plains. No more tattoos, not after he was gone.

That was long ago.

"It's only Mary St. Clair," she said quietly. "It's only Mary." As if to say, *It's not me. I'm not leaving you.*

Abe gave her a sideways glance, a kind of reproach, but he didn't say a word.

Maybe today it's "only" Mary, but who will it be tomorrow? There are only nine of us left in town. Eight after Mary goes. What will I do when everyone is gone?

But I didn't have to say anything. They knew what I was thinking. They knew my concerns.

"Maybe we should leave with her?" Miho suggested, her voice timid as the breeze, her long, slender fingers finding mine in the depths of the cool grass. "Maybe now is the time?"

"You can go anytime you want," I said, and

24

the words escaped without emotion. She didn't remove her hand from mine, but I felt her stiffen. Why was I always pushing her away?

"Dan," Abe said, and he could have gone a thousand different ways.

That wasn't a nice thing to say.

You will have to go sometime too.

Your brother is never coming over that mountain.

But he said none of those things. He was the kindest man I knew, the kindest I had ever known.

"Dan," he started again, "I am not leaving without you. Do you hear me? Miho is not leaving without you. You know that. We'll wait. We're in no hurry. Mary's leaving doesn't change any of that."

I did know it, but in the way you can know something with your head and not your heart, the way you can know a calculation is correct but still feel you've not done the work quite right. I was always second-guessing myself, always wondering why.

The breeze shifted direction, now blowing out into the plains, away from us, and it was suddenly cooler. There was an ominous feeling in the dropping temperature, the shifting of the wind. I might have suspected there was more change on the way than simply Mary's leaving.

I should have seen it coming.

The wind was trying to tell me.

The air charged around the house in gusting swirls. The long grass panicked, spinning, and out on the plains it billowed and rolled like waves in the sea, flashing white when it bent over and dark green when it stood up again. The movement was hypnotic.

I wanted to say something to ease the tension, something like, "I'm sorry" or "I know" or "Of course, you're right." I didn't want to spoil Mary's upcoming departure, and I didn't want her leaving to change anything about us or the village. It had been a long time since anyone left—I had begun to believe no one else would go, that the nine of us would spend eternity here, together.

I gently pulled my hand out from under Miho's and stood up. I stared out at the plains again, and the breeze burst around the house, this time colder and carrying drizzle. I pushed my hand back through my wet hair and it stood on end. I imagined I was a wild man setting out. The wind ripped at my shirt.

"What if he never comes over the mountain, Abe?" My voice felt empty, and the two of them felt far away. "What if I wait and wait, and he never comes?"

It was a hard question, one I ignored most days. But not on that day, and the question tied the knot inside of me tighter and tighter until my breath was hard to find.

"Did I ever tell you the one memory I still have of him, from when we were boys?" I asked. I had, many times. But they didn't stop me. "Adam and I were standing beside the creek bank, looking out over the water. The creek was swollen and fast after days of spring rain. He started climbing one of the trees—you know, the kind with branches that hung out over the water? And I pleaded with him to come down. But he didn't listen. I don't think he ever listened to me."

I stopped, and I sensed it approaching again, the anxiety.

"He kept climbing out over the water, grinning back at me the whole time, laughing at my concern. I have a feeling he did that often. And then the branch he was on broke, and he disappeared down into the water, branch and all, and was swept away." My voice trailed off. "I ran along the creek, screaming, 'Adam! Adam!' I tripped over rocks, branches scratching my face. He popped up to the surface, still holding on to the broken branch. When I saw him, I shouted his name even louder, and when he heard me, he looked over at me. And he grinned. He was being swept away, and he was still grinning."

I shook my head in amazement. "I remember pulling him to shore, pulling the branch and him and everything else. I never knew I could be that strong. I pulled him up out of the water and we sat there together, soaking wet. He was breathing hard, and I was crying and angry and relieved. I didn't know what to say to him. He scared me so bad. I think he did that a lot too. I don't know. It's hard to tell, but that's how it feels."

But it was all a lie.

I didn't have any memories of my brother apart from knowing he existed. None of us in town remembered anything of consequence about our lives before the horror of the mountain. I mean, we each had a few minor facts to lean on, maybe the existence of a family member or two, the image of a place, but the stories of our lives had been erased from our minds by what had happened to us in that forsaken range.

Abe had tears in his eyes. "The three of us, we've been here for a long time." His old voice wavered. Miho made a sound of assent, a quiet sound, and Abe continued. "I was here long before either of you escaped to this place. I've seen a lot of people come over that mountain, and I've seen a lot of people leave us, head east over the plains. This village will be here as long as you need it to be." He grunted, as if completely convinced by what he had just said.

"What if no one's left in the mountain?" I asked, agitated and shaken. "What if Adam already came over and I missed him? Or what if he's still in there but he can't leave on his own? What if they won't let him leave?"

They. I shuddered at the thought of the ones

who had kept us there, flinched involuntarily as if I could feel it all again.

Miho reached up and moved her finger in a line along the tattoo on her forehead. "We're not leaving without you," she insisted. "Not even if it's only the three of us left here. Abe and I, we'll wait with you."

I turned a short circle, not knowing where to walk. We were all getting good and wet now in the rain. I felt like I was losing my mind. Maybe sleep would help.

"Are you sure Mary's going to go through with it?" I asked. "It's a long walk. Maybe she'll change her mind."

Abe nodded. "She's leaving tonight."

"In the rain?" I asked.

"I expect if the storm comes, she'll wait until tomorrow. Don't blame her, Dan. It's her time. When it's time, it's time."

I bit my lip, nodded. A round of thunder rolled down toward us from the mountain. "And if it's still raining tomorrow evening?" I asked, feeling petulant and angry. I wanted to argue with someone. I wanted to irritate everyone close to me. I knew it wasn't Abe's fault, but I had to take my disappointment out on someone.

"She's leaving," Miho said in a soothing tone. "I talked to her too, after Abe told me. I went to her house, Dan. Trust me. She's leaving. All her stuff is bundled up and ready. Tonight, or tomorrow night, or the next. As soon as the weather's good, she's walking."

I nodded curtly. I didn't want to talk about it anymore. "Feels like the rain's going to get heavy," I said, and they glanced at each other, took the hint.

Abe stood slowly, the way an older man stands when he has been sitting on the ground for too long—a stiff unfolding, a pause when it appeared for a moment that he might sit back down. But he pushed through, stood up, and Miho rose beside him with ease.

"Shall we take our leave, my lord?" she asked Abe in a formal voice with an unrecognizable accent, as if she was a royal lady from some bygone era. She waved her arms in a flourish and bowed in his direction, extending one of her pale hands to him.

I loved her for this, her ability to lighten the mood. I smiled, and she caught my gaze out of the corner of her eye and winked at me.

Abe grinned, sheepish. His black skin had a matte finish to it, a flat sort of richness, and his smile pulled all of that back, stretched it so that he was young again. His face became bright white teeth and flashing eyes, and I could see for a moment what he had probably been like as a boy: mischievous, foolhardy. But not as lovely as he was in that moment. That would not have been possible. What had I ever done to deserve his lavish friendship?

"Yes, ma'am," he said in his low voice.

On the other side of the house, the side that faced the mountain, thunder trembled again, louder, with sharp edges and a crackling that lingered and spread its fingers through the air. Abe took Miho's arm and I felt a small pang of jealousy, even though it was Abe and it was Miho and I had nothing to be jealous about. I followed them around the corner of the house to the front, and the breeze was a chilled wind that raced down the mountainside.

The mountain. There it was, rising only a few hundred yards from the front of my house, tall and terrible and crowned with a realm of dark gray clouds that boiled nearly green around the edges. There was snow up at the peaks—I knew this not because I could see it, but because I knew those mountains the same way I knew my own face in a mirror. It was a constant in my dreams, my nightmares. The shadow of it haunted each of our faces, in the shallow space under our eyes or the dark of our mouths when they hung open while we slept. I felt, not for the first time, that the mountain might collapse on all of us.

I wondered how many remained in that pit in the mountain, how many at that moment were tortured or chased, how many were fleeing. How many were hungry and hiding and moving through the shadows, trying to find their way out, trying to find their way to us.

I glanced over toward the sliver of the canyon that split the face of one of the cliffs, two hundred yards up the hill from my house, the only break in that long line of sheer rock and crumbling rubble. The only way through. I lost myself staring up at the mountain, thinking about that thin canyon, the only way.

When I finally turned to say goodbye to Miho and Abe, they were halfway down the hill, clinging to each other. There was a long gap between my house and the group of houses that made up the rest of the town. The narrow, grassy road we called the greenway traveled from the mouth of the canyon, passed by where I stood, and meandered down to the forty or fifty houses scattered like seeds, mostly empty. Once upon a time, that green path comforted regular arrivals from the other side of the mountain, used so often by those escaping that the grass had been flattened and there had been bare patches, streaking paths of brown. But now the greenway had grown thick and lush, used only by the few of us who still lived here.

"Goodbye!" I shouted, regretting how I had turned the visit sour. They had only wanted to let me know what was happening, and I had made them feel bad. I lived in perpetual guilt about one thing or another.

They disregarded the rain—it was warm and easy to idle through. Miho waved without looking, her hair wet and flat against her head. But Abe turned halfway around, lifted his free arm, and smiled at me. It was a mischievous grin, and I could tell he liked being escorted down the greenway by a beautiful woman.

His face grew serious. His voice barely reached me before being blown back away from the mountain and swept out over the plains.

"Better get inside!" he shouted. "There's a storm comin'!"

2 Through Me, the Way

Lightning struck and I flinched. The rain came down in hard pellets, but I kept watching Abe and Miho as they drifted away. I waited until they disappeared into town before I walked inside my house, dripping wet. The sound of the storm was a steady roar on the cedar shingles above me, but the stone walls, silent and still, filled me with a sense of safety. I didn't light any lamps, and the gray afternoon filtered in through the windows.

There was a small open area inside the front door of my house. To the left, a fireplace along the outside wall. To the right was a rather long, galley-style kitchen, and at the end of it a narrow space where I ate and wrote and spent time thinking. The wide double doors that faced out the back were open, but they were sheltered by the eaves of the house so the water wasn't coming in. I stared at the plains sweeping away in a graceful downhill for a long, long way, covered in a dense curtain of rain that hit the ground before rising in a ghostly mist.

I went into my bedroom, the only separate space in the house, and changed into dry clothes. I tried to think of other things, but my mind kept coming back around to the conversation I had with Abe and Miho.

Mary was leaving.

Mary was leaving.

Mary was leaving.

After she left, it would only be Abe and Miho and me, plus Miss B, John, Misha, Circe, Po . . . was that everyone? I ran through the names again in my mind as I walked to where my desk was pushed up under the large window facing the mountain. I thought back through a handful of the people who had left a long time ago, and it filled me with a deep melancholy.

I sat there at my desk and watched the rain run in rivulets down the glass, pooling above each mullion, dripping down to the next pane. The wind came and went, rattling the wooden frames. Lightning flashed and thunder followed. It was a good afternoon to be alone.

I pulled one of my many journals from the back corner of the desk. I picked up a pen and played with it, ran it over my fingers, took off the cap and put it back on again. It was still dark in the house except for the gray light, and I didn't write anything. I thought of my brother. I wondered where he was in that moment, if it was raining on him too, in the mountain. I wondered if he was alone. I hoped he was alone. I couldn't remember much from my time there, but I did remember wanting solitude, and the terror that came when those who were in charge paid you any attention.

My house was so close to the mountain that when I was inside, I could barely see the top of the steep range through the windows. My eyes drifted over to the left, to the mouth of the canyon, the place from which all of us had emerged at some point.

And I saw something move.

I stood, stared harder through the rain. What was it? Could it be . . . someone was coming out of the mountain? I leaned closer to the glass, held my breath, willed the rain to stop.

There, I saw the movement again.

A hunched form stooped and leaned against one of the last boulders barely outside the canyon. They stopped right beside the wooden sign someone had posted next to the canyon opening a long, long time ago. I had read it many times, because I often walked to the canyon mouth and willed my brother to appear.

> THROUGH ME THE WAY
> INTO THE SUFFERING CITY
> THROUGH ME THE WAY
> TO THE ETERNAL PAIN
> THROUGH ME THE WAY
> THAT RUNS AMONG THE LOST

And then a few lines that were no longer legible, faded as they were, followed by one final line at the bottom:

Why would anyone ever enter there? Why would anyone ever go back?

The person who had just come through the canyon tried to take a step forward, but they tripped, fell onto all fours. They crawled a few feet and lay down in the rain.

Could it be Adam? A flutter of hope tried to rise in me, but I shoved it down. I stood, willed the person to keep coming, but I didn't move from my spot. It wasn't worth trying to help them yet—they had to find their own way at first, like a newborn calf finding its footing. I remembered coming through that gap and seeing the plains and the small stone houses and feeling like I could finally breathe again. I had wept and cried in agony and crawled down the grassy path when I could no longer walk. Abe had welcomed me.

Yes, it had been Abe. The memory came up from some deep place. It had been Abe. I would tell him that the next time I saw him, that I remembered it had been him welcoming me, helping me down from the canyon to his own house in the village.

This strange, unexpected person crawled down the greenway, and I could see now that the form was a woman. A stabbing sense of sadness moved through me—*This is not my brother*—and

I no longer held my breath. She was all knobby bones and stretched, naked skin, typical of those who came out. There was so little food in the mountain, and no spare clothes were ever handed out, at least not that I remembered. She was covered only by her own long black hair draping over her torso. She got to her feet, shaking. She walked like a toddler, one unsteady foot in front of the other, and came closer. Closer. After what seemed like an eternity, she reached the part of the greenway that ran directly in front of my house.

She stopped.

She was a pillar of pale skin and jet-black hair, and I couldn't see her face. She turned off the grassy lane toward my front door, wobbling with each step, and disappeared into that area close to the front door that I couldn't see through the window. I heard a weak knock.

It had been so long since someone had come out of the mountain. I hesitated.

I knew I should immediately lead her down to Abe's house—this was my main responsibility in the village, to keep watch for refugees who came down out of the mountain. Abe could assess her, help her decide what to do next, where to go, where to live if she wanted to stay. But all of that came later. First, I needed to take her to Abe.

But I felt a hesitancy I had never felt before, and it was strange, this reluctance. It scared me.

She needed to go to Abe. So why did I want to keep her at the house with me? Where was this hesitation coming from?

I opened the door with a shaking hand, and the roaring sound of the rain surrounded me through both the front and back doors. Small spits of it swirled into the shadows, small as the eye of a needle, then rose back up in the confused air. And there she was, waiting, her arms hanging helplessly at her sides. Thick black hair draped over her upper half. She raised her arms and clutched her sides, shivering, trying to cover herself. I noticed that the water where it left her feet was tinted red, blood still washing off.

"Come in, please," I said quietly. A subtle terror rose in me, and confusion beside it. Why was I inviting her in? Where did those words come from?

And why was I afraid of this helpless woman?

I should have been walking her down to Abe's, rain or no rain. But I turned and grabbed a small blanket from the rocking chair, moved toward her, and offered it to her. She shrank from my approach, seemed to be as scared of me as I was unsettled by her. As the blanket came to rest around her shoulders, her head tilted back, one hand pushed a part in the curtain of her hair, and she looked through. Her irises were dark like unlit tunnels, and the whites of her eyes were bloodshot, streaked with lightning-shaped capillaries. There were cuts on her face, red and swollen so that I couldn't easily recognize her features. She shivered, not the gentle movement of someone slightly cold, but the deep, convulsive shuddering of someone hypothermic. Her knees locked and unlocked, jerking her body this way and that like a marionette in an unwitting dance.

She opened her mouth to speak. I wanted to help her, but it was important that I let her process this new place. When I had first started welcoming people from the other side, I tried too hard to make it easy on them, and they fought me or balked from the help I offered. I learned to wait. I shouldn't have given her the blanket— even that small interference could have caused her to veer into hysterics—but she had seemed so cold and disoriented by her own nakedness. Still, I should have waited. I knew this, even now, but I couldn't take the blanket back from her.

Mary St. Clair. I remembered again that she was leaving, and I remembered when it had been her crawling down the grassy lane, the first words she said, how her name tripped its way out from between cracked lips, how her nose bled down into her mouth as she stuttered, "Mmm . . . Mmm . . . Mary. Mary Say-Say-Say. Mary Say-Saint. Clair."

I'd always had a soft spot for Mary.

But this woman couldn't even speak, and my fear died a little inside of me. Sounds simply wouldn't come out. She closed her mouth and stared hard at the ground, then met my gaze again and opened her lips. I found myself nodding slightly, coaxing her to speak. It was like watching a baby chick break out of its own egg. I wanted to reach in and help, but it wasn't time. Not yet.

"Go ahead," I whispered, not able to help myself. I reached out and touched her elbow.

That's when I blacked out.

Huge boulders sit along the walls of a gorge. Unrest fills the space, along with crushed rocks and sparse bits of crabgrass and tall cedars that are nothing more than spindly trunks sprouting dead, snapped-off branches. They stretch up forty, fifty, sixty feet to the top of the gorge where green needles dust their uppermost limbs. Through all of this, a woman comes walking, the same dark-haired woman I welcomed into my house. She's in pain. A lot of pain.

She looks broken, like the stones. She holds herself in a perpetual hug as she walks, her forearms self-consciously covering her chest. Her long black hair falls down all around her naked form, covering her arms and back, tangled and matted with something that looks like tar or dried blood. Because her hair is so long and thick, she almost looks armless.

A small dove watches the stumbling woman's

progress, hopping along the top of the gorge. It flies ahead of her, following each of her steps with interest, its head cocked to one side or the other. Gradually she passes under the gaze of the bird and walks farther ahead, only for the bird to dance along the top of the gorge, catching up. But as the woman approaches the opening where the gorge spills out into the valley, out from the mountain, the dove suddenly stops, pecks two or three times at a red vein in a silver rock, then flies away, disappearing in the cliffs.

The black-haired woman limps out through a fracture in the mountain, and as she turns the corner, finally coming out from the canyon, there is the village and a home. My village. My home. This is the woman who came to my house, and I am watching her approach, but from the canyon.

What is going on? I stir, but I cannot escape. I see a leopard creep along the edge of the gorge. A hungry lion bends over its prey, hidden among the boulders. A pregnant she-wolf, lean and starving, collapses onto her side, moaning in the shadows.

I cry out.

I woke up, opened my eyes. I was covered in sweat. Somehow, I was sitting in the armchair facing the still-open back doors, facing the plains. I couldn't shake the eeriness of the . . . what was it? Dream? Vision? Memory? The house was darker than it had been before, but not as cold. Everything was completely still—the rain had stopped, and the silence left behind was like its own sound. I could feel my pulse fluttering, and a chill spread through my body, not from the cool breeze but from something else, something deeper inside of me.

I heard a sound behind me, at the front door. A moan. I jumped out of my chair, still woozy from the dream, and turned. The front door remained wide open. There was a puddle of water on the threshold. The dark-haired woman was on the floor in the water, under the blanket I had given her, unconscious.

I took a step in her direction but stopped. I turned around, went to the back doors, and closed them. The house grew even darker. I made my way back to the woman, slowly, slowly. She still hadn't moved. I reached down to shake her shoulder, perhaps push her hair back, but that deep fear returned, made my hand tremble, and I didn't touch her.

That's when I saw it on the floor, barely outside the reach of one of her extended hands. A skeleton key, the kind used in old houses, with a small circle at the top, a long shaft, and uneven teeth at the other end. I reached for it. Her fingers were so close. I took the key and lifted it without a sound, stared at it, and slipped it into my pocket.

I had to tell Abe about this.

I eased my way around the woman's body, my eyes on her the whole time. I justified my decision to leave her by telling myself she would be fine. She wouldn't regain consciousness while I was away. I went through the front door and closed it gently behind me. The air outside was fresh and cool and the greenway grass was all bent over, heavy with moisture that soaked my shoes and the bottom of my trousers. I didn't run. But I wanted to.

There were dozens of houses in the village, including mine, and nearly all of them were empty, but we kept even the empty ones tidy, at least on the outside. There were flowers in the window boxes that we transplanted from various spots on the plains, and we swept the dust from the eaves, but there was no denying the emptiness of shades always drawn and footpaths overgrown. The tall grass from the plains had begun encroaching on our small town, growing high where the walking of so many people, so many old friends, used to keep it low.

As I walked down to the homes, all the doors were closed, blinds drawn. Dusk approached and the light dimmed. We didn't visit with each other as much as we used to. I had to admit that it seemed we were growing apart.

Miss B opened her door as I walked past, and the loud sound of the latch made me jump.

"Hello, Dan," she said in her rich voice, her dark freckles dancing, her dreadlocked hair pulled up in a massive knot above her head. She seemed to be as old as Abe, but she didn't take things as seriously as he did. She floated along, rarely offering an opinion or criticism of any kind.

"Miss B, hi." I turned toward her, slowing but not stopping. "Everything okay?"

"Where you off to? You think you're going to pass on by without giving me a hug?"

I smiled, laughed to myself, and it felt good. I took a deep breath, turned around, and approached Miss B on the short path that led off the greenway to her front door. She was a large woman, and she gathered me in. She was warm and smelled of lavender.

I returned the hug and took a step back. "Have you seen Abe?" I asked, trying not to sound worried.

"I think he went all the way down to Miho's," she said, slow and steady. "You heard about Mary?"

I nodded, started to walk away.

"Finally leaving, our dear Mary," she said in a singsong voice, and I could tell she thought it was just about the best thing, miraculous even. And maybe it was. Maybe it was the miracle we'd all been waiting for. But it was hard for me to see it that way.

45

"I'll see you soon," I said.

"That was quite a storm," she said as I walked away. I waved again over my shoulder, but then a strange thing happened.

"Dan," Miss B said, and her voice was different. Completely different. Before, she had sounded airy, light, as if nothing about the day could go wrong. But in that whispered word, everything had changed. Her voice was strained. Her shoulders were slumped, and she was using a broom to hold herself up.

"Dan," she said again.

"Miss B?" I jogged back over to her and took hold of one of her large arms, wrapped it around my shoulders. "Miss B. Are you okay?"

"Help me down. Here's fine." She motioned to the thick grass beside the front door of her house. "Oh, yes, that's good. That's good."

I brought her down and nestled her into a spot, her back against the wall of her house, both of her hands planted into the ground beside her.

"Mmm-mmm," she exclaimed. "That came on fast."

"Are you okay?" I asked again. "Maybe I should go get Abe." I wanted to leave. I wanted to get away from her. I had never seen Miss B like that before, and it made my stomach churn. Her sudden weakness reminded me too much of the woman lying in my entryway, how that woman had made me feel.

Miss B kneaded her hands, as if trying to rub out the anxiety, and swayed forward and back. "No, no," she said in the breathless voice of someone who had run a marathon. "I'll mosey on over to Abe's a little later. He'll want to know."

"Know what, Miss B?"

As soon as the words came out of my mouth, I wanted them back. I wanted to swallow them and walk away. There was too much going on—what was happening? I wanted to keep everything as it was, nothing new. But it was too late. Mary was leaving and there was a strange woman lying on the floor in my house and Miss B was having some kind of a breakdown, emotional or physical or both.

"I really think I should go get Abe," I insisted, trying to backtrack from my question.

"I remember now," she said, and I realized that what I had mistaken for weariness in her voice was actually a kind of bliss.

Miss B was enraptured.

"I remember what happened," she said, amazement in her voice.

3 The Storm

Miss B and I sat in the foot-long grass that leaned up against her house, and only after we sat did I remember that the ground was wet. I could feel the water soaking into my clothes.

"Dan, Dan, Dan," she whispered, and her voice was filled with amazement at her own recollection. "I remember it now. I remember all of it! It's been coming back to me in pieces these last days, but this morning I had almost all of it right there, just outside of my mind's grasp, and then something you did, something you said . . . You hugged me." She sighed and shook her head. "Something." She lifted up her hand and stared at her palm as if looking for a line to interpret, and I could see the wet slickness there from the grass.

"What, Miss B?" I asked. I wanted to know even though I was afraid.

"No, wait," she said, curiosity in her voice. When she spoke, it was a strange mix of words, some meant for me, some meant for herself. "It wasn't something you did. I'll be. It was something I said. 'Quite a storm.' Remember how I said that? That was the phrase. 'Quite a storm.'" She paused. "I'll be," she said, wonder in her voice. "Brought it all back. All of it."

She shook her head, and at first I thought she wasn't going to tell me.

"It was one of those beautiful days after the rain, like today. The night before, there had been quite a storm." She smiled. "Quite a storm. But that day, heavens, that golden light streamed in the windows. I looked out into the flower beds and the summer flowers were up, beaming at me, like stars that fell to earth, like solid pieces of a broken rainbow. Mmm-mmm! What a sight."

I knew she was going to tell me everything, and I felt myself tensing up, the way you might when you're reading a book and the woman is about to open the door and inadvertently let the killer inside. It's a book you've read before, long ago, and you can't remember all the details or exactly when all the frightening things happen, but you have a distant premonition. And you don't like it.

"My husband's name was Carl Bird." She let out a young laugh, the laugh of a teenager flirting with the boy who is about to become her first kiss. "Carl Bird. Dan, it feels so sweet to finally remember his name. I knew it was there. I knew he was there all along. Where he is now, only heaven knows." Tears pooled in her soft brown eyes. "He was a good man. I remember that now too. The kind everyone else thinks is too good to be true. But he wasn't. He was just

49

good. It aches me even worse now, the missing."

She wept, and I looked around to see if anyone else was close by, someone who could console her better than me, but there was no one. Only the surrounding empty houses and the greenway and the mountain behind us, although I couldn't see it now. I wished one of the other women would come out of her house, Circe or Misha. But they didn't, so I reached over and touched her hand sympathetically. She didn't let my hand come and go—she grabbed on to it, and she wept some more before gathering herself. She squeezed my fingers as she talked, and it made me feel claustrophobic.

"Maybe I should go get Misha," I suggested, but she plowed ahead.

"That morning was a normal morning, but it was also a rapture, and that's because we had recently moved out of the city into a middle-of-nowhere place. It was our Eden, Dan. And it was all for me. We did it for me. It was my choice for us to move all the way out there. But Carl loved it too, though he tried to pretend and gave me a hard time. He called me his mountain woman." Her great frame shook with barely held laughter. "Mountain woman. Psh! He didn't know nothing about mountain women. He wishes! But he moved there with me, and he flew in this tiny plane back to work, back to the town we had moved away from."

When she said the words "tiny plane," a shock wave moved through me. Like déjà vu.

"Three days a week he took that flight. Three days a week he was gone from me, Dan, flying in that tiny buzzing plane over the mountain. Three long, stretched-thin days every single week, three short flights, and I waited until long after dark on those days, begging his headlights to come dragging up the lane, through the trees."

I stared at the empty house across the greenway. These empty houses had always felt like nothing more than empty space to me, just parts of the past of the town, parts that were left behind every time someone left. But as I heard Miss B's story, as she told me more and I could see where it was going, the house across the way started to feel menacing. That's the only word that fit. Like that old house wasn't completely innocent, like it was hiding things.

Were all of us hiding things? Miss B had these memories hidden in her like the rest of us had other memories hidden away. Secrets? I had a woman in my house that no one else knew about yet. It seemed suddenly possible that even Miho or Abe were keeping things from me.

The windows in the empty house pulsated with a strange, living darkness. The eaves concealed crucial things. I imagined the attic under the thatched roof was coated in some kind of mold, something eating away at the inside of it. I wondered if maybe some of the people who we thought had gone east across the plains had actually doubled back at night and slipped into their old houses, where they now watched us through the dark panes and plotted our end.

I shook my head. Where were these thoughts coming from?

"Even though he left me in the morning, the headlights of my husband's car returned every night, Dan. They did. I sat in a chair by the window in the bedroom, and when I saw him coming, I quickly climbed into bed and got under the covers so he wouldn't know I was worried. Sometimes I pretended to be asleep, although I don't know why, now that I think back on it. Sometimes I welcomed him home, and we lay quietly in the bed for a long time, listening to each other breathe, wondering if it was too good to be true, this Eden we had created away from everyone. Everyone."

Her voice went flat. "Then came the day he left me."

The void that had found its way inside her voice scared me.

"Quite a storm."

She was empty.

"Quite a storm."

I would have run for Abe if she hadn't been holding my hand so tight it hurt.

"I knew he was in the air already, and I hoped

that storm would leave him be. What could he have that the storm would want? Leave him be. Leave him be! And behind the storm, the quietest sort of peace you've ever seen or heard."

We sat there as if she was trying to re-create that stillness. The cool air rushed around us. I heard a door open and close somewhere else in town, and a voice shouted to someone else, but I couldn't tell who it was or what they said. The sounds in our empty town were often lonely, few and far between, always distant and fleeting.

"After the storm, all day the phone was ringing. I mean, all day, ringing off the hook. And you know? I knew something was wrong. I knew someone was trying to call me about Carl, to tell me he was gone, and I couldn't make myself answer that phone. I wouldn't answer it, not for anything, because as long as I didn't answer it, nothing bad had happened. Does that make any sense to you?"

I nodded without looking over at her. It did. It made perfect sense.

"I even went outside for the rest of the day and found things to do—picked weeds, put together some more plantings, tilled a new flower bed. That night I lay in bed, staring at the ceiling, my eyes wide open, but no matter how late it got, his headlights never shone through the woods. Never lit up the window and slid that square of light along the wall like he usually did. Never came back to me. That was a dark night, Dan. A dark, dark night."

She pulled her hands into her lap like a child burned. She held them there still as stones, and her face went flat. She stared into the empty windows of the house across the greenway. My own hand ached from where she had squeezed it.

"I remember now, Dan. I remember what happened to my Carl. That's why I'm still here, why I never left. And now I don't know what I'll do."

She didn't know what she would do? What did she mean by that?

"I'm sorry, Miss B," I said, and she nodded. I stood up, but I didn't go. It was like her memory clung to me, a web holding me in place.

"What is this place, Dan?" she asked, lifting her palms and motioning around her. "What is this place? This town? This plain?"

Her voice stumbled as if she had used up all her words. But there was something else too. Something came to me, some strange knowledge, and I couldn't tell if it came from Miss B or the story she had told. Something resonated with me.

I knew her story already, somehow.

I knew it before she even told it to me, or at least certain parts of it. That's why the part about the plane had jolted through me. I was connected to it in some long-ago way. I wondered if she knew it too, if she sensed this connection I had to her new memory, the part I played in it. Maybe that's why she had grown quiet. I didn't want to press her. I didn't know what to do. So I stepped back, away from her.

"I'll talk to you a little later, Miss B," I said in a gentle voice, and she nodded again. "Let me know if you need anything." Her eyes were empty like the house across the greenway. Miss B had never been anything but grins and light, breezy sentences. Nothing but cookies and fresh bread and deep, comfortable hugs. This Miss B was different.

I walked down the greenway to the other side of the village, all the way to Miho's house. It usually took less than ten minutes to walk to her place from mine. I didn't see anyone else, but smoke rose from John's chimney, and I could hear Misha singing in her house at the edge of the village, her voice far-off and melancholy. I thought I recognized the tune.

Miho's place was the last house in the village before the greenway ended. The town's expansive garden stretched out behind her house, out into the plains. Her house was also the closest to the large oak at the edge of town with its massive, spreading branches that reached up into the now-clear sky.

I knocked on Miho's door but didn't wait for a response before walking in. Her place was bright on the inside, partially because of the fire always burning in the fireplace, but also because she kept her windows wide open and curtains pulled back. Her wood floors shone, a much lighter color than mine. I closed the door quietly behind me, still pondering the memory Miss B had shared, but I soon realized I wasn't the only one there.

There were three of them sitting at the dining room table that was partially covered in baskets of different sizes, all holding vegetables. Abe, Miho, and Mary St. Clair. I remembered again greeting Mary when she'd come over the mountain. She had moved into a house tucked in the second row off the greenway. In those days, she had a few neighbors, but now the houses in that part of town were empty. And she was leaving us. Sadness filled me again, and this time it wasn't a selfish sadness, the kind that came when I considered being left alone. No, this sadness came from knowing how much we would all miss her. Our village would be less without her. There would be only eight.

"Hi," I said quietly, frozen in place. "Hi, Mary."

"Hi, Dan," she whispered, giving me a sad smile.

The four of us remained there, no one knowing what to say, and finally Abe cleared his throat. "We're making preparations." He tried to sound upbeat and beckoned to an empty chair at the table. "You're welcome to join us. Give us your two cents."

Miho smiled.

My mouth went dry. I cleared my throat. "Of course," I mumbled. "Preparations."

"What's wrong, Dan?" Miho asked. She knew me better than anyone. She knew something was going on. I wouldn't have come down at dusk, only hours after seeing her and Abe, unless there was something I needed to tell them. For the first time since Miss B's story, I remembered the woman in my house. The woman I should have brought with me and relinquished to Abe. I squeezed the key in my pocket so hard it bit into my hand.

But I put on a dim smile. "No, no. Fine," my voice said, skipping words, a record player out of groove. "Everything's fine."

"Mary is leaving after dark, in just a few hours," Abe said, and I didn't know why he was telling me this again. Didn't everyone already know?

An irrational irritation rose inside of me. I tried to speak, tried to say, "Yes, I know," or something else along those lines, but the words had burrs on them, and they stuck in my throat.

"Would you mind gathering the firewood for the ceremony?" Abe asked. "You might have to go out to the second or third tree. I haven't seen much wood around the mountain, and this tree out here is picked clean."

I nodded, numb. "Sure." The three of them

stared at me. I felt like I should say something else, something that would explain my coming. "I had a word with Miss B."

"Good," Abe said, appearing a little confused as to why that was noteworthy.

"You should go talk to her. She had a memory."

"Is that so?" Abe sounded interested, as if he might ask me more, but I was already backing away.

I clumsily opened the door, spilled out onto the greenway, and returned through the village, toward the mountain, toward my house. I waited for one of them to come out and shout in my direction, ask me why I was going back to my house and not out toward the long line of oaks to collect wood for the ceremony. If they wondered where I was going, no one said anything. No one came after me.

After walking for a bit, I realized I could breathe again. Again I pictured the woman lying on the floor inside my front door, and I stopped. I was torn. I thought about going back to tell Abe. I had to tell him what was going on.

But something else pulled me onward, pulled me home. My walk turned into a jog, and when I passed Miss B's house, there she sat, not having moved from where I left her a few minutes before. She was staring down at her hands, as if her fingers were squeezing into fists on their own, without her permission, and she was trying to figure out how to undo the knots they had become.

I didn't slow down, and I didn't let go of the key. I ran faster when I reached the gap between the town and my own house, the heavy grass swishing with each step. And the fear was there too, that inexplicable fear, growing until it sat in my gut like a throbbing mass.

I opened the door to my house, breathing hard. The puddle was still there, sending up a glass reflection. The gray light was still there too, as the afternoon died off and darkness approached. The back doors remained closed.

But the woman wasn't lying there anymore. She was gone.

4 The Woman

An unbearable stillness settled on the house and made its way inside of me. I stepped in and stood in the puddle where she had been, my feet momentarily stirring the water, and the dying light that came in from outside reflected off the rippling surface. I felt like a foreigner in my own house, but in an unlikely act of bravery, I pulled the door closed behind me. I turned the lock. I couldn't remember the last time I had locked the door, but the metal slid home in a clean motion.

"Hello?" I said, my voice husky and fading. The air quivered around that one word, but there was nothing that came out in response—no sound, no movement. I stepped out of the puddle, kicked off my shoes, and opened the back doors, looking through them at the sky and the plains and the heavy, after-rain air. It wouldn't be long before night fell. I breathed deep. I closed the doors and locked them too, and again I wondered why. Was I locking someone out? Or locking myself in? Either way, it felt too late, an afterthought.

I walked through the kitchen to my desk, searching the mountain for any sign of the woman. Did she go back? Maybe. I'd seen it happen before, people shocked by the freedom, the cool breeze, the fresh air, turning and stumbling back into the mountain. She couldn't have gone through the village and followed the greenway east or I would have noticed, unless she had hidden among the houses and waited for me to pass, which seemed unlikely in her condition. The thought of her hidden among the empty houses made my skin crawl. She couldn't have meandered out into the plains or I would still be able to see her from my back doors. It would take a long, long time to walk out of sight in that direction. I stared at the canyon, but everything around it was as motionless as the inside of my house.

What if she hadn't left?

I moved to the closed bedroom door, stared at the knob and my warped reflection in it, held on with one clammy hand. My eye twitched at the corner, and I rubbed it with the back of my other hand. I was tired. Why was I so tired?

I pushed open the door and it swung without a sound. There, lying in my bed, small beneath the down comforter, her form barely enough to create any kind of topography, was the woman, asleep. For a moment the fear dimmed, replaced by a warming sense of concern. She was like a broken animal, something harmless, an injured bird or a lost kitten, and I wanted to take care of her, to nurse her to health. I could do that. I could help.

I walked over and sat in the chair beside the bed. I didn't want to wake her—I only wanted to watch her, to take her in. By then, I had already pushed away the vision that had overwhelmed me when I touched her arm, the strangeness of her arrival, the fear I had felt before. I only wanted to sit there and stare at her.

Her breathing was so peaceful, so gentle. Why had I been afraid of her? I couldn't remember. Was she a tangible reminder of what it was like to live on the other side of the mountain, the terror of what went on over there? Was it because she was a secret I shouldn't be keeping?

"Are you awake?" I asked quietly, my words barely above a whisper.

She tugged the covers down so that her eyes peeked out at me. She nodded slowly.

"Are you okay?"

Her head moved slightly, uncertainly. It could have been a yes or a no.

"Are you hurting anywhere?"

She paused, seemed to shrug. I waited before asking the next question, not wanting to force her memory back to the other side of the mountain too soon, but I couldn't resist. Even in that moment, even in the face of someone gravely injured, I still had to ask about my brother.

"Was there anyone else left? Did you see anyone else? On the other side of the mountain?"

Her eyes rolled back and I thought she might

pass out again. But instead she nodded, barely moving her head. She squinted in pain.

"Good, good," I said encouragingly, like a parent to a small child, wanting to coax more out of her. I paused, but the words came out before I could stop them. "A man?"

She nodded again. I felt a surge of adrenaline or emotion, and my hands shook. I wanted to stand up and clap, or shout out a hoot. But tears formed in her eyes, shimmering, welling up, and streaking along her skin.

"Yes," she whispered.

She could speak!

"Was he still alive?"

She nodded once more, and her eyes dropped below the line of the blankets still pulled up to her face. Could it be? Could this person she had seen actually be my brother? I stood up and paced around the room, feeling caged, trapped. Why was he still there? Why wasn't he coming out of that place? What were they doing to him to keep him there?

"Where?" I asked. "Where?"

She pulled the covers down even farther, down below her chin. There were wet spots on the sheet from her fingers, a damp halo around her head on the pillowcase. There were also dried brown stains in random places from mud and blood and drool. Already some of the cuts on her face had begun to soften around the edges—this was how it was on our side of the mountain. Inexplicable, really, how quickly we had all healed after arriving. How completely. Maybe it was the air. Maybe it was the grass, or the rain, or the food.

I sat down in the chair again so that my knees were against the bed. I put my palms on the edge of the mattress, consciously keeping my hands away. I was scared of the vision that had come to me the last time I touched her.

"Where?" I asked for a third time, trying to sound calm and gentle, even though I wanted to press her. I wanted to lift her by her shoulders and shake her, demand information, details. But she looked so fragile. It was like negotiating with someone on the edge, someone preparing to jump.

"The very bottom," she said, barely moving her mouth.

I sat back and shook my head. The bottom. I had so few memories of that place, but an image flashed in my mind when she said those words: a mile-wide funnel, like a pit dug into the heart of the mountain, and the road that made its way down, hugging the edge, dropping into the darkness. The bottom of that? I didn't remember seeing the bottom. I had been in there somewhere, but I couldn't imagine a bottom. It seemed endless.

What was I going to do?

"Was there anyone else?" I asked her. "Anyone?"

She looked at me as if she didn't know what I meant.

I reworded the question. "How many people did you see over there before you came here? How many people do they still have over there?"

A subtle rustling began under the blanket, the smallest of movements, and I realized she was pulling her hand up. She moved it out from under the cover in a tight fist, and one finger slowly uncurled.

"One person? He's the last person there?"

She nodded.

"How do you know?"

"Emptiness," she whispered. "Silence."

I held my face in my hands and tried to stop the tears from coming. "Are you sure?"

She nodded, her eyes closed, and she fell asleep, but there was still that one finger above the blanket, now slightly bent. One finger. One person left.

My brother. It had to be him.

Dusk grew darker, leaned toward night, and I watched it happen from the comfort of my armchair, facing out over the empty plains. I couldn't look at the mountain anymore, knowing my brother was there, alone. Sadness hung around me like a fog, and loneliness, and that new companion, fear. So I pretended the mountain wasn't rising just outside my house, and I stared through the wide-open double doors in the opposite direction.

I should have been going for wood for Mary's sending off. I should have been telling Abe any number of things, either about the woman in my bed or the memory Miss B had told me or that my brother was the last one in the mountain. But I said nothing. I did nothing. I sat there and watched the darkness drift in on us all.

There had been no sound from the bedroom since I left her there sleeping, and there were no windows in that room, so it wasn't like she could escape without me knowing about it. But I did feel like I was guarding the door. Why? What was I guarding against? Her coming out, or me going in? Or something else?

I didn't know.

It started to rain again, a steady, soaking rain, and relief washed over me because I knew without being told that Mary wouldn't leave, at least not on that night. A spark of hope murmured inside of me, the thought that perhaps she would change her mind. But as quick as that thought came to me, I knew it wasn't true. I knew she would leave as soon as there was a clear evening. And then there would be eight of us left. Nine if I counted the woman in my bedroom, but she didn't seem to count. She seemed somehow separate.

I stood up and walked forward to lean against

the frame of the back door. From there I could see down the gentle slope, to the left and into the village. The houses were quiet in the settling darkness, but I could smell a wood fire burning, and I wondered if it came from John's or Miss B's or Miho's. Miss B's house was the coziest one in town, and she was constantly bringing out fresh bread or cookies or something else she had made. I wondered if anyone else was there with her. I wondered if she had told anyone else about her new memory. I doubted it—after she had finished telling me, and when I had passed her on my way back home, I had this sense that she regretted the sharing. This is the way of secrets, an always present desire to share them and a pervading guilt after we do.

I watched Misha and Circe walk out into the rain, making a wide circle through the knee-high grass. I could barely see them in the dark. They stopped at one point and looked up in my direction. I gave them a wave, but I didn't think they saw me because they didn't wave back. Maybe they were looking up at the mountain. Maybe they couldn't see me in the darkness of the doorway. They turned, kept walking, and hugged each other at one point. The darkness got thicker and they drifted out of eyesight. Did they plan on leaving too? The town wouldn't be the same without either one of them.

I was surprised when I heard a knock at the

door. A ball of anxiety rose up in my throat when I remembered the woman in my bedroom. The woman I hadn't told anyone about. I convinced myself it wasn't the worst secret in the world, but it would have been awkward explaining her presence, especially to Miho, so I was a little relieved when I unlocked the door, opened it, and found Abe standing there, getting wet as the new band of rain became steadier.

"Come in, come in," I said. "Get out of the rain, Abe."

He came in and sort of shook himself off, like a dog emerging from a lake. We both laughed.

"Let me get you a towel," I said, moving toward the bedroom. But I remembered the woman, so I veered into the kitchen and grabbed him a small dishcloth. "Sorry." I shrugged. "Best I can do."

He waved off my apology and, while his face was covered with the cloth, asked, "You locking your doors these days?"

I swallowed hard and turned away, pretending to be busy with something in the kitchen.

I sighed. "I don't know. I guess." With that simple answer a kind of oppressiveness pushed down on me. I stared at the floor while Abe wiped off the rest of his head, his face, his arms. His hands. I stared at them as he handed the small cloth back to me. I knew where the feeling of oppressiveness was coming from: I was lying to Abe about the woman, and I was going to keep lying to him. I wasn't going to tell him about her. I couldn't see any way out of it.

When I took the cloth from him, I wanted to cover my face with it, hide my shame, but instead I carried it back into the kitchen and draped it over the counter where it could dry. I lit the lamps in the house and carried one into the sitting room, hung it on the hook in the ceiling. The flames danced and the shadows in the corners of the house came to life.

"I guess you know why I'm here," he said quietly, still standing inside the door.

"Come in, Abe. Come in," I said, motioning for him to come with me to the armchair. "Have a seat."

"You sit there," he said. "I know that's your spot."

"Abe," I said, taking a serious tone. "Sit."

He grumbled something about not getting any respect. I laughed and tried to shake off that sense of letting him down that comes with lying to someone you trust.

I sat with my back toward the back door. Cool, damp air lingered there. It had become too dark to see the plains, or the rain, or even the village, although a bit of lamplight glowed from various windows.

There had been a day when the village lit up at night. When all the windows were alight and people gathered around fires built outside of town, when the sound of laughter made its way up to where I sat. Everyone else seemed to think that people leaving indicated progress, that going east was what we were all supposed to do eventually, but I missed the old days. I wished them back, and I didn't know what was wrong with that. They had been good days. Very good days.

"So," he began again.

"Yeah. I know why you're here."

He looked at me with a question in his eyes, asking me to prove it.

"You're here because we're postponing the ceremony. The weather is too wet, so Mary will leave tomorrow evening. Or whenever this rain finally clears."

"So, you do know," he said, giving me a wry grin. His face went serious before he said, "One more day."

"One more day," I echoed, resigned. "Abe, why does it bother me so much that Mary is leaving us?"

"It's a hard thing, isn't it? This town has been good to all of us."

I could tell it bothered him too, and in some strange way that was a comfort to me, seeing that I wasn't alone. "Why do we have to go? What could possibly be better about any other place?"

He leaned his head back in the chair and stared up at the lamp. The whites of his eyes seemed especially white in the dimly lit room, in the flickering lamplight, and his mouth worked this way and that while he thought.

"You know, this is a wonderful place. I'll give you that. The friendships, the time we've had together. The way we helped each other recover from . . . over there. It's a special thing, this kind of community. No doubt about that. But can't you feel the sameness of it, Dan? Do you ever get the sense that time stands still here, that it's nothing but a place for waiting?"

I hated to admit it, but he was right. We kept ourselves busy. We grew our own food from seeds the previous harvest had left us. We gathered wood from the base of the mountain and the oak trees that stretched a straight line into the plains. We slept and talked, and the night was followed by the morning. But he was right—nothing ever progressed. If that woman hadn't stumbled out of the canyon and gone to sleep in my own bedroom, I would have even gone so far as to say nothing ever happened.

But something had happened. She had arrived. I was hiding her. Miss B had a memory. Something new was taking place. Were things changing? And if they were, why couldn't Abe feel it too?

"Yeah," was all I said. "Yeah, I hear you."

He stood up.

"You don't have to go, Abe," I said, although his leaving was a relief to me. I kept waiting for the woman to make a sound.

"Thanks. But I have a lot to do to get ready for tomorrow. I'm rather relieved Mary's been delayed. It's been a while since anyone left." He said this with a mischievous look in his eye. "And I'm not sure I remember all my lines."

"Who was the last to go?" I asked him. "I'm drawing a blank."

"You don't remember?" he asked. He even looked as if my forgetfulness was slightly alarming.

I shook my head, shrugging. "I can't. I've been thinking about it all afternoon."

"I can't believe you don't remember," he said, laughing to himself. "What a curious thing, all of this forgetting."

And all of this remembering, I thought. "At least give me a hint."

He turned to me with a glint in his eye, and his voice changed into a high squeak. "Danny! Oh, Danny! Can I come up and pick out a book to read again?"

"Oh, wow," I said, my eyes widening. "I forgot all about her. But I still can't remember her name." It was strange to me that I couldn't remember. Had it been that long?

"Does the name Moira ring a bell?" he asked.

Moira. How could I forget Moira? The woman had practically tried to move into my house with me. She had been up at my place all the time, driving both me and Miho crazy. She always wanted to peruse my books, running her pale index finger along the spines, mumbling the title names and authors to herself. She pretended she had read every book I owned—whenever I mentioned something about a book, any book, she replied with the same all-knowing words. "Ah yes," she would say. "Of course."

"Moira," I said, more to myself than to Abe. "How could I possibly forget Moira?"

Abe looked at me over his shoulder, his hand on the front door, and his face was serious again. "It's this place, Dan. It's not made for remembering. It's not a settling kind of place—it's an in-between place. This town has always been that. I know why you're here and why you're waiting. Everyone else knows too, and we understand. You want to see your brother again. Everyone else here is waiting for something too. And that's okay. But don't forget, you can't stay here forever."

"Have you talked to Miss B?" I blurted out, and he froze in place.

He turned toward me again. "Yes," he said, and I knew he was wondering how much she had told me.

"She shared her memory with me," I said. "I'm guessing you know about it too."

He nodded in a guarded sort of way. "How much did she tell you?"

I gave him the summary. He listened. After I finished, we stood there in silence.

"Seems strange," I said. "All of this in a place not made for remembering."

He gave an absent-sounding chuckle, and I could tell his mind was elsewhere. He mumbled a half-hearted goodbye, never completely returning to that place, that moment, and he was back out in the light rain, disappearing in the darkness. I desperately wanted it to be day again—I was tired of people disappearing. I was tired of standing by and being left behind.

A cold wind blew through the house while the front door was open, swept in through the frame and out the back. It felt like even the wind longed for the east.

That was the night when everything was set in motion, the night I could have told Abe but didn't. The night I could have gone down and spent a final evening with Mary. But I didn't.

That was also the night I started to remember. Not made-up memories. Real ones.

I promise. This part is true.

5 Remembering

I wish I could adequately explain how strange this all was—for a long, long time, I had lived in the village and nothing out of the ordinary had happened. Not one thing. I mean, in the early days, people were always coming over from the other side, so I would run down to Abe's and we would tend to them and help them get acclimated. Every so often someone would leave and head east, so we'd have a little ceremony and some of us would cry, and then we'd return to the same old routine.

But most days were normal days. Most days I woke up. Ate breakfast. Listened to the wind in the grass. Wrote in my journal. Read. Watched the rain. Walked down to the village and helped in the garden. Shared lunch with someone. Went home and took a nap. Stared at the mountain. Wished my brother would come through the canyon. Met up at someone's house for dinner. Sat by a fire and told stories or went home and sat in the darkness, staring out over the plains, listening to people sing down among the houses. Fell asleep.

That was it.

But then, this strange sequence of days: Mary preparing to leave, Miss B sharing her memory, and the woman asleep in my bedroom.

That was the night I started to remember things.

I was in and out of sleep. I thought I was dreaming, the kind of dream I came back to as soon as I drifted off again. I saw scenes from when I was a baby, things you wouldn't normally remember because you would be too young. But there it was, like a show in my mind: I saw me, and I saw my brother. Both of us. And in that moment, I remembered it had always been both of us. We were twins.

How could I have forgotten? I was beginning to realize how much the mountain had taken from me. The trauma I had experienced in that abyss had robbed me of any memory of the life that had come before it. In the village, we had always assumed this to be the case, that we had each had a life before the terror of what had happened in the mountain. But none of us could remember. Or if we did, the memories were brief, shallow, and inconsequential.

On that night, the memory that came back to me was dripping with detail. I saw the moment when my brother was born, and I saw my birth right after his, and even though we looked exactly alike, I could tell which one was me and which one was him. There was something wrong with me because all the nurses were crouched around the narrow table I was on, poking at me and prodding my limp arms and fastening a tiny oxygen mask to my face.

All this time, my brother was in my father's arms. My mom looked like she had passed out with exhaustion, and I guess because something was wrong with me, they had bundled up Adam and handed him to my dad. My dad stared down into Adam's eyes, stared hard, as if Adam was the only thing in the whole world, and he kept getting closer and closer until their eyes were only inches apart.

My dad. I suddenly remembered him too. He was a rough man, wild around the edges. His hands and fingers were thick, and even though they made him wash his hands before he held me, the creases around his knuckles were black from oil. He was a long-haul trucker as well as a mechanic in his spare time.

Of course, I thought. *How could I have forgotten?*

My dad wore a T-shirt, tight around his barrel chest, and his biceps were huge. His face was all blunt edges and flat surfaces. His eyes were dull and young, a strange combination. When he smiled, it looked like his teeth hurt.

My mother's beauty was disarming, to the point that men couldn't look her in the eye and women found her to be either their favorite person in the world or completely insufferable. Her attractive face was placid, like still water. Her hair was blonde, almost white, and her skin the color of milk. Her lips were a rose-petal pink. Her mouth was exquisite.

She was so still she might have been dying. Or dead. Wait, was that what happened? Was this a memory of my mother's death?

But I saw her coming back from darkness, and the movement started around her mouth. She licked her lips. Barely. She moaned. A nurse moved to her side again, and she emerged up into this painful exhaustion. I must have been doing better because some of the nurses cleared off while one wrapped me in a blanket, wrapped me tight. My mom cried as they handed me to her, and she couldn't stop nodding as they entrusted my small being into her love. And she did love me, fiercely. I could see it there, in her face, her tears. It was so obvious. She loved me.

The memory started to fade, and I clung desperately to it. It was mine now. I could keep it.

At the end, I saw an image of my father holding Adam and my mother holding me, and a thousand subtle memories returned, not in sharp images or clear pictures like this one, but in insinuations and deductions. This was how it always was, how it always would be. My mother and me. My father and Adam. Two separate teams in a single family, two sides to every problem. I never had my father, not even from day one, but I always had my mom. Adam and I were left to fend for ourselves across those clear lines, even from a young age, and we sometimes crossed them, but always as representatives seeking some kind of temporary treaty.

I woke up feeling woozy, drugged. I had slept in my clothes and was still in the armchair. The back doors were wide open, had been open all night. Cool, damp air mingled around the house. I rubbed my eyes and sat up straight. It was nearly morning, and a soft light caressed the plains, the easiest blue, the simplest ivory. The grass was rustling as far as I could see, and I wanted to walk out into it.

I thought of the woman in my bedroom. I rose up and stretched and listened for her, for any sound coming from the room. But all I heard was the roof creaking in the wind and the rush of air through the grass. It was a lonely, quiet sound. I moved to my bedroom and leaned in, put my ear to the crack where the door met the wall.

Complete silence.

I turned the knob carefully and pushed the door open, willed it not to make a sound. I peered into the room. There she was, lying on the bed, as still as ever. Was she dead? I walked in practically on the tips of my toes, trying not to make a sound. I waited beside the bed for what felt like a long time, staring at her face, the angle of her eyes, the depth of her dark hair. If I concentrated on the blanket, I could see it moving up and down ever so slightly with her breathing.

At least I thought so. I couldn't be sure. I convinced myself everything was okay. She was okay and the town would be okay, and though Mary would leave, everything would stay as it was. Which was proof that everything would remain okay, because no one else was leaving.

I leaned over the woman, put my ear right up to her mouth, and only then could I hear her breath coming and going. In and out.

"Dan," she whispered.

I jumped back.

She smiled. "Did I scare you?"

"Your breathing was so quiet."

"You take good care of me," she said in a sleepy voice. "Thank you for letting me stay here."

I looked up at the ceiling, let my gaze wander around the four walls of the room. The floor creaked as I sat down and shifted my weight in the chair. "I need to go check on some things," I murmured. "I have to go out. I'll be back soon."

"Oh, Dan," she said, and her voice startled me, because there was a kind of barely revealed longing in it.

"Yeah?"

"I've lost something."

I could feel my heart beating. I reached up and rubbed my chest, trying to hide it. I could feel the muscles tense up in my face. "Yeah?" I asked again.

"A key. I had a key when I arrived here, but I can't seem to find it."

The key was in my pocket. I wondered if she could see it, if there was any sign of its presence. I nearly reached down to hold it, but I managed to keep my hand away from it.

"I'll keep my eye out," I said. "Actually, I'll walk up to the canyon later. Maybe you dropped it when you came through?"

"Thank you, Dan." Her voice was smooth, easy to take in, like sunshine.

I stood and walked toward the door, but before I got there I turned. "Don't make any sounds if someone comes into the house. You shouldn't be here. I should have told someone."

She raised one pale finger and pressed it against her lips as if she was saying, "Shhhh."

A chill spread down my back. I couldn't remember if at any point she had asked me not to tell anyone that she was there, but it seemed important whether or not she had made this request. I didn't think she had. This was a slight relief to me. But I couldn't be sure.

I left the room. I paced around the kitchen, stared up at the mountain, paced around the living room. I stared out into the plains and listened for anything coming from the bedroom that might break the silence. The grass was inviting, so I walked out the back doors, my head no longer hazy from sleep. I was tense. Aware. I needed to talk to Abe. I wanted to tell him everything about my memory and the arrival of this woman. I didn't know if I would go through with it. But I could try.

On second thought, I went back inside the house and looked over my bookshelves. If I was down in the village all day, I would need something to give to Mary when she left that night. I scanned the shelves for a particular title. There it was, the pocket edition of a book Mary had always enjoyed. I looked at it for a moment, and then I walked out, leaving the back doors open.

I didn't realize it had gotten so late in the morning, but as I walked down to the village I could see that a few of the others were already out and about. Miss B trimmed the long grass around her house and the neighboring houses, waving absentmindedly to me when I passed, as if nothing had happened the previous day. John was repairing something on his roof, too busy to look up as I passed by. Po sat on his front stoop, smoking a pipe, staring at me. I waved. He nodded in reply and let out a long stream of smoke that clouded around his head. But he didn't stop staring at me.

I nearly turned toward Abe's place situated in the very center of the town, a little bit off the greenway toward the mountain, but I wondered if Miho was outside, so I kept walking, all the way down. I could hear her around back, behind her house. There was a rustling of tall grass, the sound of a basket being dragged along the dirt, and humming. Whenever I found her by herself, she was always humming.

Miho took me in without her normal smile. There was a strange look on her face, as if she was seeing me for the first time. "Rough night?" she asked, looking back down at the ground.

I reached up and tried to flatten my hair, realized it was sticking up in every direction. Maybe that's why Po had given me that strange stare. I shrugged. "Slept in the armchair."

"The armchair? Someone kick you out of bed?"

Fortunately, she wasn't looking at me, because I could feel the crimson rising in my face. I walked over to where she was working and joined her. For someone who avoided the truth as often as I did, I was pretty terrible at it.

She pulled green beans from a series of large, round bushes. The beans were hard to see since they were the same color as the rest of the plant, but if you bumped the fragile stalks lightly, the beans danced and moved in a way that differentiated them from the rest of the plant. I reached in and grabbed one of the larger ones, chewed the end off.

"Everything okay?" I asked.

"You going to help or eat?" she asked without looking up. She smiled to herself, but there was sadness in it, and that brought all kinds of questions to my mind.

"You sleep okay?" I asked.

She shrugged, standing up straight and wiping her face with the back of her hand. I wanted to tell her what the strange woman had told me, that Adam was on the other side of the mountain, that she had seen him, that he was the last person there, that we had to do something.

She hesitated, then blurted out, "I had some strange dreams."

I kept picking beans, hoping she'd continue. I wasn't sure if I was ready to share my own. When she didn't say anything, I tried to encourage her a bit. "And?"

"And," she said, drawing out the word so that it pulled her voice higher, "I'm not sure if I'm ready to talk about it. I woke up early and drew some pictures of what I saw. I came out here to try to work it out."

"Work what out?"

She stopped moving—no bean picking, no wiping her face, no dragging the basket. Just her standing there, still. "I'm trying to work out if it was only a dream or if it was a memory."

"You know the difference," I said.

"What's that supposed to mean?" She arched her back in a stretch, staring at me.

"You know." I smiled, trying to lighten the mood. "It means you know whether you had a dream or are remembering things. And if you're pretending not to know, it's probably because you know it's a memory you don't want to be true." By the end of my little speech, I wasn't smiling anymore.

She stared at me for a moment, as if trying to decide whether to laugh me off or accept my wisdom. The flat line of her mouth wrenched to the side in reluctant agreement. "Yeah. You're right."

I nodded. Now I really wanted to hear about it. I decided asking wasn't going to get me anywhere, so I stooped down beside her and kept working. Kept trying to find those invisible beans.

The garden was one of my favorite things about the village. We called it a garden, but that didn't do it justice. It stretched the entire width of the town and at least fifty yards into the plains. By that point, we didn't use nearly the entire space anymore, not all at once. When the village had been full, there were fifteen or twenty people out there working every day, tilling up the ground and planting and weeding and harvesting. But as the village dwindled down to the nine of us, we no longer needed the entire space. Pretty much everyone helped from time to time, even Miss B, although she found it slower going.

I loved the garden because it reminded me of

us, of how we were making our way on our own, how we didn't need anyone else. It was a picture of this new life we had created outside of the mountain. I didn't know why anyone would ever want to leave the garden, the food, the space that was so entirely ours.

I stuck another bean in my mouth, then coughed and spit it out. "That one doesn't taste right." It had a bitterness to it, an underlying wrongness to the flavor.

Miho was troubled, and at first I thought she was still dwelling on her memory, but there was something else. "Something's strange about the plants," she said, clearly puzzled.

"Strange? What do you mean?"

"Look around. The newest batch of pepper plants hasn't been growing properly, and the tomatoes aren't ripening." She pointed at a line of plants where the tomatoes had emerged from the blossoms, but they were tiny and pale green. She pointed at the bean plants. "Same with these. And the corn is a total loss."

"A total loss?" I asked.

She nodded and wiped sweat from her forehead, leaving a streak of brown dirt. "The plants grew okay, but there are no ears on the stalks."

I walked over and held out my hand so the stalks tickled my palms. A wind rushed through and set them whispering. She was right. There were no ears growing, at least none that I could see.

The sense of premonition that had been low-grade bothering me ever since I welcomed that woman into my home simmered into questions. And there was the welling up of fear again, like indigestion. I pushed it down, walking back over to Miho. I reached up and wiped the dirt from her forehead. She stood patiently while I did it, even closing her eyes slightly.

"I need to go talk to Abe," I said in a quiet voice.

"Everything okay?"

"Yeah." I paused. "I had a strange dream too."

She gave a wry smile. "A dream or a memory?"

I chuckled and admitted, "A memory."

"About your brother?"

I nodded. She took in a deep breath. Sighed. But she didn't say anything.

"I'm going." I spun around on my heel in the dirt, looking over my shoulder to see if she had changed her mind, if we could swap tales of what life was like for each of us before the mountain.

But she only replied, "Okay," picking more beans and dropping them in the basket, then dragging the basket farther along the row.

I picked my way carefully out of the garden and back to the houses.

I had to talk to Abe, but there were so many things to discuss I didn't know where I would start.

6 More Secrets

I went back up onto the greenway, walked along it for a short distance before cutting between the houses toward Abe's. The previous night's rain had left everything feeling very green and fresh and new, and anything in the shadows was still wet. I could almost make myself believe that Mary wasn't actually leaving, that nothing was changing, that today was like any other day since I had come from the mountain. It was a short walk to Abe's house, tucked away as it was among a thick cluster of now-empty houses, but even in that short distance I made a lot of progress in self-deception.

Mary will change her mind.
She's not going to leave.
Nothing is going to change.

In front of me was a house that looked more like a small compound, as if three or four cottages had somehow been pushed together into one. Each section was made of a different material—stucco and brick and wood and stone—while the roof was one long stretch of thatch, the color of slate and brittle as brush ready to be burned.

Even though the after-storm weather was cool,

all of Abe's windows were open. I smelled coffee brewing, and I knew there would be a whisper of a breeze moving around inside the house. If the breeze made the house too cool, he'd start the fire rather than close the windows. I glanced up at the chimney but didn't see any smoke. I wondered if he was home, and a kind of relief filled me at the thought of walking away without talking about any of these new developments.

But voices murmured through the open windows. Should I knock on the door and interrupt the conversation? Should I go away and come back later? I stood there for a moment, feeling the breeze, taking in the blue sky and the shadows cast by all the little houses around me. Carefully, quietly, I walked over to the side of Abe's house, sat down under one of the windows, and listened.

"It will be sad not having you around," Abe said, his voice deep and comforting.

Silence settled in the house. Had they heard me? My face flushed with embarrassment at even the thought of being caught eavesdropping. No one did this. No one. There was no reason to. If you wanted to know something, to hear something, to talk about something, you simply asked. But I thought about the memories we were recovering, how we were holding things back. Something was different in our town. Something was changing.

"I have one other thing I'd like to talk about,"

Mary said, so quietly I had to turn my ear up toward the window to catch her words.

"I thought you might," Abe said, and I could imagine the kind smile on his face. He was so receptive that it felt like you could tell him just about anything, confess to any possible sin, any act committed or omitted.

I heard something that sounded like Mary standing up from the couch and walking around the room. When she spoke, her voice had an airy quality to it. The breeze picked up, and all around me the grass bent low and made a gentle whooshing sound, nearly drowning out her voice. But not quite.

"I remembered something a few days ago. And it . . ." She paused. "It helped me. That's why I'm ready to leave. Because of what I remembered."

Abe didn't say anything. He knew when to speak and when to wait.

"It was my father," she said. "I had a memory of my father. He was old in this memory, with white hair and deep wrinkles around his mouth and eyes. They were happy wrinkles, though, the kind that stick around after decades of smiling." She laughed quietly, and I could tell it was laughter mixed with crying. "I haven't had memories of him before. I don't know what he was like when I was a child, but I like to make things up, you know? I like to pretend. But this memory wasn't pretend. This was real. It happened."

I stared up into the sky. My heartbeat quickened. It felt like I was stealing something from Mary, taking something that wasn't mine. But I couldn't tear myself away.

"There's this flash of memory that happened a little before the main part. And in that quick flash I'm driving him to work. He's starting a new job. He's sitting in my passenger seat, and he rolls down the window and holds his hand out in the rushing wind outside the car, like he's arm wrestling the day. The air coming through is warm and feels like summer, and his thin white hair blows around. I remember thinking that he should close the window because it's going to mess up his hair, and he shouldn't show up to his first day of work looking like that."

She laughed at herself. "That's all I remember from the car ride. After that, we're in this huge grocery store, and I realize he's taken a job there stocking shelves. I was still there, but secretly. I didn't tell him I was going to stay. I follow him through the grocery store, peeking around the aisles. I have this intense feeling of wanting to protect him, you know? It was like he was my kid starting his first job." Her voice ended quickly, as if she had choked on the words.

"Oh, Mary." That was all Abe said, though he said it multiple times. "Oh, Mary."

The wind kicked up, and for a moment I couldn't hear anything above its rushing. I felt a sense of panic rising. Now that I had heard the beginning, I needed to hear the rest. I sat up against the house in a kind of crouch, getting as close as I could to the window.

"I was there for a long time. It's kind of embarrassing, admitting that I spent so much time spying on him."

"It's actually quite sweet, Mary," Abe said.

"I guess," she admitted. "But I see him walk toward the front of the store and stand outside the manager's office, and I get worried. Has someone given him a hard time? Did I miss something? Does he hate the job? Is he going to quit on the first day? I'm very worried. I nearly run out and ask him what's wrong, but I don't. It seemed like he had been enjoying himself stocking the shelves, even humming. Anyway, the manager opens the door and they talk for less than a minute. I can't hear what they say, but neither of them seem upset. My dad walks away, and I see him pull something out of his pocket."

Again, the wind kicked up.

"Cigarettes! I didn't even know he smoked! He pulls out a pack of cigarettes and a small book of matches and walks toward the front door. I was shocked. It was the strangest thing seeing this, realizing my dad had this entire life I knew nothing about. How had he hidden it from me? I hated the smell. I would have known. Right? And it wasn't the cigarettes that bothered me, you know? It was this realization that he existed on his own, that he was his own person. An individual. Not 'Mary's father' or my mother's husband, but he was him. He was himself, and he contained many stories I would never know."

Abe chuckled. "That's some wisdom right there. More coffee?"

"No, thank you," Mary replied.

They sat in a long silence, and I thought that might be the end of the story. I gathered myself, getting ready to run off so I wouldn't be seen. But then she continued.

"I watch my dad and decide I'm going to leave. I'll sneak out the other side of the store. There were two large entrances, you know? He goes out one side to smoke and I go out the other, but when I get to the glass doors, I realize it's pouring down rain, a harder rain than I've ever seen. People who had been caught in the rain come in from the parking lot, and they are soaked, like they jumped into a swimming pool. I stand outside the store, under the overhang, and I wait for the storm to clear. The clouds are boiling and dark and I wonder if there's a tornado warning. I'm literally listening for the sirens. That's when I hear it."

Quite a storm, I thought. I couldn't get Miss B's phrase out of my mind. I was listening so intently to Mary that I lost track of everything going on around me. But the wind came in hard and the rustling grass drowned out her voice.

"It's okay, Mary," was the next thing I heard Abe say. "It's okay."

I heard her crying. What had she said? What had happened to her father? Why did she now feel like she could leave the village?

"I know it might not make sense, but remembering the whole story helps me feel free of it," she said. "And even though I know it was Dan's brother, I can forgive him, and I can leave."

My insides trembled. I couldn't breathe.

My brother?

She can forgive him?

"What do you think you would have done if he had come earlier, before you had this memory?" Abe asked in a soft voice.

Mary paused. "I hated him, Abe." She stopped, and when she spoke again, the words came out reluctantly, in tiny, sharp bursts. "I thought up many ways that I could kill him. Isn't that awful? But not now. Seeing what happened, remembering everything . . . I can forgive him. I can leave. I'm at peace."

My brother's fault? What had Mary remembered? I felt desperate now to know. If it involved my brother, I had to know. I scrambled out from under the window as quietly as I could, moving like a shadow over to the front walkway. I tried to approach the house as if I was just arriving. I tried to compose myself, tried to pretend I hadn't heard what I had heard. But I needed to know more.

All of that receded in my mind as the door to Abe's house opened in front of me and Mary came out. Her eyes were red, and she rubbed tears away before she saw me standing there.

"Oh, hi, Dan," she said, clearing her throat, hastily wiping her eyes. I could tell in that instant she didn't want me to know what she had been talking about, that it would be pointless to ask.

"Hey, Mary," I replied in a hushed voice.

She looked into my eyes, and it was as if she was reading my mind, as if she could see everything I had been thinking, every worry I had been feeling. Had she needed to forgive me too, in whatever story it was she remembered? Had I been at fault? Would she hate me for what Adam had done? I waited for her anger or her contempt, or even for her to simply dismiss me and walk away.

Instead, she tilted her head to the side, and I felt nothing coming from her except compassion. She genuinely cared for me. It caught me off guard.

Mary took a half step toward me—we were already standing very close—and she gently placed her hand on my shoulder, like a quiet promise, and said, "Oh, Dan."

That was all, those two words. She said them the way you might if you found out that someone had gone through something difficult a long time ago, and you had no idea before why they were who they were or why they did what they did, but now you knew and you wished you would have always known, because it would have changed things.

I couldn't reply. I wanted to talk, wanted to tell her I had heard the story. Mostly, I wanted to ask her what had happened and how my brother had been involved, but I couldn't. The words all stuck in my throat. I was afraid, afraid she might say no, afraid of what she might tell me, afraid of being discovered as an eavesdropper. So I said nothing.

The two of us stood there for a long time looking at each other, and the kindness in her eyes somehow grew even larger. She removed her hand and moved past me, back toward the greenway.

"Dan? Is that you?" Abe called from inside the house, and for a quick moment I considered not answering. But I couldn't walk away from Abe. I had to tell him about the vision I had. Or dream. Or whatever it was.

I walked through the door. Daylight streamed through the windows, and I realized the happy things made me sad. The gray days and the rain kept everything as it was, stopped things from changing, and the sun reminded me that there was nothing I could do to keep Mary from leaving, or anyone else for that matter. They would all leave, and the sunshine reminded me of this. The sunshine made it possible. It's hard to take when the things that used to make you happy start to make you sad.

I found Abe sitting at a small desk tucked up against the wall. "Did you know there's something wrong with the garden?" I asked him.

He nodded, not looking up from the papers he was examining. "So, you've been over there this morning? I don't like it, Dan. We have plenty of food for now, but I've never seen a crop fail in that rich soil."

"Are we overusing it? Maybe we should pick a different site for the garden."

He shook his head, finally looking up at me. "I've tried. I planted crops all over these plains—up by the mountain, among the rocks, on the other side of your house, even out by the fourth tree. Nothing's growing right."

"You were out at the fourth tree?" I asked, surprised. "I've never been out that far. Did you see anything?"

He shrugged and waved his hand dismissively.

"And—wait. How long have you been worried about this? Did you say you've been planting seeds all over the valley? Since when?"

The look on his face told me he felt he had said too much.

More secrets.

"I'm sure it will be fine. All will be well and

all will be well and all manner of things will be well." He smiled when he said this, as if it was an inside joke he had with himself. "Do you need something?"

I had to think for a moment to remember why I was there. All the things came rushing back, too many things to keep straight. I was becoming mired in the uncertainty of what I could and couldn't talk about. A few days ago, my mind had been a blank slate. But now it felt too complex, filled with knotted threads. There was Mary leaving and Miss B's memory and the woman in my room and the dreams I was having, and now the garden and Miho's dream and the way Po had stared at me and the fact that I had heard Mary's memory but shouldn't have, so I couldn't talk about that. I couldn't remember what I was trying to keep secret and what was public knowledge.

"I feel strange inside, Abe. I feel like I'm disappearing."

He stood from his desk and gave me a kind smile. But I wanted to weep—at my deception and my brother being the only one left on the other side and the bitterness of green things not growing.

Abe put his hand on my shoulder. "What's wrong, Dan? What's really wrong?"

I stared into his dark eyes and realized we were the same height. I had always thought of Abe as much taller than me, a presence, a force that stretched far beyond me. But there we were, eye to eye. It was a revelation.

"I had a memory last night," I told him, and I was trembling with the strangeness of it. I told him about my birth, my twin brother, my mother holding me in her weakness, and my father far away, distant, unconcerned with me. I told him about the vague knowledge that came along with the memory, the sort of knowing that it brought: the realization of the distance between me and my father, the line down the middle of our family, my mother's devotion.

Abe's eyes were soft, and I nearly told him about the woman, but that was becoming something I could never tell anyone, a secret too deep to unearth. I lied to myself, reasoning that I could keep her from everyone.

He mumbled one word. "Interesting." He said it over and over again, and he was pacing when I finished, like a metronome, back and forth, back and forth. This went on for some time, and when he finished pacing, he collapsed into a different chair, one I hadn't noticed before in all the mess. There was a silence in his house that reminded me of the silence in my own house. A silence full of nameless things.

I cleared my throat, and Abe came back from wherever his mind had taken him.

"This is all very interesting," he said.

I could tell by the hesitance in his voice that

he was weighing his words carefully, trying to decide if he was going to tell me more, if he could tell me more, or if the things he knew were best kept close.

"You will remember more soon." He motioned toward his old gray couch, indicating for me to join him among the books and crates of garden equipment and half-finished carvings. So many carvings. There were crosses that circled in on themselves and walking sticks with curving vines and eerie houses with tall windows and elven doors.

I pushed a few things to the side and sat down. Despite all the things on the cushions, despite the pressing nature of all these unfinished things, Abe's couch was the most comfortable spot in the village. I sank into it and remembered my short night's sleep in the armchair. I wanted to close my eyes.

"How do you know?" I asked.

"It would seem that something is happening," he said in a vague, wandering voice. "Ever since this last storm, that is. Everyone seems to be . . . remembering."

"Remembering?"

"Remembering. Things from life before the mountain."

"Like my memories of my birth?"

"Yes, like that, but not always births. Other memories. Sadness. Joy. Other things. Death."

He looked like he was going to say something more, but he shook his head. "Other things. And they're coming quickly now. Hard and fast and not always welcome."

"Has anyone told you? What they're dreaming? What they're seeing?" I tried to ask this innocently. I even had a small hope that he would use my questions as a launching pad to tell me the part of Mary's story I had missed. But I knew he wouldn't. When you told Abe something, it went into a heavy chest with a lock on it, and no one besides you could ever bring it out.

As expected, Abe didn't answer me. He stared at a lamp beside the sofa where I sat, a lamp that also served as a coat hook for various scarves, bags, and woolen hats.

"I can't tell you other people's memories," he said slowly. "I'm sure you understand. Maybe they will share them soon. But something is happening."

"In this place where nothing ever happens?" I asked him, remembering our earlier conversation.

"Yes," he said in a curious voice, as if that was the most alarming part. "Even here. Something is happening."

7 Another Arrival

I stopped at the corner of Miho's house and lifted the binoculars that hung around my neck, staring out into the plains. It was the middle of the day, but the town remained quiet. Everyone was staying close to home. Maybe they were getting ready for Mary's leaving party. Some days in town were like that, though, so it didn't feel completely out of the ordinary. Some days, we all just wanted to be alone. But I couldn't help wondering if these swirling new memories were driving people into seclusion.

Miho and I had eaten a quiet lunch together, neither of us wanting to ask the other about their dream. She seemed to have softened since our encounter in the garden that morning. She seemed to be more herself. I was still flustered from what I had heard Mary telling Abe. I so badly wanted to tell Miho what Mary had said, ask her what she thought about the story. But that meant I would have to tell her I had been eavesdropping. The secrets piled up inside of me. They hibernated into cocoons, transforming into things that had lives of their own.

Lunch had been earlier. Now, the two of us

planned to go looking for firewood for Mary's ceremony.

At first I had trouble finding the oak tree in the binoculars as I scanned along the horizon. I made my way slowly from left to right along that distant line, and there it appeared: massive, thick enough that the trunk could have been carved out and turned into a hut. Where we lived at the edge of the mountain and the plains, the leaves were perpetually green, although we had miniature seasons where the trees faded to something like yellow or darkened into a lush color nearly black. But on that day, the sky was bright, the plains rustling and alive, and the tree's leaves were a lively green. Far beyond the tree, the storm that had come through the night before sat like a blot on the horizon.

Miho stepped in front of the binoculars, basically a huge blob of blurry color, and held up her hand in front of the lenses.

"And then it grew dark," she said in a mysterious voice, laughing.

I shook my head in mock annoyance. "Very funny." I lowered the binoculars and pushed her arm to the side.

"What are you looking for, anyway? You're always staring east."

"I don't know. I'm not really looking for anything specifically. I'm just looking to see if there's anything to see."

"But there never is," she said, smiling again, looking at me as if I was a puzzle.

I ignored her, pretended to be miffed while I folded up a large tan canvas tarp, tied it into a bundle, and carried it under one arm. We started to walk the long path from the tree beside her house to the first tree out at the horizon. When numbering the oaks, we didn't count the one by Miho's house. The first oak tree was the one we could barely see from town.

"Tell me this: have you ever looked through those binoculars and seen something worth seeing?" Miho insisted as we walked through the tall grass.

"Of course I have," I said. "Plenty of things."

"Like what? Name one."

"Well, it's not an object. But I like looking through the binoculars because it makes me feel like I'm out there. Out in the plains. Far from the mountain."

We both walked quietly for a minute.

"What else?" she asked, her voice soft.

"My house is far from the rest of you. I like to keep an eye out, see what you all are up to."

"You spy on us a lot, do you, from up in your high castle?" She swatted playfully at me.

I shrugged. "There's a beautiful woman I have to keep my eye on."

She laughed out loud, a free kind of sound, but it made me feel sad because I remembered everything unsaid between us. She reached over and grabbed my hand, and I glanced at her. Our friendship had grown during our time together. I loved everyone in town, Abe especially, but with Miho it felt different. With her, I felt chosen. I don't know, it doesn't make much sense, but she meant a lot to me.

We got out to the first tree, but as we expected, there was no dead wood for burning. I put my hand against the oak and closed my eyes. What a tree. Its bark was rich with deep grooves. The roots spread into the earth. One side of the tree had a fine layer of moss growing at the base of the trunk. Under the spreading branches lay a thick shade, almost darkness, like an eclipse.

We'd have to go to the next tree.

I raised the binoculars again, looking out to the next tree that had now appeared on the horizon. We couldn't see that second one from the town—it only came into view as we approached the first oak. The plains were empty, so silent and vast. I felt the tug of it, a desire to keep going, one tree after another, leave the village behind without even saying goodbye. But I knew I couldn't. My brother was still over there, behind us, lost in the mountain. The last one. I had to wait for him.

Miho and I kept walking. The grass was taller in some places, reaching to our waists. In others, it was nothing more than short, green stubble barely covering the brown earth. It took us a little while, but we got all the way out to the second tree, almost identical to the first in size and height. I had only been this far from the village a handful of times. It felt like we were on an island in the middle of an endless ocean.

"It always makes me feel funny, being out this far," Miho said, her voice timid and nervous as we gathered kindling.

The storm had brought down a few large, dead branches, and Miho and I broke them up as best we could and piled them onto the tarp. To be honest, there wasn't much, and I considered going out to the next tree, but I didn't know if we'd have enough time. There was a lot to be done before Mary's leaving ceremony that evening.

"Feels really far away," I replied. It was kind of a haunting feeling, like we were the last two people.

"There's something good about it, though, don't you think? It does feel far away, but it also feels nice to get out from under it."

She meant the mountain. She was right.

Once we had the wood arranged, I slid a rope through the eyelets in the tarp and pulled it tight. We could drag it back to the village without too much trouble, but it would take us longer than the walk out.

Despite our need to hurry, I sat down at the base of the oak tree and took a deep breath, facing south. To my left, the plains stretched on, and at the very edge of my vision, at the very edge of the day, I could see the next oak tree. Nothing else. Only the next oak in a long line of trees that Mary would follow, starting tonight when she left the village. When she left us. Going where? To what?

"Do you ever want to walk east?" Miho sat down beside me, breathing heavily from the work, gazing past me in the direction I was looking. "Are you ever tempted to leave your brother and go?"

I nodded. "Sure."

"Really? You never seem that interested."

I thought about that. I thought about Abe's words from the night before. They resonated with me. He had named something I didn't even know I was feeling.

"Everything is standing still here, you know? In the village. It's like time stopped. Leaving seems somehow inevitable. It's about taking that first step."

"Yeah, I feel that way too. And I wouldn't mind getting farther away from the mountain." Miho reached up tentatively and felt along the edge of her hair where the tattoo was. "Do you ever wonder what they're doing over there?"

"What do you mean? What who's doing?"

"The ones who ran that place. In the mountain. If everyone's leaving, escaping, they can't be happy about that."

We sat with that thought for a few minutes. It was an awful thing to think about.

"Do you mean they might come out, come after us?" I asked, my voice flat.

"I don't know," she said. "Probably not. I mean, they would have come before now if they were going to, don't you think?"

"Why do we stick around?" I asked, more to myself than to her.

"I guess we all have reasons for staying." Her voice had a strange tone to it, like she wanted to say more. "But it feels safe, doesn't it?"

She was right. The plains, even at the edge of that terrible mountain, felt safe.

"What do you think is out there?" she asked.

We both stared east, away from town, and I was happy about the change of subject. There was a story, believed in varying degrees depending on who you asked, that if you followed the oak trees all the way across the plains, one after the other, you'd come to a last tree planted at the foot of another mountain, a much different mountain. You'd see an opening that led to a path that would take you up and over, to a different place, a better place. Maybe even a city. I used to believe this story. I used to watch wistfully as friends and neighbors headed east on their way to the far-off place. I used to look forward to the day Adam came over and he and I could head to this new place together.

Now I wasn't so sure what I believed. Another mountain? A city? It all felt so improbable.

"Will you ever leave?" I asked Miho without looking at her.

"Me?" She said the word in a whisper, as if it was caught in her throat.

"Yeah, do you ever want to walk, head east?"

She let out the tiniest of laughs. "Sure." She paused. "But not without you."

It made me feel good when she said things like that. But it also made me nervous.

"I don't know if you should be waiting for me. You know? I might be a while. Besides, I don't know if I'm worth hanging around for."

She didn't answer, simply reached over and took my hand again, and we sat under the oak. I wouldn't have minded if time stood still in that moment, the light of another day cresting before it faded, the mountain comfortably far off in the direction we were not looking. Maybe we should head out, Miho and I, leave our ghost town of a village and the mountain, get out of here. See what we could find. Maybe we wouldn't even have to follow the trees. Maybe we could head north or south and make a new life in the middle of the plains, the two of us in the middle of nowhere.

But . . . Adam.

It always came back to my brother.

I looked to my right, past Miho, in the direction

of the village that I knew was there even though I couldn't see it. And the mountain. There was always the mountain. It rose in a grayish purple ridge with pink hues in the midday light. A thin line of white graced the top. Snow. I imagined that I could even see the black line of the canyon that led to the other side of the mountain. The strangest part of all was how beautiful that range was from this far away.

Miho stood and stretched. "We should go."

I took an extra minute before I stood up, gathered the long rope, and pulled it snug. "Back under the shadow of the mountain." I sighed.

As we returned toward the first tree outside the village, Miho glanced back one last time, and I felt a joke rising in me, something about Lot's wife. I wondered where that phrase came from, what long-ago story I couldn't quite remember, but before the words came out, she grabbed my arm. "Dan."

I peered more closely at her, waiting for the joke or one last deep thought about the distance between here and there. But she didn't say anything. Her eyes were wide open, staring east, so I turned.

At first I didn't see anything. The light was strange, the grass blew in a hypnotic dance, and the third tree was barely visible. A strong wind came down from the mountain and blew our clothes tight up against our bodies. It felt like

110

there might be another storm on the way, ready to spill over.

"C'mon, Miho. What are you doing?" I took one step away from her, but she didn't loosen her grip on my arm.

"Dan," she said again. "Look."

An annoyed look crept onto my face and I nearly argued with her about time running short, how we needed to get back. But I gave her the satisfaction of looking one last time toward the east. The tallest branches of the oak tree lashed this way and that in the strong breeze. I dropped the rope. I took a few steps east, passing her, passing the tree, and staring. I lifted the binoculars to my eyes.

Far off in the distance, closer to the next tree than to us, I saw someone.

She was walking in our direction, a girl or a small woman, and she was stumbling with determination but also with uncertainty. A tan cloak covered her, wrapped around her body and head. She pinched it together under her chin, but long hair escaped, billowed around her. She kept looking up as if expecting someone to meet her. I couldn't tell if she could see us or not. She wiped her forehead, stumbled again, leaned hard on a walking stick. She kept coming.

I handed the binoculars to Miho. Her mouth dropped open when she saw the girl. She turned to me with a million questions in her eyes.

111

"We need to go." I grabbed the rope attached to the tarp and tightened the load.

"What if she needs help?" she asked. "I think it's a girl, maybe a teenager."

The girl wasn't stopping either. I shook my head. "No one has ever come back," I said, my hands shaking so badly I could barely grip the rope. "No one."

We moved as fast as we could, dragging the tarp filled with wood behind us.

8 Someone Is Coming

Abe met us out beyond the edge of the village. I guess he noticed our urgency from a long way off. I dropped the rope and collapsed onto the grass, taking deep breaths. Miho bent over, hands on her knees, gasping for air.

"What are you two doing?" Abe asked with an uncertain grin. "Is everything okay?"

Still trying to catch my breath, I pointed out toward the first tree. "Someone's. Coming."

"What do you mean?" he asked, looking from me to Miho and back to me again.

Miho stood up straight and held her hands together over her head, trying to make more space for her lungs to work. "Someone's coming, Abe. From the east."

His smile shifted from uncertainty to doubt. He kept looking back and forth between us, as if he was trying to decide which of us would break down and tell him the truth. The fact that we both returned his gaze without hesitation seemed to knock him further off balance.

"You must have seen something that looked like a person. Maybe a branch fell from the next tree?"

"It was a person, Abe," I said. "We saw her in the binoculars."

"But no one ever comes back," he said. "There's no reason to."

It was true. If what waited in the east was so good, why would anyone leave it? Why would anyone return to this mountain?

"I don't know what to say, Abe. We saw what we saw."

"What should we do?" Miho asked.

"I don't know," Abe said, looking away from us. "If someone's coming, we don't have any reason to fear them. But it doesn't make any sense."

The three of us took in the darkening eastern horizon. The first tree faded as evening approached. We certainly couldn't see the second tree, or the third tree, where we had first spotted the person walking. How far could she have gone since we saw her? Was she still able to walk? She had looked like she was nearly collapsing.

"Should we tell everyone?" Miho asked.

"No, not until we're sure," Abe replied.

"We are sure," I said.

"Not until we know more," Abe said.

"Is it right, sending Mary out there," I asked, "if we don't know who or what is coming?"

"I think it was a girl, Dan," Miho said hesitantly. "I don't know that there's anything to be afraid of."

"When someone's ready to leave, to make the long trek east, it's time," Abe said. "No matter what. I don't think we should say anything. Mary's time to leave has come. We should celebrate that."

I didn't know what to say. They knew I didn't want Mary to leave, even before this stranger appeared, so any objections I raised would feel loaded with ulterior motives. I wished Miho would speak up.

"It doesn't seem right, Abe," she said. "If this person is coming from the east, wouldn't it be better to find out what she knows before sending Mary out there?"

"If it's time, it's time," he reiterated. But there was something in his voice that told me he wasn't completely sure.

"Okay, then let's go out and see what this girl is doing, see what she wants," Miho said quietly. "At least then we'll know what Mary is up against."

"Up against?" Abe asked. "How do we know she's up against anything?" He was thinking again, weighing everything. "Okay," he said to Miho. "Let's go. Dan, keep the preparations going for Mary's departure."

"Did I miss something?" a deep voice called over.

It was John, who lumbered to where we stood.

"The meeting of the minds?" he declared when

we didn't reply, his voice bounding out over the plains like a mastiff.

"Just getting ready for tonight," Abe said, the tone of his voice telling Miho and me that now wasn't the time to talk about the stranger approaching. "Would you help Dan get the fire started? Miho and I need to run a quick errand."

"'Course," John said, grabbing the rope and practically lifting the tarp off the ground.

I stared at Abe and Miho, and they both looked at me as if to ask, *What else is there to do?* I turned away because I had no answer for them.

I followed John over to the large outdoor stone patio where we held our community meetings. We piled up the wood, broke off some of the smaller twigs and slices of bark, and stacked it in the iron ring in the middle of the patio.

"Do you have matches?" John asked me.

"No, but I can grab some from Miho's place."

He dusted his hands together, coughed loudly, and watched Miho and Abe as they walked away. "What are they up to?"

"You'll have to ask Abe."

The air grew cooler even though the breeze was gone, and everything stood still. I waved up the greenway when I saw Misha walking leisurely toward us. I noticed Miss B was with her, and even from that distance, I could feel a kind of coldness coming from her, a hesitance, as if she wanted to walk in the other direction. The story

116

she had told me surged back to the front of my mind.

I ducked into Miho's house. It was dark and tidy. I walked straight to one of the drawers in her kitchen and pulled it open, grabbed the matches. I turned to go, but curiosity got the better of me, so I slipped over to the large picture window that faced the plains. The light in the sky had faded, and even the first tree was nothing more than a dark silhouette against a darkening backdrop. I couldn't see Miho or Abe.

A chill shot down my spine as I thought again of the other stranger in the village, the one no one else knew about: the woman in my house. I had this feeling that I should go check on her, see if she was still resting, still there. I couldn't explain the deep desire I had to keep her presence a secret from everyone else. Why didn't I tell them? I squeezed the small box of matches in my hand. The dim gray light that remained fell through the large window and down onto the table where Miho, Abe, and Mary had met the day before.

Unlike the rest of the house, the table was cluttered, covered with papers and pens and pencils and even some paint and brushes. I pushed the papers around a little bit to see what Miho had been up to. Even though we were close, snooping through her stuff seemed inappropriate. I pushed past the discomfort and saw my name peeking out from one of the pages, so I pulled it into the dusky square of light. It was part of a question written in Miho's familiar handwriting, and as I read it, my curiosity and guilt welled up into tangible things.

Am I waiting for Dan's brother?

That was it. A question. But a strange one. Why would Miho be waiting for my brother? She hadn't known him before all of this.

Had she?

The house grew dark, but I was curious. I struck one of the matches and it hissed to life, creating an orb of light right there in my hand, like magic. I pushed a few more of the pages around. There were some beautiful pencil sketches. One of Abe, charcoal dark and shaded perfectly, his eyes looking up into mine, nearly alive and asking me what I was doing looking through my friend's things. Even a drawing of him made me feel guilty, and I flipped the paper upside down so he couldn't watch, so he couldn't ask me questions with his drawn eyes.

There was another pencil sketch under that one. It was less developed than the one of Abe. I didn't recognize the person, a woman about the same age as Abe. I looked closer. I didn't think I knew her, but she had the same almond eyes as Miho and there was something similar in the shape of her mouth. A relative perhaps? Was this the memory she'd referred to when I saw her in the garden that morning? Something about her mother?

The match diminished down toward my fingers, but I didn't notice until it burned me, and I dropped it on the table where it landed in darkness. I told myself I had time for one more. I struck a new one and held it straight up so it burned slower.

I saw the edge of a third sketch, and I pulled it forward. Complete and utter shock left me breathless. The chin and cheek lines were perfect, and the ears were fine in their subtlety. The wiry hair stood in a very specifically unkempt way, the way I suddenly remembered it. The eyes were clear enough to bring tears to my own. It was almost like looking in a mirror, but it wasn't quite me.

It was Adam.

Miho had drawn my brother. I felt like someone had punched me in the stomach. I leaned on the table with one hand and squeezed my eyes tight. A light-headedness threatened to drop me to the floor.

Another memory came to me, precise and unbidden and sharp. I remembered standing beside him, telling him he'd better get out of bed and do what he needed to do. Did I tell him to go? It felt like it. But I was earnest in my appeal. *Go. You have to. If you don't, we're ruined.* I remembered very specifically saying those words.

If you don't, we're ruined.

Miho's drawing was familiar: those same eyes, that same unkempt hair.

He'd shaken his head, and I'd grabbed him by his collar and lifted him and forced him to do what I wanted him to do.

I stepped back from the table. The match burned out, once again on my finger, and I dropped it, cursing. I got down on my knees and searched the floor for the charred end, but I couldn't find it. So many lost things.

What had I made my brother do?

"Yo!" a voice shouted from outside. John's voice. "Yo, Dan, what is taking you so long, my man?"

I left Miho's house, and suddenly I felt like a stranger in the village, like I didn't truly know anyone. Abe had said everyone was having new memories. And Miho, the person I was closest to, wasn't willing to tell me anything, not even when it obviously involved my own brother. What about John or Misha, Circe or Po? What did they know? What had they remembered?

"Found them," I shouted up to John, trying to sound light and carefree but barely succeeding. "I'm coming."

I didn't look up until I got to the stone patio. Everyone was sitting around the edge facing the plains, as they always did whenever we met there, the mountain in the distance behind them. There were houses close to the patio, huddled all around us, fencing us in. Miss B sat on an old chair that

John had dragged over for her. Misha and Circe whispered to each other, both giving me a smile when I arrived. Was something else there, in their smiles? Were they hiding something too? Po sat at the end, carving something in one of the sticks meant for firewood. He didn't look up.

"Po," I said, motioning toward the stick we were supposed to be using for firewood. "I walked a long way for that."

He finally made eye contact with me, smiled, and held the wood up to me as if in a toast. "Thank you," he said in his curling accent, his bright red hair seeming to have its own light source in the near dark.

"Is Mary ready?" I asked no one in particular.

"I saw her by her house," Circe said. "She was waiting for the fire."

That's when I noticed Miho and Abe still hadn't returned.

"And Miho and Abe?" I asked.

"They're not back yet," John said, scratching one of the matches against the stone floor. It sputtered to life.

"Back from where?" Po asked without looking up from his carving.

"The plains," John said without fanfare.

"The plains?" Circe and Misha asked simultaneously.

"What are they doing out on the plains? At this time of day?" Miss B asked.

"Don't ask me," I said, trying to deflect all the unwanted attention. "Ask John."

Everyone looked at John.

"What? I don't know."

I wondered if it was possible that even John could be hiding something. I doubted it. I didn't think he had it in him.

Meanwhile, the fire grew, moved up the larger sticks, laid down a foundation of glowing embers, and cast dancing shadows behind the group, shadows that stretched toward the mountain. *Under the shadow of the mountain,* I thought. The early evening seemed even darker once the fire rose up.

I glanced around one more time. "Well, what do you want to do?" I asked. "Should we wait for Miho and Abe or get on with it?"

"Get on with it," a firm voice said from the darkness between two of the nearby houses. It was Mary. "They know I'm leaving," she said. "It's time."

"Okay," I said, uncertain. "I can try to fill in for Abe if you don't mind, although I'm not sure I know all the words." Po grunted, his eyes still on his carving. I took a deep breath. "You sure that's okay with you, Mary?" I asked again, hoping she'd change her mind.

"Yes," came Mary's clear reply. "I'm ready."

"Okay, well, in that case," I said, holding out my arms as if I were going to embrace the entire world, "please stand with me, friends."

I closed my eyes and took a deep breath, feeling nervous and unsure of myself. It had been a long time since anyone had left. I wasn't sure if I could remember the correct order of everything. And while I considered each of them friends, I was also still feeling the uncertainty I had experienced in Miho's house—what memories had they all had? What nameless things were in that circle around the fire?

I could feel the heat from the fire, and the light flickered against my closed eyelids. What was taking Abe and Miho so long? I opened my eyes and began with what I thought were the right words. "Friends! Today we celebrate the leaving of Mary! Today we light the fire of friendship and send her on to the east, where we all will someday go. Do not mourn her passing. Do not weep."

But even as I said those words, I could feel the tears rising in my eyes. Mary entered the circle of firelight, dressed in a plain white dress with a circle of white flowers on her head, flowers that only grew up close to the mountain, hidden among the boulders. I had forgotten—usually anything involving the mountain was my job.

I walked over to Mary while Circe placed a large bowl of warm water on the ground between us. I looked at Mary, our eyes met, and she smiled a kind, sad smile. I wiped my eyes and smiled back, and in that moment, I was overwhelmed with the desire to go with her, to finally leave this village at the edge of the mountain, get out from under its shadow and move on.

But . . . my brother.

I got down in front of Mary, and the stone patio was hard and uneven against my knees. She put one hand on my shoulder for balance, then raised one of her feet over the bowl. I washed her small, very white, dainty foot. Tiny indigo veins wound their way up her ankles. She put the other foot over the bowl, and I washed it as well. The water cooled quickly, as did the day fading into evening, and I could feel the collective gaze of those sitting at the edge of the patio.

"Do not weep!" I said again, my voice cracking. I stood, drying my hands on a towel. "She travels a path we all must travel. Where her washed feet go, so must ours."

I leaned toward Mary. The others were at the other side of the fire. "How am I doing?" I asked with a smile, trying to cut the sadness. I hated feeling sad. I hated feeling like this was the end.

"Wonderfully," she whispered, reaching up and pushing back a strand of her hair. "Dan? Can I tell you something?"

I leaned closer. Her hair smelled like flowers and her skin smelled like spring. She talked so quietly that I was the only one who could hear her.

"I remembered something about your brother. I had a memory."

"My brother?" I tried hard to pretend I hadn't already heard this while eavesdropping outside of Abe's house.

"Yes." She paused and held on to my elbow. Her touch was cool, her fingertips electric. "I've been waiting for your brother too."

"Why?" I asked. If she didn't tell me now, she would leave, and I would never know.

"I didn't realize it until recently. I told only Abe. Your brother . . ." She paused again. "Your brother brought me great pain, Dan, once upon a time. A long time ago."

"You mean in the mountain?"

"Before that. He did something horrible, and I didn't think I could leave this place until I confronted him. I wanted to kill him for what he had done."

"I'm sorry, Mary." I found it hard to breathe. "I don't know what he did, but I'm sorry."

She shook her head, clearing away the past. "It doesn't matter anymore, not to me. I forgave him. I wanted to tell you so that if you ever see him again, and he remembers what happened, you can tell him for me. I forgive him. That's why I'm leaving now. I'm free to go. I can feel it."

I could feel everyone staring at us, their curiosity building.

"Is this going to take all night?" John asked with a loud chuckle. I held up one finger, asking him to wait.

"Care to share with everyone?" Po said, his voice cynical.

But I continued, whispering only to Mary. "You knew my brother back before the mountain?"

She gave me a solemn look. "Our paths crossed."

I waited for a moment, trying to think of what to say, what to do. "Can you tell me what happened, Mary?"

"No," she whispered. "Maybe someday, Dan, if we meet again, but not today. Today, I am leaving."

"Nothing?"

She shook her head in quick jerks, tears filling her eyes. "I'm sorry." She let go of my elbow and took a few steps back. "Today, I leave," she said in a loud, firm voice.

I wanted to stop the ceremony. I wanted to hear how she knew my brother, demand to know what he had done, take this story from her by force if necessary. But I also had a feeling that the memory was coming to me too, that it was on the edge of my mind.

"Tomorrow, we follow," all of us said in response.

Mary left the circle for a moment, and when she returned, she was holding a large sack. I knew that in it was everything she held dear. She put it down at her feet. Everyone walked over to her and gave her a gift, something of their own that was precious, something she would appreciate. I gave her the small book I had brought with me, the one I had put in my pocket that morning. When she saw it, she cried even harder.

Mary picked up the sack and put it in the fire, and the flames grew steadily until they were roaring. She reached down and took each of the gifts one at a time, appreciating them, then looking at the person who gave it to her. Her eyes were full of such thankfulness, and it was with great tenderness that she also put each of the gifts into the fire. It hurt me to see that book burn, I won't lie. I made myself watch it, though. I watched the pages turn brown and swell, the thin cover curling and blackening and rising in smoke. I watched the flames catch.

"You have given up anything that might keep you here," I said, still staring at the book I had given her. I felt certain that I hadn't quite gotten the wording right on that one, but I was somewhere else, my mind circling back again and again to the realization that she had known my brother, that he had done something to her. She had been waiting for him, just like me. Just like Miho too, apparently.

I tried to keep the ceremony moving forward. "Does anyone have the rocks?"

Circe walked over and handed me two rocks, both the size of a small fist. "Where do you think Miho and Abe are?" she asked me quietly, deliberately facing away from the others.

"They'll be here soon, any minute." I nodded with what I hoped was assurance, taking the rocks from her, but I didn't believe my own words. They should have been back by now. Fear for Abe and Miho fluttered inside of me. But I reasoned with myself—she was a small girl. Barely able to walk. What trouble could she have caused?

One of the rocks Circe gave me was white with dark gray veins. The other was black like coal. I handed the two rocks to Mary, and she stared at both of them for a moment. She walked up the hill a short distance, as close to the mountain as she needed to get. I watched her, but the rest of the group didn't face the mountain. Even then, they chose not to look.

Mary threw the black rock up toward the mountain, and it clattered among the shattered boulders, falling at the foot of the cliffs. She held tight to the white rock, and as she turned toward us, we formed two very short lines. I remembered when those lines used to be fifty people long, one hundred people long. But now there were only three of us on each side.

She walked between us, taking the white rock with her. Circe was crying, shoulders shaking. Miss B wiped a tear from her eyes. John kept clearing his throat. Misha nodded, as if someone was telling her something she agreed with in the deepest way. Po stared into the fire.

There was no waving, no goodbyes, no words—those had all been spoken earlier, in private. I wondered who she had met with that day, who she had spoken with. Had she told anyone else about my brother? Did one of them know more than I did?

I wished I would have taken the time to talk to her. I wished we would have sat down together. If I had visited her, would she have told me more?

I watched her walk away from the village, toward the darkness, and I was overwhelmed with anxiety for Adam, for me, for all of us. The village was emptying—how much longer until John or Po or Circe traveled east? Who would say the words for me when it was my time to go? Who would give me a gift to put in the fire or hand me the rocks?

Before Mary disappeared, I saw movement in the shadows. It was Miho and Abe, returning from the plains. And not only them—Abe carried a girl in his arms. The girl we had seen from the second tree. He stumbled at the edge of the light, went down on one knee, and laid her there in the grass.

9 Po's Theory

"I can't stay," Mary said, as much to herself as to us. She had come back to us when Abe appeared with the girl, and now there was a slight twinge of panic at the edge of her voice, as well as a kind of asking for permission. "I can't. I just can't. I made up my mind. I have to go now." She looked around with wild eyes. I couldn't make myself meet her gaze.

We were all looking at Abe and Miho and the girl lying in the grass. She was tiny, curled up in the fetal position, like a fawn that's been delivered too soon. Miho squatted down and placed her hand on the girl's shoulder, felt her neck, stroked her hair, and pushed it back behind one ear. The girl's hooded cloth poncho was disheveled and bunched underneath her, and the rest of her clothes were also a plain tan color. Her bare feet were stained green from the long walk through the plains. I couldn't look away.

Nothing felt stable anymore, nothing felt moored down. What was going on in this place? We had been there for ages, and within the span of two days Mary decided she was leaving, the black-haired woman came out of the mountain, and this girl came back over the plains. And people were remembering things. No one had ever come back. I had never kept things from Abe or Miho. It felt like someone had picked up the puzzle pieces of my life, a puzzle that was nearly assembled, and threw it into the air so that everything was separating and coming undone.

I wanted to tell Mary that she had to stay, at least until we found out what this girl's appearance was all about, that it couldn't possibly be safe out there in the dark, walking east into who knows what. What if there were others? What if this girl was trying to escape trouble? But I knew, coming from me, an appeal to stay would seem insincere.

Before anyone else could make a recommendation either way, Abe spoke up. "You're right, Mary. You need to keep going. Everything will be well. Please. Go. This is your time."

His words jarred me. But Mary nodded, unsteady, and then she walked into the night.

Misha took a few steps after her, and for a minute I thought she was going to leave too, without any fanfare, simply vanish into the darkness with Mary. But she stopped where we could all see her. She watched Mary walk off, and her voice came out tiny, barely a squeak. "Mary?"

"Are you sure Mary should leave?" John asked, but Abe cut him off.

"I need some food and water, right now. Hurry."

Miho slipped into her house and came out with half a loaf of bread and a glass of water. She bent down close to the girl.

"Out of the light," Abe mumbled, and we shifted where we stood so that the dancing firelight made its way down the bank and into the midst of our small gathering. John lumbered back up to the stone patio. I could tell he was miffed at the way Abe had ignored his concern. He threw a few more logs on the fire, sending up a shower of sparks. Soon the fire roared again, but John didn't come back down. He stood there, staring into the fire, his massive paws fisted on his hips.

I moved closer, staring again at the girl. She had long, light brown hair. Her arms were lean with muscle, and even though she was small, her shoulders were strong. Her face was lined with determination, even when she was unconscious. A deep bag was on the ground beside her. Abe put a hand under her neck and raised her head, and with his other hand he put the glass of water to her cracked lips.

The girl's mouth moved, barely, the way a leaf might flutter when there is no wind, so subtly you could hardly see it. Then her lips moved toward the water, and her tongue flashed between them. Abe tipped the glass a little more so that water trickled into her mouth, and she swallowed, wincing. He went on like that for a long time, giving her small sips, until some kind of relief washed over her. She became less rigid, and her head turned to the side.

Abe bent even closer, whispering in her ear, "You're okay now. We will take care of you."

Her eyes fluttered. Her mouth opened again with a kind of yearning that we all felt and understood. Abe raised the water, and she drank in a thirsty way this time until it was gone. She opened her eyes, looked around at us in confusion, and closed them again.

I stared off into the darkness, looking for Mary, but she was gone. It was night, the traditional time of day for heading east. The great, empty plains had swallowed her. I hoped she could find the first tree in the darkness, but I also knew that if she couldn't, she'd wait for morning and then find her way east, one tree at a time, all the way across the plains. How long would it take her? What waited for her on the other side? There was so much that we didn't know.

"She's awake again," Circe whispered.

"What do you need?" Abe asked the girl.

That's when I noticed she was staring at me. She didn't say anything, but she stared with intensity, as if she knew who I was.

Abe turned to Miho. "Can we keep her in your house for now?"

Miho nodded. The others murmured questions

and thoughts to each other, but no one had anything productive to offer. We were all stunned.

The fire dimmed and a log fell by itself, collapsing in the space of things already burned. John hadn't moved. He still stared into the fire. A cloud of ash moved upward in small wisps and sparks. Po had returned to his seat beside the fire not far from John, carving quietly. We had all become stir-crazy. No one wanted to go home and sit in the heavy silence that waited for us.

I walked over and sat beside Po. "What's going on around here?" I asked him, shaking my head. "This is absurd." I thought of the strange looks he had given me earlier that day. It seemed awkward to ask him about that directly, but I thought that maybe if we spoke, some explanation would come out.

John glanced over at us, opened his mouth to speak, then closed it and stared back into the flames. Po peeled away a small slice of wood with his knife, and it dropped to the stone patio, joining a small pile of similar shavings.

"Feels like we're coming to the end," he said without emotion, blowing on the walking stick, eyeing it critically before shaving off another piece.

"The end?" I asked.

He grunted, kept carving, and didn't say anything else for a little while. There was something tender about the way he carved, something intimate, as if he wasn't cutting the wood but coaxing it.

"What do you mean, the end?" I asked again.

He sighed and spoke without looking at me. "Think about it, Dan. What happens when that place empties out?" He motioned with his head back toward the mountain, and returned to his carving.

"You mean what happens once the last person comes out?"

He nodded.

"I haven't given it much thought."

He gave a wry grin. "I don't think anyone has."

"But you have?"

"For years now, as long as we can remember, people came out of the mountain. Right? You've seen them. Beaten down. Tortured. Bloody. You came over, I came over. We can barely remember what happened to us over there, but it's pretty clear it wasn't some kind of party going on. 'Escaped,' we call it. 'Escaped from the other side.' "

I nodded.

"Now, it also seems pretty clear to me that there were some nasty folks running that place over there. Judging by the state of us when we came over. Fair to say?"

I nodded again. "That's fair. From what I can remember, it's true." I tried to sound like I'd been

135

thinking of this for a long time. Images of some of the worst abuses came to mind, and I squeezed my eyes shut instinctively, trying to push those images back. But they never went anywhere. Not really. I could close my eyes, but I couldn't keep the nightmares at bay. So I opened my eyes and stared into the fire.

"Okay," Po continued, "so put all of that together and then ask yourself, when's the last time anyone came over the mountain?"

He said this as a kind of final point in his argument, but I couldn't help picturing the dark-haired woman who had come over the day before and was lying in my bed. The woman who had told me my brother was still over there alone, that he was the last one.

"It's been a long time," I said, trying to go along with his game, my voice faltering in the lie.

"What if they're running out of people to torment?" Po asked. "What if there's no one left over there? What if they're gathering their forces and preparing to come over the mountain and retrieve us, take us back, use us for whatever it was they were using us for before?" His eyes grew wild and he stopped carving, punctuating his words with his knife, a stab in the air for each question mark.

I sat there as his words sifted through the air. There was no breeze. The fire burned straight up with very few sparks. John stood, walked over

136

to the pile of wood, and threw a few more large pieces on.

"Do you think that's what's going to happen?" I asked Po, my voice low, not wanting to bring John into the conversation. And if that's what he thought, why had he been glaring at me? What did I have to do with any of this?

"Makes sense, doesn't it?"

"So what are you waiting for? Why stay so close to the mountain? Why haven't you headed east yet?"

He looked at me, squinted, and stared back at the walking stick, but he didn't carve. "For a long time, I didn't know why I was staying. But last night, I remembered something."

"Really?" I asked. Po too. Not only me and Miss B and Miho and Mary, but Po was remembering too. "Something about the other side of the mountain? Or before that?"

"Before."

"Really?" I said again, and this time I couldn't keep the fascination out of my voice.

He nodded.

I waited. He was silent.

"Can you tell me?" I asked hesitantly, already knowing what he would say.

He gave out a small laugh. "It's mine. I'm not giving it away, Dan. But that's why I'm still here, why I can't leave. I had a feeling about it for a long time, but that memory confirmed it for me."

"Fair enough," I said, disappointed and feeling spurned. Again.

Miho walked up to the fire. "You guys okay?" she asked.

"Anything new?" My voice came out weak and tired. Po was back into his carving, sitting right there yet also somewhere far from us.

Miho shook her head. "Do you have that book Abe likes to read to people when they first come over?"

It had been a while. I had to think about it. Did I have it, or had I last left it at Abe's?

"Yeah, I think I do," I said.

Po's words still occupied my mind. What if he was right? What if we were moments away from those horrible slave masters coming out of the mountain and hauling us back to that hell?

"I'll run up and get it. Where do you keep it?" she asked.

Po peeled back another long piece of wood and it curled in on itself, fell down onto the stone patio. I was drowning in all the recent realizations—Miho's drawing of Adam and Mary's memories about Adam and Po's theory about those on the other side and the woman's revelation that my brother was the last one.

"It's probably on the first bookshelf by the door, up toward the top. Red spine," I said absentmindedly. I was trying to think through some flaw in Po's theory that would keep me from worrying about it. I'd never been able to visualize our tormentors, but that neither supported nor undermined his idea that they were coming back for us.

Minutes passed before I realized Miho was walking to my house to get the book. She was walking by herself, to my house, where the woman slept in my bed.

I ran after her, wondering what made me think I could ever keep all these lies and half-truths straight in my mind.

10 You Never Told Me Your Name.

The breeze returned in the darkness, coming back at us from the plains, and it was sweet and melancholy. It pulled a deep sense of nostalgia from me, a kind of remembering, but not of specific things: nebulous, old memories of tears and great happiness, of devastation and celebrated rebuilding. I wondered if my memories of those old days would ever come back to me, if I would ever remember everything, or if they would always be made available in fits and starts, small pieces here and there.

The grass was nearly dry, and my feet swished along quickly as I ran first through the dark village, then through the short empty space that led to my house, and finally up to my front door. I opened it, breathless, just as Miho came out.

"Oh!" she shouted, jumping.

"I'm sorry," I said, laughing nervously. "I'm sorry." I looked into her eyes to see if she had found anything, to see if she had seen the strange woman in my house.

"What is wrong with you?" she asked with a laugh, raising one hand to her chest as if to slow her heart. "You scared me, Dan."

"I'm sorry," I said again, bending over, still breathing hard. "I . . . I wanted to make sure you could find it."

She held up the book by its spine, her laughter shifting into a small suspicion. "What is going on, Dan? You haven't been yourself lately. What's wrong?"

I couldn't look up into her face or she would have convinced me without saying anything to tell her the truth, so I stayed bent over and stared down, catching my breath. "It's Mary," I said. "Just Mary. And now this girl."

Miho put her hand on my head, a kind of blessing. "Dan," she said in a quiet, breathless voice. "Oh, Dan."

We stood there like that for longer than made sense. The two of us, I knew, were looking for something to connect to, someone to trust. And guilt seeped through my entire being. She was that for me. She was someone to trust. And I was so utterly not.

But the guilt was also compounded by a feeling of indignation that she knew more than she was telling me. I kept seeing in my mind that sketch of my brother on her table. What did she know? And why wasn't she telling me? I felt this growing chasm between us, and I wasn't sure what to do about it.

"I have to go," she said, regret in her voice. "I have to take this down to Abe." She raised the book again. "Do you want me to come back up here? I feel like we need to catch up."

Concern etched itself around her eyes. I felt it too, the distance.

"No," I said, standing up and shifting so that I stood between her and the rest of the house. "That's okay. Just grabbing a few things. I'll be right behind you."

She reached out and touched my arm, gave a small smile I could barely see in the dark, and drifted toward the village, swinging the book by her side while she walked.

I watched her disappear into the darkness. How could she remain so carefree? When I went inside and closed the door quietly, the latch barely made a sound.

I meandered around in the kitchen for a bit, taking out some bread and gnawing on the crust. I walked over to the rear door, opened it, and looked out over the plains. I couldn't see very much in the dark, but the grass rustled in the wind.

I left the back door open and walked to my bedroom, paused for a moment, then went inside.

She was still there, and it looked like she had barely moved since I had left earlier in the day. She was on her side, eyes closed, hand still reaching over toward the chair where I had sat. I walked slowly to it and sat down. Why was I so afraid of her? What could she possibly do to hurt me?

Her eyes opened slowly. They were beautiful

eyes. I could see this, finally, since they were healing. The redness had gone out of them. Her dark irises were soft, even inviting.

"What are you going to do?" she asked in a drowsy voice.

"About what?" I replied. There were so many things on my mind. I couldn't narrow them down to what she might be referring to—telling everyone about her? Going east? Trying to find out more about the memories everyone was having and not telling me about? Finding out more about the girl?

"Your brother," she stated.

"I don't know."

"Your brother needs you," she said, and I felt like crying. What was there to do but wait? I couldn't go back over the mountain, not back into that hellish place. When I thought of it, screams echoed in my mind. Pain frayed my nerves. I didn't think I could bear it, going back in there.

"How did you make it out?" I asked. "Do you remember anything?"

She coughed, moved her hand to cover her mouth.

"Wait, let me get you some water." I walked back to the kitchen and returned with a glass. "Would you like to sit up?"

She shook her head. She leaned to the side and managed to drink some water like a bird, tipping her head back. "I don't remember much.

I remember the path going up and up and up. I remember hiding. I don't know how I did it." Her eyes went momentarily wild.

"I wish we knew more about it," I said, more to myself than to her. "I wish I could remember something."

She coughed again. "When I left your brother, he was at the very bottom. The very bottom." The darkness in her eyes shifted to sadness, the way a sunny day can suddenly dim.

I leaned toward her. Again I was taken by her beauty, her vulnerability.

"I wanted to bring him with me," she said. She licked her lips, and they, too, were soft, healing. Tears formed in her eyes. I leaned closer. "But he wouldn't come. He was too afraid."

Something about her courage latched on and stirred up a longing in me. I moved to kiss her cheek at the same moment she turned to look up at me, and our mouths came together. She was warm, and she kissed me back. I felt a rush of confusion and the soft delight of intimacy.

I see him kneeling on a mound of rock, and he looks like he's been there for a hundred years. His clothes are tattered, and when he looks up, his eyes are wild. I wonder if he's sane anymore—there's something about him that looks missing, vacant. I want to walk toward him, but something is between us, something is keeping us apart.

This vision was quick, like a stabbing pain. I leaned back in my chair, shocked, existing on some other plane.

"You should go get him," she whispered. "You could convince him to follow you out."

"I can't go down there on my own," I murmured, trying to catch my breath. My heart was pounding. I wanted to kiss her again but knew I shouldn't. I thought of Miho. What was I doing?

"You wouldn't have to go alone," she said, and her voice was relaxing, mesmerizing, convincing. "You have friends here who would go with you if you asked them. If you all went together, you would be safe."

"I couldn't do that," I said, but I didn't sound convincing, not even to myself. Would they do that? Would they come with me? Maybe the horrible ones waiting on the other side wouldn't expect us. Maybe we could sneak in unobserved and bring back Adam. Safely. All of us together.

My voice emerged empty, distracted. "If you want to get cleaned up, there's a bath in there." I pointed mechanically toward the bathroom no bigger than a closet.

I stood up. I had to get out, take a walk, clear my head. I moved to the door, but when I got there I stopped and turned. "You never told me your name."

But she was already asleep.

"You never told me your name," I said again, this time in a whisper. I stared at her placid face, my hand on the doorknob. I wanted to stay, but I left.

In the middle of that dark night, Miho's house became the new center of our small universe. Misha and Circe sat in the soft grass outside her front door, talking earnestly, quietly. Miss B walked in circles around the stone patio not far away, every so often looking down toward the house. As I walked up, John and Po passed by.

"Where are you guys going?" I asked, worried for a moment that they were leaving too.

"We're going for wood," John said.

"You'll have to go a long way," I warned them. "I was at the second tree and there wasn't much left."

"We'll check it out," Po said dismissively. There was an edge to his voice that seemed unwarranted.

"Everything okay?" I asked their backs as they walked away, but they didn't reply.

"Should they be going out there right now, in the dark?" I asked Misha as she came up beside me. "I can't even see the first tree."

She shrugged. "What can we do?" Her voice was so slight that her words melted away.

I sighed. "Anything new in there?"

"The girl woke up a bit ago," Circe said. She clenched her jaw. "I've been hounding Abe for

146

an update. I'd love to know what they're talking about."

Misha nodded in agreement.

"Why would someone come from the east?" I asked. "After all this time, after all of these people leaving, why come back?"

Could it be there wasn't anything on the other side of the plains? What if the promised haven didn't even exist?

But if there wasn't anything over there, why didn't more people come back, and sooner? Were the people over there sending for help?

Miho's face appeared at the door. "There you are," she said to me in a calm, kind voice. "Thanks for the book. It's helping her relax."

"Is she okay?" Misha asked.

Miho nodded. "She's sleeping now."

Abe came out, walking past Miho. "Why don't you all get some sleep," he suggested. "There's not much else going on here right now. Let's meet at the patio in the morning. We'll give you an update."

"Sleep? Abe . . ." Circe replied, clearly ready to interrogate him about the woman, but he interrupted her with a tired voice.

"Circe, please. We're all tired. Let's talk in the morning."

"Do we have that long?" she asked.

He stared at her for a moment. "In the morning, Circe."

"The guys went out for wood," I told him. "I think they'll have to go out to the third or fourth tree."

"I wish they hadn't done that. Listen, let's all stick together until tomorrow, okay? Stay in the village. Stay together. I'll keep the fire going to make sure John and Po can find their way back."

The women glanced at each other nervously.

"Can I stay with you?" Misha asked Circe.

Circe nodded as Miss B came over.

"Miss B, we're having a slumber party," Misha said, smiling, trying to lighten the mood. "You want to stay with me at Circe's tonight?"

"And sleep on that godforsaken sofa of hers? No thank you, ma'am. I will enjoy my own bed quite well, thank you."

Everyone laughed, and for a moment the air felt more breathable.

"Well," Misha said, "can we at least walk you home?"

"Of course."

The three women walked up the lonely greenway into the darkness. They walked slowly, accommodating Miss B's easy pace. I made a mental list of where everyone was: Miss B at her own house; Misha and Circe at Circe's house; John and Po on an unadvised wood run; Abe and Miho in the house with the girl. Who was I missing? I was convinced I was missing someone.

Oh, of course. Mary. But she was gone, walking east, somewhere in the dark, maybe at the fourth or fifth tree by now if she had walked straight, if she had found her way.

I turned to walk home, wondering if the woman in my house had fallen asleep for the night, but Abe called my name.

I turned around. He motioned for me to come back to Miho's door. "You need to come in. We have to talk."

Three lamps lit the inside of Miho's house, and their softness caused a seed of homesickness to rise again. I loved our town, and I was heartbroken at how empty it had become. There were times we had picnicked out by the first tree, well over a hundred of us. Maybe even two hundred at one point. People had shared houses in those days. The greenway had always been full of people—barely green, in fact, usually trampled to dust by all of the coming and going, the visiting. There had been the constant sound of laughter and even, sometimes late at night, singing.

I could barely see the girl lying on the small couch against the wall, resting in the shadows. I took a step toward her, but Abe held out his arm like a small barrier. I stopped.

"Wait," he said, motioning toward the table where Miho sat, her face in her hands. She looked up at us, her eyes tired, more tired than I'd ever seen them, and she gave me a sad, uncertain smile. She reached out her hand to me, and I crossed the space and took it with a pang of guilt, remembering how I had kissed the woman in my house. The woman without a name.

Abe pulled out a chair for me and I sat in it. I glanced around the table, but the sketch was gone, as was the note with the question about my brother. How could Miho possibly know what my brother looked like? Why was she waiting for him?

The three of us sat still for a few moments, saying nothing.

Abe broke the silence. "She can't speak," he said quietly, and I could tell he was trying to keep our words from reaching the girl.

"What?" I asked.

"Or won't," he clarified. "Can't or won't."

"This isn't good," Miho whispered to herself, as if it was the only thing she had been saying since the girl arrived. "This isn't good."

Abe seemed to consider disagreeing, then thought better of it. "We don't know what it means," he said to me.

"But everyone's already freaking out," Miho said. "What will they do when they find out she can't talk? What if she can't talk because of something that happened to her on the other side of the plains?"

I knew immediately what she was implying—that the other mountain, the faraway respite we had heard so much about, might simply be a mirror image of the one we had escaped from. Another place of torment. If that was true, we were trapped in between them, mountains to the east, mountains to the west. Where could we go?

"We don't know anything for sure," Abe said firmly.

"But that's the whole point," I said, anger or cynicism or despair rising in my voice. Or all three. "We don't know anything. She's here, and we still don't know anything. What could be more discouraging than that?"

We sat in the quiet. The lamp in the kitchen burned down too low and winked out, and the shadows that formed in its wake felt like living things drawing closer, predators closing in.

I felt the key in my pocket. I gathered myself. It was time to tell Abe and Miho the truth.

But then I heard a sound from the sofa. The girl was sitting up, staring at me with eyes wide open. She was either terrified of me or surprised to see me, and neither response made any sense.

"Hi," I said to her, glancing nervously over at Abe. He nodded at me, encouraging me to keep going. I realized he was hoping we might get her to say something, to explain why she had come back.

She didn't reply, so I tried something else. "Are you okay? Would you like something to eat?"

She stood up and limped toward me.

Again I thought of how far she must have come, the toll the journey must have taken on her small body. She moved more fully into the light, and when I saw her face, I felt the tug of familiarity, but it was a flash, here and gone. There were tears in her eyes as she raised her hand to touch my face, but just like that, the light went out of her eyes. Her hand fell back to her side, her mouth closed into a straight line, and her eyebrows furrowed in confusion. She turned and went back to the sofa, curling up under the blanket with her narrow back facing us.

I looked over at Abe and Miho. We stared at each other. No one knew what to say.

What I didn't say was that I had experienced this before. I knew that old familiar feeling of someone looking at me, thinking they recognized me, only to apologize and walk away.

It happens often when you're a twin.

So, she knew my brother. I considered telling Abe and Miho this revelation, but it became another nameless thing.

"Tomorrow morning," Abe said, weariness in his voice, "let's meet up at the patio. We'll tell the others everything we know."

"We don't know anything," Miho replied, but it wasn't a protest of any kind, simply a statement of fact.

"And that's what we'll tell them."

• • •

My house was dark and quiet, and there was an undercurrent of something I couldn't identify, like a high-pitched sound I heard for an instant and then lost track of. I assumed the woman was still sleeping in my bed, and I felt guilty because of my recent treasons, so I didn't even go back into the room. I didn't trust myself. Why should I? No one should trust me. Not anymore.

I pulled the armchair over to the back doors and opened them, sat in the chair, and stared out over the plains. Since it was night I couldn't see anything, but I could hear the wind moving madly through the grass. It whipped in the door and stirred the air in the house, so I got up, found a blanket, and sat back down.

I fell asleep, drifting into a shallow snooze. I tossed and turned all night. I even watched the sky brighten in fits and starts as I slept and woke up, slept and woke up. Finally, as light took over the morning, I found a place of deep sleep.

When I woke up, I had it. Another memory. One that filled me with dread and a deep, deep sadness.

11 A Real Shame

I saw the sunlight glaring off the windshield and felt the warm summer air gusting through my passenger-side window. My arm rested on the window ledge and my chin was propped on my forearm. I stared out at the passing fields and it gave me an empty feeling. The wind blew my hair around as we drove through a cloud of dust, the specks rising up and stinging my face and eyes.

I could feel the resentment of my father, who was boiling in the driver's seat of the car. I was old enough to drive, but if he was in the car, he was driving. On that particular trip, he was a tornado of pent-up energy, twitching and biting his fingernails and muttering the beginnings of sentences that never came to fruition. I was sixteen, and he was afraid I was about to let him down.

Finally, he managed to actually say something, real words, and he had to shout to be heard above the wind rushing through the open windows. "I don't care what happened. He's your brother." His words simmered there in the air, spitting hot, before being swept out of the car. We left them behind, or at least I wanted to leave them behind. But words have a way of keeping up.

The car carried us around bends and over bridges, and for a moment I was a child again and pretended we were launching into space. I closed my eyes and felt the darkness around me, the earth moving away faster and faster, the encroaching stillness of space and the pinpricks of stars all around. I felt like I was floating, and I had to catch my breath when I looked down and saw nothingness for all eternity. The earth became a tiny blue dot, remote, and I felt a great sense of freedom.

But my imagination could only take me a certain distance from reality, and when the car stopped abruptly and my father shut it off, I had to open my eyes. We were at my high school. He pulled violently on the parking brake, even though the car had come to rest on flat ground. I wondered if you could break the parking brake by pulling on it too hard. He might pull the handle right out of the car and carry it with him into the principal's office.

"C'mon," he growled.

As we crawled from the car, I knew a couple of things.

I knew my father believed you should never rat out your brother—never, never, not for any reason.

I knew we were going inside so I could tell a lie.

We crossed the baking pavement. My father treated the handle of the front door much the same as he had treated the parking brake. We entered the air-conditioned lobby, and the cold air clung to the sweat on my forehead, under my arms, on the small of my back. I followed my father as he plunged through door after door, never knocking, never waiting.

Then, the door to Principal Stevens's office.

"How can I—" his assistant began, but my father ignored her and pushed through the door.

I followed, my shoulders hunched over apologetically. I stared at the floor tiles.

"Gentlemen," Principal Stevens said, unfazed by my father's entrance. "Have a seat."

My father paused, as if he was considering the most brazen way to reject any seat ever offered to him by this no-good principal, but he scowled and sat. I sat beside him. In the remaining seat sat a police officer.

Principal Stevens looked across the desk at us. "As you know, Jo Sayers has accused your son of . . ." He hesitated, weighing his words. "Of violating her at a party three months ago."

"Why'd she wait so long?" my father hissed.

"I'm sure we can sort all this out," Principal Stevens said, somehow managing to remain completely removed from my father's spite.

My dad glared over at the officer. "What's he doing here?"

"He's here to collect your son's statement and make sure there are no . . . inconsistencies."

We lived in a small town, one that didn't give too much standing to things like Miranda rights or the right to have an attorney present.

"Boy?" the police officer said, staring at me.

"I was with my brother all night," I said quietly.

"Which night?" the officer asked.

"The night Jo claims he . . . was with her."

"That's right," my father muttered. It was the closest thing to encouraging me that I had ever heard slip from his mouth.

"A few kids say they saw him at the party," the officer said. His voice was neither skeptical nor believing.

I glanced at the principal. I had the sense that this was a performance they had all created, and all I had to do was play my part.

"I heard there was a lot of alcohol there." I shrugged, staring back at the floor. "Easy mistake to make."

"This isn't just any violation," the officer said, a sternness entering his voice. "This is rape, boy."

I didn't reply.

"Where were you boys, if not at the party?" Principal Stevens asked in a completely unconcerned voice, but he did lean over his desk toward me.

"Camping. Sir. Up at the state park. We left right after school and didn't come back for two nights. I was with him the whole time."

"You sure?" the police officer asked.

I swallowed hard. "Yes, sir."

The principal leaned back, and it was clear he was immensely relieved. "We don't need a good boy to be kept from graduating, not over something like this," he said. "Thank you, Dan. Officer?"

The police officer shrugged. "This clears it up pretty good."

We all stood at the same time. I was amazed at how easy it had been, not only the process but also the telling of the lie. A shiver ran through me, as if I'd swallowed something raw, something not meant to be consumed.

"Why'd that little swine wait to come forward until now?" my father asked as we all shuffled toward the office door.

Principal Stevens shrugged. "No one knows for sure," he said. "Maybe because she's pregnant."

The officer shook his head. "It's a real shame," he said, and the other two men grunted their assent.

I couldn't tell what it was he referred to as being "a real shame"—the fact that she had come forward, the baby, the rape, or the lie we had all agreed on.

It was a quiet morning, and I knew they were probably waiting for me at the stone patio, waiting for me to come down so that all of us could decide what was next. What would we do in the face of so many unexpected things?

But the new memory gave me so much more to think about, and I needed to sit with it a bit. I wondered how I could do that, how I could lie for my brother, but then I remembered the look on my father's face while we drove. The images swirled in my mind—the wind in the window, the anger of my father, the baking pavement as we got out and walked toward the school. The sense that I had to fix what my brother had broken. Anxiety at the impending lie.

I stalled. I woke slowly and rose even slower, weighed down by what I remembered. The day was already there, and it was bright. The grass was still and the air had warmed, now that the storm was two days gone. The horizon formed a line where the deep blue of the sky rested on the rich green of the grass, barely moving. I stood in the doorway, shading my eyes with one hand, staring out into the emptiness.

There was something about the light of a warm day that scattered the fear from the night before. Po's theory, that those who had held us captive were returning for us, had felt so true in the flickering shadows beside the fire, but here? In the daylight? It seemed ludicrous. The valley was too peaceful to imagine some kind of impending invasion.

I heard rustling from my bedroom, a sound that caused nervousness and other feelings to flutter in my gut. The woman. I walked to the door and stood there listening before raising my hand and knocking lightly with two knuckles. "Hello?" I said in a hushed voice no one could possibly hear from the other side of a door.

But she must have heard my tender knock, because her voice called out to me. "Come in."

I pushed the door open. She sat in bed, her back against the headboard. She had combed her long black hair and it was straight and shining. Her dark eyes searched mine. She pulled the covers up around her and sighed.

"Thank you," she said, her voice rich and purring.

"For what?"

"For taking me in. For helping me. For letting me stay here without telling anyone else. I needed this rest. I'm still not ready to be interrogated."

She was a vision sitting there. Stunning.

"Have you found my key?" she asked in a distracted voice, as if it was the last thing on her mind.

"No," I managed to get out, even though the key was right there in my pocket where it always was.

"Have you decided?" she asked me, her eyes wide with curiosity.

"Decided what?"

"Decided what you're going to do."

"About what?"

She smiled, and it was the closest she had come

to condescending. It was a smile that said, *You silly boy. What would you do without me?*

"Your brother," she said, and the blanket lowered so that I could see her bare shoulders. "What are you going to do about your brother? You can't leave him there."

"I should probably go find him," I said, looking away from her. My voice was noncommittal, not convincing in the least. In fact, the words surprised me—I could never go back into the mountain and look for him. Where had that come from? Still, it was embarrassing that I hadn't gone for him as soon as she told me where he was.

"To be honest, I don't know if I can do it," I muttered.

"Of course you can! But you can't go alone," she replied, and there was an urgency not quite hidden in her voice. "You need to take them with you. You will need help."

"Them?"

"Your friends. All of your friends who live here with you. They should all go with you."

I nodded, but my words went in a different direction. "I can't ask them to do that. It's too terrible. I can't."

She looked at me as if I had said something very noble, and she nodded at the truth of it—the deep, aching truth. "But you can't go alone," she repeated.

"I know." I wanted to tell her I didn't think I could go back there at all, on my own or with an entire crowd of people, because what was over there was simply too awful.

"It wasn't as bad as you remember it," she said in a soothing voice, looking down and to the side as if she was afraid to make eye contact.

"What?" I asked, confusion all over my face. "Are you kidding?"

There was a sincerity in her face that I couldn't argue with. "I know you have terrible memories of it, but you've made it much worse than it really was."

"You just crawled out of the canyon a couple days ago," I said. My voice sounded like someone else's, someone far away, someone rather silly. "You were bleeding. You could barely stand." Why did I sound silly to myself? I made a resolution not to say anything else.

"What are you talking about?" she asked. "I'm completely fine. Look at me. You found me in the plains and brought me here. Don't you remember?"

She was right. Her skin was like white soap, clear and soft. Her face was untainted by anything. Her eyes were sharp and black, and her hair glowed. I squeezed my eyes shut and shook my head, trying to loosen this grip of confusion. I was getting mixed up between finding her and seeing the girl out by the third tree. How long had this woman been in my house? Where exactly had I found her?

"Dan," she whispered. "It's okay. Look at me." She paused. "Dan, look at me."

I opened my eyes. Her gaze was a deep pool. Her hand moved up my arm until it stopped behind my shoulder. She pulled me down toward her and kissed my cheek, my forehead, and then my mouth. Softly. So softly. I closed my eyes and fell into visions of other times, other places.

But always, at the heart of everything I saw, was my brother, alone.

My heart pounded when I locked the house and walked down the greenway toward the cluster of houses. I felt all emptied out, turned around, and disheveled. It was like someone had taken my mind, with everything it knew and believed and felt, and shaken it, so that all the papers mixed up, all the files opened, all the pieces jumbled.

The day couldn't have been more beautiful. The air was the perfect temperature, cool on my skin. The sky was blue and clear, and the grass on the plains rippled in gentle waves. I wanted to go lie in it, stare up into the blue, feel the blades of grass against my arms and ears and fingers. I took in a deep breath and let it out, another deep breath, another letting out. Yes, this was it. No matter what else was happening, this was the village I loved.

I walked through the houses. No one was there, and this went beyond the normal quiet of our near-empty town. Even the places where people usually moved around were empty. No one peeked out to say hello, no one invited me in for a chat, no one offered me a drink. The doors were closed and the alleys were empty and the blinds were all drawn. Even Miss B's. Even the women's.

By the time I approached Miho's house, I could hear them. I looked up the small hill to the stone patio, and they all were sitting in a circle, talking in murmurs and whispers, their voices mingling with the breeze that moved through town, stirring the long grass, sounding Circe's wind chime. I felt like a kid late to class.

I walked toward the patio and everyone stopped talking. Now I felt like a defendant entering the courtroom. Their eyes were on me. When I returned John's gaze, he looked down at the ground nervously. Po didn't look away, though. Neither did Circe. Misha swallowed hard. I kept walking toward them and took in each person in the circle. Finally, Miho pulled her mouth up at one side in a kind of apology and started crying softly. Then she pulled her knees to her chest, her feet coming up onto the seat.

"Hey," I said, the one word a question. I stopped walking and stood at the edge of the small circle. The charred remains of the previous night's fire sat black and lifeless.

"Dan," Abe said, standing and motioning to an empty spot right beside him, "where have you been all morning?"

I shook my head slowly, not answering.

I noticed that the girl sat on the other side of Abe. Someone—Miho, I guessed—had brushed her hair and braided it. Her skin was clean. Her eyes seemed cooler in the daylight. She was biting her fingernails, and her eyes kept flitting up, looking at my face, and then looking elsewhere quickly. She didn't say anything.

I walked across the patio, and I had never felt so self-conscious of each step. I was sure I'd catch an edge and trip. But I made it to my seat and sat down.

Abe walked to the other side of the small circle so he could face everyone. But he spoke mostly to me. "Dan, we've all had memories in the last two days that need to be shared."

"I thought we were going to talk about her," I said, motioning toward the girl. "And try to figure out what's going on around here."

"I think it's important that we take some time today and share our memories because, well, as it turns out, they all pertain to you." He paused. "Or your brother."

I couldn't have been more confused. But I thought about Miss B's memory and how I'd had a feeling it was connected to me somehow. And I thought of overhearing Mary's memory. Miho's drawing of my brother. I looked at the rest of them: Circe, John, Po, Misha.

Now what?

"Dan, if you don't mind, we're going to have everyone take turns sharing their new memories."

I was relieved and terrified. Relieved because I would finally know what everyone was thinking about, what everyone else had remembered. Terrified because . . . well, I wasn't sure. What was it about these memories that had anything to do with me?

I had a sense that their stories might change me, make me into something entirely other than what I was. Could stories do that?

12 The Daughter

I looked across the circle at Circe. She couldn't hold the connection, and her eyes dropped to the stone patio. The whole time she told her story, she stared at the ground, then at Abe, then back at the ground again. But never at me.

"My daughter used to call me Susie," Circe began, her voice almost apologetic, as if she'd rather not share all of this. "It was just her two-year-old way of squeezing out 'Circe,' and it always made me smile. I don't know why I'm telling you that. I guess it all comes together, doesn't it? It always does.

"The memory that came back to me doesn't have a sharp starting point. It's like trying to remember a dream. There are all these dull edges, things I can't quite see, but up out of those came this memory. It's been right there on the edge of my mind all week. You know how sometimes you can't quite remember a word? That's what it felt like. Then, last night, I was pacing through the house, thinking about all of this, and, *pop!* There it was."

She paused and took a deep breath. She sounded nervous. I leaned forward. I wanted to know now. I was hungry to know.

"I've known for a long time that I was waiting for Dan's brother, that I couldn't go east until I saw him again, confronted him, whatever. But I didn't know why until this memory came. I still don't know exactly why, but I know it's connected to this somehow.

"It was her birthday. I remember that now. She was turning three, and she loved giraffes. Everything was giraffes. Her curtains, her pillowcases, her blankets. She had a dozen giraffes, anything from stuffed animals to small plastic toys. How strange to remember all of this now. It seems impossible that I ever could have forgotten. I feel guilty for forgetting. I feel guilty that something as selfish as the pain I experienced in the mountain could take her from my mind, could eliminate her from my thinking."

She stopped, and I wasn't sure if she'd be able to continue, but Abe spoke up. "Pain isn't selfish, Circe."

She sniffled, wiped a tear from the end of her nose, and nodded. "What happened to us in the mountain that could have made us forget all of these things?" she asked, and for once she scanned the group, but no one offered any answers.

"Anyway," she continued, "the two of us were at the grocery store picking up a few things. She was only three, but she understood it was her birthday. She was a big fan of birthdays, actually.

I guess most kids are. And she was never one to sit in the grocery cart. At this store, they had miniature carts for children, so she would push it along behind me, clipping my heels or knocking things off the shelves. I tried not to get upset, but it always hurt when she caught my heel with her cart, and I think I was a little stern with her about the mess she was making. I wish I wouldn't have been so harsh. I wish it wouldn't have bothered me."

She was crying, but she kept going. "I saw her too, got a really good glimpse of her in this memory. She was so beautiful!" Circe held both hands over her face, and Misha moved to go to her, but Abe held up his hand and shook his head.

"I'm sorry," Circe said. "I'm trying not to get emotional. It's hard and good, seeing her in my mind again. She had wispy blonde hair pulled up in a precious little ponytail. Her eyes were a kind of icy blue, a sharp, piercing blue, and she was sassy! My, she was sassy. She'd fill her cart up, and I had to make a pile at the register of all the things we weren't going to buy." Circe smiled, then laughed. "She'd pull it all from the shelves, anything she could get her hands on, and at the checkout I had to figure out how to get rid of it all."

A few people in the circle chuckled. I felt a slight sense of relief at the idea of her not finishing. I didn't know if I really wanted to know any more, and her silence took away some of the apprehension I was feeling.

"The strangest, most maddening part of the whole thing is that I still can't remember her name. I can't remember my own daughter's name. Not knowing what I named that beautiful little girl is almost the worst part. Almost.

"It was a Tuesday. That much I remember. The exact date, I'm not sure, but it was a Tuesday. The woman at the checkout was so kind to both of us, not making a big deal of all the groceries in my daughter's cart that would have to be put back on the shelves. The woman smiled down at her, asked questions about the things she had chosen, and complimented her on her choice of shirts—it had a cartoon giraffe on it—and the perfection of her ponytail. She looked at me when she said this, and we smiled at each other. I felt a kindred connection with that woman, the two of us going about our daily lives, neither of us having any idea what that morning was about to hand us. And we both laughed when my daughter explained her need for nearly every item. I laughed and laughed, and it felt so good."

She was smiling. I felt strangely happy that something about this memory, which had to do with me, brought that smile to her face. I wished it would be happy all the way to the end, but I knew that wasn't where Circe was going. She wasn't going toward happiness.

"I needed that laugh," she said. "I can't remember why, but there was something about the other parts of my life, something missing or sad, that made that laugh important somehow. That woman helped me to laugh, and it felt like a big glass of ice water on a summer day. What a gift laughter is. I've never thought of it like that before.

"My little girl and I walked outside, and it took me a little while to convince her to leave her cart inside the store. She always wanted to take those things home with us. I think I found some treat or other from the groceries we had actually bought and managed to bribe her with that. When we got outside, I realized the wind was gusting. There was a storm coming, but not a normal storm— the horizon had these swirling green clouds, like boiling water, and the gusts of wind would stop for a moment, then come back harder than before. We had parked far out in the parking lot, so I scooped my daughter up and put her in the cart, preparing to run through that charged air to our car and quickly load up the groceries before the rain came. But we were too late."

She paused.

"We were too late."

Even the mountain seemed to be listening in on her story. It seemed like it might be nearing the middle of the day, maybe even later, and I wondered if I had really stayed in my house for that long. Where was the day going to?

"Lightning struck and the thunder came right after it. Before we even left the shelter of that overhang, the rain came down in buckets, and we stopped where we were. Anyone walking toward the store was drenched in seconds. The sound of it was a roar overhead, and all around us the smell of the steaming pavement rose up as the water pounded down. It was raining so hard that the raindrops were exploding where they landed, creating this misty coating everywhere. I didn't want to take my daughter out in that rain—she'd get soaked in seconds. Why would I do that? Right? And the groceries too. Everything would get soaked. So I thought maybe I could run out quickly to the car and leave her there with the cart. It would just take a moment. Only a minute.

"I looked around for someone who would stay with her while I went for the car. A woman and her elderly mother had come walking in from the parking lot after being caught in the storm, both of them wet through. But they were laughing, pointing at each other's soaked-flat hair. Their eyes were shining.

" 'Excuse me?' I said to the woman. 'My name is Circe. This is my daughter. Would you mind watching her and my groceries while I run out to get the car?' Or something like that. I don't know. Was I a terrible parent? Would any of you have done this?"

"Oh, Circe," Misha whispered.

"She agreed. She was very kind. Her mother immediately took to my daughter, chatting with her in a very grown-up way. When the next round of thunder rumbled around us, she jumped. But the woman was kind and reassured me that the two of them would watch her and take care of her. How often I thought of those words! How often I cursed myself for leaving her with someone else!"

A breeze made its way down from the mountain, stirring every loose thing: the grass, our clothes, the ash in the fire pit. A gray cloud of it burst out and swirled in a funnel shape before blowing past Miho's house and disappearing in the plains. I looked over at the girl. She was listening intently. A strand of her hair blew into her face, and she pushed it behind her ear.

Circe got a firm look on her face, like she was determined to see this through. "I stared out into the downpour and gathered my courage to run, but then an older man came over and asked if I would like him to go out and get my car. I thought about it, but it was still raining so hard, and I felt bad asking him to do it. He was sort of hunched over, and I didn't want him to get pneumonia or something from getting wet when I was quite capable of getting the car myself. I thanked him and told him I would do it. And I didn't mind. It was warm, and it would only take me a moment.

"He turned, and he smiled real big when he saw

my daughter. The mother and daughter who were watching her both sort of squealed when they saw him, and then they were hugging because apparently they were very old friends. As the three of them stood there chatting, the older woman had her hand on the man's shoulder, and he was acting very bashful about it. 'Are you sure you don't mind watching her?' I asked the woman again, partially to make sure and partially to remind her about my daughter. The women both seemed completely caught up in this unexpected reunion with the older man. She smiled and waved her hand at me, saying they weren't in a hurry and I should go on."

Circe took a deep breath as if going underwater. "I felt like I was diving into a pool as I started to run. Even when I wanted to breathe, the whole thing sort of took my breath away—the lightning and thunder, the ridiculously hard rain, the way it splashed up off everything. I was drenched in a second. My feet got heavy from the water soaking into my sneakers. I got to the car and frantically tried to work the key. I ripped open the door and fell into the driver's seat, banging my head on the door frame.

"What if I had run faster? What if I hadn't fumbled with the keys? What if I hadn't bumped my head? Would I have gotten there faster, in time to pick up my daughter and get her out of there?

"I sat there in the car, rubbing the sore spot on my head. The sound of the rain was like a waterfall. It ran down the windshield, blurring everything around me. I thought of my daughter and started the car. I backed out of my space, turning toward the store. And that's when I heard it."

Circe swallowed hard, as if she thought she might throw up or her body was trying to consume the words she meant to say. "The sound seemed both far away and right overhead. At first it was a dim kind of humming, like a mosquito getting closer. But I noticed that the humming was choked back at times, making it sound irregular, sputtering. It turned into a whooshing sound that came in over the parking lot, and I saw this thing drop from the sky and land right where my daughter had been sitting in the grocery cart."

Tears streamed down her cheeks, but Circe made none of the sounds I associated with crying. It was haunting seeing her like that, her eyes suddenly empty, staring out over the plains.

"It was a small airplane. It seemed so absurd, so out of my normal experience that I almost couldn't comprehend it. I sat in my car and screamed. It's kind of embarrassing, but that's what I did. I had my foot on the brake in the middle of that parking lot. I didn't get out and run to her. I didn't get out and call for help. I just stayed right there and screamed.

"The strangest part of it all is that I know Dan's brother had something to do with it, and that's why I'm here. That's why I'm waiting."

Her eyes were flat. It was as if she was talking about some other Dan, some other story that had nothing to do with me. I squeezed my eyes shut, pressed on my temples with my index fingers. I felt like more was coming back to me. Circe's memory stirred the dark bottom of my subconscious, and things were rising.

"I'm sorry, Dan," Circe said, and I didn't understand why she was apologizing. I glanced at her. She didn't look like she knew either.

"No one's at fault," Abe said. "These things are from long, long ago. If having these memories and talking about them will help you move on, then that's a good thing. If hearing someone's memories stirs up more recollections of your own, good! We're here to talk and, by doing so, move forward."

While my initial response to Circe's memory had been to recoil and not want to know any more, a kind of hunger remained. If these people were somehow connected with my brother, I wanted to know how. Maybe it would help me find him. Maybe it would help me bring him back.

"Would anyone like to go next?" Abe asked.

A few of them glanced at him, hesitation on their faces. A few kept staring at the ground. There was a long silence.

Po spoke, his normally whimsical accent terse and sharp, as if he was trying to hide his anger and doing a very poor job of it. He scared me. I finally understood why he had given me such a glare yesterday morning.

"I'll go," he said, running a hand through his red hair. His fingers trembled. "I'll tell you what happened. But I'm not rushing it."

13 Po's Story

I watched Abe, hoping to get something from him, anything that might bolster my spirits. A smile, perhaps. A nod. But he looked intently at Po, and I felt very much alone. Po cleared his throat, and I felt a kind of helplessness, like I was being carried along on a river in rough water, not knowing how much longer it would be until I was sent careening over the falls.

"Jan and I had spent the previous week hiking in America," Po said, his words deliberate, rehearsed, "in some of the most remote areas we could find. All we had with us, we carried on our backs. She was a trooper too, and carried as much as me. She insisted on cooking, not because I thought she should but because she hated my food. 'You're always burning things,' she would tell me with a smile. 'You're always running too hot.' She giggled after she said that, and I would protest. 'What? My food is just fine, thank you very much.'"

Po stopped and smiled to himself, now fully immersed in his own story.

" 'It's true,' she'd say, and she'd try to make up. She'd come over to me, hug me, and then pull away so she could look at my face. 'Maybe it's because of your red hair. Everything about you is burning.' That always made me laugh. At night by the fire, she'd run her fingers through my hair and talk about how much it looked like flames.

"Anyway, there we were, making our way on a trail, and she was hopping from one rock to another when she hurt her foot. I thought it was a pretty straightforward sprain—it didn't look like anything was broken—but it was bad, so I tried carrying her for a while. We weren't getting anywhere. She was trying to tough it out, but I could tell her pain was getting worse.

"We cut through the woods toward a spot on the map that indicated a road, and it was really slow going. The day was dying, and her foot was swelling, like a sausage ready to split. It definitely seemed worse than a sprain. I was afraid because I had no way to stop the pain. We'd rest every so often and elevate her foot to relieve the pressure. Eventually we got to the road where there was this narrow shoulder, so we set up camp there in the dusk and hoped a car would come. She was moaning and biting her lip and trying not to make a fuss, but she was hurt bad."

In the silence between sentences, when he stopped for a moment, all I could hear was the wind coming down over the mountain and sweeping past us. Sometimes when it picked up, the girl held her cloak so it wouldn't flap and Miss B held the corners of her shawl close to her chest. I could see the edges of the garden from where I sat. The corn tassels flailed wildly. I realized Po had stopped talking, and he was staring at me, not saying a word. It sent a hollow jolt through my stomach.

"It didn't take too long for a car to show up. It was this old woman," he said. "She drove past and went far enough that I was disappointed, like she had decided to leave us behind or hadn't seen us, but her brake lights came on and she eased to a stop. I saw her bright white reverse lights, so I walked toward her. I could tell she was afraid I might hurt her. She only put her window down an inch or so.

"I told her my wife hurt her foot pretty bad, and she asked if I was going to murder her. So I asked her if she planned on murdering me, and she chuckled, a nervous little sound. I thought she might drive away. I was sure I looked terrifying after being in the wilderness for as long as we had been. But I went back and told Jan this old lady was going to help us. I lifted her up, carried her to the car, and the old lady got out. I guess she had decided to trust us and let fate take its course. She opened the rear passenger door for me and I gently eased Jan in. I walked back to get our stuff, brought it to the car, and climbed into the rear seat with Jan. It was almost completely dark by this point.

"The old lady explained our options. The

closest hospital was a five- or six-hour drive, and I couldn't tell if this was because it was that far away or because she drove slow. She was willing to take us there in the morning—she couldn't make the trip that night because she had already been away from home for too long and had to care for her husband. There was a small, private airstrip not too far off, and she thought they might be able to fly us to an airport close to the hospital. If she remembered right, the small plane flew back and forth twice a day, once at night and once in the morning.

"I honestly thought I was in some kind of a nightmare. We were in America but couldn't get to a hospital? It was so frustrating. We decided to look into the plane option, so she drove there gingerly. Jan whimpered every time we hit a bump, and the old lady emitted a kind of sigh when she heard Jan, as if trying to apologize without words."

Po stopped, and the sudden silence made me look up, but this time he wasn't looking at me. He was staring up at the mountain. I followed his gaze and let my eyes roam the cliffs high above us, the snowy peaks, the fractured angles and jutting faces.

"I can't believe I'm remembering all of this," Po muttered. "Where did all of this stuff vanish off to? I feel like if I had remembered before now, I could have done something about it.

"Anyway, it was late when we got to the airstrip, which was nothing more than a large warehouse-type building flanked by a chain-link fence. I climbed out of the car and walked through the dark. There were trees all around. It was hard to imagine a clearing large enough for a plane to take off.

"A voice called out to me from inside the building, so I turned and walked toward it. As a man came toward me, I told him my wife needed to get to the hospital. He said the plane had already come back and wasn't leaving until early in the morning. I asked if he was the pilot and said we'd be willing to pay extra, but he said that wouldn't work. They didn't fly at night. When I pressed him, he gave me this sarcastic little grin and said his brother was the pilot and was drunk."

When Po said these words, a jolt went through me.

"I wondered how I could get Jan through an entire night. That's when he told me they only had one seat on the plane. I was so frustrated. This wasn't what I had in mind at all. I started pacing. Maybe one of the other passengers would sell me their seat in the morning. I asked him what time the plane left, and he told me six a.m. sharp."

Po ran his hands through his hair, looking frustrated, as if having the experience right there in front of us for the first time. "I asked him how I was supposed to get to the hospital.

" 'We have a neighbor who sometimes rents out his car,' he said.

" 'Why can't we just take it now?' I asked.

"He shrugged. 'You can, but it would probably take us just as long to drive there with the storms that came through.'

" 'We'll take that last seat,' I said, and then I asked him if they had a place we could sleep. He said they did. I asked him if they had any Tylenol. He said they could do better than that."

I glanced around the circle. Everyone was caught up in the story. Misha's head was tilted to the side and her eyes squinted in a kind of wincing sympathy. Circe nodded.

"That night was like hell on earth for Jan. She was in so much pain, and I was really worried for her—a sprain shouldn't have been like that. Her foot was purple and green, and the painkillers weren't working. I didn't sleep all night.

"The plane was a Cessna 172. Don't ask me how I remember that when there are other things I can't remember and should be able to recall. That name and model number are stuck in my mind. Cessna 172. The runway was paved, kind of, with lots of loose stones. The pilot was barely sober, but we didn't have any other options. Jan was so out of it that she couldn't have had any concerns anyway. I watched them take off, and the wings dipped a little one way, then the other, and they were off. It killed me to send Jan off that way in her condition. He had promised me that his brother the pilot would make sure she got to the hospital. I had sent a wad of cash along to help him remember."

He looked over at me. "I guess by now you know you're the brother."

Po waited as if he needed my nod, my acknowledgment, before he could continue. I stared at the ground, closed my eyes, and nodded. Then he continued with his story.

"I was worried about the storm, and I told Dan that. He told me it would be fine, and he claimed storms moved in a certain direction there, pointing vaguely away from the spot where I had last seen the Cessna. I stood there for a long time watching the storm, noting how it wasn't moving the way he said it would. After that, he drove me to the other guy's house and I rented that car he had told me about."

Po stopped. He tried to speak again, but his voice had tiny fractures in it. He took a deep breath, raising his shoulders deliberately to take in more air. A sense of panic rested on me. I wanted to run. I didn't want to hear the end. I had a sense of what happened, and that was all I needed.

"I first heard what had happened on the radio. I was only a few hours into my drive, and the rain was coming down in sheets. I knew it when I heard it. I knew it was her plane. But I kept driving. I didn't cry. I didn't break down. Something in me thought that if I could keep driving, it wouldn't be true. I'd never have to face it as long as I didn't push the brake."

He nodded as if trying to convince us that every single word he said was true. He nodded over and over again.

"I drove around for a long time, just kept driving in circles."

14 When the Plane Fell from the Sky

We sat there for a long time, and no one said anything.

"Are you okay, Dan?" Abe asked, and I nodded, though it wasn't true. I wasn't all right. Their stories weighed on me. I tried to look out over the houses, stare into the plains, but there was no escape, not even there. I wished Miho would come over and comfort me in some way. I needed something. Anything. But their words were everywhere. They were inside of me. And a picture was revealing itself in my mind, an understanding of where these stories were going. I didn't know if it was because I was putting the clues together or because the memory was coming back to me.

"Let's take a break," Abe suggested, and there was a collective sigh.

Miss B stood up and stretched. Po slumped farther forward, his face in his hands. No one looked at me. No one knew what to do with my presence. I felt as if I had become superfluous to the proceeding, as if everything would move along better if I wasn't there.

"I'll get some food," Miho said, even though

it was well after lunch. The sky had reached its brightest point a while ago. The afternoon was upon us, and at this rate dusk would settle with us still here, sitting around the fire pit. I glanced over at John and Misha and watched Miho walk away.

Even when Miho returned with the food, no one else said anything.

"We're getting somewhere, aren't we?" Abe asked quietly, but no one replied, so he took a bite of bread and passed the bowl of raspberries to his right.

Was Abe trying to work everyone through their issues so they would go east? But he knew I wasn't going anywhere without my brother. Did he want me to be here on my own? Did he think that if everyone else left, I would change my mind?

I watched the girl eat. She moved in tiny motions, like a mouse holding a small morsel, nibbling.

"Her name is Lucia," Abe said, and by the lack of reaction from everyone else, I could tell I was the last to learn this.

"Really?" I asked. "Did she tell you?"

"She wrote it down." Abe was clearly trying to be patient with me.

"Did she write anything else down?" I asked sarcastically. I couldn't help it. I felt cornered and defensive.

"She can't speak," Miho said in a flat voice, "but she can hear, Dan."

I sighed and closed my eyes. "I'm sorry." I couldn't remember Miho ever talking to me in that way, disappointment in her voice.

For a little while, the only thing I could hear was the sound of people eating, a fresh breeze coming in over the mountain, and eventually, when everyone was finished, John pacing in the grass behind us.

"John, your turn," Abe said, and his voice sounded hoarse.

John's massive bulk was striding back and forth with a nonsensical urgency. He was wringing his hands, muttering to himself. He nodded at Abe and came over. It didn't look like he was going to sit for this one.

"So . . ." He cleared his throat. He took up his pacing again, as if trying to decide exactly how to begin. His feet sounded like soft pads on the stone. His gaze roamed from one person to the next, finally landing on Abe. "I can't," he said.

"Take your time," Abe encouraged him.

But John had made up his mind already. He shook his head firmly. "I can't." He walked away, past Miho's house, past the tree, out onto the plains.

"John!" Abe called after him, but he didn't look back.

Abe seemed deflated. Why couldn't we all have hashed these things out privately?

"Well," Abe said, his voice a quiet breeze, his eyes vacant and far away. "Well."

"I can go," Misha said.

"Yes," Abe replied absently. "Yes, of course."

She looked at me the entire time she spoke, as if it was only us.

"The memory came back to me first in numbers," she said. Her voice was calm and deliberate, like a surgeon's. "The date, the hours of my shift, and the blood pressure of the woman we were helping in the back of the ambulance. I can't remember her name, but I remember another number—it was our third visit to her that week, and it was early in the week. She was always calling the ambulance. Sometimes we could placate her in the house, other times we put her on the stretcher, and occasionally we had to wheel her out and actually load her into the vehicle before she came around."

This was the most I had ever heard Misha speak at one time.

"I tightened the cuff and pumped it up and watched the dial drift down, stethoscope buds in my ears as I listened to the strong beating of her very old heart. I told her she was recovering, playing along with her as I had learned to do. My two colleagues had already returned to the front seat. They were less patient. She nodded, sighed, made some excuse, and I helped her back to the sidewalk, holding her arm as we climbed the three steps to her front stoop. She went in and closed the door without a word. I looked at the guys in the front seat and shrugged. They were laughing. I started laughing. But by the time I came around and climbed in through the passenger door, they had stopped laughing."

Misha's words came out calm, but her hands were busy: smoothing the fabric of her pants, tracing the veins in her wrist, squeezing into tiny fists.

"The driver pulled away quickly, and I told him to take it easy. My friend in the middle seat held up his cell phone and I stared at it. He had received a message from a friend at the grocery store before the call even came in. 'Small plane down in Kellerman's parking lot. Get here fast.'

"More numbers come back to me. The siren was on and the lights were flashing, and we flew past 4th Street, 5th Street, and 6th Street. I glanced at the speedometer—45, 50, 60. I was never afraid of blood, and my stomach never turned at injuries, no matter how gruesome. I could pull a stitch through someone's flesh without balking. I once held someone's scalp onto their head while we raced to the hospital. But there was one thing I could never get used to: speeding through red-light intersections, passing cars on the wrong side, slipping along the shoulder."

She paused. "The rain began to fall. Quite a storm." She exchanged looks with Miss B and

Po. None of them smiled or cried or gave any kind of expression.

"Smoke already rose from the grocery store parking lot. We had to wind our way among the other vehicles blocking the way. Some people fled, afraid more planes would fall from the sky. Others sat in their parked cars, staring but not wanting to get close. Others did gather close and stood in the open as if the rain wasn't pouring down on them. There was no fire, but smoke rose from the plane's engine. Sadness rose in me as I saw multiple bodies lying motionless, but the mechanical, numbers side of me pushed the sadness down. I became a robot. We set up a small triage area, the three of us making our way from body to body. I prayed another ambulance would arrive, but none came, not right away. There were a few we moved on from. A baby. An elderly man. They were clearly gone."

I thought the man must have been Mary St. Clair's father. A small sound came from Miss B, like the homing signal on a piece of electrical equipment. Nothing more than a chirp or a hiccup. Circe was weeping hard without making a sound.

"I got to the plane first," Misha continued. "A pilot and three passengers. They all appeared deceased, but I tried to pry open the door to get closer, checking vitals with my hands, looking for signs of life. Through the shattered window of the plane I could see my colleagues working on two people. I cycled through the three passengers. They were gone. I reached for the pilot to confirm that he, too, was dead. You know those dolls made of cloth with sewn joints, full of cotton? You know how their legs fold and bend in any direction? That was the pilot's legs. They were folded and rolled up under him as if they had no bones."

She paused again. "Then he gasped. The pilot, I mean. He was alive. I shouted for the others to give me a hand. He screamed, the pain bringing him back to consciousness. We pulled him from the plane. I knew right away, when I grabbed under his arms and pulled, that he was intoxicated. I could smell it. We placed him gently on the pavement. The crowd had grown. Another ambulance arrived. And another. And another. We loaded up the bodies."

She shook her head. "I was soaked through, and my anger at the pilot rose up in me like a storm. He screamed the entire time he was being loaded into the ambulance. We covered three bodies, and I stumbled as I walked away from them. I heard a mother cry out for her little girl whose body was still under the sheet. 'But she's getting wet,' her broken voice said. Two officers held her back. I went over and held her close. It was Circe. 'But she's getting wet.' She kept saying that over and over again, and her voice turned into a whisper. But she didn't stop."

15 The Fire

Circe let out a sound, a tiny sob, and Misha leaned over and put an arm around her. A tightness wrapped itself around my chest like a constricting band, and I found it difficult to breathe. My brother had done this. My brother had caused all of these people, my friends, tremendous pain. I wanted to run away, but I sat there like everyone else, not saying a word, not knowing what to do next.

That's when I felt something else—anger at these people who had called themselves my friends. These stories they were telling me, about how my brother the pilot had ruined their lives or stolen someone they loved seemed to invalidate my waiting. All this time! All these long days! I had been waiting for someone they now found despicable, unworthy. They had turned my brother into a monster.

Evening approached, with the dusk spilling in over the mountain. Shadows pooled around us, some filling up the alleyways and the hollows, some creeping in behind the rocks that lined the base of the mountain. I found my anger deepening into something close to hate. I couldn't look at them. I hoped Miho wouldn't tell her story, because I didn't think I could stay any longer if someone else spoke, if someone else piled their own bitterness onto my brother.

John returned wordlessly from the plains, a massive bulk of firewood in his arms. He knelt in silence before the fire pit, spread the wood, struck a match. I was suddenly glad he hadn't told his story. I didn't need to hear it all again from a different angle, over and over.

We all watched the fire grow as if it was the most interesting thing on earth, this concentration of heat, this speeding up of molecules, this splintering of wood, the way it turned into ghostly smoke. Our fire made the approaching shadows feint back and forth, this way and that. But out over the plains, a nameless darkness gathered, thick and new and frightening.

I thought of Mary, now one day's journey away. It seemed like ages since she had left. How many trees had she passed? How many long, empty stretches? Could she still see the mountain, or was it only a thin purple thread on the horizon?

I put my face in my hands. I felt spent, like I had run a long way, and I could tell the others all felt the same. Lucia sat hunched and almost disinterested, the way teenagers often do. She picked at the skin on her knee. She stared up into the sky.

Miho leaned toward me. Her hand moved, and

I thought she was reaching for mine, something that would have given me a lot of comfort, considering everything that was taking place. But in the end, her hand dropped to her side.

"Miho?" Abe said. "Are you ready to tell your story?"

But I interrupted. I didn't even know what I was going to say. I would make something up. "I . . ." I began, but there was nothing. What words would make sense following all of that? What could I say that would make them stop? Miho of all people! I didn't need to hear her version of how my brother had ruined her life.

Then I started to worry. What if my brother showed up now, in the midst of all this? What would they do to him? Tear him to pieces? Only minutes ago I had been paranoid about being left here in town all alone, but now I wanted them to leave. I wanted them to go east without me, every single one of them, so I could wait for my brother in peace and welcome him. I could nurse him back to health. He would see what he had done and he would be sorry.

It's hard to remember the exact sequence of events after that. Everything seemed to happen simultaneously. Miho was staring into the fire, and its orange light spilled from her eyes. But it was too much light, and I realized she wasn't looking at our small fire—she was looking beyond it, out over the village roofs, and the fire reflected in her eyes wasn't the one in between all of us. No, there was a larger fire, growing like a monster.

"What's that?" she asked in a flat voice, dread leaking out.

Everyone stood, and sounds of surprise and alarm rose. A fire burned among the houses, the flames moving in a strange kind of synchronicity, darting up and down, flowing in and out of the shadows, peeking around corners and playing with each other.

While we had been speaking, a fire had started, spread out through many of the houses, and rose above the roof lines, seemingly everywhere. The flames farther up the hill rose higher, as if that was where the whole thing had started.

Farther up the hill. Toward my house.

"Grab your things!" Po shouted. "We have to get out of this place! It's time to go!"

"Wait a minute!" Abe replied, raising his hands, trying to calm everyone. But he was too late—the group had scattered. Even Miss B limped quickly down the hill toward the greenway, but she barely made it twenty yards down the greenway when the smoke clouded the sight of her and overcame her, and she collapsed. Her form came and went in the gray billowing, and I thought we might lose her.

"Miss B!" Circe screamed, running to her side and pulling her back.

The others, too, had scattered into the smoke

and the flames. Abe followed one person, then another, trying to call them back to him. But it was total chaos. I could hear voices shouting, first for each other, then for help. Some of them came back to the patio after attempting to get to their homes, coughing and retching.

"We have to stay calm," Abe insisted, wiping sweat from his dark face.

Soon everyone had returned. No one had been able to get anything out of their houses. No one had even been able to get close. We gathered beside Miho's house, which by that time was also in flames, and the heat forced us farther away, back beside the oak tree. The crackling sound grew louder, the beams of her house split, and the roof caved in like a piece of rotten fruit.

"We have to leave. Now," Po said. "We need to head east. Something's going on. Maybe they're coming for us from inside the mountain. We have to go."

John echoed his agreement. The women nodded too. I looked out into the darkness, in the direction of the first tree. Is this how it was all going to end?

Abe nodded, but he didn't look convinced. "Let me think. Just give me a minute."

"What's there to think about?" Po demanded. He paced and ran his hand through his blazing red hair. "How did this happen?" he practically screamed, waving his hand toward the flames.

Miho sat on the grass and wept, pulling her knees up to her chest and rocking back and forth. Lucia fell to the ground beside her, hugging her. I wanted to go to them, to comfort them, but a sudden suspicion entered my mind.

The fire had begun at the top of my hill.

Toward my house.

I sprinted away, following the greenway through the flames and the smoke.

"Dan!" I heard Miho shout, and the voices of the others joined her, calling out to me.

It was like another world in there, a foggy place full of nightmares and heat and flames. I pulled my shirt up over my nose and mouth and tried to run with my eyes closed, but they still teared up. The flames reached for me and my sleeve caught on fire. I slapped it until it went out, running the whole time, feeling the sting of hot embers glancing off my face.

The rain was the only thing that saved me. It came down in hard pellets, and while it didn't drown out the fire, it diminished it enough to clear the air. Soon I was on the other side of the scorched and burning village, running up the hill to my own house, the greenway slick beneath my feet. Everything smelled of smoke and heat and, somehow, also of spring rain and new life. It left me feeling incongruous, disconnected, and unsure of myself or of what to do next.

I ran to the front door and pushed it open. My

house was not on fire. I saw her immediately, sitting in the chair that faced the glass doors, looking out over the plains. When she spoke, the pitch of her voice was willowy and light. I didn't recognize the sound of her at first, and I turned to see if someone else had walked in behind me, if someone else was speaking.

"You have to go get your brother," she said again, and this time I realized it was her.

"I can't," I whispered. "I can't go back in there."

"Not alone," she said, standing, and something of her old voice returned, soft and imploring. "Not alone, no, you can't go there alone. But you have friends. Good friends. They'll go with you."

I didn't think they would. No matter how sweet her voice, no matter how convincing, she didn't know them. I couldn't picture any of them coming with me back over the mountain, back into that hell. Nothing could get them there—not Po's anger or Circe's sadness or Miho's disappointment. We were all too afraid of that place. And besides, now they all hated my brother. Why would they save him?

No, wait. Abe would go with me. Abe would do it if I asked him. But I couldn't ask him. I couldn't.

And so it was just me. The thought of going over there alone sent such violent shudders through my body, I thought I might collapse.

"Did you do this?" I asked, trying to look into

her eyes and failing. "Did you start the fire?" My voice was weak and tired, where hers was firm and unrelenting. But there was something there that seemed to be at its end. Was she losing patience? Did she feel something slipping through her grasp?

She gave a half laugh and shook her head. "No. Why would I have done that?"

"I don't know."

She looked at me with a smile that was almost sad, as if she felt bad about what she was going to say. "It was Abe."

"Abe?" I asked, shocked.

She nodded, and I thought I saw her smile turn a shade less sad.

"Why would Abe do this? And how? He was sitting with us the whole time."

She didn't say the question back to me, but it was in her gaze, as if the answer was inside of me somewhere if I would only look honestly. So I did. I don't know why I let her direct me in this way, but I followed the question as it looped around in my chest and my mind, and the answer came to me. When I spoke, my words came out in a whisper.

"Because he wants us all to go east?"

Again, she didn't confirm my answer with a nod or any sound. But the look on her face said, "And?"

"And Abe thought we'd stay here forever if he didn't do something drastic?"

She sighed. Anger swelled in my gut, pumped into my face, red and pulsing. I paced frantically, moving in a kind of frenetic pattern of distracted anxiety.

"He wouldn't do this!" But my words were shallow and had no bearing on what I had started to believe. "He wouldn't."

She didn't argue with me. She sighed again.

"But what about my brother?" I asked, again in hushed tones.

She shook her head. I thought of all the times Abe had reassured me there was no hurry. He would stay with me as long as I wanted to wait. Had even Abe reached his breaking point? Had he and Miho conspired without me, tried to figure out how they could motivate me to go? Were all the stories changing the way they felt about me? Maybe now that they knew what my brother had done, even they couldn't imagine staying with me.

Maybe Abe had instructed John to go around and start the fire, then come back with wood he had arranged beforehand. It was all coming together in my mind, and because lying came so naturally to me, it was easy to see it in others.

"Come," she said, holding out her hand. She led me to the front door of my house, out onto the greenway, and up the hill toward the canyon that led back into the mountain. I looked over my shoulder once, but all I saw was the village burning down, the flames already lower, the houses collapsing in on themselves. Smoke billowed up as the rain fell, but even the rain was slowing. I could hear the drops hissing in the charred ash.

Could Abe really have done that? Could he have destroyed everything that made up our lives?

We approached the gap in the mountain, the sliver of an opening that went back into the canyon. The woman's hand was soft and cool, and sometimes she reached over with her other hand so that she held on to me with both of them, leading me, beckoning me. The sign welcomed us to the opening.

THROUGH ME THE WAY
INTO THE SUFFERING CITY
THROUGH ME THE WAY
TO THE ETERNAL PAIN
THROUGH ME THE WAY
THAT RUNS AMONG THE LOST

The unreadable lines seemed to grow sharper, but the letters were still jumbled or too close together, or perhaps the words were written in another language. But the last line was still there, clear, breathtaking.

ABANDON EVERY HOPE, WHO ENTER HERE

"I can't," I said.

She reached up and touched my cheek, the

gentlest nudge, moving my face toward hers. "You have to."

"I can't," I repeated, shaking my head.

"If you don't, your brother will stay there forever. You are his only chance."

I stared into the canyon. For as far as I could see, it was nothing special, only a narrow path through the rock that seemed to widen out the farther along it went, gently going uphill. Maybe it wasn't as bad as I remembered?

"If you go in, if you go and look for him," she said, "I will convince the others to follow you. They'll be along soon to help you find your brother."

"How?" I asked, but I already knew.

"I convinced you, didn't I?" she said. Her words were like those of a mother to a toddler, finally letting him in on her secret when it is too late for him to escape bedtime.

I sighed. She had convinced me. It was true. I was standing there picturing my brother, and there was no way I could turn and leave him. Not now. The village was gone—there was nothing there for me. Miho was gone. My brother had destroyed her life, and she wouldn't be coming back for me. Even Abe—surely the revelations about what my brother had done, the pain he had distributed to our friends, had turned him away from me. I had no one besides my brother, and if I didn't go find him now, I would have no one, forever.

I didn't even say anything. I took one step, then another step, then another, and before I knew it, I was inside the canyon. I was leaving the village behind, leaving Abe behind, leaving Miho behind. I was going to find my brother. I was returning to the suffering city.

The dread of it filled my stomach like a ball of lead. My hands were sweating. My tongue felt scorched from the fire, swollen and dry. I could still smell smoke on me, and I wondered, too late, if I should take things with me: food and water and supplies. But I kept going, one step after another. The sounds of the burning city vanished, and all that remained was a gray, filtered darkness, the pattering of heavy raindrops at the tail end of the storm, and a sense that everything had turned to bitter ash.

PART TWO

PART TWO

16 The House

I expected my first steps into the canyon to be difficult or heavy, as if the terror would be waiting for me as soon as I crossed over some imaginary threshold, but even though the light was dim and smoke followed me in from the burning town, I found the going strangely easy. And quiet. I knew the way in led uphill, into the mountain, but it felt like I was walking downhill. My senses were confused, so I turned around and looked back toward the opening. There was the split in the mountain, a dark line of nearly black sky between the shadows of the cliffs, the space that led down and out into the plains.

Was I actually doing this? Was I actually going back into the mountain?

The farther I went, the darker it became, until I couldn't see the difference between the cliffs on either side, the sliver of sky above me, or the boulders that lined the path. I kept tripping over dead stumps of trees. There was a short stretch of what felt like tall, brittle weeds that rustled and snapped off when I meandered through them.

I thought it might be best if I waited until morning to keep going, so I felt my way to the side of the canyon, waving my hands in front of me. It was narrow at that point, but the dark was so thick I couldn't see from one side of the canyon to the other. I found a series of breaks in the rock wall and cleared the ground of larger pebbles, sweeping them to the side with my bare hands. Even then the ground remained rocky and hard. But I was exhausted. Hearing everyone's stories, running through the fire, and my last conversation with the woman in my house weighed heavily on my mind. I fell into a fitful sleep, worried about Miho and Abe and everyone else. Worried that they had already left without me. Worried that they were following me.

When I woke up, an anemic light illuminated the narrow crag of sky at the top of the canyon, the color of blue-gray smoke. Everything was completely still. I realized that what I had been walking on was not dried-out weeds but rubble-strewn ground covered in old wasps' nests. A surge of panic filled me. There were hundreds of nests scattered along the canyon, so many that it was nearly impossible to walk without stepping on them. In a panic, I walked quicker, trying to avoid them.

But when I did hit them with my feet, their gray, honeycombed surfaces peeled apart like ash or tissue paper and floated around, lighter than air, so that I left behind me a wake of shimmering, sheer flakes hovering in that liminal space. I saw nothing alive among the remnants of the nests, nothing moving. As I walked farther into the canyon, they thinned out until there were only one or two here and there, hidden among the boulders or resting in the cliffs. I had a distant memory of walking through this same area when it was full of wasps, when they filled the air with their writhing, their buzzing, but it was too far away in my mind to grasp properly.

The tiniest of movements caught my attention, over along the edge of the cliff. One of the dead hives had twitched, but not in a way that was consistent with the movement in the wind or any other kind of natural trembling. I changed directions, drifted over toward the movement, but I lost track of where it had come from, so I stood perfectly still, close now to the right-hand canyon wall. I waited.

Again, the same twitching, and I saw where it came from. I moved closer. One of the gray wasps' nests sat precariously on a boulder that was about waist height. It shifted again, and a tiny black wasp crawled out from under the nest. I glanced around, a bit afraid that this was not the only one, that I might now find a million other lonely wasps crawling out from under those million dead wasps' nests. But no. Nothing. Only this one last wasp hovering above its dead nest, then landing again on the surface, spinning, exploring, and crawling back under.

It gave me a lonely feeling. It would die. I left it there, peering over my shoulder a few times with the strange sense that it might follow me, but it didn't. For as long as I could see the nest, it was dancing as if in the wind, but I knew better.

I remembered my dream again, the one in which I lied for my brother. Adam was clearer to me than he had ever been. I could see his face as if he was standing right in front of me. Wait. Was he standing right in front of me? Something seemed to be moving in the shadows, something with form, something human. I walked toward it, up the canyon. The place smelled of smoke and dust, and I could see a wind blowing up above the canyon walls, but the air down where I was remained still.

The shadows shifted, and what I had seen was gone. But I could still envision his face. I felt like I had found my way in among nameless things, as if all that I had forgotten would now come back to me. It was exhilarating and new, and again I had the sensation of walking downhill, even though I knew the path was heading up into the mountain.

The sky brightened as I continued, and the air cleared a bit, seemed more breathable, but my eyes were still watering from the dust and the lingering wisps of smoke. The canyon widened gradually, so that at first I didn't notice the extra space. But there were trees all around me, tall and thin, and they made it difficult to see both sides of the canyon. All of this transitioned into an even wider space that felt more like a forest than a narrow chasm.

That's when I saw the house in the woods.

I stopped for a moment, leaned behind a tree, and peered at the house only fifty yards or so in front of me. It was covered in weathered wood siding that was gray and split by the dry air. The windows were dark, and the front door looked like it might be partially open, but I couldn't tell from where I stood. From the chimney, a narrow, twisting thread of smoke rose up into the sky.

I stayed there for a long time. I sat down, waiting to see if anyone would show themselves. I peeked around the tree and pulled back again. But there was also a huge sense of relief building in me, even in the midst of the fear—after waiting for my brother for such an incredibly long time, I was finally doing something about it. I was no longer sitting in my own never-changing house at the edge of the plains, wondering if he would be the next one to come out.

There was no way to pass the house without going within view of the windows. If someone was in there, they would see me. I could sneak from tree to tree, but then the house would be behind me, and I still wouldn't know if anyone was in it or if they had seen me. Or if they were following me. Going farther without knowing what was inside that house unsettled me more than the thought of walking up and knocking on the door. I had to search the house before I could pass it by.

I stood up and went out into an open space between the trees, where I had a clear view of the front porch. "Hello!" I called out.

The resulting sound was alarming. I should say the lack of resulting sound was alarming. The canyon swallowed up my shout in an instant. It was the polar opposite of an echo, as if I had not even said anything. The sound of my voice died the moment I stopped shouting, the "o" of "hello" cut short. It sent a shiver down my spine.

I took a few steps closer to the lonely house, walking under some low-hanging branches. The trees, while being alive and having leaves, drooped in the heat and the stillness. I reached up, pulled down a leaf, and realized it was brittle, even on the branch. It crumbled in my hands.

"Hello!" I shouted, and again my voice died in the air. I was closer to the house now. The light reached its peak in the sky above me, and I nearly forgot I was in a canyon.

The door of the house creaked open a bit, an abrupt sound that set my heart racing. I felt my muscles tense instinctively to run. I steadied myself by reaching over and holding on to one of the trees. The bark disintegrated under my fingers, and the fragments fell to the ground without a sound.

If it wasn't for the house, I felt like I could have lost track of which way I was going. I looked out from behind the tree again. I was still thirty or forty yards from the house, but I saw a woman come out to the porch. She wore a black dress, and her long, dark hair was up in a tight bun. She peered out into the woods as if looking for something specific.

I opened my mouth to shout again, but I wondered if she would even be able to hear me. I gathered my courage and walked toward the house and the woman. She watched as I approached, but she didn't say anything. I got closer, so close that I could see a thin layer of dust covering everything—the rails, the wooden porch floor, the front door handle. Her narrow feet had left a path through the dust from the door to where she stood. The inside of the house was dark.

Above us, the light was fading. I needed to get moving. I needed to travel farther before the darkness fell again.

"Hello," I said, and when the word was swept away, I said it louder, trying to lodge it in the air. "Hello."

She nodded. Her face was plain, and once I was close I could see she had dark rings around her eyes. Wrinkles radiated out from their corners. She gave a weary sigh, closed her eyes as if she had already had enough, and crossed her arms, not in a defiant way but in the way small children sometimes cross their arms when they are cold.

"Hello," she said in a wispy voice. "Who are you?" Even though it was a question, it came out more as an exasperated statement. *Who are you, and why are you bothering us?*

I swallowed hard. I hadn't expected to see anyone on this side, at least no one besides Adam, and certainly no one living here, this close to the entrance. Why would anyone stop here? Why would anyone live here?

"I'm Dan," I said. It gave me a breathless feeling, talking in that quiet place where any words spoken were caught up in an unseen river and swept away.

"Dan," she said quietly, as if she could decide everything she needed to know about me simply by saying my name. "Dan."

"What happened to the wasps?" I asked, and immediately I wondered why that particular question had escaped.

Her eyebrows raised, and I thought I could almost see a smile gathering at the corners of her mouth, an amused expression. It felt mocking. Or something else, something I couldn't put a finger on.

"The wasps?" she asked, tilting her head back and appraising me. "The wasps are gone. We are nearly at the end. Yes, nearly."

"The end?" I asked, but she ignored that question.

"In the next strong wind, more and more of their fragile nests will be swept away. Dan." I had the feeling she was trying to decide what to do with me. "They crumble and are blown away like dust. From dust they have been made . . ." Her voice trailed off.

A creaking came from inside the house, along with the slow knocking of labored footsteps and a rhythmic *thud, thud, thud.* If anything of the grin remained on her face, the tiny hint of a smile that my questions had nearly brought out of her, it vanished at the sound of those footsteps, and a deep sense of dread was pounded into me, deeper with each wooden knock. I considered running back the way I had come, back through the trees and the dust and the lifeless wasps' nests, back through the narrow part of the canyon and down into the plains. Could we begin again? Could we rebuild our town and return to what we had?

A man came through the door. He wore a red flannel shirt faded to almost pink under denim overalls covered with rips and snags and holes. Neither the man nor the woman wore shoes, and their feet were cracked, calloused, and cinnamon colored from the coating of dust. He had a white beard, a bulbous nose, and gray eyes. Red varicose veins crisscrossed under the translucent skin of his cheeks and seemed to continue into the whites of his eyes, which were bloodshot and irritated and had large bags under them.

He clenched his jaw—I saw it in the way his beard bulged around his cheekbones and his lips bunched up each time, the way lips will scowl on the face of someone who has no teeth. He leaned on a weathered gray cane. When he saw me, he breathed hard, taking in great gulps of air and blowing them out through his nose like a winded horse.

"Hello," I said, but he didn't move from his spot just outside the door. He didn't stop that labored breathing. He hated me. I knew it as clearly as I had ever known anything, but I had no idea why.

The woman looked at the man and waited. When she seemed to accept the fact that he was not going to stop all that blustering and blowing, she turned back to me. She might have been beautiful once, a long time ago, but her hair had been pulled so tight, and apparently for such a long period of time over and over again, that she had bald spots above her ears and a bald line down her part. She had a strand of a scar that ran from the corner of her left eye almost to the edge of her left ear, a shallow scar not easily spotted at first, but when the light hit it in a particular way it flashed like a vein of silver in rock.

"I'm Sarah," she said, looking at me with a question in her eyes and then glancing away quickly. Was that a bashful look? Had she expected me to recognize her?

"Does your friend have a name?" I asked, surprised at the forwardness of my question. I was getting used to the fleeting nature of my own voice in that stifling air, and somehow it made it less intimidating to speak. The words were gone almost before anyone heard them.

He seemed to be calming down, not because of any kind of acceptance of me but because he appeared to be growing tired. "His name is Karon," Sarah answered.

We stood there for an awkward time.

"Karon?" I asked.

She nodded.

"Why are you here?" I asked. "I thought everyone had left."

When Sarah spoke, it was with great reluctance. "Come." She turned and walked through the door.

The man didn't look back as he followed her into the house, his cane louder against the wooden floor. It seemed his anger at me had been transferred from his heavy breathing and blowing to the force with which he thrust his cane against the floor. *Thud. Thud. Thud.*

They left the door open to me, but I hesitated. I could still see the rock wall of the canyon hidden among the trees. I took a few steps away from the door to the edge of the porch and glanced toward the back of the house. There, farther into the woods, I could see the other side of the canyon wall. I couldn't see the top of either side of the canyon, because the canopy of the forest was high and thick.

"What should I do?"

A whisper of a breeze moved through the canyon, only a few seconds' worth, but enough to lift the fine dust and swirl it around. The brittle leaves seemed to whisper, "Shhhh." The dust settled all around me, on my shoes, my arms, even my face. I closed my eyes, reached up with both hands, and wiped my skin, finding a thin layer of the finest powder.

When I opened my eyes, the woman was standing in front of me. I jumped.

She almost smiled again. "Come," she said, but this time she didn't turn around until I moved to follow her.

17 The River

A great sadness filled the house. There was an emptiness, not only in the corners but even in the areas where we stood or sat. Even when the rooms were full of us, they felt vacant. The sadness coated everything, like the dust or the shadows that deepened as darkness fell.

I followed Sarah through the front door into an old kitchen, the counters warped and yellowing around the edges, the cabinets misaligned with doors that didn't close quite right. Beyond that was a kind of dining area, as sparse as you can imagine, with a small round table and four chairs. The walls were yellow, whether by choice or due to age, I couldn't tell.

Karon had already sat down, his mouth scrunched together, his old, watery eyes looking past me through the door that Sarah had left open. She walked in a kind of glide, never in a hurry, and pointed toward a chair, indicating I should take a seat. But I didn't sit down right away—I put my hands on the back of the chair and stood there. I watched her sit down, quietly, calmly.

The two of them were quite a sight.

"Why are you here?" I asked again. I realized

in that moment that they had given me the seat that would leave my back facing the still-open door, and something else followed me into the house along with the dust and the sadness and the emptiness—a pinprick of fear that started in my gut and moved outward, threatening to make my hands tremble. It was the same fear I had felt ever since the woman had come into my house. Was she out there somewhere?

Sarah took a deep breath, looked at me and then over at Karon, glanced past me almost imperceptibly, and rested her hands on the table, one on top of the other. She had wonderful posture. She sat there like an etiquette teacher.

"That's not important," she said.

"Well," I began, but she interrupted me.

"We have been here for a long time. A very long time. From the beginning, in fact, and now time has nearly run its course. The important question is, why are you here? You do know you are walking the wrong way?"

Again, the hint of cynicism—or was it sarcasm or genuine amusement?—crept in around the corners of her mouth, the edges of her eyes. I decided to be completely truthful with her, and it was a strange sensation, this letting go of all the lies I had clung to for so long.

"I don't remember seeing you here when I left the mountain the first time," I said.

"You wouldn't," she said. "The condition

people found themselves in when they were leaving was . . . overwhelming. It would have been difficult to pay attention to anything but your pain and your guilt."

I nodded slowly, accepting her explanation. "I'm here for my brother. He's the last one, the only one left."

She looked at Karon as if he might want to weigh in on the subject, something that surprised me, considering his inability to speak. She turned back to me and stared hard into my eyes, looking for something. Maybe trying to detect truth from lies? I couldn't tell.

"Have you considered that it might be important for people to leave this place under their own volition? Under their own motivation?" she asked.

I shrugged. "I can motivate him."

This time she smiled for real, a smile full of pity. "Oh my."

"What?" I asked.

"This is not a place you can be rescued from." She hesitated. "That's not exactly the right way of saying it. Maybe this is closer to the truth— this is not a place where someone can come and whisk you away."

"What kind of a place is it?" I asked, not sure what she was getting at.

"It's the kind of place you have to leave on your own. Everyone who has ever left has battled their own way out. In this place, our guilt consumes us."

"Do you mean guilt as in that sense of feeling guilty, like shame, or as in being found guilty? A guilty verdict?"

The old man practically roared at this one, and I jumped at his outburst. Sarah reached over and held his shoulder in a gentle grasp, but she did not look away from me.

"Yes. Both. It is through the maze of guilt that someone must find their way out."

"So, it's some kind of motivation? Determination?"

"Do you really remember nothing about this place?" she asked. Something about it felt like an insult, but I didn't feel offended as much as embarrassed.

"No. Nothing," I mumbled.

She clenched her jaw and shook her head in a barely perceptible way. "The only thing that can rescue anyone from this deep darkness is grace."

"Grace?" I asked. That didn't sound like anything nearly strong enough to bring my brother out safely. But I didn't say that. I stared down at the table. If I somehow managed to find my brother in this hellhole, was I sure I could persuade him to come with me? Doubt made its way inside of me and settled, a seed.

The three of us sat there in the silence. Karon worked his mouth from side to side and up and down, his lips twisting in on themselves something fierce, so heavy was his hatred toward me. Or so I imagined. Sarah sat completely still for long periods, her unflinching nature interrupted occasionally by deep sighs, during which she closed her eyes and tilted her head back.

A strong breeze blew through the canyon, coming from the direction of the plains, the direction I had come from. It rustled the leaves of the trees, at first gently, then sending them into a chattering panic. It was a loud, roaring sound, one that the stillness could not sweep away. I looked at Karon once again, and for the first time he seemed calm. Perhaps by the sound. His shoulders slumped and his eyes crept toward closing.

A grayness came with the wind, a tangible dimming of the light, and a weightless substance like flakes drifted around and through the house. It was like ash or a very fine dust. I reached up and caught an especially large piece, and it disintegrated in my hand.

"What's that?" I asked.

"The old wasps' nests," Sarah said.

When the wind subsided, the gray flakes were everywhere—on the table, the countertops, the floor, even our shoulders and the tops of our heads. Sarah stood and brushed herself off, but most of it clung to her clothing until she ground it in with all the brushing. I did the same. But old

Karon just sat there, the lighter-than-air wisps resting on him, fluttering slightly even after the breeze had passed.

"How do you expect to get to your brother?" Sarah asked.

I didn't know what to say. I didn't have much of a plan except to go back in, all the way, and then go all the way down.

"There's only one way in, isn't there?" I asked.

"Yes. But there are . . . obstacles."

"Like what?"

She picked up a larger piece of nest, a shred resting on the table, and it disintegrated. "Only one that we might be able to help you navigate," she said, glancing at Karon.

Again he began huffing and puffing through his nose and toothless mouth. His indignation only minutes ago had terrified me, but now I realized there was something endearing about it.

"What is it?" I asked.

"You don't remember?"

I tried to think back, but there were still so few distinct memories of my time here in the mountain. I shook my head.

Karon rested his knobby, weathered fists on the table. His knuckles were like knots in thin branches, and all the ash-like wasp paper that he hadn't brushed off drifted backward as he leaned forward suddenly.

"The river," he said in short gusts of breath.

He barely moved his mouth, so at first I wasn't sure what he had said. I glanced at Sarah, but she was still looking at Karon.

He erupted again, this time incorporating a kind of groan that added body to his words, if not clarity. "The . . . river . . ."

A sense of drowning overcame me, and the smell of blood, and the warmth of muddy water, and a desperation to rise, rise, rise. I stood up in response to this overwhelming sense of claustrophobia, and my chair fell over backward. Had his words awakened a memory? Or a kind of nightmare?

A premonition?

I turned to pick up my chair, and the open door caught my eye. All of the light had fled, and I realized that complete darkness had descended, the kind I had only ever seen and felt in the canyon during the previous night. Or was it two nights ago? Or more than that? I exhaled with disappointment. I had wanted to make more progress before the light left. I had so far to go.

"You will spend the night here," Sarah said. "Tomorrow, at first light, Karon will take you to the river and help you cross."

What could I say? The darkness was so thick outside that the opened door looked like a portal into an ocean of black mercury. There was a small lantern lit on the kitchen counter, and I didn't know if she had only just lit it or if it had been burning when I first walked in. Its light was tepid.

"What has happened to you?" I asked. I stood behind my chair, and the dark doorway behind me felt like another person, someone else I needed to be mindful of. "Why are you here?"

She stared hard at me again, as she had been doing almost the entire time. I was becoming used to her gaze—something about it grounded me in reality, kept me from becoming lost in the dizziness and the dark. If she saw me, then I was.

"Sit down," she said. "I can tell you a little."

I eased into the chair, and at the same time, Karon stood. He stared at me, his mouth wrenched into that same old scowl. His breathing had dimmed along with the light, so that each exhale seemed to illustrate his weariness, deflating him slowly. He turned and thumped his way into another part of the house, and all went silent.

"He doesn't like to talk about this," Sarah said, her voice suddenly kind. "Where did you go when you left the canyon?"

"Not far," I answered, shaking my head. "I stayed in the same town, the one barely outside. I wanted to wait for my brother." My weak words vanished quickly in that dark soundlessness.

"I know the town. If you stayed there, you understand how many people traveled through. Karon and I have waited here for a long, long time. He has helped more people cross the river than either of us could ever count. This was what we chose."

"Why didn't you ever come all the way out?" I asked.

"We took a few steps out, once. I saw your town. But we have been waiting for a long time too, and this is where we decided to do it. You understand how this feels. Some time ago, a woman came along, worse off than many, perhaps not as bad as some. But she bore a great resemblance to the one we were waiting for, and Karon immediately went to her and brought her into the house. Once I saw she was not who we had hoped, I thought we should send her on her way. It didn't make sense for someone to stop here. There is nothing here, in this house or in this canyon, for anyone."

I began to ask if there was anything there for her and Karon, but I stopped. I felt like I was asking too many questions.

"We nursed this woman to health, against my better judgment. This is no place to grow healthy. It's much too close. But we did it, we took her in and helped her, and the past is the past."

I heard Karon's knocking again. At first I thought he was protesting our conversation, but I realized it was the thudding of him walking the floor above us from one end of the house to the other.

"Her name was Kathy, and she soon became

like a daughter to Karon." Sarah said this with great loneliness in her voice, and deep regret. "For a long time she stayed here with us, a very long time, and when she was well she took care of us. I began to doubt my doubt, so to speak. I wondered if I had misjudged her. She was very pleasant, and Karon was happier than I had ever seen him."

I found it difficult to breathe. I knew what was going to happen.

I knew who she was talking about.

"She began going out whenever someone was passing by, someone making their way out of the canyon. She would walk up to them and have long conversations, even though they were barely rational. It seemed to me that she was asking a lot of questions, and again, I thought it inappropriate. Karon and I had always let these passersby go along their way. Of course, Karon helped them along the river, but after that, they were free to go. But Kathy would sit with them. Some of them became disoriented after talking with her, wandering the woods here around the house, calling out the names of people they were looking for. Sometimes I can still hear them."

Her voice had not changed, but her face was pale.

"I spoke to Kathy about this. I told her she shouldn't distract the people walking by, that they were on the right road and would find their way. Once across the river, they did not require our aid or intervention. Do you know what she said to me?"

I shook my head.

"She smiled a nice smile and whispered, 'Through me you pass into eternal pain.'"

A chill spread from my neck all the way down my arms. I swallowed hard.

"Soon after that, people stopped coming. I assumed no one was left. Or very few. Once the flow of people stopped completely, only recently, she left us alone." Sarah stared vacantly past me, over my shoulder. "Karon fell into a bottomless sadness, not because he missed her but because he was convinced she had passed beyond the canyon in order to bring people back into this place. He thought we should have stopped her. And so we remain, no longer helping people leave but guarding the way back."

"Why do we let our guilt consume us," I whispered. It was not a question but a kind of statement.

I felt a numbness moving throughout my body. The woman didn't seem to notice my distress. She kept talking.

"This is why Karon was so upset by your appearance. You are the only person to ever come back through the canyon. He assumed she had sent you back this way. His hatred for her is difficult for him to contain."

Finally, she looked at me, and her gaze was piercing. I could tell she wanted to ask if I had returned because of Kathy. I felt frozen in place. I was thinking of all my friends outside the canyon, our destroyed village. I suddenly wondered if Kathy was trying to convince any of them to come back in as well. Perhaps to save me?

As we sat there, I felt a kinship with her and Karon. If I had not been on a search for my brother, I would have stayed with them for a long time, perhaps forever. It was lonely there, and dark, but there was a peace to be found among the shadows of the trees, and the confines of the canyon seemed a welcome enclosure. The feeling I had identified as a deep sadness was something else, something I couldn't put a name on, but it wasn't entirely negative.

"You can stay here, but you can't live here," Sarah said, as if she could read my mind. "There is no life here. Only dim light and ash."

"But you're living here," I said.

"Not much longer," she whispered. "Come." She stood up from the table and walked into one of the side rooms. I followed her, and miniature clouds of dust swirled up under each step, as if the world was decaying and its remains were rising in slow motion, trying to re-form it into something new.

It was a tiny room, more like a closet. There

was a dingy window, the glass so dirty I doubted I'd be able to see through it even during the day. On the floor was an unrolled, navy-blue sleeping mat an inch thick. I did not think of myself as being tired, but as soon as I saw the mat, a weariness split my marrow and my eyelids sank. Again I tried to remember if I had slept for one or two nights in the canyon on the pebble-strewn ground. I was fairly certain it had only been one. But I couldn't be sure.

I turned to look at Sarah, and I realized she had moved closer to me. I saw for the first time what it was that made her beautiful—those flat gray eyes, in the dim light, were like horizons. I felt myself leaning toward her, falling in, so tired I needed someone to lean on. But she lifted her hands in the space between us, held me away from her, held me up.

"Lie down," she whispered. "Sleep."

And from there I descended, yes, down onto the mat, but I went deeper than that. Deeper than the floor of the house, deeper than the foundations of the canyon, deeper than dreams or nightmares or memories. I stayed there in that depth, and I slept like I never have before and will probably never sleep again, there on the edge of the river Acheron.

When I woke up, I rose up through all of those layers of darkness, back up to the floor of the house, back up to where I slept on the mat, back up to the canyon. I realized something hard was jabbing me. First it prodded my leg, so I pulled my leg away, and then it was in the middle of my back, a straight rod grating against my spine. I rolled over, and the thing rammed my eye. I howled, reached up, and grabbed it. Karon was scowling down at me. We both held tight to the cane, and I could feel his anger trembling through it.

"The river," he said. Whether it was because I had heard him say it before, or because a good night's sleep had cleared up his speech, or because he wasn't as angry as he had been, I could understand him. The words even sounded like actual words people use in real sentences.

I released his cane. He looked me over as if trying to decide where next to deliver additional pokes, then let out a burst of air, disgusted at my laziness or some other shortcoming, and turned, limping out.

I sat up. A dusty light came through the window. I stood, walked to it, and peered through the dirt, but all I could see were smudges of dark trees and the empty spaces in between them.

The room where we had sat the night before felt new, completely different. Because of the light, it was almost cheery. Someone had spent a good amount of time mopping and cleaning the countertops and dusting the high spaces, evidenced not only by the shining room but also by the four wooden pails of dirty water sitting beside the open door. There was a loaf of bread on the table, but the house didn't smell like someone had done any baking. I tore off a piece. It was stale but I was hungry, so it tasted delicious. I gulped down a cloudy glass of water.

The air outside was somehow new. Sarah and Karon sat on the chairs on the front porch, staring out into the dim day and the rustling trees, now clean.

"What happened to all the dust? And the wasps' nests?" I asked.

"Didn't you hear the wind last night?" Sarah asked.

I shook my head.

"You must have slept well," she replied, that small smile finding the corners of her eyes and mouth. "A strong wind blew for most of the night."

"Does that happen often?"

It was her turn to shake her head. "No. Very rarely, in fact. And it's a beautiful thing when it does. Karon thinks it's a good omen for you."

The trees seemed not so dead in that early morning. The forest was actually quite beautiful now that everything had been cleared away—the brittle leaves were gone from the forest floor, the dust had been removed from the leaves, the remains of the nests no longer clung to the roots and the trunks.

I sighed. I needed to leave. I didn't want to, but Sarah's story about Kathy concerned me. I didn't know how much longer it might be until she convinced the others to follow me, and I needed to find Adam before they did.

"I have to go," I said. "I want to stay, but I have to go."

"Yes, of course," she said. "We're ready."

They walked off the porch and I followed. I kept looking behind us, down the canyon path that cut through the mountain to the town and the plains. I kept waiting to see someone walking out from among the rocks or emerging from behind a tree. I listened. But I knew I wouldn't hear them until they were right up next to me, not with the way sound died so soon in that heavy air.

I turned to see where Sarah and Karon were going, and they had already stopped, the house still visible through the trees. In front of us was a river more wild and alive than any I had ever seen.

"We never expected to take anyone this way, back over the river," Sarah said quietly. She paused, and it seemed to me she still wasn't sure about helping me go back, farther into the mountain.

"Have you always done this?" I asked. "Have you always helped?"

"One day we were standing here, the two of us, and we saw someone approaching from the other side."

I peered across the raging water. It was hard to see the far bank.

"I turned to Karon to see what he thought we should do, but he was already in the boat, pulling himself across. When he returned, he had a young man in the boat with him. The boy was badly beaten. We didn't ask him what his name was or what he was doing. He simply climbed out, crawled a short distance on the ground, rose up on shaky legs, and continued along the path."

Sarah smiled. Even Karon seemed to have a pleasant look hidden among the deep wrinkles on his old face. "The river," he said.

"Yes," she said in a whimsical voice. "The river. After that, we came down every day, and if someone was at the far bank, Karon went over and brought them across." Tears were in her eyes, but she didn't move to wipe them away. They sat there like diamonds. "Soon we were bringing them over in boatloads, every day, twice a day, three times a day. Sometimes all through the night. Yes, even in this inky darkness. We could hear their cries."

The sound of the river was loud and alive. I thought the cries must have been very loud, to hear them all the way from the other side.

"If you want to know why Karon looks so old, it's because he worked so hard for so very long."

I looked over at him, his white hair, the wrinkles etched in curving lines around the movement of his face. He stared back at me, and this time he didn't growl. He seemed content to let me stare at him, to let me explore, but I couldn't hold his gaze for long.

"Even after Kathy arrived, we kept bringing more people over, although by then the flow had slowed to a trickle. She was here, as I already told you. And after she left, there were no more from the far bank. Now, you."

Karon's mouth curled up in anger and he snorted, but it wasn't so scary now that I knew his anger was not aimed at me.

"I'm ready," I said.

Their faces held a subtle pity that said, *You can't possibly be.* Karon looked embarrassed by my ignorance. He turned away and bent over, and I realized he was reaching for something. I had not noticed the boat, shallow and gray, bobbing against the bank. Mist from the raging water had partially hidden it. When Karon moved toward it, I nearly laughed, thinking he must be joking. There was no way that boat would make it across. I might as well hurl myself into the water and hope for the best.

If Sarah noticed my doubt, she ignored it. "Over there, that's where it truly begins," she said. "This is nothing. This darkness, this ash, this dust: it's only the wild edge of what's waiting for you. Once you cross, you will see things you can never unsee. You will hear sounds and silence that will split you in two. It is a horror." She paused. "I will ask you this only once."

I saw again the beauty in her gray eyes. Again I wanted to stay. "What?" I asked.

"Will you please reconsider? Stay with us. Wait here for your brother. When he is ready, he will come out."

In that moment, it wasn't her gray eyes that struck me, and it wasn't the fact that she reached out and put her hand on my arm. It wasn't even that, when I glanced over at Karon, he had tears in his eyes. What struck me was the sound of the word "please," the way it sank into me, the way it latched on to my better nature, my best self. It was the "please" that was so convincing. I couldn't say no, but she could see it in me, I guess, because she turned away.

I helped Karon drag the boat to the bank. The ground was slick with mud, and as we struggled with the boat, Sarah put something around my neck. It was a knapsack made of burlap, and heavy. We situated the boat so that it pointed down into the water.

"Food and water," she said. "For your journey. It won't last long."

I nodded my thanks. I didn't know what else to do, what else to say. Karon grunted, motioning for me to sit at the front of the boat, and I climbed clumsily aboard. The inside was wet. There was a small bench that ran across, up toward the front. I sat down and realized I was terrified. I gripped the sides and closed my eyes, trying to breathe slowly. I looked over my shoulder to see if Karon was going to push us off, and I caught him leaning toward Sarah, kissing her cheek. They were both crying.

The boat shifted backward as Karon crawled in, bearing a long oar. "The river," he growled, and we slid down the short bank and into the rapids.

The water immediately lashed our boat to the right, downstream, and I nearly went overboard in those first moments. The front of the boat rose and fell once, smacking the water. I shouted my alarm, holding even tighter to the sides, leaning forward so as not to get tossed into the muddy, churning rapids. We moved from side to side, mostly facing downstream but also making our way to the far bank. I heard a loud sound from Karon.

He was laughing. His white beard was wet and blown to the side by the strong wind that now swept over us. His wide eyes burned with a strange fire, and he was smiling a fierce, almost delirious grin. Every time a large wave hit us and I thought we would turn over or take on too much water, he would laugh uproariously, his eyes flashing. He was no longer the bent old man from the dusty house in the canyon—he was Karon, some kind of seafaring master. Something not human. Something beyond human.

I turned back around, and the boat slammed into another huge wave. I pitched forward, striking my head on the bow. Everything went black.

18 Into the Abyss

In the darkness of my mind I heard a gritty scraping, and I realized only once it stopped that the sound had been that of my heels sliding along a sandy beach. Someone's hands were under my arms, dragging me along, and then they dropped me to the ground. I groaned. I could hear them walking away, their feet scratching along the sand, then the long, slow sliding of something into the water.

I opened my eyes, reached up tenderly to touch the side of my head, and groaned again. My head felt split in two, and as if to mirror the feeling, a long grumble of thunder crackled around me. But there was no rain, no lightning. Only the pealing of thunder, one long, low sound after another. It was a persistent, faraway call, and it filled me with loneliness.

The satchel Sarah had given me weighed heavily on my neck, an anchor. I sat up, looked out over the river, and was surprised to find that the water had calmed. Karon stood in the prow of the boat, steady and strong, his white beard billowing out to the side. I wanted him to look back, wanted him to wave, but his stoic silhouette never turned toward me. Soon he was a tiny speck at the far side, and I saw him pull his boat up onto the bank. Sarah must have already gone back to the house.

There, on the far banks of the Acheron, I sat for what felt like a long time, thinking about all that had happened. And all of it in such a short time. I wondered about Miho and Abe, where they had gone after the fire in the village. I thought about the woman whose name I now knew, Kathy, living in my house, her dark hair soft and shining. I thought about sitting beside her when she was in my bed, kissing her, and shame smothered me. I dwelt on the story Sarah had told me about how Kathy had deceived them. Or had she? I still had trouble placing any blame on her. Maybe she had been trying to help.

A sound moved around me, and at first it moved so subtly I was unaware of it, focused on my own thoughts, my own problems. But gradually I became conscious of it—a deep sighing, a long, heavy moaning. Was it the river? The wind was strong, drying me off, parching my lips. Another gust of wind, another long, low sigh, so heavy it ached in my bones.

I turned away from the river, my head still throbbing. I thought of my brother. I had to keep going. I couldn't turn back now.

The thunder continued to rumble, though the sound of it seemed to come farther and farther apart. My clothes still clung to me, and a mist moved in, a fog that made me feel even more alone.

What was I doing? Why did I think I could go back inside and even find my brother, much less bring him out with me?

I thought again of Sarah's words. *It's the kind of place you have to leave on your own. Everyone who has ever left has battled their own way out. In this place, our guilt consumes us.*

Our guilt consumes us.

I was guilty. I had lied to my friends, kept secrets from everyone. I loved my brother, the same brother who had hurt so many people. Was that a guilt? Was that a transgression? And now I was there, on the other side of the Acheron—even that seemed some kind of sin I would have to atone for. Having barely entered this foreign land, I could already feel my guilt rising up around me, an acid eating away at me.

The mist settled on my skin, and the satchel swayed against my side, bumping me with each step. The day was cool even as it rose toward midday. Distant thunder moved around me like the sounds of a faraway battle. I waved my hand gently through the mist, and a kind of dew gathered on my fingers. I licked a finger, but it tasted almost stale. Not quite salty, but there was a sharpness about it, and it sat on my parched tongue. I shook the satchel and could feel the slosh of water, but I knew I needed to save it for as long as I could.

The mist became so heavy that when I arrived at the edge of the abyss, I nearly fell in. It was an immense hole, wider than the river, so deep I couldn't see down into it. This was the place from which we all had fled. I would have to be quiet now. I would have to be careful.

Were they still down there?

Our tormentors?

The wind picked up, the mist melted into strands, and the strands sifted up and away. For a moment I could see all the way across the hole. It was like a caldera, except there was no visible bottom, and it was not the black color of hardened lava but granite gray. Was it a mile across? Two? I couldn't tell, but as I took it in, I saw the path that wound its way down into the great hole, clinging to the edge of the rock like a thread.

I stared at the path and found where it spilled out of the hole, not far from where I stood. I walked to that ledge and started down, then stopped. I looked back toward the river one last time. I couldn't hear it. I couldn't see it. I almost couldn't imagine it anymore, that river I had been sitting alongside minutes before. Or had I been walking through the mist for hours? My mind was weighed down with the unknowing. The place had a way of making me forget.

The mist descended around me again, cool and heavy. I stayed there at the edge an extra moment, remembering Sarah's words and wondering if perhaps Kathy had persuaded someone else to come back to this side of the canyon. Maybe she had persuaded all of them. I stared into the mist, looking for someone, anyone. Part of me wished someone had come so that I wouldn't be alone. But another part was frightened for my friends, frightened about what would happen if they did come with me or what they would do to Adam if we found him.

Then another thought.

What if Kathy had followed me in?

Another rumble of thunder. Another gust of wind.

And down I went.

Every so often, as I followed the path down into thicker mist, it widened out. I hadn't circled the great pit even once before I came to the first one: a small glade of trees up against the face of the cliff with four seats made up of wide, cut logs. I stared at them for a minute. I thought I should know why they were there or who they were for. Everything about this place felt familiar, which made sense to me because I knew I had passed that way once before, but nearly all of it was so deep in my mind I couldn't quite remember it.

I sat in one of the seats and stared out over

the narrow space, out over the abyss. The mist seemed lighter there in that place, but it hung heavy higher up. The bare wooden seat was worn smooth, as if it had been used over and over and over again, so often that it had been buffed into something that felt like silk. I touched the rough bark of the sides. I felt like I could sit there for a long, long time, going even deeper into my thoughts.

I heard a sound up the path, the direction I had come from, but I couldn't see anything through the mist. What had I heard? Footsteps? Or perhaps the dew had gathered on a crumbled ledge and the ledge had fallen? Maybe it was only another rumble of distant thunder? The thunder never seemed to stop.

The remarkable thing about loneliness is how the mind begins to turn further and further inward. I found myself latching on to memories, following them to their source. I remembered getting the news about the plane crash, and the long way into darkness I followed after that.

I went deeper and deeper inside of myself. I could stay here forever. I could sit here for a long time until I remembered everything, until the mist cleared. Perhaps my friends would come and find me, and this suddenly seemed like a good thing. I imagined four of us sitting there on the wooden seats, perhaps me and Kathy and Miho and Abe. We could tell stories, talk about the old days in the village. The hint of a dazed smile lifted the corners of my mouth, I took a deep breath, and I sighed.

There was no better place to be than right here.

A loud crack of thunder seemed to come from right above me, and I ducked my head, nearly falling off the wooden seat. I was bent over so low that I felt the ground under my hand, rocky and solid, and the movement also caused Sarah's knapsack to move on my shoulder.

What was I doing?

Why had I stopped?

I shook my head, trying to clear some space for the present moment. I stood up and was surprised at the effort it took. I felt like I was waking up from a dream.

I remembered again the morning of the crash, the morning my brother had wrecked the plane. I thought about helping the injured woman into the plane. Po's wife. I remembered the two businessmen climbing in, long-limbed and cramped in the small seats, made even more uncomfortable by the woman moaning in pain. The black man leaned forward, put his hand on her shoulder, and whispered a few questions. Miss B's husband. She answered without opening her clenched-tight eyes, nodded, bit her lip.

I waited impatiently for my brother. Where was Adam? What was taking him so long? I looked over the plane once, twice, even though I had already checked it twice that morning, and stared down the runway. This was what sat at the heart of our brotherhood: his constant return to failure like a dog to its vomit, and me waiting, waiting, waiting, the responsible one, clearing his path of all obstructions. Lying to keep him free.

The truth was, we were staring down the end. This last business venture, this tiny warehouse and adjoining airstrip in the middle of nowhere, was one that I had sunk every last penny into. And we were walking the edge. I hadn't slept well the night before and ended up roaming restlessly around the building, listening to the woman's quiet pain, Po's insistent caring. I tried to think our way out of our debt. But there was no way. We had to keep going and hope our luck broke through.

And the morning found me waiting beside the plane, waiting for Adam to come and fly it, to keep this dream going. One more lost flight and we were finished.

I was confused. I had thought I was back at the airstrip with my brother, waiting for him beside the plane. But the lashing wind and the drenching rain reminded me that I was walking down into the abyss along the narrow path. But no, I wasn't walking, I was sitting, huddled up against the rock face. The darkness I thought existed only in the pit itself had crept up to the path. A storm shook the rock. Water rushed down over the edges in small waterfalls, formed small rivers that ran along the path or plunged over the dark edge.

I didn't care. The memories swallowed me.

I walked around the plane one last time. It was sunny there, in my memory. It was warm.

One of the businessmen poked his head out the door. "Are we leaving soon?" he asked, concern in his voice. "I don't think this woman is doing well."

I stared at him, wanting to shout at him in frustration. I slapped the tail of the plane twice, not hard, but it still made a sound. He leaned back into the plane. But I knew he was right, so I walked to the warehouse, back toward my brother's room.

The early morning sky was cool blue on that day when I found my brother passed out drunk on the floor in his room. I went out and retrieved a bucket of water. I didn't care anymore. I threw the bucket of water on him, and he barely made a sound. It was the lightest of groans, as if he was lost so deeply inside of his body that not even a bucket of cold water could find him. I got another one. And another.

By the fourth bucket, he was sputtering, sitting up. He wiped water from his eyes, shook it from his hands, and stood unsteadily in the small lake I had created. He looked at me with tired eyes, eyes pleading to let him sleep, let him go, let him be. Let him live his own way. He had chosen his lot in life—that's what his eyes seemed to say. And I almost did. I almost gave him what he wanted. But there was still that thing inside of me that had to keep going, had to keep pushing, had to make sure this little flight got out, had to keep my brother on the right path.

"Adam," I said quietly, "if you don't go fly that plane, we're done. We can't take another loss like this. We'll lose these customers, and that will be the end of it."

And after much pleading—and a change of clothes, a hat, sunglasses on his bloodshot eyes, and help to the plane—he agreed. He crawled in, he taxied, and they took off.

I sat there on the path, in the storm, and the realization of it all took my breath away.

It had been my fault.

Everything that had happened, all of that death, had been because of me. Everyone waiting in the village to exact revenge on my brother should have been waiting for me. When I forced him to take that flight, I had sent them all to their deaths.

I was the guilty one.

I leaned against the rock. The rain came down so hard that I didn't even hear the person approaching. I didn't hear their feet on the wet ground. The only reason I knew they were there was because they reached down and touched my shoulder.

19 Voices

My initial response to the light touch was terror. I flailed my arms and legs and pushed myself farther down the path. The wall left deep scrapes along my spine, but I didn't slow down until I was far enough away to stand up. I ran, and all that time the rain was coming down harder and the wind sounded like voices shouting up from the bottom of the abyss.

I got about twenty feet down the path, moving as fast as I could while keeping one hand on the cliff wall so I didn't plunge over the edge, before my feet slipped out from under me, my head hit the ground, and a black curtain drifted down, covering me along with the rain. The thunder seemed to be very far away—perhaps I was dreaming it? The sound of it echoed inside my head, a comfort. I moaned and rolled onto my side.

Again the soft touch of a hand on my shoulder. But this time I was too exhausted, too hurt, to move. The hand was small, but it was filled with strength, and it seemed to be trying to lift me to my feet.

"I'm not going back without my brother," I mumbled.

Again the strong, gentle tug on my arm. I tried to look up, tried to find the face that was behind this soft encouragement, but the rain was blinding. I could barely open my eyes. I was confused. Had Sarah followed me across the river? Was it Kathy?

"I'm not going back," I said again, my voice fading. "Not without Adam."

I stood and the hand moved down to mine, and the person led me along. The rain stung my face, and as we made our way down, the wind seemed to always be at our back, pushing us farther into the depths. We stayed as close to the rock face as we could. I closed my eyes and let myself be moved along. The farther down we went, the lighter the rain, the calmer the wind.

Suddenly, all went still. I looked over at the person who had helped me travel down the path.

It was Lucia.

The insides of my eyelids burned and scratched like sand whenever I blinked. The muscles in my neck ached, and my head felt heavy on my shoulders. Every so often I tried to stretch, arching my back and straining my neck from one side to the other, but nothing loosened up. Every other breath seemed to emerge as a sigh. My legs were heavy and on the verge of cramping. But we kept walking.

I took off the knapsack and rummaged through

it. I pulled out the water, took a swig, and offered it to Lucia. She barely took a drink.

"Go ahead," I encouraged her. "Keep drinking."

She shook her head, her quiet eyes staring into mine. I couldn't hold her gaze. It felt like she might see inside of me.

Ahead of us the path narrowed, became more of a ledge than anything else, and I peered over the edge. There was a gray sort of undulation running toward the other side of the abyss as far as I could see.

"Is that the bottom?" I asked her. I didn't know why I kept talking to her. She obviously wasn't going to speak to me. But there was comfort there, even in the sound of my own voice, even in my own unanswered questions. We both looked over the edge, and Lucia's mouth drew tight. She shook her head. She didn't think it was the bottom.

"What is it?" I asked. "Wait. Are those . . . clouds?"

A sadness filled her eyes and she nodded. She took a deep breath and let it out, then another.

"So, you mean that even once we get all the way down there . . . we'll still only be in the clouds?" I asked, as if it was her fault.

We stared down into the depths. Lucia didn't move. She didn't look at me. She just stood there at the edge of the abyss.

I sat down. "I can't," I said, although I

couldn't even vocalize exactly what I couldn't do. I couldn't go on? I couldn't keep hoping? I couldn't bring myself to slink along that narrow ledge with the entire abyss waiting for us to fall in? I couldn't bring back my brother?

Lucia sat down beside me, put her head back against the cliff that rose at our backs, and quickly fell asleep. The air was clear around us, although up above, high above, the mist we had descended through stretched out like a flat white covering. A breeze came down the path, and wisps of Lucia's hair trembled around her face, her fair skin, her small ears.

"What are we going to do, Lucia?" I whispered. The words had barely escaped my lips, hadn't even risen up in the cool air, before I, too, fell asleep. It was a sweet feeling, giving in to that weariness, resting my head back against the rock, feeling the dust of the path under my palms.

Sitting there with Lucia, I felt something I hadn't felt in a long time: hope. Her unexpected appearance in the abyss, her kind face, her gentle disposition, awakened something lovely in me, something peaceful and patient. I wasn't sure what to do with it. I wasn't sure how to be. I wondered if this was how it felt to have a daughter. While I sat there, her head against my shoulder, I felt like I could breathe again.

It was a heavy, dreamless sleep, more like a fog than a darkness. My eyes shot open. I thought

I had heard something, and it seemed strange, this idea that a sound had woken me, because everything was so still. The air was clearer than it had been when we were higher up, but there was still a humidity to it, a kind of mistiness, and the cliff walls were damp, shining in the dim light.

I sat there staring out over the abyss. Lucia was still asleep. My legs were stretched out in front of me, and my feet nearly reached the edge. I looked down the path, and my heart raced again as I saw how narrow the ledge became. If it continued to narrow, we'd never make it down. Even if it stayed the same, I wasn't sure I could trust myself to walk along it, when one wrong step, one tipping of the balance, would send me into the abyss itself. How long would it take me to fall to the bottom? Could I count to five? Ten? Twenty? One hundred?

Was there a bottom?

I heard the sound again, the sound that had woken me up. I sat up straighter, and Lucia slowly lifted her head off my shoulder. She cleared her throat, coming up out of sleep, and it was a tiny sound, pebbles tumbling. I held up my index finger.

"Quiet," I whispered. I heard it again. "Voices. Did you hear that, Lucia? Voices. Or at least one voice."

She nodded, propping her hands underneath her as if she might spring to her feet at any moment and run. She trembled like a deer aware of a predator, trying to remain still, struggling not to spring away. I could feel the energy of it course through her body, a jolt.

"Slowly," I whispered. "Slowly."

We stood like children playacting, moving in exaggerated slow motion. I bumped the cliff and a small rock fell out, striking the ground at our feet with a miniscule thud. It terrified me, the thought that I might have given us away. But the faraway sounds I heard didn't change, didn't come more quickly.

We looked up along the cliff, but the way the rocks jutted out and the mist hovering above us meant it was impossible to tell how high above us the path had last circled by that spot. I couldn't tell if the voices were straight up, which meant they still had a long way to go to catch up to us—one entire revolution of the abyss—or if they were up the path from us, which meant they would see us at any moment.

"We should go," I said, adjusting the knapsack on my shoulder and moving toward the place where the path narrowed. It was too thin to walk forward on—with only a foot or two to work with, we had to turn sideways and shuffle, our backs to the cliff, our faces looking out over the abyss. I told myself again and again not to look down, but the gaping space in front of us almost had a personality of its own, one I could not look away from indefinitely, so after we had made our way twenty or thirty yards along the ledge, I looked down.

The curved cliff walls were wet and shimmering. A fair distance below us, those clouds sat thick as a blanket. Would they hold us if we fell? Maybe Lucia was wrong. Maybe they weren't clouds but snowdrifts or rolling plains covered in white ash. Or frost. I wanted to jump, and the desire scared me. I wanted to fly through the air and feel the breeze on my skin, the weightlessness of falling, the plunging into those clouds. The disappearing—that was it. I wanted to disappear. I wanted to feel the end.

But Lucia was beside me, and again I felt that calm surge of hope. She shook her head, but whether she had read my mind and was telling me not to jump or had heard the same call and was saying no to it, I couldn't tell. She swatted her hand about her head as if trying to clear off a stinging fly.

The whole oppressive place, with its shimmering granite rock and its narrow ledge and its mist and its hopelessness, was like a voice in the back of my mind. *Jump. You can do it. It would be so easy. Not even a jump—a fall. A slow leaning forward. Go on. Let go.*

"No!" I shouted. I couldn't help it. I had to do something to scatter the voices, and for a moment I felt that presence, whatever it was, withdraw as if cut. The air cleared, and even the mist seemed to dissipate. A brighter light came down to us from above, through the haze. But only for a moment.

"Dan, is that you?" a voice called out, muffled and far away. I thought it was a woman, but I couldn't tell for sure who it was. Miho? Kathy?

"Hurry," I said to Lucia. "Hurry, we have to get going."

We descended faster, our feet shuffling, almost reckless. My breathing was labored, and not only from exertion—the air itself became harder to breathe.

A long time passed—hours? days? weeks?—and we were down among the clouds, disappearing into the fog. Yet always above me, fainter and farther away than the first time, I kept hearing the voice.

"Dan! Dan! Is that you?"

20 Dad

A memory came to me there on the ledge, my back to the cliff, my hands sliding along the damp rock. In the memory, a woman came out of my father's bedroom.

"You can go in now. He doesn't have long," she said. She was a nurse or a caretaker. I nodded, and after she passed by, I took a deep breath and went into the room.

The lights were dim. It was the house I had grown up in, and the walls were the same dark paneling, the ceiling fan still swaying back and forth as it turned. Mom was long gone by then. I knew that as the memory came back to me. My mother had died. Did she pass before or after the airplane crash? I thought it was before, but I couldn't be sure. I hoped it was before.

My father didn't move when I entered the room. His eyes didn't open. His hands were still on top of the beige sheet. The place hadn't changed much. Mother's old figurines were still on top of the dressers, the old lamps she had chosen still sitting on small bedside tables on either side of the bed. Neither of them were turned on.

"Dad," I whispered. It was strange speaking

to him like that, calling him "Dad." We hadn't spoken in the weeks leading up to that moment—maybe it had been months—and I couldn't remember the last time I had called him "Dad," but I didn't know how else to address him. "Man"? "Mother's husband"? His name was Virgil, but I never called him that either.

He stirred, and his lips parted, seemed to mumble some words, but no sound escaped. I moved closer, leaned in over him, and for the first time felt genuinely sad at his passing. We had never understood each other. Had we ever loved each other? I wasn't sure. I didn't think I could remember ever loving him.

"Dad," I whispered again.

There was a chair positioned beside the bed, and I pulled it over, sat in it, and put my hands on the bed, close to his right arm. He had always been a very hairy person, his arms practically furry in his old age. Hair sprang out of his ears, and his eyebrows were wiry with strands standing up here and there. Tufts of chest hair came up out of his shirt collar. His hands were still the hands of a trucker, cracked and etched with deep lines of dirt, the kinds of stains that would never come out no matter how much soap was applied. His fingers were thick and his hands were powerful. His nails were a mess, chipped and raw around the edges.

Even as he slept, his hand sought mine out,

drifting toward my arm. "My son," he said, and tears rose to my eyes. He had never, ever called me that. He had always spat my name out like profanity: "Dan!"

But there, he called me "son." I leaned closer. His eyes wouldn't open, although his forehead seemed to be trying to lift his eyelids by sheer force.

"I'm here, Dad," I said, and the word "Dad" came easier that time. "Are you okay? Are you in a lot of pain?"

His head shook, lulled around, and it took some effort for him to steady it. When he spoke, his words were slow and slurred. "No, fine. I'm fine, son."

Again, I melted at the title of "son."

"Can I get you a drink? Anything?"

He held tight to my arm and didn't answer. He took in a breath and moaned the exhale, not a painful sound but a tired one. "Just wait," he said, trying again to open his eyes, to no avail. "Just wait."

I sat there for quite some time, so long that I thought he might have fallen asleep. Or died. Had he died? I put my ear next to his mouth and nose and thought I sensed some stirring, like the air outside a cave that has another entrance miles away.

"Son," he said again, the word a balm. "Adam."

Wait. What? I wasn't sure. "What did you say, Dad?"

"Adam." The word escaped from him like a breath.

He thought I was Adam. That's why he had called me "son."

"That's not me," I whispered. "That's not who I am. Dad, Adam's in prison. He killed a lot of people in a plane crash that was his fault."

"Adam," he continued, his voice otherworldly, breathless. "You are the one. I have left everything to you."

I tried to speak, but I could no longer use the word "Dad." It wouldn't come out. I couldn't say it. I hated him. In that moment, when he thought I was my brother, when he called me "son" only because he thought I was Adam, I hated him with everything inside of me.

"You have had a hard time of it," he mumbled.

"Yes," I whispered, even though I knew he wasn't speaking to me.

"Oh, Adam."

And then he died. I didn't have to check his pulse or lean in close to know it. There was an incredible stillness that settled in his flesh, a kind of anti-animation where every one of his cells appeared to harden. Lifeless doesn't even begin to describe it. He seemed to immediately turn gray, a darkening that blended into the wood paneling and wooden furniture. The room dimmed, perhaps because a cloud passed over the sun, or perhaps because the ghost of him shrouded the window on its way out. I didn't know. To be honest, I didn't care. He was dead. I thought that might rid me of the voices, the ones that had told me throughout my entire life that I wasn't quite enough, that my father didn't love me, that I had no one.

But the voices never left.

21 Crossing Over

The mist grew more and more dense as we made our way down, and the ledge became narrower. My toes reached over its edge at some points, with only my heels finding space to stand. Lucia and I leaned back into the cliff face. I didn't know how much farther we could go. I kept peering into the fog, hoping to see a place where the ledge opened up again to something the size of a normal path, but I could see nothing beyond the next ten feet.

"Are you okay?" I asked Lucia over and over again, looking back at her, hoping she had enough bravery for the both of us. She nodded, nothing more than a twitch of her head. Sometimes she looked at me, her soft eyes almost smiling.

Smiling. And there it was again: hope.

I could still hear the voice calling my name, but it was much more distant now, faint, and I wondered if it was a real person or some trick of the mountain.

"Dan!"

It called to me like something from the past.

"Dan!"

When we reached the bottom, at first I thought

the ledge had vanished. I thought we had gone all that way for nothing and would now have to shuffle our way back up to the path or jump. But the ledge hadn't left us stranded. It had led us to the bottom. There it was. Flat ground.

The fog still hung about us, but now it held a sickening smell like rotting mud. It was the smell of composting vegetation and dead fish and lingering water. We stumbled off the ledge and I fell to the ground, my legs trembling. Looking up, I could see nothing but mist. The walls of the abyss, the sheer cliffs, spread out and away from us on either side.

How long had it taken us to get to the bottom? A day? Two days? A month? Without any change in the light, it was impossible to say. We stood there for a moment, both of us completely still. I tried to peer into the fog to see if our tormenters would show up, come racing out of some cave and tie us up, carry us away. But after all the time we had spent in the pit so far, I hadn't seen signs of anyone. It was so strange.

"Now where?" I mumbled, but Lucia was already off and running, plowing through the fog. I hoped she wouldn't run into anything or over any other cliffs, but I could hear her feet in the distance, and they were a continual patter. Searching. Wandering.

"Come back!" I shouted, and immediately covered my mouth, not wanting the voice that was following us to know we were there, that we had reached the bottom. I had hoped that the narrow cliff would prove to be too much for the person to navigate. But there was no response to my shout. The bottom of the abyss seemed to have the same sound qualities as the area around Sarah's house—the sound of my voice was immediately swallowed up.

Lucia emerged from the fog and grabbed my hand, pulling me after her.

"What?" I asked. "What did you find?"

I followed her into the haze, and when the ledge disappeared behind us, and then even the walls of the cliffs, I felt disoriented. There was nothing around us but the swirling mist. No sound. Even the light seemed too dim, so that we were cloaked in a grayness. The ground went from rock to packed clay to pebbles on a kind of wet dirt, but we hadn't walked far before the mist cleared a bit and I saw the water.

I couldn't tell if it was a river or a lake or an ocean, although I would have guessed lake because the water wasn't moving. Reeds grew along the bank, oozing up out of the muddy mess. Beyond them, the water seemed a bit deeper, but still very brown and full of silt, a gray kind of mud. In front of us, as if placed for our purposes, was a small rowboat.

Lucia bent over and lifted an object out of the mud. It came up like something peeling and hung from her hand. It appeared to be a shirt coated in the gray muck. She threw it out into the reeds and it spun end over end, making a wet slapping sound where it landed. I realized the whole bank was coated in mud-covered clothing. I had thought they were only strange shapes in the mud. I bent over, grabbed a wrinkled ridge of mud at my feet, and lifted a pair of jeans up.

We moved closer to the boat grounded among the reeds.

"Can we get to it?" I asked.

The boat was only ten or fifteen feet out from us, but the mud was oozing and liquid, nothing that could support us. I shuddered. It seemed a particularly horrible way to go.

I took in our surroundings, paying closer attention. There were tiny white flowers growing up around the reeds, barely out of the mud, concentrated in circles. The sheen of their spiky white petals, even in those dire surroundings, was not beautiful. The bright red stamens rising from their throats looked hazardous. I glanced down at my feet to make sure I wasn't getting close to any of them.

The reeds were brown and jagged, the same color as the mud, or perhaps a bit more yellow. I touched one to see if we could perhaps lay them down as a kind of bridge to the boat, but their edges were sharp and slicing, like upright blades. The air was almost unbreathable, and I coughed, trying to hide the sound in the crook of my arm. I listened again for the one coming behind us.

A strange coldness pooled at our feet, moving in like a breeze, and the slow pace of it made it seem sentient, as if it was picking its way along, choosing where to go, where not to go. The cold unsettled me, but it did seem to clear the air, the mist rising above our heads so we could see farther in both directions.

Lucia gave a quiet coughing sound as if the air was catching in her throat after her run, but soon she was off again, this time along the edge of the undefined bank between land and mud. She bent down and seemed to be pulling article after article of clothing from the mud, throwing them over her shoulder. Was she digging a hole?

"Lucia," I said, trying not to be too loud. "What did you find?"

I walked carefully in her direction. This place had that effect, with the ascending and descending mist, the creeping cold, the knowledge that all around us, the cliff face rose hundreds of feet, thousands of feet, with the only way out being that narrow path. The voice behind us. The always-present question about what had happened to those who had tortured us. And the bog. Even the bog seemed to hate us, to hold a seething animosity. I wondered if anything living swam in its dark depths, out in the middle.

A long-lost phrase came to mind like a memory.

I will put you in the cleft of the rock and cover you with my hand until I have passed by. I could not remember where those words had come from.

Lucia was down on her hands and knees, tugging at something, wrestling a shape from the mud and the clothes and the smell of the bog. I arrived where she was and reached out to touch it, my fingers sliding along the muck. It looked like an oar, the long kind a gondolier might use to direct a flatboat along a shallow canal.

"How did you see that in the mud?" I marveled.

She didn't quite smile, but it was there in her eyes.

I followed her back along the soft bank to where we had stood staring out at the irretrievable boat. She dropped the oar to the ground and worked over it, wiping as much of the muck from it as she could, leaving small piles of mud that sank back into the earth without a sound. The wood, partially cleaned off, was quite light colored. It reminded me of pine.

Lucia placed the oar between us and the boat and walked on it, balancing herself above the mud. Moving along it like a water bug, she got to the end and hopped into the front of the boat. When she turned to look at me, her eyes were wide with exhilaration, almost joy.

The cold came in deeper, approaching from the far side of the water, and it was rising, no longer swirling around my ankles but rising to my waist, my shoulders. With it, the bog smell lessened. But it was cold. Very cold. I clutched my arms to my sides.

Lucia's smiling face flattened out in a way that said, *Come! Hurry!* She reached over the side, lifted the oar, and laid it back down in a new spot so it wouldn't be implanted in the mud. All around us, the little white flowers seemed to bloom in the cold, opening their petals, turning toward the swamp like rotating red eyes. The reeds made a whistling sound, or seemed to, even though there wasn't a discernible wind. I could see no far bank.

The cold was deeper, up to my chin. I could feel it the same way someone who cannot swim would feel the rising tide gather over their shoulders, their neck, their mouth. I could still breathe, but my exhale clouded out of my mouth. I glanced at Lucia perched at the very front of the boat, looking as though she was prepared to jump out and retrieve me if I fell off the oar and sank. She made me brave, though I doubted she would be strong enough to pull me from the muck.

I took a few steps out onto the oar. It was slick, and one of my feet slipped off, went into the mud. I pulled it out, back on the oar, another step.

Lucia looked at me anxiously.

Another step, another. The oar was sinking in the mud. I walked faster, arms out at my sides for balance, feet sliding here and there, one step off the oar, quick back on before it sank, another step.

"Dan!"

The shout came from behind me.

"Dan!"

It was Miho. I knew it. I looked back. I had to see her. And because the cold had driven away the mist, I could see all the way across the flat space, all the way from the edge of the boggy lake to the cliff wall and the thread of the tiny ledge.

Miho edged her way down quite quickly, twenty feet from the bottom. Fifteen feet. Ten. She jumped from there, hit the ground hard, fell, stood, and came running.

I turned back toward Lucia. I slipped but then reached the boat. Her skinny arms pulled me in and I fell into the bottom, hitting my shoulder on one of the crosspieces. She leaned out over the edge and I clung to her legs to keep her from falling in. She hauled in the oar, and it was longer than I remembered—it didn't even fit in the boat.

I sat up on the seat and watched Miho come running. Closer, closer. Lucia's eyes filled with questions, and she thrust the oar into my hands. I nodded without really knowing what to do, but I wedged the oar into the mud and pushed, leaning against it with all of my might.

"Stop!" Miho shouted, standing on the bank only fifteen feet away, close enough that I could see the tattoo that edged her hairline. I missed her. An ache filled me, and I wished I could go back and do it all differently. I wished I would have told Abe the second I saw Kathy coming down the greenway. I wished I would have shared my memory with Miho.

She didn't look well. She was so thin I could see her collarbones clearly, and her arms were sticks. Her eyes were weary, and she kept giving her head a little shake as if trying to wake up. But even with her in that condition, even with the affection I felt rising in me, I knew we couldn't bring her along. I had no idea how Adam's actions had hurt her or what she would do to him given the chance.

"Don't stop," I whispered to Lucia, though she wasn't doing anything. "Keep going. We have to keep going."

She stood and grabbed the oar below my hands, and we both pushed. The boat edged backward, away from the bank.

"Dan, I'm coming to you," Miho said in a determined voice, as if she couldn't believe I would leave her there. She took a few steps toward us into the mud. Her feet sank immediately, down to her shins.

I didn't say anything. I couldn't. Again I leaned against the oar with Lucia, we both pushed, and the boat moved. The farther we went, the less muddy the water and the easier we moved.

Miho took another step. She sank up to her knees. "I'm not stopping, Dan," she said, and her voice was calm. "You can't do this. You have to come back. You can't bring Adam out. He has to do it himself. You know it's true!"

"Why don't you want him to come out!" I screamed, and emotion split my voice. I was crying and I didn't even know why. "Why do you want to keep him here?"

I had so many more things I wanted to say, but I knew if I kept speaking, I would lose the argument. I shook my head, a poor defense against the sadness and doubt gathering inside of me. The reeds made a rasping sound against the wooden sides of the boat. We went through a pool of white flowers, and their stamens burst in a cloud of red pollen.

"Dan!" Miho shouted. "Dan!"

"I can't!" I finally said. "I'm sorry!"

I watched as she wrestled her way backward and fell onto her back, her arms sinking in the mud. For a moment I thought she might be going under, and I grabbed Lucia's arm, holding the oar still.

"Dan!" Miho screamed, and there was an edge of terror in her voice. One arm vanished into the mud all the way up to her shoulder, but she wrestled backward, rolling, plunging, like a wild animal struggling to stay up out of a swamp. Eventually she dragged herself back onto the bank. She was covered in the brown-gray muck, and she stayed there on her hands and knees. I could tell she was sobbing, though I couldn't hear it.

"How could you leave me in that?" she shouted, but the mist around us swallowed up her words.

"I'm sorry!" I shouted again, my voice cutting short, and there were so many things I was sorry about that I didn't even know which one I was apologizing for. But the bog swallowed up my words too, and I didn't think she heard my apology.

The boat drifted slowly away through water almost completely clear of any reeds. Above us, the mist descended again. The cold grew sharper.

I let go of the oar. Lucia pushed us out, one hand over the other, the oar reaching deep. Then she sat, and the oar trailed in the water as some current tugged us away. I put my forehead against her back and wept.

22 Adam's Rock

"I can push for a little bit," I said, moving toward the back where Lucia had settled after turning the boat around and setting out across the muddy water. She slid forward to the bench where I had sat and handed me the oar. I thought for a moment how disastrous it would be to drop it.

My legs wobbled underneath me as I stood, and I grabbed the oar with two hands, stabbed it into the water. The shallowness surprised me. I had expected to have to reach far into the depths to find the bottom, but it was only three or four feet beneath us. I got into a slow rhythm of plunging the oar, pushing the boat forward, lifting, bringing the dripping oar back beside the boat, and dropping it in again. The movement helped keep me warm.

Lucia sat completely still, staring forward. All around us the water moved, creating small crests. I looked back, but the bank was far off. I couldn't see Miho.

In front of us, far in the distance, a dark rise became visible, a thin line along the gently swelling surface. I had nearly forgotten about the knapsack. It had become a part of my body, an extra appendage, and the way it bounced against my side as I walked had become a kind of comfort. We reached in and took what we wanted, and soon the small bits of food were gone. A small amount of water remained. How would we ever hike back up with so little water, with no food? But this was not a question my mind attached itself to. The only remaining desire was to get to the bottom and see if my brother was there. After that, who knew?

The far bank came up on us quicker than I expected, and our boat ground up against rocky beach. Lucia and I crawled out, dragging the boat farther in until it was lodged firmly between two boulders. I pulled the oar up onto the flat slab that made up the rest of the bank. I wished Lucia would say something—I thought I would feel less lonely if she did.

"Here we go," I said, hoping for some kind of an answer.

She nodded, her eyes bright again, eager. She took off in a slow jog, her feet padding ahead, away from the water and into another narrow canyon. It was maybe twenty feet wide, flanked by the same kind of cliff walls that made up the rest of the abyss. I wondered how she could run—gravity felt heavier there. My feet were a burden to lift with each step.

I had lost track of the shape of our sur-roundings and the direction we were walking.

Our wanderings had gone down, that I knew, but once at the bottom of the ledge, once we crossed the bog and left Miho behind, any sense of direction disintegrated.

Beneath our feet was hard rock, and the path twisted and turned even deeper into the mountain. I had a sense that if I could see high enough up, there would be a sliver of blue sky, but the cliffs rose up all around us. The light was dim.

"Lucia," I said.

She slowed, turned to look at me. But I had no other words. I had only wanted to hear my own voice, to make sure I wasn't disappearing.

We came to an iron gate. It was tall, too tall to climb over, and its imposing doors swung on hinges somehow attached to the stone. They were tall and narrow, formed with metal fastened to itself with rivets. There were no signs of rust.

I walked up to the gate and stared at it. I swung the knapsack around in front of me and reached deep inside, my hand sliding along the seams. There it was. The key I had found, the key Kathy had always been asking me about. I pulled it out. It was cold in my fingers, and something about it made me afraid. I handed Lucia the knapsack, and she slung it over her shoulder and watched me with expectation in her eyes.

I put the key into the lock. It didn't go in smoothly, but as I struggled to turn it, the entire gate groaned, and there was a loud splintering sound as the latch was freed. The gate moved toward me almost imperceptibly, and I reached my fingers along the inside edge and pulled. It was heavy but swung soundlessly, as if it had recently been oiled. Lucia didn't run ahead of me. She nodded, and I couldn't tell if it was a movement of agreement or a lifting of the chin indicating, "You first." I reached back and slipped the key into the knapsack now dangling over her shoulder.

We walked through the gate, and I noticed there was no lock on the inside. This gate was not for keeping people out of the area we had just entered—it was for keeping people in. I stared at it. Would it stay open? If it closed, would it lock us in automatically? I searched for anything to wedge in the gate and hold it open until we returned, but there was nothing.

I turned away from the gate, and Lucia sidled up beside me. We put our arms around each other to stay warm, and I felt such a fatherly affection toward her. Her presence was a gift. I wondered again where she had come from, why she was here.

The cliff walls pressing in on us widened into an open space of what appeared to be deep, rich soil, and the light increased, if only a little. I could feel my spirits rise. There were large, beautiful trees everywhere, their heavy limbs swaying in a breeze. The cold that had felt nebulous or intangible solidified there in that glade, made itself present in a way it had not been anywhere else.

A light snow fell as we walked among the trees. They were shaped almost like people. The wide bases of their trunks split into several exposed roots before plunging into the frozen earth. Could there be a warm undercurrent of water? But what of the lack of light? It was a strange and nonsensical place, the lime-green leaves coated lightly in white snow, the rich earth carpeted with grass and filled with glassy puddles, the trees whose branches moved and shifted like arms.

Lucia ran off, vanished among the trees, and her absence left a lonely, frightened space inside of me. The shadows in that place were strange. They seemed to move of their own accord, somehow separate from the object that made them. A tree's shadow might appear to be billowing in a storm while the tree itself was standing nearly still. Or the dim shadow cast by the walls where we had entered shimmered and moved like a liquid, but the walls were fixed.

From some of the deeper shadows I thought I could hear something. Voices? Or maybe it was only the wind? I was so cold. So cold. Could I even trust my senses anymore? How much longer until my body gave in to hypothermia?

"Lucia!" I shouted, a sense of frustration rising toward the girl. I did not like being left alone in that place. Why was she always running off?

The snow fell heavier, and I moved farther in among the confusing trees with their incongruent shadows. It was like a swirling of my vision. I realized the ground had gradually gone from grass to icy puddles and then to a solid block of ice—the trees somehow grew up and out of that shallow, frozen lake. The trees looked more and more like terrified people waving me off, motioning for me to go and never return. Warning me.

"Lucia!" I shouted again. The wind blew harder, and the snow stung my eyes, blinding me until I stumbled out into a clearing, all of the trees shrinking back from this open space. Here the ice was clear all the way down to the depths, and the snow stopped suddenly. I wondered if I was dead or alive. The stillness was vast.

"Lucia!" My voice was weak and hoarse, scratchy in the cold, and puffs of steam escaped every time I shouted. But she did not reply, and I grew more frustrated, nearing anger. Where was that girl?

Across the vast pool of black ice I saw movement. Lucia? But no, it wasn't movement so much as something that didn't blend in with the complete stillness, something that didn't move so much as shift. I looked closer, peering through the darkness.

Adam?

I walked forward carefully, skeptically. Could my greatest hope be right there? But I hadn't taken more than five or six steps forward when a sound made me stop suddenly. I was awakened by fear. It was the sound of creaking and a grinding split. The ice under my feet was not as thick as I had thought, and a gentle thread of water oozed up through the crack. I stopped. I peered into the darkness again.

Could it be him?

A man Adam's size, with long black hair, down on hands and knees, was isolated on a tiny rock island in the middle of the frozen lake. I took another step toward him, and this time the ice cracked in the shape of a spiderweb. I took a step backward.

"Adam?" My voice came out tenuous like the ice, cracking in the cold.

Somehow in that great stillness, he heard me, and he looked over. It was too far away to see his eyes. He didn't have a shirt on. His pants were torn and frayed and sliced so that they hung around his legs like rags. He seemed to be looking for the source of the voice, then turned his face upward, toward the nothing sky, and gave a maniacal laugh.

"You fooled me again!" he screamed, and in his voice I could hear every torment known to man. "Well done! Yes! Well done!" He slammed his hands against the ice and his shoulders shook. I thought he must be weeping. I wanted to shout for him again, but I didn't want to cause the same reaction. He was obviously hurting himself.

But I couldn't help it.

It was him.

"Adam!" I shouted, looking frantically around for another way across the ice. I took a few steps back, slid to my right ten or fifteen yards, and walked forward again tenderly, leading with my toes. The ice was turning to fire under my feet. But when I had walked the same distance forward, the ice groaned and split.

"No," I groaned. "Adam!"

Immediately I wished I hadn't called for him again—my voice seemed to be making him crazy with agony. He struck his forehead on the ground in front of him. He screamed. He grated his fingers along the rock.

I felt it before I saw it, a blur of movement to my left, coming out of the trees. Lucia ran across the ice, and as she did, a word erupted from her. It seemed to have the force of all the gathered words she had held in.

"Daddy!"

I caught my breath. I stopped blinking. The world spun.

Lucia, running toward Adam, was shouting "Daddy!" over and over again.

My throat swelled and I knew it was true. Maybe I had known the first time I saw her, recognized something in her eyes or the way she looked at me or how she pushed her hair away in some familiar gesture of Adam's.

"Lucia!" I shouted, trying to warn her. "The ice!"

But she didn't stop. She only glanced at me and sprang from side to side, here and there. In some places I could tell the ice had split under her while in others it remained flat and firm. She didn't run straight but seemed to follow some pattern. Maybe she could see where the ice was thicker. Maybe a shallow place ran from where she had emerged out to the small island where Adam knelt. Or maybe she was simply lucky.

I watched the knapsack sway and bounce on her back, the precious knapsack holding the last of our water. And the key.

She arrived at Adam's rock, clambered up, and sat quietly beside him. He did not look up. I wondered if he could see her. Maybe he thought she was simply another in a long line of hallucinations. She studied him, her head tilting to the side, then she reached out a hand and, with the gentlest touch of her index finger, lifted his chin so that his eyes rose to hers. They were like a precious statue, the father on his knees, the daughter lifting his face so that he could see her.

Even from where I was, I could see him begin to tremble, first in the weakness of his arms, and after that his hips, and eventually his whole body. Lucia lifted her other hand and held his face, her tenderness propping him up. She leaned forward and kissed his forehead.

The ice under my feet cracked further, and I shifted back and away from Adam's rock, alarmed at the distance growing between us. I stared down at the ice to see if things were stabilizing, but hairline fractures were still forming, so I took a few more steps back. When I looked back up, Lucia was taking off the knapsack and placing it on the rock. She took out the water and funneled some into Adam's mouth. I worried about how much she was giving him and if we'd have enough to get us back out.

Adam drank, sat back on his haunches, and stared at her as if she was a vision come to life. He said a few words I couldn't hear, and she leaned forward and hugged him, even in his wretchedness, his filth. This time his shoulders trembled, but in sobs. He kept leaning his head back and looking at her in amazement, then embracing her again.

The water under me churned, which was strange because I hadn't moved. I looked out over the black expanse of ice, and it all seemed to vibrate as if in an earthquake. The ice trembled. Some distance off, at the edge of what I could see, a large piece of ice broke from the rest and stood up on end. The whole earth seemed to groan.

"Lucia!" I shouted. "The ice!"

We must have realized it at the same time:

this was not a lake we were on but a river, one so massive I couldn't see the far bank. The water beneath us was moving, and the ice was beginning to break up. The sound of it was like the splitting of the mountain. I became more and more frantic as the seconds passed, as the river moaned, as the ice fractured.

"Hurry!" I screamed, my voice as broken as the river, and yet still they remained on the rock. I could tell she was pleading with him, and he was shaking his head, his long black hair swaying in pendulum movements. She wept, she pleaded, she hugged him, and still he remained, sitting back on his heels, refusing to move.

She pointed across the ice. He looked at me. Our gazes locked, there at the bottom of the abyss, with the world collapsing around us. I wanted to shout to him to get moving. I wanted to raise my hands and gesture wildly for him to hurry, the ice was breaking, this was his chance. I wanted to get on my knees and plead. But all I did was stand there, my shoulders slumped.

I had caused this. He was here because of me, because I had forced him to fly that day, because I was more concerned with my own reputation and possessions than anything else. I wondered if he had somehow discovered that it was my fault, that the accident never would have happened without my insistence that he get out of bed that morning and fly the plane.

He stood. Lucia was tiny next to him, but strong. He leaned on her and they climbed gingerly down the shallow side of the rock and began making their way across the ice. She ran ahead, I guess because their weight together would have been too much, and beckoned to him. As they grew closer, I could hear her voice encouraging him, pleading with him to keep coming, telling him he could do it. He followed her, barely able to walk, sometimes falling to his knees. At one point his legs went through the ice, and he sprawled forward, spreading out his weight, inching himself forward.

It started snowing again. Lucia arrived to me before he did, and we backed up, hoping to find thicker ice or shallower water farther back toward the trees. Still he kept coming. Now he could walk, his bare feet white on the ice. I was shaking with cold but also warm from the exertion, the stress, the emotion.

There he was, standing in front of me. Could it be true? I waited for him to evaporate, a mirage. I had waited so long for this moment.

He wouldn't look directly at me. His eyes flitted here and there, nervous and unstable, and I understood why Lucia had reached out and taken his chin in her hands, directing his uncontrolled glances. But I waited, and eventually our eyes met.

"Adam," I said, my voice shattered, miniscule, lost.

"Dan," he said.

For a moment I thought I was truly looking at myself, another version of me, one that had never made it out of this place but had withered away here at the bottom for endless years, endless decades, tortured by all the wrong I had done. It should have been me. All along, it should have been me.

"I'm sorry," I said, and his gaze sharpened, but he said nothing. "I'm sorry," I said again, and I put my hands on his shoulders as if I was going to shake him. He seemed so lost.

"The knapsack," Lucia whispered, her voice barely registering in the midst of the river's chaos and my overflowing emotions.

"What?"

She didn't answer. She sprinted back onto the ice that continued to break up, clashing against itself, upending in sharp angles and shards.

"Lucia!" I shouted.

Adam, too weak to continue in the midst of everything, fell to his knees and broke through the ice. The ice around my own feet followed, and I plunged through. For a moment we clawed at each other, trying desperately to rise. The water was dark underneath the ice, and in a panic I lost my sense of up and down. But it was shallow there where we stood close to the trees, and my hands soon found the muddy bottom. I pushed off, up, and burst through the surface.

My brother had already pulled himself to safety and crawled the rest of the way to the trees. He sat there, his back against a trunk that resembled a forlorn mother with branches reaching down like arms. The trees' shadows were darker then, like bottomless ditches. I pulled myself aching and frozen from the water. How long could we survive, wet as we were, hungry as we were, cold as we were? I gathered myself on all fours and the ice creaked. I didn't think I had the strength for another submersion.

I crawled along a line where I thought I would be safe, looking toward Adam's rock for Lucia, wishing she would show herself. I choked back tears at the thought of losing her there, in that lowest of places. Just when I gave up, she appeared, coming up out of the icy water, gripping the rock, pulling herself up. She lifted the knapsack and started to put it over her shoulder but stopped. She stared at it. She peered through the darkness and spotted me.

Freed from its icy bonds, the river flowed faster than before, and the flat spaces of ice had become bobbing, miniature glaciers sliding away. Lucia seemed to gather her courage. She jumped from one floating ice island to the next. She vanished into the water, then pulled herself up again, crawling onto a slowly spinning slab. She was swept toward me briefly, jostled by other moving pieces of ice. She prepared herself to make another running leap, had second thoughts. Her face was sad. Her lips were a straight line. All around us was the sound of ice colliding, cracking, creaking.

She threw the knapsack hard in my direction, her arm a slingshot, and I crawled toward the spot where it landed, on ice in shallow water. I grabbed it, and a wave of relief washed over me so that I almost felt warm again. I looked at her, a smile on my face. She gave me a thumbs-up. Throwing the knapsack had knocked her to her knees, and she paused there for a moment on all fours. She tried to smile, but I could tell she was afraid.

Then the ice she was on tipped up at one end. She slid toward the other edge, bracing herself, clawing for something to hold on to.

"Lucia!"

She went under, and I lost sight of her.

23 How Far We Have Fallen

I don't know how long I waited in that spot, holding my breath. The water was a mess of ice collapsing in on itself, mounding up in some areas, spreading out in others. It was like a flat field full of debris left behind after a village is leveled in war. I gasped for breath. I held the knapsack in one hand. I wanted to scream.

But the cold, the cold was breaking my bones. I turned and crawled, and my body creaked with the weariness of it. Once I was closer to what I thought was solid ground, I stood gingerly and walked toward where Adam still sat against a tree. They were haunting, those trees. Their roots, where they showed through the black ice, seemed to pulse like veins. I knew it was some trick of the light, perhaps the shimmering of the ice, but it still repulsed me.

I stopped beside Adam and sat down. The snow had been coming and going ever since Lucia and I had arrived in that place, but in that moment, it was so light that I thought it had stopped. Except every so often a lone flake would fall, lost. The sky was only low, gray clouds, like a hovering fog. I thought about the rim of the abyss beside the river Acheron and the immeasurable distance between us and that place. I wondered how far we had fallen.

Adam mumbled something that sounded like a question. I looked at him again, trying to find the brother I remembered hidden there among the gaunt flesh, the long hair, the broken skin. His knees bled from kneeling on the rock for who knows how long. He flinched every few seconds as if being prodded.

"What?" I asked him quietly. I wanted to hug him. I wanted to hold him. After so much time with Lucia and her silence, the sound of another human being's voice, even indecipherable, was like balm. But there was something between us, something I couldn't identify. There was a kind of strangeness there, and years, and misunderstandings that might be too far gone to clear up.

"The girl," he muttered, his voice still hoarse. Saliva pooled in the corners of his mouth. He was crazed. Would the hike out help him heal, or had he left whatever shred of sanity that remained on that rock in the middle of the frozen river?

"Where is she?"

I took in the shifting ice. When I didn't see her, a sob came out of me, a wave of grief, but I cleared my throat to hide it. I knew in that moment I could never tell him about her, or he wouldn't leave. I was the only one who knew she was his daughter. Had been his daughter. There was no reason to tell him now.

"What girl?" I whispered.

"The girl," he said, his voice stronger, his eyes searching mine. "The girl who came over to me."

I shook my head slowly. "I don't know, Adam." I paused, swallowed. "I didn't see anyone."

He stared hard into the deep blackness of the ice beneath us. There was another blistering crack from the river, a moaning creak, and Adam shivered convulsively. The ice was on the move. I wondered what had set it off.

"I've seen a lot here," he said. "I've imagined a lot."

I nodded.

"Are you sure?"

"I didn't see a girl," I insisted. "I saw you look up at me across the ice, drag your way through the river. That's all I saw."

He clenched his jaw. Shook his head. "I could've sworn . . ."

"We should go." I stood up, moving gingerly away from the tree on the ice, but my caution was unnecessary. The water there remained solidly frozen.

"No use," he said.

What?

"No use," he said again. "There's no way out. The gate is locked."

"Have you been to the gate?" I asked.

He nodded. "Once. Long after everyone left. Long after she left. I managed to crawl all the way there. When I found the locked gate, I gave up hope. So I crawled back out to the rock."

"She?" I asked.

"What do you mean?"

"You said, 'Long after everyone left. Long after she left.' Who's 'she'?"

He shuddered. "The one in charge. The one who ran this whole place, every circle of it, every tree, every corner."

"It was a she?" A sense of dread slunk through me. "Did she have a name?" I asked in a hushed voice.

He nodded again.

I raised my eyebrows in a question. *What was her name?*

"Kathy," he whispered.

Kathy. I had left everyone with her, and they didn't even know who she was. A thought dropped into my mind—what if I was here because of her? I was, wasn't I? Hadn't she been the one to convince me to come back in, to get my brother? But he couldn't have gotten out without me, could he?

What if she was now convincing the others to come in and retrieve me? What if she walked east and found others to convince?

She would fill this place again.

"We should go," I said. I was filled with fresh

urgency to get him out, get us out, and find the others.

"Who are you?" he asked with none of the urgency I was looking for.

"Me?" I asked. "I'm Dan." I decided to leave it at that. For now.

"Dan," he whispered, and he was lost again, searching through hidden realms in his mind, perhaps searching for me. He emerged moments later. "The gate." He sighed.

I reached into the knapsack, searched the bottom corners of the cloth, and pulled out the key. I held it up in front of him, and he looked at it in awe, as if it was the strangest of all the strange things he had seen, the least believable.

He reached up, not to take it but to touch it. "Is it real?"

"Yes," I said, again seeing the movement of Lucia's arm as she threw the knapsack. I saw her clinging to the ice, sliding toward the edge. I saw her going under.

Adam tried to stand, and when he couldn't do it on his own, I reached down and took hold of his arm. He felt like a bundle of twigs. We both continued to shiver, so I put my arm around him and we tried to live off each other's warmth. I didn't know how we would walk, how we would leave this place. I thought of the bog we had to get through, the ledge we'd have to maneuver. The river. Maybe Karon and Sarah could help us. If we made it that far.

The ledge. I had left Miho by the ledge, assuming she wasn't a figment of my imagination. And now we had to get past her too, make sure she didn't exact some sort of revenge on Adam. I had never heard her story, but I could guess. The crash had affected her in some way. She hated my brother. She was waiting for him like all the others.

"Do you see people a lot down here? Imaginary people?" I asked.

He nodded as we walked stiffly through the trees and over all those strange shadows. The ice felt solid under our feet, but I was still expecting it to break at any point. The water that was on me felt like it was freezing, turning me into a block.

"Do you think I'm real?" I asked.

"No," he said, and as we shuffled along, this was the closest he'd come to giving me a smile.

"Fair enough."

We found the entrance to the narrow canyon and left the trees and frozen river behind. And Lucia. We left Lucia behind. The guilt was crushing me, even though I knew there was nothing I could have done. I could not have walked across the ice. I could not have jumped in and pulled her out. I could not wait here long enough—she was gone. Not telling Adam about her felt like both a gift and a terrible betrayal. I told myself I would tell him someday. Far in the future. Far from here, when everything else was better.

The gate was still there, open, just as I had left it. Adam seemed so intrigued by it that I slowed and let him lead the way. He stopped directly in front of its opening, walked from side to side, and caressed its cold metal. He examined the lock, the doors.

"I stood at this gate, beating on it with my fists." He rubbed his hands together. "I screamed until my throat bled. How did you get the key from her? How did you come here?" He seemed to finally be accepting the fact that I was real and that I was with him.

"Do you know who I am?"

He nodded, his face blank, his hand still on the gate.

"You do?"

He nodded again, but he still didn't say anything.

"We have a lot to talk about once we get out of here," I whispered. I glanced away from him, feeling my face form a kind of wince, before walking over and gently taking hold of his elbow to guide him farther along. He kept looking over his shoulder at the gate, as if it might transform into a monster and chase us down, devour us in that rocky canyon.

"You should lock it," he said, his voice suddenly lifeless.

"What?"

"The gate. You should lock it. We can't leave it

open. What if she comes back down? What if she brings someone else here to keep them prisoner, like she did to me and all the others?"

"I don't think we have to worry about that," I said. I would have locked it had it not been for Lucia in the frozen river. Somewhere among the ice. Locking the gate suddenly felt crucial. Every evil I knew would come through if I didn't.

"There are horrors there," he said, stopping. "There are things in there, in the water, in the woods, you cannot even imagine. They will follow us. They will get out."

His voice was quiet, but it was impossible for me to ignore the terror he clearly felt in that moment. Have you been with someone who is in the midst of a panic attack? There is no rationalizing, no explaining. Nothing I said would convince him that all the things he had seen had been illusions, the constructs of a broken mind. But I could not lock Lucia into that place. It was the very bottom. If she had somehow survived, the way needed to remain open for her.

To appease Adam, I walked over to the gate and pushed the doors against each other so that they appeared to be closed. I held up the key so he could see it, then inserted it into the gate. I turned it so that it locked, but I also turned it back so that it unlocked again. When I took out the key, the unlocked gate budged only a fraction.

When I turned to look at him, relief left him

sagging, like someone who has finally relaxed. He had not seen the slight movement of the gate shifting open. In his mind it was locked and all the horrors of this place would be contained. Seeing the gate from that side, he raised his hands and covered his face, and the sound of his weeping echoed off the rock. I did not go over to him, not that time. I only watched and waited. His crying went on for a long time.

We finally continued through the canyon and had nearly reached the bog when I noticed that the cold was not so cold. My feet and fingertips were no longer numb. I put my hands up to my mouth and blew into them, and I could feel the warmth spreading. I looked over at Adam and could tell he was feeling it too. His joints didn't seem so locked. His face had regained some color, although his black hair did still emphasize the paleness of his skin. He reached up with a swollen finger and pushed a thread of hair out of his face.

"I can't believe this is all here," he said. "A way out."

We walked slowly, and the scuffing sound of our feet on the hard earth was lonely and peaceful. Every so often, one of us would need to stop to rest, and the other would stop as well, leaning against the canyon wall or sitting on the ground. We had reached the limits of our exhaustion. I could not let myself think about how far we still had to go.

I pulled out the water and we each took a sip. I put it back in the knapsack and thought about the price of it.

"How long?" he asked, staring at the ground between his feet.

"How long?" I repeated.

"How long was I in there?"

That was a good question. I had no idea. The passing of time in the small town on the edge of the plains had felt immeasurable. It could have been ten years. I thought of all the harvests we had seen, all the times we had pulled vegetables and fruits from the garden and the orchard. It must have been longer. Twenty years? Could it have been longer than that?

"I don't know," I said. "Time doesn't pass the same way anymore."

"Why'd you decide to come and find me? Why now?"

"Things were ending. Our village was destroyed. Kathy was there."

"Kathy?" He didn't actually say her whole name out loud. He said it the way a child might whisper a curse, knowing they'd be in trouble if anyone heard.

I nodded. "She burned down our village. At least I think it was her. She was trying to cause chaos, trying to break us up. I don't know. I don't understand completely. I think she wants everyone back in here again."

"But you're here because . . . of her?"

"No. I'm here because of you. I waited a long time, Adam. For you. I couldn't come back here. I couldn't. But then, when everything fell apart . . . I don't know. I had to do something."

We walked on, and I could tell he was thinking hard about something, thinking through all I had told him.

"You shouldn't be here," he said. "Nothing she wants to happen is good."

I didn't know what to say, so I didn't say anything.

He spoke again. "If she wanted you to be here, you shouldn't be here."

24 Broken Things

The rocks rose up in front of us, a kind of jetty that held back the bog waters. We made our way up, exhaustion stiffening my fingers, but after the cold of the forest and the canyon, the rocks felt almost warm. We got to the top and spotted the boat and the extra-long oar, and we wound our way down among the boulders. It took both of us to lift the boat and slide it into the water, and I'd imagine we both looked pitiful in our pain and weariness.

Adam climbed in gingerly, and I followed, dragging the oar with me. It took one easy push and we were back in the water. Again I searched behind us for Lucia. I willed her to appear. How could she ever cross this water without a boat? How could she ever leave this place on her own? I took heart in knowing that anyone who had ever escaped from this part of the abyss before had done so on their own, perhaps even without a boat. But it all felt so unlikely.

We drifted silently across the still water, and after a while the bank we had come from disappeared behind us. It wasn't until this moment that I realized there was no fog, no haze. The clouds were so high that they looked like a flat sheet, stretched, without any breaks in them.

Adam sat in the front, his back to me, leaning forward with his arms out and his hands gripping the bow. He could have been in prayer. He could have been asleep. He could have been plotting some escape. I wondered how his clothes still clung to him after all that time, torn and shredded as they were. His hair had dried in coarse clumps like wet straw, and between the strands I could see long, deep scratches on the back of his neck. Were they the marks his abusers had left, or were they gouges of guilt, self-inflicted? This place was even stranger than I had imagined, and what had happened to all of us seemed less and less clear.

He whispered something in his hoarse voice.

"What?" I asked, not even sure if he was talking to me or to himself.

"The water." He pushed the words out. "The water. Do you remember? The lake. Do you remember the lake?"

I was about to say no, but an image came into my mind. Adam and I in a lake house that one of my father's trucker friends had said we could stay in. It was a rough hunting cabin, and there was no running water inside, although there was a pump out front and an outhouse. Thirty yards down the hill from the house, the lake lapped up against a stony beach, and a long, narrow pier jutted out into the cold blue water.

Adam and I were roughhousing one afternoon, and in a series of events that happened too fast to replay in my mind, our wrestling caused a large pair of elk antlers to fall off the wall, strike the floor, and break. The two of us sat suspended in time, me on the bottom, nearly pinned. We craned our necks to find the source of the loud snapping sound.

We could fix it, I told myself. We could glue it, or hang it back up and pretend nothing happened, or throw the entire thing into the lake. But neither of us could move, because we heard the creaking of the bedroom door, and our father emerged without saying a word. He didn't even look at us—we still hadn't moved from the floor. He stared long at that broken set of antlers, his friend's fractured trophy.

"Come on," he mumbled in a voice that terrified me more than any shout could have.

We disentangled ourselves from each other, and I felt alone, afraid, and somehow naked. With Adam, even when he was pinning me to the ground, I felt part of something, something strong. But standing and following my father, walking wordlessly behind Adam, I felt even less than what I was, which at the time was a frightened twelve-year-old boy.

Still not looking at us, our father walked

outside and down to the pier. It swayed under our weight, and I nearly fell in a couple of times. I considered turning around and running, once even looking over my shoulder into those wooded hills. I imagined the feeling of safety I would have, running through the shadows of the trees, building a shelter in the wilderness where I could stay. Escape.

But I didn't run. And neither did Adam. We trailed behind our father, all the way to the end of the pier, by which point my legs were trembling. He climbed into the motorboat, also owned by his friend, and motioned for us to get in with him.

"The rope," he said, and I knew he meant for me to untie the boat from the dock.

I tentatively untied the rope, and the boat bobbed for a moment in the water, independent of the pier, independent of me. Again I considered running. I could be halfway back to the dock by the time he climbed out of the boat. I could be in the woods before he could catch me. Would he even chase me? Probably not. Maybe that's the real reason I didn't run—I couldn't face such a tangible sign of his indifference.

I jumped in and the boat shook. Adam and I moved to the front, gripping the sides, and the motor roared to life, easing the three of us out into that flat, beautiful lake. Soon we skimmed the water, and there were no waves to slap the bottom, no waves to skip us up into the air. It was a droning, constant propulsion to the deepest section, where the far banks were barely visible in all directions. A cold mist blew into our faces. I looked at Adam. He couldn't help but grin.

Our father cut off the engine unexpectedly, and the boat limped to a stop, pitching this way and that ever so subtly. There was no wind. The sky was huge, a beautiful blue dome that held everything, the entire universe. There was even happiness in that moment of quiet, that moment of peace, and I could nearly forget that Adam and I had broken something important.

"Get in the water," our father murmured. Had he been drinking? I couldn't tell. Adam reached for one of the life jackets, but our father stuck out his foot and stamped it down in the bottom of the boat, where an inch or so of water had gathered. "You won't need that."

We looked at each other. We had on normal clothes—khaki shorts and T-shirts. We had planned on going out for dinner. I reached into my pockets to make sure they were empty, taking out only a few small pieces of lint, a penny I had found on the dirt road that led to the cabin, and a movie stub. I moved to take off my shirt, but a hand ripped it back down.

"Get. In. The. Water," he said again, each word existing entirely on its own. When Adam and I paused at the side of the boat, he shouted so that his voice broke the dome and brought the universe caving in around us. "Get in the water!"

We jumped in, our splashes nearly synchronized. The water was clear and cool but not cold, a perfect day for swimming. I could feel the colder currents moving around my legs like fingers reaching up for me. We both hovered there, treading water, waiting to see what we were supposed to do next. But our father sat in the boat, staring off at the distant horizon.

Adam and I drifted closer, but as soon as one of us came within arm's reach, our father cleared his throat and said in a light voice, as if he was wishing us a good afternoon, "Don't touch the boat."

"It was an accident," Adam said, sputtering as a small swell rose up over his mouth.

"You two. You just go through life thinking you can have or take or break whatever you want. You're like two little animals. It's pathetic."

"We didn't try to do it," I chimed in. "We're sorry."

"You're right, you're sorry," he said, staring down at me.

My arms and legs ached, and the water was cooling. I hadn't noticed when we first set out, but the end of the afternoon was near. I wondered if he was going to make us swim home. The shore was nearly invisible from where I was, down in the water. I put my head back and floated, eyes closed. The water drowned out all other sounds, and I was gone, far from there, in a bathtub or a swimming pool or hunched under an umbrella after the rain has stopped. It was quiet there. Peaceful.

I stayed that way for a few minutes, and when I looked up, I found it hard to believe how far I had drifted away from the boat. Adam was still there, still treading, although the look on his face was strained. His skin had gone pale. He floundered, coughed, righted himself.

"Adam!" I shouted. "Float on your back. Get some rest."

But he wouldn't. His dark hair was wet. His breathing was hoarse. His arms splashed. Then he was under.

"Dad!" I screamed. "Adam!"

Our father eased his way over to the edge of the boat and stared into the depths. He plunged his hand in and grabbed Adam first by the hair, then by the scruff of his T-shirt, pulling up on it so that it came up under his chin, a noose. He dragged Adam into the boat and dumped him like a marlin. I heard Adam coughing over and over again until he threw up. Our father sat at the front of the boat as if nothing had happened. He wasn't smiling or frowning. He was sitting. Waiting.

I floated on my back, trying to preserve my strength. I knew in that moment what he wanted— he wanted me to feel that gentle slipping under, the panic of no air, the sense of him saving me from death, literally pulling me up into life. And I would not give him that satisfaction. I floated on my back, the water plugging and unplugging my ears, the sky cool and far above me. I treaded water for a few minutes. Then I floated again.

The boat coughed to life. I straightened up, kicked in the water, moved my arms around. I felt instantly suspicious because my father never gave up, never at anything and especially not when it came to waiting. He showed Adam the motor, how to steer, and sat in the front of the boat again.

He had never let either of us drive the boat, no matter how many times we begged.

As they trolled past me, he spoke one last time, and again he did not look at me but sent his words out to some other place. "You little cheat. Floating isn't allowed."

The boat powered past me, leaving me in the middle of the lake. I caught Adam's glance and could tell he was worried for me. He looked nervously over his shoulder to see if our father was watching, then he pushed a life vest over the side. It bobbed in the water, pushed aside by the wake. Our father turned toward Adam again, and at first I thought he had seen the life preserver, but he only instructed Adam on how to give the boat more throttle. It stood up out of the water, a higher pitch, before sitting and speeding away.

I swam, exhausted, to the life vest and tangled myself up in it. It held me, and I could finally catch my breath. I started kicking slowly, asking myself if it was even possible for me to swim all the way back to the shore in front of the cabin.

There is a particular feeling that comes in the night as you float on your back, when the deep water is still and the sky is reflected back to you. I moved slowly, sometimes using my arms to paddle, sometimes my legs, and I made it through the dark, all the way back.

The boat thumped against the pier in a gentle rhythm. There were waves, tiny ones, enough to lift and lower the craft. A hand reached down and helped me up, and once on the pier, sitting on that solid thing, I felt like jelly, like my entire body might melt. I was so tired.

"You okay?" Adam asked.

I nodded. We sat there for a long time, saying nothing. Then we stood and walked back inside. Our father never said a word about it. He used glue to reattach the antler. No one ever noticed the difference.

"I should have come back for you," Adam said as we approached the muddy banks of the bog. "I should have brought the boat back out and found you."

"It was dark," I said. "It was a big lake. You wouldn't have found me, not at night."

"That's not the point. You came back here for me."

Back here. For a moment, in that memory, my mind had escaped to a place where the sky was bright blue and the water clear, where the trees that lined the distant banks were green and full and the cabin's red metal roof was like a siren's call. Back here, though, the muddy water was thick. The only bank that was visible was the one coming into view, loaded with those sharp reeds growing up out of the mud. The sky was dull, a kind of brown-gray, and while the cold had dimmed, the warmer air smelled of rotten mud.

"If you are real," Adam said, staring straight ahead, leaning into the bow of the boat, "if you are real . . . where did you come from?"

"Outside of the mountain."

"And what is it like there? Outside?"

"It's very green," I said. "It's quiet, and the air smells of living things. From there, the mountain looks like something beautiful. I live in a small stone house at the edge of a village." I paused and decided not to tell him about going east, not yet. "There are a few others there."

I wondered if they were still there, if all of the houses had burned or if any had been saved. Was Abe still waiting for me, as he always said he would?

"You can choose a house. There are some empty ones. But we still have a long way to go to get there. You were at the very bottom."

Adam turned around and faced me, leaned

back, and wedged himself into the bow. I could tell he was on the edge of passing out.

"You know what I miss the most?" he said, his voice weak and see-through.

"What?"

"The birds," he whispered. "The swallows swooping down over our heads like bats, the pigeons in the barn, the doves in the eaves, the robins hopping along, eating worms."

"I never knew you liked birds."

He nodded. "I stared into the sky for years here, or decades, I don't know, just looking for the birds."

"Mother loved birds," I said quietly.

He nodded. He leaned his head back on the point of the bow and spoke toward the flat clouds above us. "You know, I remember how Mom used to stand beside the window and watch the birds."

"Yeah," I said. "Me too."

"One day I saw her standing there, and there was such love in her eyes. She held a cup of coffee close to her face, and the steam moved around her mouth, cheeks, and ears. I had never seen such love before. I wondered if she was looking out the window at Dad, but we both know that wasn't what it was." He gave a wry chuckle. "I walked over to stand beside her and see what she could possibly be looking at with such love, such fondness." He laughed as he said "fondness," as if he knew it wasn't a word he usually used. "Do you know what she was looking at?"

I shook my head.

"She was looking at you, Dan."

The oar stopped in the water, and our forward motion slowed. For a moment we were adrift, and the boat, because of the distribution of weight, an underwater current, or something else, slowly spun, pointing us back toward the far bank, the path through the gate, the frozen river, and Adam's rock.

She had loved me. And yet, I had only ever been concerned about my father's love.

I gripped the oar and braced my weight against it, sending us in the correct direction, back toward the muddy side of the shallow brown lake. When we weren't speaking, there was nothing but the sound of the boat in the heavy water, the oar dipping in and drops falling from it when I lifted it out.

I did not want to tell him that there were no birds in the plains.

"Have you seen Father in any of your travels?" Adam asked me.

I shook my head. "No."

"So, he found his way out."

This was something I could not contemplate. If he had left the mountain, if he had been in this place and fled, it must have happened before I had found my way to the village, because I had seen many hundreds or perhaps even thousands of people come through, but never him.

"I guess."

"I thought I saw him here, once," Adam said. "But it was from a distance, and it was when there were still a lot of us. I don't know. Probably my imagination."

Now Adam was looking right into my eyes. He scared me, because I couldn't tell if he was sane or not, if all this time in the abyss had unhinged his mind or if this was the brother from my childhood. If it was him, I didn't recognize him.

"I hated him," Adam said, his words reluctant to come out. "I don't remember much about this place. I've been here for so very, very long. But I do remember that I wasn't always so deep inside the mountain. It was my hatred for him that drove me down here, looking, searching. I wanted to find him. I planned on killing him. But this place . . ." He motioned all around us. "This place was so full of people moaning, screaming, pulling on me, needing, needing, needing."

He ran his hand through his long, tangled hair and winced, gritting his teeth. He was getting himself worked up. I wanted to say something that would calm him.

"I wish you would have come out. I wish you would have joined me."

He shook his head, put his face in his hands, and sat there like that for so long I thought he might have fallen asleep. But then he spoke.

"I do too. When I heard your voice, and the voice of that imaginary girl, it was like all of that hate broke up inside of me. The fog lifted. I don't hate him anymore." He paused. "Do you, brother? Do you hate our father?"

I didn't know what to say. I had barely thought of him, except perhaps when my memories came back to me. I was so focused on Adam that my history with our father slid easily through my fingers, but here, deep in the abyss, I could feel that hatred rising. It threatened to pull me down.

I shook my head uneasily. "No," I said, frowning. "I don't know."

I didn't want to talk about our father anymore. "What else do you remember? What else do you miss?" I asked.

He looked at me, squinted, and I knew I had been found out, that he could tell this was me grasping for a change of subject. But he went along with it.

"I miss the sunrise. Remember when we had that airplane business and I'd go on an early morning run? The plane lifted easily off the runway, barely clearing the trees, and there it was—the sunrise. I can't tell you how many times I wanted to keep flying, all the way into it."

I was amazed at how many memories he had.

I was amazed at how quickly he seemed to be recovering, transforming from that torn man kneeling on the rock, and I didn't have the heart to tell him. This place we were going to had no sunrises—only the soft dimming of light in the evening, which was beautiful and peaceful but was no sunset, and the dark of night, and the early morning brightening, which was gentle and quiet, but it was no sunrise.

Would we ever get out of this place? Would I ever see the green grass of the plains stretching out in front of me?

I felt a nagging sense of fear that something was coming for us, that I should have locked the gate no matter what that might have meant for Lucia. The desire became so strong that I nearly turned the boat around. Again I scanned the horizon for any sign of our tormentors. I dug in the oar, and now it was a struggle to pull it out, because it sank into the muddy bottom. Bubbles rose in the water every time I lifted it. I scanned the bank for Miho. Nothing.

We got the boat as close as we could. I told Adam to avoid the reeds and the flowers. After we had struggled to push the boat farther through the mud, we lay in the bottom, exhausted, panting. I arranged the oar the same way Lucia had placed it, on top of the mud, stretching out to the bank.

"You have to walk along it or you'll sink," I

said. I took off my shirt and threw it to the bank. "In case you need an extra step."

Adam scurried along the wooden oar, his feet slipping, and he did not have to step on the shirt. I followed him, and the oar sank in. My last few steps were in knee-deep mud, so tight, resisting each step with such powerful suction, I thought I might lose the skin on my legs. But soon we were resting on the bank, the bog and the gate and the icy hollow behind us. Now there was only the long, steep ledge, the climb to the top, and the river Acheron.

But . . . Miho. Where was Miho?

Maybe we didn't see her coming because we were exhausted. Maybe we didn't sense her approach because she was still covered in mud, blending in with that whole place. Maybe I didn't want to see her, frightened of what her presence might mean. But she was there, and she came out of nowhere. Before I knew what was happening, she had leaped onto Adam, pulled him backward onto the ground, and had her arms tight around his neck, choking him. Adam's eyes bulged out of their sunken sockets. He held tight to her forearm, the one that was choking him, but he didn't have the strength to pull it away.

25 Leaving

We became a blur of bodies, of arms pulling and scratching, of lungs gasping for breath. Someone bit me. I grabbed hair and pulled. A rake of fingernails tore lines in the side of my face, and I yelped, turned away, kicked with both legs. Three of us, on the ground, and Adam barely fought back. Miho wasn't going to let go—she was like a python, squeezing, squeezing, even after death. The only thing I could think to do was to put her in a choke hold as well, and soon she released Adam's neck and started hitting me.

This was what I remembered about this place. This was the abyss—not the quiet passing over water or the insistence of cracking ice. But this. This fight to stay alive. This confusion. This self-preservation. This pain.

I fell away and rolled over again and again, trying to create distance between us. She heaved three loud sobs, let out a scream muffled by her own hands, and ran to the cliff wall, wedging herself into a narrow space in the rock beneath the ledge. Her body shook with cries and tears and sobs.

I glanced over at Adam. He was curled up on

his stomach, twitching as if he had the hiccups. Moaning. I took a deep breath and sank onto my back, relieved that it seemed to be over if only for a few moments, staring up into the gray sky. The cold air swirled around us, but there were touches of something warmer.

What was happening to us?

I reached up and held my face, touched the cuts, then looked at my fingers and saw thin clouds of blood. I could taste it in my mouth too, perhaps from the shot I had taken to the lip. I spit it out. I searched for the knapsack, picked it up, and crawled over to Adam.

"Are you okay?" I asked.

He nodded without looking up, without moving.

Miho was ten yards away, still crying, still pulling on her short hair. This place would destroy us. I didn't know how I knew that, but I did. We had to get out.

"Miho," I called out.

Adam looked up slowly, not in fear but in resignation. He had bright red marks on his cheeks from where someone had struck him—it very well could have been me in the confusion. I didn't know. One eye was swelling. His neck was raw, and he kept rubbing it, gently clearing his throat.

"Miho," I said again.

She stilled herself and sat down, her knees

pulled up to her chest, her face down. The three of us sat in that silence for a long, long time. I focused on my breathing. Adam lay back down on the ground. I stared out across the water, thinking of when my father had left me in the lake. Thinking of Adam waiting for me on the pier. Thinking of Lucia going under.

Miho's silence turned again into sobs, and her voice choked out words in a strange rhythm. I stood on shaky feet, held the knapsack over my shoulder, and shuffled toward her.

"I can't," she said. "I can't. I can't. I can't."

I sat down wearily beside her. I didn't care anymore if she hurt me. I was too tired to care.

"Miho," I whispered, "we have to leave. We have to get out of this place."

Adam made his way over to us and sat beside me, so that all three of us were resting in the shadow of that cliff. Again I thought of the long, narrow way out. My muscles were so weary they trembled and cramped every time I tried to move. I couldn't imagine how we would ever make it up.

"I hated you for so long," Miho said.

"Me?" I asked.

She shook her head. "Him. I hated him for what he did. He killed her. My mother. She was at the store the morning the plane crashed. She was killed along with all the others you heard about. She was the sweetest, kindest woman."

Miho paused. "I tortured myself for years over that, blaming myself for not taking her inside the store faster. I wished I hadn't agreed to watch the child—if we only would have gone in, she wouldn't have been there when it happened. I couldn't get the sound of it out of my head for years. Any loud sound would send a panic through me."

She took a deep breath. "I always had a hunch that I was staying in the village because I was waiting for someone. It was this idea hovering at the edge of my mind. But after the memories came back that night, I realized I was waiting for your brother. And once I realized that, once I remembered his name and all that he had done, all that he had taken from me, I hated him."

"What changed, Miho?" I asked. I was so tired.

She looked at me without any expression. "I hated him until I saw him here on the bank, and I saw you."

"If you didn't—" Adam began.

"I attacked you because I couldn't hate you anymore. That made me so angry. The thought of revenge had sustained me, but when I saw you, I knew I couldn't hate you anymore."

"Why not?" Adam asked.

"Because of love." She said this simply. Matter-of-factly. "In the village, I came to love Dan. Even though my love wasn't for you, love changed me."

I felt many things in that moment. I felt a rush of love for Miho, the old feeling that had grown between us. But I also had a sense that it was leaving, that everything that had happened was putting a small crack in the glass, and anything special we'd had between us was slowly fading away.

"What happened in the village?" I asked her. "What happened after the fire?"

"The rain came. A woman walked toward us through the embers and the ash." She looked at me as if she knew I would never believe something so ludicrous. "She said she had just come through the canyon, but I knew she was lying because she seemed fine. She didn't look tortured at all. She looked rested and, well, good, like she had been out for at least a few days. Maybe a week. She told us we should all go after you, because she saw you going into the canyon. She said you told her you were going to look for your brother, but that we should go in after you and stop you. She asked if any of us had a key."

Miho spoke in short bursts. She sounded confused by her own story, even though she had been there.

"I don't know, Dan. It was all so strange. But she was adamant. We needed to go in after you. All of us."

"I think I know her. This lady," Adam said.

We both looked at him.

"There was a woman, when the place really started to empty out. She was actually trapped in the ice all the way up to her chest. She never made a sound, but I saw her digging at the ice until her hands were bloody. Clawing at it like some kind of animal, or like a machine that couldn't feel any pain. I shouted at her a few times and told her to stop, she was hurting herself, but she didn't listen." He nodded softly to himself. "That's her. That's who you're talking about. She broke free somehow. I don't know. She found a rock or a shard of ice and picked her way out with it. She was the last person I saw down there."

I looked over at Miho. I didn't want to dwell too long on Kathy. I didn't want them to know that I had kept her in my house, sheltered her, helped her.

"And only you came?" I asked Miho, my voice timid.

"We all went up to the entrance. You know, beside the signpost. We had a long conversation about what we should do. Abe was saying that it wasn't smart for all of us to go in. Po said he wouldn't go in anyway, whether it was smart or not. Most of the others didn't seem to think they could make the trip. They were too afraid. John wanted to come with me. Lucia, the girl? She ran in before any of us could stop her. We all ended up having a terrible fight about it. I wanted to follow her in. Abe said to wait. John wasn't sure."

She paused, and I looked up. The clouds were coming down.

"That woman was there the whole time," she said, "not saying a word."

"But you came," I said.

She nodded, shrugged, as if her trek here was nothing worth mentioning. But then her eyes lit up. "Lucia was with you in the boat."

"What?" I asked.

"When you left me on the bank. Lucia was in the boat with you."

A surge of panic raced through me. Somehow I had completely forgotten that.

"I don't know what you're talking about," I said quietly, firmly.

"This place will mess with your mind," Adam whispered.

Miho looked at me, glanced away. "I could have sworn I saw her."

"It's strange you both would have seen the same thing," I admitted, trying to sound confused by their visions of a young girl. What would they do if they found out I had left her behind?

"What about everyone else?" I asked, trying to steer the conversation back. "Where did they go?"

"Everyone else went east. They said they had waited long enough. They thought Adam was probably dead, and even if he wasn't, they were ready to move on. Kathy kept saying these things that tugged at all of us, things that made it hard to walk away. But eventually they did. Then it was only her and Abe and me. As I walked into the canyon, I could see the two of them there, standing side by side."

Adam's voice sounded groggy. "What do you mean, they went east?"

"I'll explain later," I said. I couldn't imagine trying to explain one more thing to him. I closed my eyes, rubbed my temples. The scratches on my cheek were stinging, and I rubbed them gently with the very tips of my fingers.

"Are you sure you didn't see her?" Miho asked Adam.

"See who?" Adam asked.

"A girl. Lucia. She's only a teenager."

"The person you were just talking about is a girl?" Adam was suddenly alert, leaning forward so he could see Miho on the other side of me.

She nodded. "She showed up a few days before all of this happened."

Adam's voice was full of confusion. "I saw a girl when Dan came for me. She crossed the icy water and helped me to the bank. When she ran back out to the rock, I lost sight of her."

I shook my head. "I told you, Adam, it was your imagination. You were seeing all kinds of things down here. Kathy in the ice up to her chest?"

"What did she look like?" Miho interrupted me, throwing the question at Adam.

"Thin. Light brown hair. A pretty face. A soothing voice. When we were out on the rock, she told me I could do it—I had to do it. It was time for me to leave. And for some reason, I believed her." Adam gave out a half laugh, disbelieving. "So I did."

"What's going on, Dan?" Miho asked, turning to me.

"I have no idea," I said emphatically before sighing. "Anyway, Lucia couldn't speak, remember?"

This seemed to turn the tide of Miho's belief. "True," she said.

"We have to get out of here," I continued. "We shouldn't be waiting here. When you stop moving in this place, it's so hard to get started again."

"Dan," she asked, doubt in her voice, "did you see Lucia?"

"No." My jaw clenched. My heart raced.

Silence. They both stared at me.

"We have to go," I said. "Can't you feel this place? It's coming for us. Something here is coming for us."

That part I was not making up. They could sense it too. I stood up, walked over to the ledge, and started inching my way up, pressed along the wall. Enough. I would leave, even if that meant leaving alone.

"C'mon, Adam," I said. "You next. Stay close."

When he started up the ledge behind me, he

324

was so shaky I couldn't imagine him ever making it all the way to the top. But with one sliding step in front of the other, up we went.

I looked at Miho now fifteen feet below me. "C'mon, Miho," I said, trying to speak in a steady voice. "We have to go."

She sighed, stared back over the bog. The clouds were so low now that my head was nearly in them. I thought that was probably helpful—none of us would have to worry about a fear of heights if we could barely see down past our feet.

Miho walked over to the ledge and started up behind Adam. Our backs were to the cliff wall. She took a few sliding steps up, stopped, and held her face in her hands. She cried again, softly, and I thought I knew why: she knew I was lying. She knew we were leaving Lucia behind. But she didn't have the strength to go back and find her.

26 Up

We inched our way up the ledge, small pebbles falling in front of us and disappearing into the fog. Soon we were so high up we couldn't hear them hit the ground. Every so often I stopped and waited for Adam and Miho to catch up—Miho always looked calm, sometimes closing her eyes, taking centering breaths. But Adam grew less steady the higher we went. His legs trembled from exhaustion and fear.

I thought about the view we would have if it wasn't for this impenetrable cloud we were climbing through. The short, dusty space between the cliff and the bog. The long brown water that Lucia and I had crossed together, and the thread of a canyon that led to the final, frozen river and the island of rock where Adam had knelt. Could we see it all from here if the clouds cleared?

I doubted it. There was something about this place that seemed to operate outside of reality, as if the journey into the abyss was actually taking place inside of me, in a place you couldn't see from far away. I thought that if the clouds cleared, we would probably see a long emptiness, a dreary landscape, and maybe a small brown puddle.

But the clouds never cleared. Adam constantly wiped his hands on his torn pants. He licked his dry lips quickly, like a reptile. I could count the ribs in his side. He looked up the ledge at me, his eyes wild, before looking at Miho. Sometimes the mist was so thick I couldn't even see her.

There was a particularly narrow section of the ledge, and after I shuffled my way through it, I waited to make sure Adam would be okay. He came sliding along, his feet scraping the stone, and small bits of dust and tiny pebbles bounded off the edge. At the space where the ledge was less than the length of his feet, he balked. Trembled. Swayed out but somehow caught his balance by bracing himself against the cliff face.

He froze.

"Adam!" I moved back down toward him, but the change in direction threw me off for a moment, and I nearly fell. "Miho!"

She came up, a calm look on her face. "You're fine, Adam." Her voice sounded like a gentle breeze moving through the mist.

"I can't," Adam said, the words coming in short bursts, his lips pursed. "I can't."

She reached up and took his hand. He looked so shocked by her touch that it nearly sent him over. "We can do this together."

If she wanted to kill him, I thought, this was when it would happen.

But she didn't. She spoke quiet words to him,

327

so smooth and low I couldn't hear them, the way a trainer speaks to a spooked racehorse. He nodded, seemed to find himself, and shuffled one side step, another side step.

"Take his other hand," she told me.

I hesitated, because if he fell, I didn't want him dragging me over the edge with him. But I thought of all those years, all that time I spent waiting for him in that stone house. This was my brother, my long-lost brother, and if I returned without him, what was the point?

I took his hand, and his fingers felt the same as mine. I had the strangest feeling, almost like vertigo, that he was me, that it wasn't him we were leading out of the abyss, but me. I took my eyes off the ledge and looked over at him as we moved along, and I wondered why I wasn't happier in that moment. I had waited so long for him. And now we were leaving, escaping the abyss, both of us alive. But I couldn't shake this deep sadness, so heavy it nearly pulled me off the ledge. It turned every breath into a sigh, every thought into a spiral.

Miho held his other hand. Our eyes met, and it felt like the first time we had really seen each other in that place. She was sad, I could see that, and disappointed. I couldn't help but feel that it was there on the narrow ledge that all of my lies finally ended whatever it was we had been so close to having.

That was how we made our way along the narrow ledge, sliding up until we reached the place where the path widened. We fell to the ground with exhaustion and relief, sitting side by side once again, our backs to the cliff. I reached into the knapsack and took out the water container. It was nearly empty. I handed it first to Miho, and she took a small sip, the tiniest of draws. She licked her lips, trying to spread the moisture around, and handed it to Adam. He took a large gulp, and I could see his throat lurching. I closed my eyes and imagined the coolness of the water, the smoothness of it running over my tongue, silk on the sides of my throat.

Adam handed it to me, but I knew before raising it to my mouth that it was gone. I sighed and pretended to drink, because I didn't want Miho feeling sorry for me. But nothing came out, not even a trickle. I held it up for an extra moment, then put it slowly back into the knapsack. I glanced over at Adam. The smallest drop rolled down from the corner of his mouth, but I could not tell if it was water, sweat, or the buildup of moisture in the air. It was now on his skin, drifting down. It was like a globe, like a small world to me. He reached up and wiped it away.

Without saying a word, we stood and trudged upward, the abyss now to our right, the clouds thinning as we climbed, until all at once we were in clear air again. Clearer air than I had seen at any point inside the mountain. I could nearly see to the far side of the round abyss. Once again, the clouds filled the abyss like drifts of snow.

A realization snapped into my mind like lightning. "Miho," I asked, "are they waiting for us?"

"Who?" she said, her voice cracking. I didn't think it was from lack of water.

"The rest of the group. Abe. Kathy."

"Why would they wait?"

"You said the rest of them went east, but do you believe that? Or are they waiting for Adam?"

"Why would they wait for Adam?"

I stopped walking and turned on her. "Can't you answer a simple question?" I demanded. "Why do you keep asking me questions in return? Are they waiting for Adam? For revenge?"

She shook her head, but her words were less assuring. "Maybe, Dan. I don't know. They said they were leaving."

"But they wouldn't have gone far unless they forgave him. They wouldn't have left the town behind unless they were free of that."

Adam glanced back and forth between us. We were talking about him as if he wasn't there. "It's okay," he said in something like a whisper. "It's okay. I'm getting out—that's all that matters. I remember now. Remember it all. What can they do to me that's worse than this place?"

Miho and I stared at each other for quite

some time, as if we were feeling each other out again, trying to decipher where each of us stood, whose side we were on, and who we should be concerned about. But Adam seemed genuinely unaffected by the conversation.

Up we went, up and up and up, and finally there was the top, way ahead of us on the curving path, up above us like the lid of an eye. The roaring of the river became audible in the still air, a kind of fearful rumbling. I had tried not to think about how we would cross.

Once we scaled the path and stood at the top of the great abyss, we all looked down over the ledge, the clouds far below us, nearly invisible in the shadows. Lucia came to mind, little Lucia with her soft face and quiet eyes. I had to turn away.

We followed Miho toward the Acheron. She walked straight to the river, made a sharp right at the bank, and kept moving. Up ahead, I saw Karon's boat.

"How?" I began, not knowing what else to say.

"I found this boat on the far side when I came in after you," she said, shrugging.

"Did you see Karon?" I asked.

"Who?"

"The man who belongs to the boat. Or the woman who was with him?"

"I didn't see anyone," she said. "Help me turn it around."

The three of us grabbed the smooth wooden sides, and in our weakness it took a great effort to drag it, turn it, hold it. There was Karon's one small oar, the bench where I had sat at the front, the bottom of the boat where I had passed out. Across the river, above the foaming white rapids, I could see the far bank, the trees.

"Didn't you go to the house?" I asked Miho.

She shook her head. "There was no way I was going in there. Are you kidding?"

"Sarah lived there," I said quietly.

"What?"

"Nothing," I said. "Nothing."

As usual, Adam watched us, his eyes taking us in, his long black hair swaying like a pendulum.

I felt a sort of numbness as we climbed into the boat. I imagined it was the same feeling someone might have before they take their own life, knowing the end of all things is only moments away. I couldn't see us surviving this river.

We all shifted our weight together as best we could, and the boat lurched once, twice, three times, four times. Finally we were in deep enough to drift, and already the current yanked us downstream. Adam and I sat in the front and Miho perched in the back, small yet strong with the oar, thrusting it in and pulling, pulling, pulling against the current.

The white water was rough and choppy. I noticed then—and it seemed a strange time to see such small things—that the wood of the boat was smooth, and the metal sheath that held the bow together was burnished from so many crossings, bearing dents and scrapes from collisions with rock. The bottom of the boat was slick with a kind of black-green algae, like moss, and slippery as ice.

On the far side, in the direction Miho fought to take us, I thought I saw Kathy waiting.

I stood to get a better look. I slipped, striking my head again, and darkness took me under.

27 Forgiveness

My eyes opened, and everything was silent. I was in an uncomfortable bed in a drab room, staring up at a yellowing ceiling. The only light came in from a window along the wall behind me and a bit to the left, and through it fell tan, dusty rays. My vision went blurry and I blinked to correct it, and with that blink a searing pain radiated from the side of my head, down and out my arm. A few realizations settled on me like birds returning to a wire after being frightened off.

I was in Sarah and Karon's house.

I was in Sarah and Karon's house alone.

Miho and Adam had left me.

I deserved it.

I was hot, so hot, and I pushed the blankets down off my fevered body, but as soon as I did, I realized how cold it was in the room. How had I not noticed this before, not seen my breath rising like the clouds in the abyss? My body trembled, and I pulled the covers back up. The cold had followed us all the way from the icy lake, the stone island, and had caught up to me here.

I felt an absurd relief at my pain, my loneliness, my confusion, because finally this place inside the mountain had become what I always remembered it to be: a place of horror, of ongoing dread and sickness and lack. I was somehow relieved to know I hadn't made up that part in my mind. This was a horrible place, and I was back in it, and I would never be able to leave.

Lucia walked into the room, her skin a whitish blue. "It's your fault," she said. "It always has been. Your brother. The accident. Me falling in. It's your fault."

I knew it wasn't her. I knew it was a vision handed to me by the mountain, but I still wept and trembled. I pulled the covers up over my face before plunging into a feverish sleep.

I woke again, and this time it was dark except for a weak, trembling light that came in through the doorway. A candle? A fire? I no longer cared. The pain in my head was a constant companion, a worm working its way deeper into my mind. I scratched at my scalp to try to find it, dig it out. I scratched until I bled.

I heard the sound of footsteps on the creaking floor, and I went from a state of fevered numbness to sharp fear. Who was coming for me? Was it Lucia again, to torment me? A shadow stretched across the dim light, a firm shadow of utter blackness, and fear eclipsed the pain.

Kathy.

I knew it. She would pick me up and carry me

to the boat, throw me into the abyss, drag me through the gate, and lock it with the key I had in the knapsack.

The key! What had happened to the key! I groaned in despair. She came across the room, lifted her hand, and again everything went black.

I stood from the bed and walked outside, walked through the cold, and there among the trees was the large building my brother and I had used for our airplane hangar. *Where is the runway?* I kept thinking. *Where did all of these trees come from?*

I walked through the oversized garage door into the barn where we parked the plane, and there was a bright light in the back corner over the door that led to the room where my brother used to sleep. I stopped outside the room, my hand on the knob, frightened of what I might find.

The door eased open silently, and I looked inside. He was there, passed out. His eyes opened. He tried to talk, but his tongue slurred all the words. He stopped, shook his head, and tried again.

"I cannnn't do it todaaaaaay. Not nowwwww. Leave meeeeee alonnnnne."

But I picked him up, surprising myself. Wasn't I sick? Wasn't I weak? I carried him to the plane and stuffed him in, not finding the sudden appearance of the plane remarkable in the least. His arms and legs were limp and refused to comply.

"You have to!" I screamed. "You don't have a choice!"

Then the plane was taking off, and I realized what I had done. I chased it through the trees, but he was gone, flying away, disappearing into the sky.

I opened my eyes, wincing at the light that came through the window. It wasn't exactly bright, but my eyes weren't used to it. I blinked again and again.

I heard someone pushing a chair in under the table in the dining room, and the sound had a particular quality of realness to it, the untidy feel of concrete reality. This was not a dream. I was still in Sarah and Karon's house, but I was not alone.

I sat up slowly, trying to remain silent, but the bed creaked slightly. I froze. I didn't think the sound was loud enough to alert whoever was in the kitchen, but I waited to see. As I came up from under the blanket, I realized just how cold the air was. I looked over at the window to see if I could open it, if it was low enough for me to crawl through. I would make my getaway, escape before my captor knew what had happened.

I became convinced that Miho and Adam had left me behind, which was no surprise after my never-ending lies and refusal to own up to what I had done. Kathy had come back. I was sure of it. In a strange reversal of roles, she was in the kitchen and I was in the bed; she would tend to me while I recovered, as I had tended to her. But I didn't want to see her again.

The cold air would have been refreshing if it wasn't so dusty, and when I pushed the blanket down off my legs, it was the cold that woke me completely. The pain in my head still throbbed. My fingers explored sensitive, deep cuts from where I had scratched too hard in my dreams, trying to get to the pain in the middle of my head. The gashes down my cheek from when we had fought with Miho were dried out, but they burned when I touched them.

I moved my legs around and gingerly put my feet on the floor beside the bed. I waited again. The person in the kitchen took a few more steps, the floor giving them away, but the sound moved to the front door. I heard it open. I heard them go out onto the front porch. I tried to stand, but my legs turned to jelly and gave out under me. A rush of blood to the head and I fell to my knees. I felt disoriented and dizzy. I hoped I hadn't made too much noise, but I heard footsteps coming quickly through the house.

Tears filled my eyes, but I didn't know why—desperation? regret? sadness?—and I tried to claw my way up, pulling on the windowsill. But my arms were hopelessly weak, and I fell to the dusty floor again. Sobs wracked my body. The footsteps stopped inside the bedroom door. I didn't even want to look. But I did.

Miho stood there with Adam. They stared at me, and I didn't know what to think or what they were thinking or why they had stayed behind.

"Why are you here?" I asked quietly.

"You're hurt," Adam said.

"We couldn't leave you behind, but we're too weak to carry you," Miho explained. "We tried."

"You wouldn't be here if you knew me, if you knew what I did," I said, not daring to look at them any longer.

"We know," Miho whispered.

"No, you don't," I said.

"We do," Adam said. "You practically told us your life history while you were sleeping. Your dreams, your nightmares, you talked about it all."

Shame dropped me farther to the floor, if that was even possible. They knew it had all been my fault from the beginning.

"Lucia?" I asked, staring hard at the floor.

"We know," Miho whispered again.

"So why didn't you leave?" I asked, my voice barely strong enough to muster the words. "You should have left me."

"We love you," Miho said.

"We forgive you," Adam said.

A harsh wind kicked up and blew the front door open, and a bitter cold raced in around us.

We forgive you. Those words soaked into me

like sunshine. *We forgive you.* Had those words ever been uttered in this place, in this mountain? I didn't know how to respond. I didn't want to believe it could be true, but I was too weak to run away from it. I wondered if that was the only gift this place could offer—a weakness so intense that you simply could not do anything on your own. You could not flee when penance was paid on your behalf.

"Did you see Sarah or Karon?"

"Who?" Adam asked.

"They lived here before. This is their house."

Miho shook her head. "We haven't seen anyone."

We waited in that house for a long time, trying to recover enough strength to go on. Days. Maybe weeks, I don't know. We used Sarah and Karon's meager stores of food and water. Inside the mountain, it was often hard to tell if night had come or if clouds had simply shadowed the canyon, choking out the light. At other times, night seemed to stretch on endlessly, and the three of us would sit at the kitchen table, quiet, staring intently at the dark windows, feeling a nameless fear.

Sometimes, when the light came around, we sat on the front porch. I always stared in the direction of the Acheron, silently pleading for Lucia to come across. I hadn't gone down to the riverbank, so I assumed the boat was still on the near side, which meant she had little chance of coming across. Still, I wished I would see her small form coming through the trees.

While we sat on the porch one afternoon and the light faded and the ominous shadows of the trees gave way to a broader darkness, Miho looked over at me. She was sitting on the other chair. Adam stood at the corner of the house, leaning against the wood siding. I thought I could sense something between them, something new and growing, a green sprout pushing up from under a small stone. It made me feel unsettled, and happy, and jealous, and sad.

"I think we're ready to leave," she said, and she did pretty well at keeping any semblance of a question from her voice. But it was still there. I knew it. They wondered if I felt ready.

I nodded slowly, cleared my throat, decided not to say anything.

"So, in the morning?" Adam asked, and there was a childlike eagerness under the surface of his voice. I could understand that. He had been here in the mountain for a long, long time. I couldn't wait for him to see the land opening up in front of us, the plains stretching out as far as he could see, the green space alive and warm and calm.

"It's colder," I said, hugging my arms to my chest.

"That's another reason we should go," Miho said.

"And Lucia?" I asked, barely able to say her name.

"We'll talk to Abe," Miho said in a determined voice, as if she had already argued this point many times with Adam. "Abe will know what to do."

I sighed, a kind of quiet acquiescence. I was ready. Truth is, I had been ready for some time, but I found it hard to leave Lucia behind. I thought for a second of going back, of boarding the boat and crossing the Acheron again, making my way down the path, down the narrow ledge through the clouds, to the bog, across, through the canyon, through the gate, to the frozen lake. But I didn't even know if she'd be there, if she had somehow managed to survive. The thought of the journey, or perhaps the memory of her—I couldn't tell which—brought tears to my eyes. And I couldn't have done it anyway. I was too weak.

I stood and limped back into the house, into the bedroom, and crawled under the covers. They had seemed much too thin recently, the cold reaching under them. The cold was growing. It felt like it was spilling up and out of the abyss.

When I woke up and walked into the kitchen, the small bucket of water we had kept in the corner was frozen. Miho and Adam stood on the front porch, clapping their hands together and blowing into them for warmth. We were clothed in leftover garments we had found in the house, Karon and Sarah's final gifts to us. We looked at each other and no one said a word, but Miho led the way off the porch, into the trees, and toward the narrow canyon that led to the village and the plains.

As we walked, it started to snow.

28 The Crossing

I wish I could tell you about the look on Adam's face when we walked through that canyon and came out into the great wide open, how awestruck and happy he was, how he fell to the ground weeping and smelling the grass, feeling the sunshine. I wish I could tell you how he hugged Miho and me, how he started healing immediately, and how we sat out back just like the old days and looked out over the plains.

I wish.

Truth is, when we got to the opening that led into the plains, right beside the wooden signpost, I wasn't even looking at Adam. I was looking out into that wide-open space, and I felt nothing apart from shock, confusion, and sadness.

Because there was nothing to see except snow.

But it was beautiful. Yes. The landscape was pristine, the snowflakes fell heavy and thick, and before we knew it, our hair and shoulders had a fine layer of white gracing them. Glaring white for as far as we could see, completely covering the tall green grass.

"Is this it?" Adam asked.

Miho and I didn't say a word. The village itself didn't look any more welcoming. Most of it was blackened, charred from the fire, and the snow only served as a greater contrast against that burned wreckage.

"What happened?" Miho whispered as I walked out in front of them. Somehow the snow had been light in the canyon, but once I stepped out into the greenway, it was ankle deep at its most shallow points. Some of the drifts reached my knees. I pushed through it, the cold wetness soaking into my pants, leaking down inside the shoes I had taken from Karon's room. It had drifted up against my door, and when I opened it, some fell inside the house and began melting on the wooden floor.

That reminded me of when Kathy had first arrived, how she had let in the rain, collapsed inside the door, and lay there in the puddle.

Miho and Adam came in behind me, and after I pushed the door closed, everything went silent. The three of us stood there without moving, looking around. The white snow glared its light in through the back doors, but the rest of the house was dim and gray. I held my breath, waiting for Kathy to emerge from the bedroom, but after waiting a few moments and realizing everything was deathly still, it was clear no one had been in the house for a long time.

"Is this it?" Adam asked again. "Is this the village where you live?"

"It's not usually like this," I said.

"It's never snowed before," Miho said, as if explaining away some small defect.

"It's never been this cold before," I added.

We searched the house for anything we could burn, and soon a blaze glowed in the fireplace, crackling legs of wooden chairs and smoldering pieces of the oak bed frame and hissing smoke from the spines and pages of books. That hurt me the most, nearly caused a physical pain—when Miho pulled the books from the shelves and tossed them into the fire, splayed open, pages moving. But we were cold and tired, and long after the other two had fallen asleep on blankets on the floor in front of the fire, I watched the paper blacken and curl. I stabbed at the books, pried them open with the metal poker, so that the pages would burn completely. Even then, I could see that some of the words would survive.

Long after dark, I heard a knock on the door. At first I wondered if Adam or Miho had gone outside. But they were sleeping, and neither moved at the knock. Was it Abe? Or one of the others, come back to have their revenge on Adam? I walked to the door and stood there for a full ten seconds before reaching down and taking the knob, turning it, opening the door.

Kathy.

We stared at each other as she stood in the snowdrift, light from the dying fire flickering on her face, her back to the mountain and the nighttime shadows. I felt gaunt and stretched, filthy, worn down. I felt like she must have felt when I had first seen her.

"Hi," I said in a tired voice. My knees were suddenly weak.

"Dan," she said, compassion in her voice. She looked like she might cry. "You're back."

She filled me with competing desires. I wanted to slam the door in her face. I wanted to embrace her. I wanted to care for her. I wanted her to care for me.

"What happened?" I asked. I couldn't help it—accusation slipped into my voice.

Her dark eyes hardened like water freezing in fast motion. "Whatever do you mean?" she asked, her voice barely louder than the wind that swept the snow into the house. I could hear it, the icy rasping of the snow scraping along the floor. The cold breeze rustled the fire, fanning it.

"All of this happened after you arrived," I said, but the accusation had taken a backseat to genuine confusion. "The fire. Me going into the mountain. The chaos." I paused. "The snow. Everything fell apart."

She gave a mocking grin. "You think I caused the snow?" Her voice was the one used to speak to older children about nighttime monsters and fantastical creatures.

I stared at her. Yes, actually, I did. I did think she had brought the snow. "You started the fire. I know that."

Her mouth hardened. She blinked once. Twice. Her piercing eyes took me in, devoured me. "I know what you did," she said. "I know who you left behind."

My face flushed with shame.

"You should rest here, recover your strength, and go back in. Find her." Her voice was very convincing.

"I can't," I said.

"You left a small girl in the abyss. Think about it. What chance does she have?" She turned and walked through the snow as if it was warm water, as if her body was nothing more than a mechanical shell made to transport her mind through any condition. I walked out into the snow and watched as she vanished into the darkness, down the hill, in among the burned buildings.

A voice called to me from the house. I turned in a daze.

"Dan!" the voice shouted again. "What are you doing?"

I walked slowly back through the snow, feeling as helpless as I ever had. At the end of me. We could not stay here, that was clear. I did not have the strength to go back and retrieve Lucia. But without her, I didn't think I could go east.

I came to the door of my house and walked past Miho, her confused, beautiful face. She leaned aside to make room for me to go through. "Dan, what were you doing out there?"

I sat down in front of the dying fire. I threw in another book. And another. And another. "I thought I heard someone," I said.

In the morning, we stood by the back doors and took in the plains. Because the sky was a glaring white, it was almost impossible to distinguish the horizon. The entire world was a white space, empty and never-ending. The first tree outside of town, off in the distance, was black against the white backdrop.

"We have to go east," Miho said, and neither of us replied. We stared out at the snow.

In the stillness, I heard the sounds of someone approaching the front door through the snow, pounding their hands together, kicking through the drifts. I didn't think I had the mental fortitude to argue with Kathy one more time. If she insisted I go back, I would. I would take a flask of water and whatever food I could find in the burned houses, and I would return. I knew I would die there, either drowning in the river or falling from the ledge or starving. But if it was her, I knew I would go back.

Adam and Miho looked at me as the sound of knocking echoed in the quiet house. I wondered why one of them didn't go answer the door, but I was also afraid of what Kathy might do to them, what she might say to them, so I took on the mantle of their expectations and crossed the room. It was my house, after all.

I opened the door.

It was Abe. His arms opened wide, and I fell into them, weeping.

Abe sat in the armchair. Miho sat on the floor beside him, closer to the fireplace. Every so often, she leaned over and plucked a book from the shelf and threw it in. It hurt a little, how easily she did this.

Adam sat across from them, his back to the fire, facing the back doors, staring out over the plains as if it was the most beautiful thing he had ever seen. Even when he spoke, he barely shifted his body.

And I sat wrapped in a blanket, my back against the wall across from the fireplace. My gaze went from Abe to Miho to Adam to the fire and back again to Abe. He was the only one who made eye contact with me. When Miho's gaze met mine, it flitted away like a doe into the undergrowth. Adam refused to look at me. They had forgiven me in the canyon, but here, where our trip east became real, where we would turn our backs on the mountain and Lucia for the final time, the reality of what I had done was hard to forget.

When Abe first arrived, we'd greeted him and said a few pleasantries. We'd settled into our current spots. And then we'd said nothing. Where were we supposed to begin?

"How did we end up here, Abe?" I asked quietly.

"Here?" he asked.

"This place. The mountain. This village. What is this? How is it connected to the memories of these lives we lived so long ago?"

His face was almost expressionless. "I think you already know."

"Maybe, but I want to hear it from you."

He seemed to be considering his options, and he started nodding before he even spoke. "Yes, you know. I think you all do, if you're honest with yourselves."

Miho held her hand up over her face, tears rising to her eyes.

"The memories you have," Abe said in a kind, hesitant voice, "are from a life you lived before you died."

"So this . . ." Adam began, his voice trailing off.

"This is all in a time and place after life," Abe said.

"We're dead?" Miho's words came out with a kind of dread. But Abe's smile warmed us.

"Do you feel dead?" he asked.

Miho shook her head.

"That's because you died, but you're not dead. You're here. You came through the mountain. You lived in this town for a long, long time. And now you have to decide what to do next."

I knew that Abe was talking to all of us. I had died. This was not a surprise to me. In some ways, him saying that out loud felt like the final piece in a puzzle that I had been able to see for quite some time. But even though Abe wasn't delivering a revelation, we still sat there in silence for a long time, trying to connect everything.

Finally, Miho broke the silence. "What now, Abe?" She sounded like a lost child.

"There's not much food," Abe cautioned. "The others took most of what they could find with them for the journey. I hope they made it out in front of this snow." His voice faded, and I imagined our friends forging through knee-high drifts, collapsing in the cold. How could Miss B ever make it through this?

"So, we can't stay," Miho said in a matter-of-fact voice.

"Why would anyone stay here?" Adam asked.

"You should have seen it." My voice erupted almost without my permission. "You should have seen this place when times were good." I stared into the fire. "I could hear the laughter from up here. Everyone down in the village on a cool night, the fire roaring. Sometimes there was singing." I looked over at Adam. "Sometimes there was singing," I said, as if that alone would be enough. My voice sank down into a whisper. "You might as well know it all now. There's no reason to keep it from you. You already know I left Lucia behind, not that I could have done anything, but I lied to you about it and I accept responsibility. But there are other things too."

I felt Miho stare at me in that moment, and it felt like everyone was holding their breath.

"I knew Kathy was here. I welcomed her into my house when she came from the other side." I waited for admonishment, yet there was nothing but kindness in Abe's eyes. "I don't know why I didn't tell you all about her. I thought I was doing something good. At least in the beginning."

This time Miho didn't look away.

"She kissed me." I shook my head. There were so many things I wanted to say, and all the words were getting clogged up in a drain too narrow to accommodate the flow. "But that's not even the worst of it." I laughed, as if the extent of my false life was ludicrous. And it was. It suddenly seemed almost comical to me. "The worst is that the plane crash wasn't even Adam's fault."

Now they all looked surprised. Even Abe.

"It's true!" My voice started sounding maniacal, even to me. "It's true. Adam wasn't fit to fly that plane. He was drunk. Do you remember that, Adam? You were a raging alcoholic."

He nodded. "Yeah," he said, but he didn't seem ashamed. That made me even more jealous, and I felt like I was losing myself, like my sanity was tethered to me by a thin string and the tension was building, and if the string snapped, all would be lost. "I do remember that," he said.

"Well, I found you that morning, and I forced

you to fly. I laid it on thick—we'd go under, we'd be broke, you had to do it. And so you did. If I hadn't walked you to that plane, you never would have flown, and no one would have died."

I looked between the three of them, my heart racing, my eyes bulging. I stared at everyone again. "So. That's it. Everything—Lucia, Kathy, the crash. It's all my fault."

We sat there in the silence that rushed in after my outburst. The fire died down, and I willed Miho not to throw any more books in it, and for some reason she didn't. She was staring into the glowing embers, somewhere far away. Adam had stood and walked over to the doors, standing so close to them I thought he was going to pull them open and go blundering into the snow. Only Abe returned my gaze. He said something under his breath, to me or to himself, I couldn't tell. But the shape of his words seemed to say, "Well done."

He sighed. "All of this is in the past. I'm glad you've said what you've said, Dan. There is nowhere to go now but forward. In this moment." He waited to see if Miho or Adam would say anything. When they didn't, he continued. "It seems to me," he said in a humble voice, as if he was completely open to disagreement, "that the most important question is the one Miho asked a moment ago. Namely, what now?"

Miho shook her head, still staring into the fire.

"I'm just along for the ride," Adam said.

"Our options have not changed much." Abe smiled. "They are, in many ways, what they have always been. We can stay. We can go back into the mountain, this time to find Lucia. Or we can go east."

"We?" Adam asked.

Abe shrugged. "I think, at this point, the best thing we can do is stick together."

I weighed the options. I could try to go back and get Lucia, but that seemed impossible. I had used up everything I had to get Adam. I had nothing left. Going east felt equally as difficult, and I didn't know the path or what was at the end of it. Staying seemed the easiest thing to do yet the least feasible.

"How far can we get without food?" Miho asked, and I assumed she meant east.

"I didn't say we are entirely without food," Abe said.

"I'm not going back in the mountain," Adam said, and there was a lining of panic in his voice. "I wish I could. I wish I could go back for the girl. But I don't have it in me." His words came out in short thrusts.

Miho shook her head sympathetically.

"Honestly?" I said. "I don't think I could do it either."

"So we just leave her over there?" Miho asked.

"She fell into the river," I replied. "Under the ice."

"So we just leave her over there?" Miho repeated, her voice swelling.

Our words at a deadlock, we looked to Abe.

"This is what I think," he said gently, shifting his tone. "This is what I would like to see. I would like the four of us to rest here today, tonight, maybe one more day, until you're ready. Then I'd like to pack up the food we have and any supplies that might be helpful, and head east."

Miho started speaking again but, uncharacteristically, Abe held up his hand to stop her. "I will bear responsibility for Lucia. I will make sure that anything that can be done will be done."

"What's that supposed to mean?" Miho said, and it was the harshest tone I'd ever heard her use with Abe.

He looked her full in the face, and there was nothing but love in his eyes. He said it again, this time somehow both quieter and firmer. "I will bear responsibility for Lucia."

I started to speak, to say that wasn't fair, that Lucia's fate was my responsibility. I wanted to argue with him, to tell him they should all go on while I went back for her. But I didn't have the strength. I had to let him assume that burden, and I had to admit, it was a relief. When he said those words, it was the closest I'd felt to free in a long, long time.

Miho stood up and paced back and forth. She

356

stopped beside Adam and put her hand on his shoulder. "Abe's right," she admitted.

Was she talking to Adam? To me? To all of us? I couldn't tell. But in that moment, it was decided. The air in the house held still. Outside, the wind stopped and the snow on the plains glittered. I felt an aching sense of relief now that the burden of those lies had been scattered.

We would go east.

I don't know who decided that we should keep track of how many trees we passed, but at some point between the fourth and fifth tree, it was decided that I should use the charred end of a piece of kindling and mark one tally inside the front cover of the only book I had brought with me. I had pulled it from the shelves before we left and looked at Miho. "Not for firewood," I had said, not even knowing what was behind my need to say it. Was it to make her feel guilty for all the volumes she had burned? Was it an attempt at humor? Whatever the case, she had given me a sad smile as I nestled the book in the knapsack that Sarah and Karon had given me.

Would I find them again sometime in the east? Or had they vanished into some in-between place in the canyon or here on the plains?

I took the book out, clumsily held the crooked stick with the black end, and marked five long straight lines on the page inside the hardback book. I blew the black dust away and stared at those five lines for an extra moment before putting everything back in the knapsack and following Abe, Adam, and Miho. Their forms were almost indiscernible, wrapped as they were in the bulky garments of other people's clothes, so many layers that their appendages were unnaturally short and plump compared to the hulk of their wrapped bodies. We were like astronauts.

They forged ahead in the snow, and already it had become shallower the farther we walked from the remains of our village. I did not hurry to catch up, content to place my feet where theirs had gone and watch from a distance.

At every tree, we changed out the leader, and it was slow going. At the sixth tree, I made the mark in the book and then took the lead for the second time. On the first day, we only made it to tree number nine, but we hadn't left until well after dawn, and we stopped while the light was still bright in the gray-white sky.

We hollowed out a place in the snow, piling it up around us as a shelter from the wind that occasionally rose. There were plenty of fallen limbs under each tree we had passed now that we were so far from town, though they were covered in snow and challenging to light. But with enough care and attention, we were able to start an anemic, smoking fire. We huddled close.

Miho seemed to be further inside of herself than usual. Adam, on the other hand, was coming alive, gaining health, and eager to help in any way that required movement or action. Abe seemed always to have a small smile on his face, as if he had finally received a long-sought-after gift.

I felt like a clumsy butterfly only recently emerged from my chrysalis. Wings still bent and folded over. Walking with uncertainty and a kind of vague knowledge that there was another way. Confession had broken me free, but navigating the pain I had caused was no easy thing. And I sensed that whatever had existed between Miho and me could not be recovered.

Although we were all close together, she seemed to always lean toward Adam. I felt a peace with this. It seemed a deserved, almost welcome penance for the lies I had hidden behind. I wanted to pay for what I had done. This seemed fair enough.

"Any guesses on how many trees until the next mountain?" Adam asked as we huddled together in the dark.

"One hundred and seventy-nine," Miho said, and we all grinned. Adam groaned.

"Did Lucia ever say how many?" I asked. As soon as I said her name, I could feel a heaviness descend on the group, and I wished I could retrieve those words and put them away.

"No," Abe replied.

After a long period of silence, Adam ventured again. "Any other guesses? Closest one wins the prize."

"I'll take two hundred," Abe said. The fire grew in the midst of us, bringing with it a sense of home and comfort even though we were surrounded by snow and the dying evening light.

"Two hundred and one," I said, and Miho burst out a kind of one-syllable laugh, punching me in the shoulder.

We sat there for so long, leaning against one another, that I thought everyone but me had fallen asleep. But then I heard Miho whisper, "What's the prize?"

No one answered. The cloudy shape of her words rose along with smoke from the dying fire. I reached into my knapsack, took out the book with the marks in it, and threw it onto the embers.

We started passing other villages at about the thirtieth tree, which I found interesting. It meant people had left our village beside the mountain and, after walking for some time, decided to stop and create a new life in the plains. But every village was empty, and we found few supplies to gather up and take along with us.

A few weeks later, our habit hadn't changed. Wake with the light. Eat a small amount of our food, the supply dwindling. Walk east, changing leaders as we passed each tree, although since the shallow snow no longer required forging a path through drifts, the shift changes were mostly unnecessary and done out of habit. I no longer counted the trees.

Abe was in the lead, moving ahead at his slow but steady pace, when he stopped. We nearly bumped into each other, so unaccustomed were we to stopping between trees.

"What?" Miho asked.

The snow was not deep, only a few inches, and the air was warmer. I had shed a few layers that morning before leaving the last tree, laying my clothes at the base of it like an offering.

"Look," Abe said, and we peered around him, shading our eyes from the glare coming off the grass.

There was a large crowd of people walking toward us, coming from the next tree—coming from the east.

29 The Other Mountain

"Howdy, friends," Abe said as the group stopped a few yards away from us.

The leader was a man with a short beard, small eyes, and a mouth that wore a frown as its neutral position. He grunted some kind of a response.

"Where're you headed?" Abe asked in a nonchalant voice.

"Back," the man said, curiosity and skepticism making his tiny eyes even beadier.

"Huh," Abe said, as if the man's response concerned him but he didn't want to say why. "Mind if I ask where you're coming from?"

"The east."

"I can see that," Abe said, nearly letting out a chuckle.

"The mountain in the east," the man replied. I could tell by the tone of his voice he didn't enjoy being laughed at. But if his first response had amused Abe, his second answer brought the seriousness back.

"The mountain?" Abe asked, now in earnest. "The far mountain?"

The man nodded, looking satisfied that he had

finally said something that apparently wouldn't be mocked.

"So, it's there." Miho let her words out in a quiet wave of relief. Adam leaned closer to her, and she whispered something to him before speaking to the newcomers. "How far?"

"Maybe twenty trees," the man said. "Maybe less."

We were so close. I could feel the weight lift from my shoulders, but almost immediately it returned. Why were these people leaving the far mountain? It was supposed to be a good destination.

Abe was thinking along the same lines. "What's waiting for you in the west that you would go back?"

The man hesitated, seemed unsure of himself, or perhaps didn't know if he wanted to answer. "Nothing special about the east," he mumbled.

"Nothing special?" Abe said, not trying to hide his disbelief. "Did you even go up the mountain?"

The man shrugged. It was clear he had not. A few of the people behind him sat down on the wet ground. I was ready to do the same, wondering how long Abe and this man would keep talking.

Abe took a few steps toward the man and held out his hand. "Abe," he said. "You?"

The man paused. "Jed."

"Jed," Abe echoed. "Jed. Forgive me if I keep coming back to this. I just find it hard to believe someone would walk all the way to the mountain in the east and then turn around."

"She told us the truth," a voice shouted from the back of the pack.

"She?" Abe asked, his eyes narrowing.

"Black-haired woman," Jed said. "She explained what was actually waiting for us up in the mountain. Nothing better or worse than what we've always had. She said the old place was cleaned out and ready for anyone who wanted to return."

"We've come from back there," I blurted out. "Look at me. Does it look to you like a good place to be?"

I could feel their eyes on me, feasting on me, taking in my gaunt frame, my scabbed face. I could feel Miho look at me.

"Snow gets deeper too." Adam shrugged, acting as if he didn't care whether or not they believed him. "You can go if you want. Gets pretty cold over that way. You'll need something to get through the snow. And warmer clothes than what you've got on."

"And our village is burned," Abe said. "Yours might be too."

"What?" Jed asked, looking confused, doubting us.

"She did it," I said. "That woman. She's destroyed everything. And now she's trying to get you to go back."

We all stood there in the silence, taking each other in. Beyond them, I could see the next tree. Beyond that, on the horizon, a narrow purple strip the width of a thread. Was that an illusion? Or the eastern mountain range?

"Is that the mountain?" I asked. "Can you see it from here?"

Jed turned around, moving so that he could see through the crowd behind him. He looked at me again, and I could tell he was weighing my appearance with the promises Kathy must have made about how good it was back there.

"If you can see it from here," he said, "you've got good eyes."

I turned to the others. "You all ready? I'm not going back. Not for anything in the world."

Miho nodded, and for the first time I felt a softening in her toward me. Adam, too, seemed inspired by my action.

"Fair enough," Abe said. "Wait a minute."

I had already taken a few steps forward, so now I was even with Abe, could see his face, and it emanated peace and goodwill.

"Don't believe her," Abe said to Jed. "Come back with us. I'll show you the way into the mountain. Please." He finished by nodding a kind sort of greeting, something he gave each and every person who made eye contact with him as we made our way through their midst.

"Abe?" I heard someone ask. "Did he say his

name is Abe? Is that Abe from the first village?"

Soon the crowd was behind us, and still we walked on, now with a clear view of the tree. Thinking about them going back into the old mountain nearly had me in tears. The dust. The bog. The cold. I wished I could tell them. I wished they would believe me, but I knew the way Kathy's words could whisper to you.

I tried not to look back, but after two or three minutes, I couldn't help it. I glanced over my shoulder.

Every single one of them was following us.

They weren't the last group we met. In between nearly every one of those final trees, we crossed paths with a group that had been persuaded, always by Kathy, to leave and go back. Sometimes the groups were large, hundreds of people. At other times they came in twos and threes.

And every single time, we were able to convince them to turn around.

So it was that we finally arrived at the last tree, in plain view of the eastern mountain, with a crowd behind us that numbered in the thousands. As we got closer to the mountain, I could sense the difference between it and the range we had left behind. There was something calming about it, welcoming. It was bathed in a purplish hue as the light faded, and the trees were of every kind. There were maples and sycamores, oaks and birches. Farther up the mountain, where the rocky outcroppings became more dominant, evergreens swept the stone with their graceful boughs. And everywhere, flowers.

At the base of the mountain, I saw a woman standing beside a fire.

When we got closer I noticed that the mountainside was teeming with people. Soon the glow of a thousand fires lit the mountainside. There were more people there than I could have counted. The fires were like stars in the night sky.

We walked up to the woman. It was Kathy.

Abe turned to those behind us. "Go ahead," he said. "Make your way up. We'll join you soon."

It took a long, long time for all of them to file past. I could hear the sounds of reunifications on the mountainside, people calling out in loving surprise to returning friends or family. Names cried out with tears in their voices. Hugs. The pounding of backs. The rustling as people made more room around a fire.

It was the sound of coming home.

"You all go ahead as well," Abe said solemnly to the three of us.

"What? No," Miho said. "We're with you, Abe."

Abe looked at me when he spoke. "Thank you, Miho, but I have some unfinished business with Kathy. You all make your way up the mountain. I'll sort it out."

We turned to walk away, and I heard his voice again. "Dan."

He held out his hand, the same way he would have reached for me if I was falling. "I'll need that key to make sure everything goes back where it belongs."

I walked over to him and dug deep in the knapsack. I pulled out the key and laid it in his palm.

He nodded.

That was it. We walked up into the trees, into the smell of a thousand fires, and I felt emotion clogging my throat.

30 And We Begin Our Descent

Miho and I remain at the back of the crowd, walking slowly through the trees, always farther up the mountain, farther in.

We hike during the day, sleep on the warm ground at night. We walk for a long time, maybe weeks? Could it be months? It's hard to say. But it's very slow going. It didn't take many days for the others from our village to find us, and now we walk together, a small cluster at the very back of this rustling sea of humanity. The old crew. We keep our distance from the rest, the way my house was always separated a bit from the rest of the town. John and Po, Miss B, Circe, and Misha. Miho and Adam. Me. Even Mary St. Clair. Together again. Everyone except Abe.

He went back for her. A sob catches in my throat.

No one walks at night, and at first it bothered me. I kept looking in the shadows, wondering if Kathy had somehow managed to trap Abe inside the mountain. If she did, I know she'll come for us, and I don't know if we have the fortitude to resist her without him. So I keep my eyes open most nights, as long as I can, waiting for her to emerge. What will I do if I see her? What will I do if she walks into camp and starts filling our heads with nonsense about the old mountain range, how things are better there? I don't know. But if she does come back, I want to know the moment she arrives, so I keep my eyes open.

It is night, and we are all sitting around the fire. John gathers wood and makes a large pile. He will sit there and tend the fire all night. It's what he does. Po sits at the edge of the light, carving something, humming to himself. Our eyes meet through the dancing shadows, and his gaze is softer than I remember. There is nothing there but acceptance. He nearly smiles, then looks back at his carving. Adam sits beside him, watching, occasionally asking questions about all this time between what happened before and now. Miho comes over and sits beside him.

"The air is thin," Miho says.

"And dry," Adam replies.

"We're close to the top," I say. Soon we'll have to decide if we're going to cross over the mountain without Abe and Lucia. On the one hand, this feels like a silly concern. On the other hand, crossing to the other side of the mountain feels like something monumental, something that should only be done with serious consideration.

I look over to where Circe and Misha sit with Mary. The three of them whisper to each other, not because they are trying to keep secrets but because it is a quiet dusk that calls for gentle voices. It is cool, but perfectly so, without a chill. If this night is like the last few, everyone will sleep on the ground without blankets. I try to stay awake as long as I can, on the lookout for Kathy, but most nights I fall asleep staring up through the forest canopy, at the stars that have become visible ever since we started climbing, wondering if I could have brought Lucia back with me. What if I had kept the knapsack? What if I had gone to retrieve it? I remember Adam kneeling on the rock island and, after that, Lucia running back to me. I remember her disappearing. It is something I see in my sleep, her sudden dropping, the entirety of her vanishing.

We scavenged for mushrooms and berries during our walk that day, and there is always plenty for everyone. Wild fruit trees can be found standing in the open places, and we help ourselves to apples and cherries. The path is not treacherous. But it does sometimes feel long and winding.

"Where are we going?" Misha asks the group, and we gather closer to the fire, the darkness growing deeper behind us like a steadily filling pool.

"Only a little farther," I say, although I can't know for sure. "We're nearly at the top."

John smiles. "Now this reminds me of the village." He shrugs as if to preemptively ward off questions about why he's thinking about the village. But I was thinking the same thing. And no matter how far up the mountain we walk, there is still a part of me that longs for the old days. Is it because Abe is gone? I can't tell. I can't sort these things out in my mind. Any thought of Abe leads to my eyes welling up, my throat aching.

"Up front," Mary says, "before I came back looking for you all, I heard people say there's a city on the other side of the mountain."

"Like the village?" Miss B asks.

"Maybe," Mary says. "Maybe better, without that old mountain looking over our shoulder all the time."

Miss B shudders and moves closer to the fire. I look at her. She seems younger now.

"Do you think she'll try again?" Circe asks. "Do you think she'll try to take us back?"

There is a pause. No one wants to answer.

"I'm not going back," Adam says. "No matter what she tells me, I'm not going back." His is the voice of a child, convinced he has learned how to fly.

"What do you miss the most?" Circe asks.

"You're full of questions," Po replies, but good-heartedly, with a grin. A few of us snicker.

"No, really!" Circe smiles. "What do you miss? You first, Po."

Po raises his eyebrows in mock surprise. "Me? I don't miss anything."

Po is a changed man. We are all changed. When we first met up as a group, soon after I stared out from the rocky outcropping, everyone eyed Adam with suspicion. They seemed to evaluate his every move, his every step, his every word. And that first night, when we all stayed together around one fire, an awkward silence fell among the dancing shadows.

That was when someone started talking, and it was the person I least expected.

Po.

He looked over at Adam and said in a firm voice, "I know what happened. I've asked around. We've compared stories. And I want you to know that I, that all of us"—he paused and looked at the group, received nods and sincere looks from everyone—"forgive you and your brother. That's all behind us now. We're ready to keep walking up this mountain." He stood up, walked over to where Adam sat, and shook his hand.

"Oh, c'mon, there has to be something," Circe insists now, staring at Po with laughter in her eyes.

He snorts, sighs, and stops carving. He stares into the fire, then looks around at each of us as he talks. "You know, I miss the plains. I miss the mornings, waking early with the light, and walking out into the high grass."

We all sit quietly in the wake of this unexpected revelation. He returns to his piece of wood, the knife peeling away shavings like butter.

"I miss the big sky," Mary whispers so that I can barely hear her.

"I miss the gardens," Miho says.

"They'll have gardens there," I say.

She looks at me with surprise, and it's the closest she has come to looking at me in that old way, back when we were friends. "How do you know?" she asks, giving me a curious smile.

"I don't know, I just do. Big gardens too, inside tall fences, and you can spend all the time you want in there, harvesting and pruning and planting. There are orchards there, and quiet corners."

"That sounds nice," Miho murmurs.

"And birds," I say, reaching out and patting my brother's knee. "All the birds you could ever want, singing and chirping. You can sit there and watch them all day if you want."

"I miss my oven," Miss B says in a sad voice.

"I miss your oven," Po says, and we all laugh.

A lightness moves in among us, binds us closer together, begins to heal these nameless things that have come between us. Circe, smiling, leans forward and throws a handful of dead leaves on the fire. They smolder and smoke.

There is a rustling in the woods down the hill from us, the sound a deer might have made if it was wandering up to see what the light was all about. But we have not seen any animals on the mountain. We all freeze.

"Anyone else hear that?" Mary asks, her voice a creaking door. A few of us nod. All of us stare into the darkness, and a shape emerges, the shape of a human being, standing at the edge of the firelight.

"Who are you?" Po asks, tensing up. John stands beside him.

The person falls to their knees, but they are now inside the light, and I get my first clear glimpse of who it is.

"Abe?" I stand, wanting to go to him but still holding back for the same reason that everyone else remains motionless. He is almost unrecognizable. His nose is broken and there is dried blood on his face. He holds up his wounded hands so that they do not touch the ground. His head is covered in deep scratches that have healed only partially. His clothes are mangled and torn.

But it is Abe, and we are all a rush of movement to get close to him. We bump into each other. Mary trips, picks herself up.

I'm there first. I stop, and everyone else stops with me. It's as if we cannot touch him, as if an invisible barrier is around him.

"Dear one," he says in a husky voice. He turns as if we're not even here, looks over his shoulder into the shadows, and gives out a weak call. "Come along."

A rustling sound in the leaves makes the hair

stand up on the back of my neck. We all flinch at the sound, wanting to retreat back to the fire. But we are frozen there, congregating around Abe.

He sways and calls out again, "It's all right. Come out where they can see you." He coughs, a low, wheezing retch from the depths of his lungs, and lifts one of his hands. A wave. A beckoning.

I hear the rustling sound again—the sound of a squirrel dancing on dry leaves, or a bird flapping its feathers without leaving the ground. And then she emerges.

Lucia.

Abe passes out, collapsing face-first onto the forest floor.

We stare at Lucia, look at Abe, look back at Lucia again. They both look like they have come through a battle, but she has healed quickly or perhaps did not bear the brunt of it. She is wispy, as I remember her, and ready to run. But she looks around at us, and when she spots Adam at the fringe of our small group, she can't keep her voice from springing out of her.

"Daddy!"

A light rises in Adam's eyes, like the morning sun easing up over a mountain, and he just stands there. That's all he does. The two of them stare at each other in the darkness, the fire burning lower behind us. I can tell he is finally remembering everything. All of it. She takes a hesitant step toward us on her toes, and I can tell she's holding herself back, until Adam lets out a sound like a laughing cry and runs to her.

She vanishes in his embrace, and he is whispering to her over and over again. We watch, unable to look away. I feel like my heart might explode.

"Abe," Mary says. "We have to help Abe."

We take turns sitting with him through the night, and when it's my turn, I get on my knees and stare at his closed eyes. Circe and Misha took water from a nearby stream and washed him, so the Abe I am looking at is scarred and battered but no longer bloody. He appears to be sleeping. But I'm worried we might lose him. His breathing is so shallow. He seems so far away.

I reach over and take his hand. His weathered fingers are cracked and worn, and the wounds on his hands are wrapped in strips of torn clothes some of us donated to the cause. I want to say something. I want to say everything. But all I can say, with long pauses in between, is, "I'm sorry" and "Thank you."

John and Po rise early, when the fire has burned low, and build a makeshift stretcher out of poles long enough for eight of us to hold, four on each side, bearing the weight of our friend Abe. More than a friend.

And that is the day we come to the top of the mountain.

At first the trees clear, the sky growing large

above us, the ground more rock than dirt. Then there is a flattening, and we realize we are crossing an open space. We do not even take a moment to look back. I can hear the people who have gone before us exclaiming and shouting to one another as they make their way down the far side of the eastern mountain, and there is joy in their voices. Astonishment.

We come to the edge where the path begins its descent, and we stand there for a moment, every single one of us. It is a vision to behold.

"You've got to see this, Abe," I say. Someone gives out a loud sob, but I can't see who it is through my own tears.

"C'mon," Adam says, his voice catching. He clears his throat and tries again. "C'mon. Let's take him down."

And we begin our descent.

Author Note

I have always found Dante's *Inferno* intriguing, and as soon as I imagined that it might be possible to escape from it, *These Nameless Things* was born. I thought about Dan and Adam for many years, from around 2011 until 2018, before being able to finally wrap my mind around the story.

If you have read the *Inferno*, doubtless you recognized things in this book: the signpost at the entrance to the mountain; the vision of the leopard, the lion, and the wolf; a few of the various circles, settings, and bodies of water; and some character names.

More importantly, I hope this book serves as a mirror to the *Inferno*, providing hope for those of us going through our own personal hell and leading us to ask questions about guilt, hope, and forgiveness.

Acknowledgments

Does anyone recognize the toll a book requires better than the family members of a working writer? Thank you to Maile, Cade, Lucy, Abra, Sam, Leo, and Poppy for loving me well, reading my words enthusiastically, and allowing the space for stories to thrive in our home and in our lives.

Shawn Smucker is the author of the award-winning novels *The Day the Angels Fell, The Edge of Over There,* and *Light from Distant Stars.* He has also written a memoir, *Once We Were Strangers.* He lives with his wife and six children in Lancaster, Pennsylvania. You can find him online at www.shawnsmucker.com.

Center Point Large Print
600 Brooks Road / PO Box 1
Thorndike, ME 04986-0001 USA

(207) 568-3717

US & Canada:
1 800 929-9108
www.centerpointlargeprint.com

For once, no one would look for her—thanks to a runaway who'd taken her bed at the shelter. Even if the impostor was discovered, foster care wouldn't search too long or hard for her. In fact, if she guessed right, they'd mark Reagan Moore off their rolls by noon as if she were resting in Resurrection Memorial Cemetery in northwest Oklahoma City. The druggie who'd climbed in to sleep in Reagan's bed had found a place to rest, and Reagan had found a way to disappear.

Flinging her backpack over one shoulder, Reagan slipped into the shadows. Harmony had been her goal for almost a year and, finally, she was here. It didn't matter if the place measured up to her dreams—nothing ever had—but at least she'd made it. She'd accomplished what she set out to do. She found the little town in the middle of nowhere. Reagan couldn't help but smile.

Six months ago she decided this place was her hometown, so she had to at least see the small farming community. No one would ever know this was her first time to set foot in town. For her, and for them, she was simply and finally coming home.

Walking in the shadows, she took in the place like an art student taking in the Louvre. Brick streets. Storefronts without bars that pull down at night. A movie theater at the far end of Main with lights blinking. Traffic moving as slow as if passing time and in no hurry to get anywhere. She felt like she'd stepped into an enchanted world.

This street was called Old Main, she remembered from an article she'd read. New Main was at the other end of town, where tire stores, a shopping mall of four one-story stores, and five small restaurants had been built. But here, on Old Main, was the way she always imagined the town to be.

The jukebox music from a diner, almost a half block away, drew her like a pied piper toward the center of town. A painting of a midnight sky and a full moon ran the awning. Above the shade were the words BLUE MOON DINER. Reagan felt as if she'd stumbled blindly into a picture-book story. She'd heard the words but never seen the drawings, and now they were coming alive around her.

The place was ten years past needing a coat of paint, but the light glowed golden from windows in need of washing just as old Miss Beverly at the Shady Rest Home had said it would.

The old lady would always say, when she talked of the diner, "You ain't been to Harmony until you've eaten at the Blue Moon."

Reagan walked inside feeling like a preacher who'd studied heaven all his life and finally set foot in it. The diner even smelled like she thought it would. A mixture of grease, baked apples, and burned toast.

A year ago she'd been cleaning rooms in a nursing home in Oklahoma City for eight bucks a room when she'd found a newspaper, the *Harmony Herald*'s Centennial Edition. Reagan had read every article, what happened in the past, what was happening in the fall of 2005, what folks hoped would happen in the future. Somehow, the town filled a place inside her. A place that had always been empty.

Home.

"What can I get you?" The waitress startled her as Reagan stuffed her backpack under the table. "We ain't got much pie left, but if it's fries and drinks, we're still open."

Reagan looked at the menu written on the wall. "Fries," she said, "and a water."

"Chili or cheese?"

Reagan stared at the chubby middle-aged waitress who looked like she'd already had a long day. Her apron was spotted, her eyes tired, but her smile was real.

"You want chili or cheese on them fries? It doesn't cost extra after ten." The waitress tapped her pencil on her pad in rhythm to an Elvis tune.

"Both," Reagan answered, thinking the doughnut she'd had for breakfast had been far too many hours ago.

The woman winked. "You got it."

Reagan leaned back in the booth and took a deep breath. "Finally," she whispered as if she could wish it true. "I just know this time I'm home."

She'd cleaned that nursing home room for a week before she'd met Miss Beverly Truman and began to stay after work to read the old woman her

9

mail. Beverly must have been pen pals with half the town.

After they'd read all the gossip, they'd talk about Harmony. Miss Beverly might forget where she put her teeth, but she remembered every detail about the town where she'd lived most of her life.

Reagan closed her eyes as if filling in a blank on an invisible test: The night waitress at the Blue Moon Diner was named Edith. Miss Beverly always said she had a good heart and a husband who wasn't worth the iron in his blood.

She pulled her tattered manila folder from her pack and spread it out on the table. Someone had handed it to her years ago when she'd been moved from one foster home to another. It had a big label on the front with her name and nothing else. Like no address had ever belonged to her long enough to stick to paper.

She'd hidden the folder away while in transport and kept it. One envelope held all that was her. Birth certificate listing father as unknown, a copy of her mother's death certificate, a school picture from the fourth grade, and an award she'd won once in an art class. Tugging out a pencil, she scratched out her last name and wrote *Truman* in its place, then, with a bold hand added *Harmony, Texas* under her new name.

"I put the chili in a bowl so it wouldn't get your fries soggy." The waitress was back.

Reagan slid the envelope aside. "Thanks, Edith."

The woman seemed in no hurry to leave. "You from around here?"

"Yes." Reagan ate, chewing down the lies along with the fries. "But I've been gone a long time."

Edith studied her for a few minutes. "You must be one of the Randall kids that used to live north of here. Their youngest girl would be about your age."

"No," Reagan said just before she shoved another spoonful in her mouth. "This is great chili."

The waitress was on a quest and refused to be distracted by the compliment. "You Willa May Turner's granddaughter? I heard you might be coming to live with your grandparents."

Reagan shook her head. "As far as I know, I don't have a single living relative here now. Not one that would claim me, anyway."

The woman smiled. "You never know. Everybody's related in this town. We laugh and say if the gene pool gets any shallower in these parts we'll have to declare a drought."

Reagan swallowed down water and began her new life with another lie. "I'm Beverly Truman's granddaughter."

"I thought I saw Truman blood in you. Don't know where you got that red hair, but your nose is shaped just like every Truman I ever knew. Old Jeremiah Truman still lives on the homestead place a few miles out on Lone Oak Road. He's as mean as Beverly is nice; it's no wonder no woman in the county would marry him. We all miss Beverly, but we don't blame her for moving a state away just so she wouldn't have to live with him and clean around his collections."

Edith slid into the booth across from her. "How is your grandmother? We used to buy all our cream pies from her. Folks would come in here after the movies just for a slice of Miss Beverly's coconut pie. Cut our profits in half when she moved."

Reagan chose her words carefully, thinking of how Beverly would have answered. "I haven't heard lately; she may have passed on to be with the Lord." In the year she'd known the old woman, Reagan had never seen a visitor and, when she died, Reagan was the only one who cried. She guessed that made her more a relative than anyone else.

Edith leaned over and patted Reagan's hand. "We all have to make that journey, child, and you can bet your sweet grandmother made it on the express flight if she passed. Both her grown children and her husband going before her must have left her in a powerful hurry."

Before the waitress could start asking questions Reagan didn't have the answers to, the front door bumped open and the number of customers in the diner doubled when one man entered. He looked like he could have been a model for western wear except for the anger in his eyes. Tall, broad shouldered, and furious.

Reagan took one look and fought the urge to slide under the table.

The waitress just smiled at him as if he were cute as a newborn pit bull.

"Edith!" he yelled from the doorway. "Get a thermos of coffee ready. I'll be back for it." He plowed his hand through jet-black hair and shoved his hat down hard as if about to face a storm.

The Blue Moon Diner door slammed closed and he was gone.

"Who was that?" Reagan asked, figuring this would be the first name on her list of people to avoid.

Edith laughed. "That's Hank Matheson. He's headed across the street to Buffalo Bar and Grill to break up a fight." The waitress laughed. "It's Saturday night and Alex McAllen is either passed out drunk or starting a brawl. One of the bartenders calls Hank every time to come get her before she gets in too much trouble."

"Why don't they just call the police?"

Edith giggled. "You *have* been gone a long time. Alexandra McAllen has been the sheriff for three years. Barely had time to accept her master's in criminal justice down at Sam Houston State before she pinned on the badge."

Reagan smiled and quoted a line from the Harmony paper she kept. "Three families settled in to work at the Ely Trading Post in 1887: the Trumans, the Mathesons, and the McAllens. When old Harmon Ely died, he left a third of his land to each family and together they founded Harmony."

"Good." Edith smiled. "You do know your history. Most folks driving by think we was named Harmony after a mood, but in truth, folks just got tired of calling the town Harmon Ely and shortened it to one word. Kind of a private joke for locals, being the old man was as mean as a two-headed snake on a hot rock."

Edith stood and moved around a long counter to make the thermos. "If you know that much, you also know the three families have never gotten along."

"But Hank's helping Alex, and she's a McAllen."

Edith wobbled her head so far from side to side she almost tapped her shoulders. "Yeah, and she'll hate him for saving her in the morning. Once she got so mad he rescued her that she tried to get him fired as the town's volunteer fire chief. When that didn't work, because it's impossible to fire someone who's not paid in the first place, she blacked his eye with a wild punch."

"And he still goes into that bar on a Saturday night to save her?"

Edith screwed on the top of the thermos. "I guess he figures it's the best way to irritate her."

A scream and a string of swear words could be heard from outside.

"That'll be Alex." Edith rushed to the door.

Reagan watched through the window as the waitress hurried out with the thermos to give to Hank. He was shoving a woman, fighting and kicking, into the passenger side of a Dodge Ram.

He slammed the door and climbed in on the driver's side.

When he opened the window to accept the thermos from Edith, the wild woman he'd trapped managed to open the door and was halfway out before Hank jerked her back.

Edith didn't seem concerned. She just nodded at Hank and hurried back toward the diner.

Two feet inside, she ordered, "Truman, if you want a ride out to your great-uncle Jeremiah's place, Hank said hop in and he'll take you. He's headed that way anyway."

It took Reagan a moment to figure out who Edith was yelling at. Then she remembered. She was a Truman. She'd been one for at least ten minutes now.

"Great," she said, and pulled her pack out from under the table. She couldn't stay here; it would look strange. Maybe she'd just hop out of the truck and find somewhere to sleep until morning. Down the road seemed as good as any place to go.

Edith walked her out and held her pack as she climbed into the bed of Hank's huge pickup truck. Reagan settled in between saddles and serious-looking riding gear.

She noticed that Alex, looking tall and blond, sat perfectly still in the passenger seat, but Hank was swearing that he'd handcuff the sheriff if she tried to get out again. Reagan wasn't sure either of them even noticed her hitching a ride.

She leaned toward Edith. "Doesn't anyone think they're a little strange?"

Edith frowned and looked at them, then shook her head. "He's the only one brave enough to stand up to her when she's had a few, and she's the best sheriff we've had in forty years. Besides—"

Hank threw the truck into drive and roared down the road before Edith finished.

Reagan leaned back on one of the saddles and tried to figure out the couple yelling at each other just beyond the back window. Somewhere in an old paper she remembered reading that a McAllen had died in the line of duty. A highway patrolman maybe, or a marshal. Or maybe, she guessed, the last sheriff of Harmony.

By the time Hank turned off on the farm-to-market road, he had to be going eighty. He hit the first pothole so hard Reagan almost bounced out of the truck bed. Three minutes later he was braking and she was rolling around in the back like the last pumpkin on the way to market.

He was out of the cab before she could settle enough to sit up.

"Sorry, kid," he said as he offered her a hand down. "Alex is threatening to throw up. I can't waste any time."

Reagan grabbed the strap of her pack and let him

16

lift her down. He couldn't be much over thirty, but the worried tone in his voice made him seem older. When she put her hand on his shoulder climbing out, he felt solid as rock.

"It's all right. I understand. Thanks for the ride." She thanked her stars that Jeremiah's house wasn't farther from town.

"Will you be all right from here on?" Hank asked. "The old man's house is a hundred yards up that dirt road. I'd turn in there, but he's left holes wide enough to swallow the truck."

"I'll be fine." Reagan fought to keep her voice from shaking. The shady lane he pointed to looked like it could easily make it onto the "Top Ten Most Likely Places to Get Murdered" list.

Hank reached into a toolbox and pulled out a flashlight. "You can leave this at the diner or the fire station next time you're in town." He hesitated, then added, "Good luck with the old man."

Reagan took the flashlight. She didn't want to go on down the road, but she wasn't about to climb into the bed of Hank's truck again. One more mile and she would have had brain damage for sure.

They both heard someone vomiting.

Hank groaned and climbed back into the vehicle. He was gone before Reagan could figure out how to turn on the light.

Chapter 2

HANK DIDN'T SAY A WORD AS ALEXANDRA threw up into his best Stetson while he drove across the bridge and onto McAllen land.

She lived in a cabin on the north rim of a small canyon when she wasn't sleeping at the office. McAllen land wasn't fit to farm, but when her big brother, Warren, had been alive, he'd run cattle. Alex and her kid brother, Noah, pretty much let the cattle run wild now. She was too busy in town, and Noah still had a few years of high school before he could even think about being a rancher.

The cabin that Alex now called home had been used as a line shack years before and converted to livable by her big brother. No one who hadn't been to the place could have found it in the daylight, much less in the dark, and of course, she hadn't bothered to leave a light on.

Hank pulled up to the long porch and left his brights on. Carrying her through the unlocked door, he flipped on the living room switch with his elbow. In mud-covered boots, he stomped straight to the bathroom. Without a word, he dumped her in the tub and turned on the cold water, then walked out to clean up the cab of his truck before the smell of vomit sank into the upholstery.

By the time he'd finished and walked back

inside, Alex was wrapped in a robe on the couch, her face resting atop her knees. Her beautiful blond hair now hung like wet roots about her head.

"Want a fire? I could bring in some wood. It's getting cold."

She didn't answer.

"You can't keep doing this, Alex." He'd sworn he wouldn't argue or preach at her again, but she made him so angry. "What if that trucker had taken you out of Buffalo's?" Half the drunks in the place wouldn't have noticed if she'd been screaming and the other half wouldn't have challenged the guy.

"I wasn't going with him. I was just having fun. I would have stopped it without you."

"Another drink and you might not have been able to stop it."

"I could have." She sounded tired. "And if I hadn't or couldn't, what difference would it have made? I was off duty. I wasn't the sheriff. I was just a woman looking to get picked up. Last I heard, that wasn't a crime." She glared at him. "Or any of your business, for that matter."

He fought down words he knew he'd regret. "You want a cup of coffee?" he asked after a moment.

"No," she said. "I'm going to bed." She walked to the bedroom door. "Alone, thanks to you, Hank."

He glared at her.

She turned and added, "How long does Warren

19

have to be dead before you stop being my brother's best friend and let me live my own life?"

"*Screw up* your own life, you mean."

"Whatever." She waved a hand. "I don't care what you think anymore. I do my job all week. I should be able to do whatever I want on my own time."

He didn't argue. Grabbing a blanket, he headed for the couch.

"You're spending the night again, aren't you? Guarding over me so I don't break out and go back to town."

"Something like that." He tugged off one boot and tossed it toward the doormat.

"Well, you'd better be gone by morning or I swear I'll arrest you for breaking and entering." She slammed the bedroom door so hard it echoed off the rafters.

Hank barely noticed. It had been the way she ended every conversation they'd had since her brother died. Warren had been her hero, her big brother, the only father she claimed, but Warren had also been Hank's best friend. Alex couldn't seem to look at him without remembering Warren, and he couldn't look at her without remembering his promise to a friend.

When Warren died, something had shattered in Alex. She'd turned all her energy, all her talents, all her soul into doing her job better than anyone else ever had. Except for one tiny part of her time.

Her Saturday nights, she'd turned into her own brand of hell. The wound to her heart hadn't healed, but festered with time.

And Hank had fallen right into the fire with her. He didn't allow himself one drink, one solid night's sleep on the weekends. Somehow when Warren died, Hank had become Alex's guardian. He'd butted into her life, where he knew he wasn't welcome, and they'd been slugging it out with neither one of them having any idea of how to stop.

Hank sank down and spoke to the closed door. "The next time you want to sleep with an idiot, Alex, all you've got to do is open that door. There's one waiting right here on your couch."

Chapter 3

REAGAN WALKED INTO THE BEAM OF LIGHT from the borrowed flashlight, feeling like Indiana Jones. Huge old evergreens permanently bent by the wind blackened most of the path. An ancient house, with half the windows boarded up, waited at the end like a troublesome shadow in a horror film.

Not one light flickered from the direction of the house. Old Jeremiah was probably dead, she thought. Probably had been for weeks, but he was so mean no one bothered to come check.

Miss Beverly never talked about her brother,

other than to say he would drive a saint to swear. He'd served in World War II and brought his army ways home with him when he returned. Beverly said once that he hated farming but, as far as she knew, he'd never tried anything else after the war. "Some folks," she'd said, "had rather stick with what they can complain about than wander off into something new that they might enjoy."

When Beverly Truman's divorced son had died of lung cancer, she'd decided she'd rather move up near Oklahoma City, where she knew no one, than have to move back in with her brother, Jeremiah.

Reagan remembered that Beverly had mentioned once that Jeremiah collected something, but she couldn't remember what. Probably skeletal remains of teenagers.

When she got out of the line of trees, Reagan was surprised by the yard around the house. It seemed orderly, the kind of stiff, planned arrangements of an institution, not a home. She spotted several chairs and tables turned in different directions, all facing away from the house, and a hammock stretched across an opening between two trees. Both ends of the porch drooped, making the place appear to frown. Rusty wind chimes clanked in the midnight breeze.

The hammock looked as safe a place to sleep as any. She wasn't about to knock on the door and wake up the old man. A blanket she found in the hammock smelled of rain, but nothing else.

Reagan wrapped it around her and crawled in with her pack cuddled against her. She'd figure out what to do in the morning. Right now, she needed sleep.

Closing her eyes, she whispered, "Harmony, I'm home."

Dreams drifted in her thoughts as they always did. She was walking through a house trying to find her room, but every night, every dream, it was a different house. Some big, some small, some with secret turns and hiding places, but in one way they were all the same. None seemed to have a room for her.

She'd just cuddled into a corner somewhere in her dream when a bright light woke her. Reagan opened one eye and watched the sun spread across an open field that shone between the tree branches. The ground looked pink, then violet, then golden. The sunrise was so bright it sparkled white and, for a moment, the light turned the earth to a shining lake of silver.

Reagan smiled. It was the most beautiful thing she'd ever seen.

She heard a clank and turned to see an old man sitting in a chair five feet away. He'd put down his cup and lifted a metal coffeepot that looked like it had been used on open fires since the Civil War and never cleaned.

"You want some coffee before you start explaining what you're doing on my land, kid?"

His hands were big, and tiny scars flashed white against his tanned skin. He could have been eighty or a hundred. Once some people get so old, they kind of fossilize.

"Yes, I'd like some coffee . . . please." She almost tumbled out of the hammock trying to sit up.

When her feet were planted firmly on the ground, she walked close enough to him to take the cup and took a seat in the other metal lawn chair facing the sunrise. It was so rusty she couldn't make out what the original color had been.

The sun was a ball now, sitting on the horizon, and the morning pushed all shadows away.

The old man watched the dawn and didn't seem too interested in her. He also didn't seem worried or afraid she might try to rob him. Maybe the seventy-pound German shepherd at his side accounted for some of that. The dog watched her as if he thought she might be a take-out breakfast.

"You got the Truman nose," Reagan finally said.

"I've been told that before. It's the only nose I got and I'm a Truman, so ain't no surprise to me that I got a Truman nose. You come all the way out here to tell me that?"

"No," she answered, wondering what she could tell him. "I hadn't planned to come out at all. I was just talking to Edith at the diner and she asked some guy named Hank to give me a lift out here. I guess she thought because my name is Truman that I might be welcome."

"Well, you ain't," Jeremiah said. "I welcome company about the same as I do black mold."

"I figured that." Reagan really hadn't expected the world to change just because she made up a hometown and a last name, and a dead grandmother. "I guess I was just wishing."

"What were you wishing for?" he asked, not sounding like he cared much what the answer was.

"Oh, I don't wish *for* things. I gave up on that years ago. Never got me anywhere." She drank a long draw on her coffee and added, "If I do anything, it's reverse wishing."

He raised a bushy eyebrow on a face so wrinkled a mosquito would have trouble finding a landing spot.

"You know," she said, just to talk. She'd never see him again after a few minutes, so she might as well tell him her thoughts. "People are always reverse wishing around me and they don't even know it. Like them saying, 'I wish you'd never been born,' or 'I wish I didn't have to take care of you,' or 'I wish you'd move on and leave me in peace.' That's the only kind of wishing that I've ever seen work. So I don't wish for good things to happen, I just wish the bad things would leave me alone for a while."

"And if you were doing this reverse wishing, kid, what would you wish for?"

She couldn't look at him. His eyes were so hard and cold they could have been frozen marbles.

She'd be better off to go back to the diner and ask Edith for a job. Maybe she could even find a place to rent a room somewhere and tell everyone she was eighteen. Only problem with that was she was a sixteen-year-old who could pass for twelve. Half the people she met couldn't even tell if she was a boy or a girl.

"I'd wish, if I were reverse wishing, that I didn't have to leave this place."

He was silent for so long, she thought he'd surely died on the spot. Then he said, "You can stay for breakfast, and then I'll take you back to town. Looks like it might rain today, and I wouldn't want you falling in a mud hole on my land and suing me."

Reagan looked at the cloudless sky and decided the old man had floaters in his eyes. Miss Beverly had floaters. She was always swearing there were bugs in her oatmeal.

Jeremiah stood slowly, as if testing to make sure his legs still worked, then walked toward the house. "We're having eggs." He didn't turn around. "Damn chickens keep laying them faster than I can eat them."

She watched him, not believing he'd invited her to breakfast. Somewhere an ounce of Miss Beverly's goodness must have been in him. She ran and caught up to him just as he stepped in the side door.

She wasn't sure what she'd expected, but a spotless kitchen with long countertops and linoleum almost scrubbed off the floor hadn't been on her list. Everything, from the walls to the appliances, was in black and white. She felt like she'd stepped into an old, old movie.

Jeremiah rolled up his sleeves. "You think you can make yourself useful by squeezing the oranges while I cook?"

"Sure," Reagan answered as she reached for the top orange in a white mixing bowl.

"Wash your hands first, kid."

After she did that, he had to show her how to cut the fruit and grind them over this strange bowl with a bump in it. "I didn't know you could do this to make the juice," she said, loving how easily the center of the bowl ground out orange juice.

"Where'd you think orange juice comes from?" he asked.

"The store," she answered.

He turned his back to her, and she wanted to believe that he was smiling. More likely, he was thinking she was the dumbest kid ever born.

They didn't talk as they ate eggs and toast made with homemade bread. He'd dotted it with butter, then sprinkled sugar and cinnamon over it before sliding it into the bottom of the oven. The sugary mixture had bubbled and crusted over the bread. She decided it had to be maybe a hundred times better than toast made in the toaster.

"You in school?" he finally asked.

"I was," she answered between bites. "I dropped out. If I wait a year I can take the GED test and it'll be just like I'm a high school graduate."

"Smart, are you?" He didn't sound like he believed she was.

"Smart enough." She took a breath and dove in. "If I could stay around here, I could help you to earn my keep. I wouldn't be any trouble, and I don't eat much."

He glanced at the empty plate he'd shoveled five eggs onto a few minutes ago. "I can see that."

"I could clean and I could learn stuff that needs to be done." She fought to keep her voice from shaking, thinking of all the times in her life she'd begged to stay when someone was telling her to go. She knew all the excuses. *There's not enough room. You're getting too old. It's time to move along before you get too attached to one place.*

She straightened. She'd be fine without him. She'd find somewhere in town to stay.

He frowned at her. "What's your name?"

"Reagan Truman."

He scratched his beard. "Got saddled with two presidents, did you?"

She forced herself to show no reaction.

"Well," he finally said as he stood, "I guess you could stay for a while. There's a ton of work to do on the orchard before spring. I always have more work than I have time to do, and spring may come early this year. I can't pay you much, but I'll give you room and board for two hours' work on week-days and pay you for up to eight hours' work on Saturday."

"I can work more."

"I wasn't finished. I got one rule, other than if you mess up the kitchen, you clean it."

"All right, what else?"

"You go to school every day. Folks who think they've learned everything they need to know are usually dumber than chickens."

"But . . ."

He turned his back on her and moved to the sink. "That's my terms. Take them or leave them. I don't much care. If you're going, don't slam the door. If you're staying, bring that plate over here and wash it."

Reagan didn't know whether to laugh or cry. He was letting her stay, even offering to feed her, but she'd have to go to school and she hated school. "I could work all day every day." It would be easier than being the outsider with tattered clothes. The child no one talked to. The student in the back of the room trying to be invisible all day.

"No." He snapped out the words like a drill ser-geant. "It's not open for discussion. My house. My rules."

She had a hint of why his sister might have left. Only Miss Beverly must have had money to move to Oklahoma and get a room at the nursing home. Reagan had four dollars in her pocket. "All right.

I'll take your offer and am grateful to have it." To her surprise, she meant it. She'd somehow survive school if she could stay in Harmony, and this seemed the only way.

"How dumb are chickens, anyway?" she asked as she washed her plate.

"They'll stand in the rain watching until they drown." He almost smiled. "And believe me, kid, you don't want to be that dumb."

Chapter 4

TYLER WRIGHT HATED SUNDAYS ALMOST AS much as he hated Halloween.

Folks probably thought since Sunday was the only day he didn't do funerals that he'd like the time off, but they'd be wrong. As the town's only funeral director, he never had a day off. More often than not he'd have to drive somewhere and pick up a newly departed, or get ready for a service on Monday morning. On weekends when he didn't have a corpse waiting in the morgue, there was always a mound of paperwork he never seemed to finish.

"Morning, Tyler," someone said from behind him.

Tyler moved up the line toward the counter before he turned around and smiled. On Sundays the only place to get a good cup of coffee was at the shop in the bookstore, and Tyler loved any kind of brew he didn't have to make himself. The problem, of course, was that he'd run into people if he went out. There was always someone who'd been a member of the family from a funeral he'd done last week or ten years ago. They'd know him, sometimes even hug him. After all, he'd done them a great service during their time of grief. He'd been there, he'd handled things, he'd been their rock in stormy seas.

Only problem was, Tyler never remembered them. He was one of those cursed people in the world who didn't remember names or faces. They'd be bawling on his shoulder, telling him how hard it had been since the death of their loved one, and he'd be trying to place them.

"Morning, Mr. Wright," a pretty teenager said as she took his coffee order.

"Morning," he answered with a smile while he tried to remember where he'd seen her before. The great-granddaughter of someone he'd laid to rest about six months ago, he decided, or maybe she sang in the Baptist choir. They were always pulling the whole choir in for a Baptist funeral.

"You want two blueberry muffins with that, like usual?" she asked.

Great, he thought. *She remembers my order and I couldn't swear in court that I'd ever seen her before.* With a lucky glance, he noticed her name tag. "Yes, thanks, Gracie."

She handed him the muffins and Tyler tried to find a chair that faced the wall. Otherwise, he'd be talking to every third person who walked by. There weren't more than a dozen people in town that he could relax enough around to enjoy talking to, and it looked like none of them came in for Sunday-morning coffee.

Why don't these folks go to church, he wondered, then the coffee shop would be empty and he could enjoy his breakfast and *New York Times* without having to talk to anyone. Tyler rarely went to church. He'd usually filled his quota of visits by Friday every week.

He slipped out the side door planning to eat in his car, as he did almost every Sunday.

"Something is wrong with me," he said aloud as he wiggled beneath the steering wheel. Whoever heard of a funeral director afraid of people? He didn't like idle talk with folks dead or alive.

Tyler almost spilled his coffee laughing as his employee Calvin came to mind. That man usually talked to the customer all the way from the embalming to the dressing as if he were a shoe salesman trying to get the fit right.

Taking a bite of one of the muffins, Tyler decided his problem was he didn't know how to have a real conversation with most people. All he ever talked about was death. *I'd kill myself, but then I'd feel bad about someone else having to drive to Harmony to take care of my body.* Tyler smiled and

thought, with his luck, Calvin would do the job a talk to him until they closed the lid.

A lady with two little boys walked in front of car and waved at him.

Tyler smiled and waved back. There were e too many people in the parking lot these da Starting his car, he headed for the Wright Fun Home, an impressive white stucco building West Street.

He was the son of a son of an undertaker. H known how to act and what to say to peo crying over a body since he crawled out of crib. His ancestors had moved to Harmony a Harmon Ely died, slicing the town up and giv it to the residents since Ely had no kin. His gr grandfather had been penniless after the C War and missed old Ely's funeral by a matte weeks. In so doing, he also missed out on split of land.

Tyler thought about how his family ha missed a funeral since. Great-Grandfather cam Texas looking for a fresh start. They would starved if he hadn't hung a sign in front of shack that read: WILL UNDERTAKE ANY W OFFERED.

The offers were made for several kinds of l but the job no one else wanted to do was to graves and prepare bodies for burial. Ty ancestor took on the responsibility. Within a he'd learned to build a coffin overnight

33

embalm a body in the kitchen before the women started preparing the funeral meal.

As the town grew, so did the Wright family. In thirty years, two sons worked with their father. They not only made caskets for the dead of Harmony, but shipped them all over the state. They'd built a funeral home as grand as any business in town. Tyler's father, the only male heir, took over the reins of the funeral home while his three sisters married and moved away. He'd planned to have a big family, but he'd waited until almost fifty to marry. Tyler was his only child. So for Tyler there was no one else to take over. Four generations had built up a business, a trust, a life in Harmony.

Tyler had no doubt that all before him would haunt him if he sold out and left, but still, he imagined living in a beach house down on the gulf. He dreamed of talking to a woman who forgot to ask what he did for a living, but at forty years old and fifty pounds overweight, he doubted the dream would ever come true. He longed to have a conversation that wasn't related to dying.

He pulled his Cadillac into his space outside the three-story building. The first floor consisted of offices, a chapel, and staterooms for viewing. The basement housed the embalming room and storage. The second and third floors were the only home he'd ever known: a five-bedroom rambling apartment, where he lived alone.

Tyler unlocked the door to his office and sighed as he stepped inside. He might as well get some of the paperwork done; then he wouldn't feel so bad about spending the afternoon and evening with his hobby. If he went upstairs before dinnertime, his seventy-year-old housekeeper would glare at him as if she were sorry he hadn't died of a heart attack while out.

Alone in the huge oak-paneled room his grandfather had built, Tyler sat in his desk chair, turned on the computer, and did what he did every morning. He checked his e-mail.

He began deleting. Thank-you notes from families. Advertisements. He'd moved through twenty before one caught his attention.

The subject line read: *Hi from Quartz Mountain.*

He knew no one from Quartz Mountain. He'd stopped at a lodge there almost a year ago. He'd been on his way to pick up a body in Elk City and decided to take some time and wander the back roads. Both his employees had offered to go, but he looked forward to the drive, only the ice on the back roads had forced him to pull over and a lodge tucked away in the hills around the lake had been his only choice.

The stay at the lodge had been uneventful, except for the dinner he'd shared in a darkened bar with a woman also traveling. They'd been about the same age, early forties and all business in a room full of fishermen and vacationers. They'd sat in a shadowy corner near the view of the water and talked of the Native American artwork lining the walls of the lodge and of their childhood vacations spent on lakes. Tyler remembered shaking her hand and introducing himself, but he didn't remember her name. Her e-mail address was simply a jumble of numbers and letters offering no clue.

Her eyes though, he'd never forget . . . warm hazel like a cloudy day in late summer.

He clicked on the e-mail.

Stayed at the lodge again and thought of you. Since I remembered your last name, the clerk gave me your e-mail. Just wanted to say hello.

Tyler smiled and wrote: *How is my hazel-eyed dinner guest?* He watched wondering how long it would be before she answered.

When the screen blinked, he jumped in surprise.

Fine, she wrote. *Do you remember the art?*

Leaning back in his chair, he described a few of the wonderful pieces that had drawn him that night. She answered back with details on some of the artists she'd learned on her latest visit. The lodge was gearing up for a big weekend and the halls were full.

He told her of the tribes he'd looked up in southwestern Oklahoma just because of one painting that had seemed so alive it could have stepped from the frame.

He wasn't sure how it happened, but they e-mailed back and forth for a half hour.

Finally, she wrote: *Have to work. Loved talking to you. Let's do it again. Kate.*

He stared at the screen. Kate. Her name was Kate. Glancing over at his forgotten coffee and muffin, he smiled. If he had a few more conversations that were this interesting, he'd be below two hundred pounds in no time.

Three hours later he wrote Kate back. *How about taking a break and having lunch with me?*

Staring at the computer, he waited until she blinked back. *Give me five to get my salad.*

Pulling a Coke and a couple of candy bars from the break room, he waited. When she came back, he lied and told her he was also eating a green salad.

They talked about food and the weather and how much they both wished they were on a beach. Neither asked any personal questions. She'd told him a great deal without writing a word. She was working on Sunday and in no hurry to go home. He knew without asking that she lived alone.

When she finally wrote: *Have to go.*

He asked: *Tomorrow?*

She answered: *You bet. Is nine too late? I've got a hell of a day, but visiting with you would be a nice way to end it.*

I'll be waiting.

Tyler turned off his computer and grinned. He'd talked to someone, really talked . . . well, almost talked . . . and they hadn't mentioned death once.

Chapter 5

⟨≈⟩

REAGAN HATED HAVING TO GO TO SCHOOL. She'd enjoyed Sunday working in the orchard with Jeremiah. He didn't talk much. He just showed her what he needed her to do, and she did it. In a strange way she liked taking care of the trees, mothering the saplings and trimming up broken branches.

Old Jeremiah gave out and had to sit a while about mid-afternoon, but told her he thought she should learn to drive. She picked up leaves and threw them in the back of a cart he called his little truck. She felt like she was really driving for the first time, even though her truck was the size of a golf cart with a pickup bed welded on the back.

When she circled by him to ask what to do with the dead branches, he was sound asleep. By the time he woke up, she had another load of limbs stacked and ready to transport.

They'd stopped at sunset and had a supper of ham sandwiches and fried potatoes, then he'd showed her a room with all the furnishings covered in sheets.

"This used to be my sister's room. If she comes back, we'll have to find another place for you."

She didn't have the guts to tell him Beverly was dead. He'd ask too many questions.

38

They took the sheets off everything and he gave her a fresh stack of linens to make up her bed, then closed the door without a word.

The place should have made Reagan feel creepy with all the old pictures and old furniture, but everything reminded her of Miss Beverly and nothing about the old woman had been creepy. Reagan pretended she'd come to visit Miss Beverly and been welcomed.

She slept without waking all night. At dawn she awoke to Jeremiah pounding on her door.

"If you're going to have time to eat before you leave for school, you'd better hurry up."

She pulled back on her same clothes she'd worn working the day before and ran downstairs. In the shadows of boarded windows, she saw the other rooms. All were covered with sheets as if no one lived except in the kitchen. A light shone beneath a closed door down a dark hallway. She guessed that must be Jeremiah's bedroom, but didn't ask as she moved to the counter in the kitchen and began making juice.

"I don't want to go to school," she complained as he shoved oatmeal and toast in front of her.

"I don't care," he answered.

"I don't have any of my papers to transfer in."

"I'll take you. They'll let you in."

She wasn't so sure. "If they don't, can I come back here? There's still a ton of work to be done out in the apple trees."

He didn't answer. By the time she finished washing up her breakfast dishes, he and the dog were waiting outside in an old green pickup.

A few minutes later, he walked into the school and told the assistant principal that Reagan Truman was enrolling. No one questioned him. In fact, half the people in the office looked afraid of him, making her wonder just how mean Jeremiah Truman was.

She shrugged. He was good to her. That was all that mattered. She didn't care if the volume on him was broken. Reagan almost laughed. She'd been tossed around so long that anyone who didn't hit her was considered a saint. Jeremiah had fed her, given her a place to sleep, and driven her to school. So what if he didn't talk to her? He was high on her list of friendly.

When they passed her paperwork to fill out, he walked to the exit without saying a word to her, then turned at the door and bellowed, "You got a bus that goes down Lone Oak Road after school?"

"Of course," the assistant principal answered.

"Then see that she's on it."

Reagan wrote her name without looking up when the door slammed.

The assistant principal glanced down at the paper. "Reagan Truman," he read aloud. "You related to that old man?"

She nodded. "He's my great-uncle."

"Sorry about that," he answered.

Reagan raised her head and glared at him. "Don't you ever say anything about Uncle Jeremiah. Not ever."

The assistant principal looked surprised and more than a little angry, then took a breath and answered, "You're right. I was out of line. You got a right to stand up for your kin. Welcome to Harmony High."

If anyone else had anything to say about Jeremiah Truman, they kept their mouth closed. Reagan had a feeling they were thinking that she was definitely related to the old man.

Chapter 6

TUESDAY MORNING AT SEVEN FIFTEEN, HANK Matheson walked into the diner with his four-year-old niece on his shoulder. Two days a week he drove her into town for preschool, and on Tuesdays that always meant breakfast out.

He removed his straw hat as he shoved the door closed with his foot. He missed the felt Stetson, but Alex had ruined it. He had no idea when he'd have time to drive over to Lubbock for a new one. It was too early in the year for straw to feel right.

"Let me hang it up," Saralynn squealed.

He leaned forward so she could reach the rack, his hands firmly on the metal braces around her legs. "Thanks, Princess."

41

"You're welcome, Horse. Now gallop on."

"Morning, Saralynn. Hank," Edith said as they passed her. "Hope you can find a seat this morning. Place is hopping."

"I'm a princess today, Edith, and this is my horse."

Edith's quick one-second smile told Hank she didn't have time to bother with the kid's fantasies this morning. Last week Saralynn had been a frog and would only croak. "Find a seat, I'll get to you when I can. The morning waitress quit on Cass as he unlocked the door. Said she'd thought about it and decided she was a night person. When he told her he'd see if I'd be interested in trading shifts, she also decided she wasn't a waitress person. If he don't find someone soon he'll be serving the meals as well as cooking."

Hank moved down the row between booths. Cass lost several waitresses a year. Some said the only reason Edith stayed around was because she worked nights and didn't have to put up with him much. Others thought Cass might be easier to get along with than Edith's husband waiting for her at home.

The place was packed. He saw one empty seat in a front corner booth that held only two. Trouble was, Ronelle Logan was in the other chair. No one in town ever sat at the same table with Ronelle. She wouldn't have allowed it if they tried. Ronelle worked at the post office sorting mail. If you wanted your mail, you left her alone, so Hank kept moving down one of the center aisles.

Hank noticed that the only other open seat was half of a booth in the middle of the room. The other half was taken up by the local undertaker. Hank moved through the crowd, relieved to find a seat across from someone who wouldn't talk his ear off.

"Morning, Tyler. Mind if the princess and I join you?"

He carefully lifted his little passenger down. Hank would have sat her next to him, but Saralynn pointed to the space next to Tyler.

The chubby man grinned. "I'd love to have royalty join me for breakfast."

"I'm Princess Saralynn," the thin child said. "And you are Sir Wright, my most trusted knight."

"Great." Hank gently moved her legs beneath the table without bumping anything. The slightest bump would cause a bruise on her legs. "I get to be the horse and you're knighted."

"Can't win them all, Chief." Tyler Wright laughed.

Hank nodded while he tried to think of something to say to Wright. "How's business?"

Tyler looked up from his paper. "Business is slow. Only one pending."

"Anyone I know?"

Tyler shook his head. "You know what they say, the young leave this town for the big city and the dead return to be buried with their kin. This newly departed had been gone from Harmony for sixty years. Half his kin don't remember him."

"Well, it's only Tuesday. Maybe business will pick up." Hank smiled. He liked the undertaker. He considered Tyler Wright a friend. They'd shared breakfast at the Blue Moon more times than either of them could count.

His chubby friend asked Saralynn, "How's your mother?"

"Fair," Saralynn said as if she were grown and not four. "She's stopped crying and started painting."

Hank studied his menu. He didn't like talking about his newly divorced sister, but he guessed everyone in town knew she'd moved back to the ranch. She'd repainted her old bedroom for Saralynn and turned the attic into a studio loft, where no one was allowed. In the four months she'd been back she'd done six paintings, all of men dying horrible deaths.

"Glad to hear she has a hobby." Tyler pulled a quarter from his vest pocket. "I've been saving this for you, Princess Saralynn." He handed it to her. "It's the new one."

Saralynn smiled. "Thanks. I'm going to collect them all." She turned it over in her hand. "Do you collect anything, Sir Knight? I could help you."

Tyler shrugged. "I like old maps. I'm kind of a cartophile."

"Really." Hank was taken aback. He'd known Tyler all his life and never thought to ask if he had a hobby.

Saralynn lost interest in the conversation and began playing with her quarter. Tiny hands slid it from one hand to the other.

Tyler looked embarrassed. "Yeah. I got maps of this area that go all the way back to the cattle drives. Sometimes I drive out trying to see how much of the original roads are still around."

Hank wanted to know more, but Edith was back. "What'll it be?" She pointed her pen at Saralynn. "The usual for you, one pancake with blueberry eyes and a banana smile."

"Yes." Saralynn straightened. "And oats for my horse."

"That's right, the usual for your uncle."

She turned to Tyler. "And you, Sir Knight?"

"I'll just have coffee for now." He folded his paper.

A few minutes later, Edith slid a diet special of two egg whites, dry toast, a cup of blueberries, and oatmeal across to Hank. He ordered the same meal every Tuesday.

"There you go, Hank, try to enjoy it." She turned to Tyler. "Did you decide what you'll be having, Mr. Wright? We got biscuits and gravy with sausage in it for the special this morning."

"No thanks." Tyler closed his eyes as if forcing himself to forget the offer. "I think I'll have what Hank's having."

Edith stared at him as if she saw proof of alien occupation. "All right. Anything else?"

"No," Tyler answered.

As the waitress walked away shaking her head, Hank was smart enough not to comment. He wouldn't ask. One of the things he liked about sitting with Tyler was neither got too personal with questions. That and Tyler always remembered that Saralynn collected state quarters. Anyone who was nice to his niece was all right as far as Hank was concerned, even if he did have a strange hobby.

Tyler straightened the gap in his shirt. "I'm thinking of taking off a few pounds."

"Oh." Hank put jelly on his bread, then took a moment to clean syrup off the princess's face.

"Yeah. I know it won't be easy," Tyler added as he winked at the little girl pouring more syrup on her smiling pancake. "I'm invited to every family meal after the funerals, and everyone knows there's no better food than funeral food."

Hank nodded. "If you decide to work out some, you're welcome to come down to the fire station. We got some pretty good exercise equipment." He didn't add that he'd bought most of it and moved it to the station, hoping the other men would use it. Some of the volunteers were barely fitting into their uniforms.

"I might do that," Tyler said. "Thanks for the offer."

Hank drank his coffee, thinking that Tyler wouldn't exactly fit in with the firemen. Willie, just a kid whose parents made him move out the day he turned eighteen; Brad, bunking there because he was in the middle of a divorce; and Andy, who stayed around because he didn't want to go home alone. Twenty other men made up the volunteer fire department, but they came when needed and then left.

Edith set a box down on the end of the table. "Sheriff brought this by and said to give it to you when you came in."

Hank looked at the box. He didn't have to open it. He knew what it was.

Saralynn lifted the lid with sticky fingers. "Look, a hat, just like the one you have, Uncle Hank."

"Had," Hank answered without offering any further explanation. The town had enough to talk about without him telling everyone within hearing distance what happened between him and Alex in private this weekend.

Edith leaned her head over as she studied the Stetson. "What I can't figure out is how she guessed your size."

"It's not the first she's bought," he answered, wishing they'd move on to something other than the Stetson.

Tyler helped him out with the first thought that crossed his mind. "They say it may rain this weekend. We might get some relief from this dry spell. If it comes with a cold front, I wouldn't be surprised if we don't see a late snow."

Edith looked bored and moved on down the line of booths.

Saralynn picked up her napkin. When it stuck to her fingers, she began waving the paper square, letting it dip into her plate of syrup and dribble about.

Both men decided not to notice.

"I wouldn't mind rain," Hank said to Tyler. "Fire danger signs have been up so long they're starting to look wind-worn." The grass had browned enough to burn fast and hot if sparked. "A grass fire could cost dearly in lives and property." His volunteer forces hadn't been trained properly to fight the hundred-acre fire two years ago that had taken one life, and they weren't trained now.

Hank wondered if Tyler, too, could still smell the odor of burned flesh. Hank and his men had fought the fire, but when one man suffered a heart attack and fell into the flames, it had been Tyler and his crew who'd tended, with loving care, to the blackened remains.

Edith walked by and took the napkin away from Saralynn with a stern look at both men.

"Don't look at me," Hank snapped. "I'm just the horse."

Tyler straightened. "And I would never question a princess." He placed his paper over the sticky table, hiding the evidence.

Edith looked at the mess. "I expect royalty tips double?"

Both men nodded. As soon as the waitress moved on, Tyler moved his paper away so the princess could continue her syrup painting.

"Did you hear old man Truman's great-niece is in town?" he asked Hank.

"I thought she might be since I dropped a kid out by his place a few nights ago. Couldn't imagine anyone going out to the place unless they were kin."

"They say she's grumpy as Truman, but that couldn't be possible." Tyler laughed. "The last time I asked Jeremiah how he was doing, he accused me of trying to drum up business."

Edith passed Tyler his plate and all conversation stopped while they ate.

A few minutes later, Alex McAllen walked in dressed in her tan uniform. She looked all business with her hair tied up and her gun belt around her waist. She looked around, her eyes narrowing when she spotted him. She headed over.

Official trouble, he thought, wrapped in a body he couldn't keep out of his dreams lately. One of these days he'd voice his thoughts and Alex would probably get so mad she'd shoot him, putting them both out of their misery.

"Move over," she ordered, looking like she might flash her badge if he didn't make room for her.

Hank did so without comment, but Tyler smiled a welcome. "We'd love to have you join us,

Sheriff," he said motioning for Edith to bring another cup. "I'm having breakfast with Princess Saralynn."

Alex winked at the tiny girl. "Morning, Princess. Morning, Tyler."

She didn't look at Hank. He might as well have been the horse in the room.

"I just have a second. Phil called in a few minutes ago from his patrol south of town to tell me there's a cow in that grave you dug last night."

"Great," Tyler mumbled as he scooted out the far side of the booth. "I've got until two to get it out before the graveside service. Won't be many at the service, but they're bound to notice a cow in the grave."

Hank bumped her leg with his, forcing Alex to look at him as he laughed. "Whose cow is it?" The cemetery was bordered by McAllen land. It had to be one of the half-wild cattle that ran over her land.

She turned her sky-blue eyes directly at him and said sweetly, "Yours."

He frowned, but didn't move his leg away. Neither did she. He couldn't tell if she liked his touch or was just calling his bluff. "How's that possible? My field's five miles from the cemetery."

"One of your men was hauling a dozen head in this morning and it appears he forgot to latch the trailer gate. There are Matheson cattle scattered out for half a mile along the cemetery road."

50

"Any hurt?"

"Phil said they're all standing, except the one who fell in the open grave." She slid from the booth and smiled. "I wanted to be the one to tell you."

He stood. "I'll just bet you did." He grabbed the new hat without saying another word and lifted Saralynn out of the booth and onto his shoulder.

"I want to go see the cow," Saralynn yelled as she tried to clap her sticky hands.

As everyone at her table left, the sheriff called out, "You're welcome!"

Hank stormed to his truck trying to figure out which he disliked more, Alex drunk or Alex sober. He waved as Tyler pulled out. "I'll meet you there."

He had no idea how to get a cow out of a six-foot hole, but they had until two to figure it out.

Chapter 7

TWO DAYS, REAGAN THOUGHT, TWO DAYS AND no one had said anything to her. She'd seen them watching her. Knew they talked about her. But not one person at Harmony High had been mean to her.

She walked out the side door of the cafeteria and found a bench to eat the apple she'd brought with her for lunch. She'd thought of asking Jeremiah for lunch money, but her pride wouldn't let her. He already fed her breakfast and dinner.

A dry wind blew from the west. The warmth of it surprised her because she'd felt like the temperature had been almost freezing at dawn. She watched dirt from the field next to the school whirl in a tiny dust devil. The baby tornado widened and rose, blending with the wind. Reagan shifted, not wanting to be pelted when the dirt blew over her.

A tall, thin shadow crossed the ground in front of her. She looked up.

"Hi." A boy, so thin he looked stretched, folded to the ground in front of her like some kind of double-jointed metal chair. He pulled a bottle of juice from his pocket. "Mind if I join you?"

Reagan ignored him. She'd seen him before. How could she have missed him? The guy was a head taller than almost everyone in the sophomore class. He had a bad complexion, a farmer's tan, and a lopsided smile. All he needed was an *L* painted on his forehead and he'd be the complete package.

"It's nice out here." He looked around and lowered his hat against the dust. "I can see why you'd like leaving all the noise behind." He took off his battered cowboy hat and propped a corner of his backpack against it so it wouldn't blow away.

She stared at him. "Maybe I just want to be alone."

Stretching out one booted foot, he nodded as if agreeing with her.

"Completely alone," she added, hoping he'd get the point.

After a long draw on his drink, he asked, "What's your name?"

"What do you care?"

He laughed. "I care because if you're about to walk into traffic or fall off a cliff, I could yell at you." He gulped down more juice.

She glanced at the road in front of the school. "Don't have much traffic around here, and I've yet to see a cliff."

He tossed his empty juice bottle in the trash next to her bench, then stood in front of her as if waiting for her to look up at him.

Reagan refused. He could stand there like a pole all day.

"I'm Noah McAllen, but most folks call me Preacher," he said finally, in a low voice flavored with determination.

Great, Reagan thought. The only thing worse than being picked on by a bully was being recruited by the school religious nut. Despite her resolve, she looked up at him.

"You got the most unusual color of hair." He frowned. "No offense, but it kind of reminds me of the color of the mud down at the Salt Fork of the Red River. Kind of red and brown at the same time."

She thought of snapping something back at him, but she wasn't sure he meant it as an insult.

"Look, Preacher, I don't need saving, I'm not interested in dating, and I'd just as soon not be your friend, so why don't you go peddle 'Let's be friends' somewhere else."

A grin spread across a face that could almost grow a beard. "They call me Preacher because I seem to get religion when I ride bulls. I'm the junior state rodeo champ. Not to hurt your feelings, but I don't want to date anyone—but I wouldn't mind having a friend."

"Why?"

He shrugged. "Maybe just to have someone to talk to that's been outside the city limits."

"I'm not good company." She'd spent far more time in her life arguing than talking. "I'm not easy to talk to."

He shook his head. "That don't matter. If I liked easy, I'd go out for football or track."

She hid a smile as she took a bite of apple. "Reagan," she said as she chewed. "Reagan Truman."

He nodded, and she was pretty sure he'd already known her name. "Trumans and McAllens don't get along in this town, but I guess I could make an exception. After all, you may be the last survivor in that clan, and McAllens grow like weeds." He offered her his hand. "Friends."

She stared at him for a long moment before she shook.

Leaning down to pick up his hat and backpack, he

54

added, "Don't worry about the way I look. In a few years, when my face clears up and I get a little more muscle around these bones, I'm going to be a hunk. Then, Reagan Truman, we'll talk about dating."

Reagan laughed.

He raised an eyebrow. "Don't you believe me, Rea?"

"Sure," she answered. "The way I see it, you've got nowhere to go but up in the looks department and, as far the dating, I'll pass on that."

He fell backward as if shot, then lifted his head and smiled at her.

Just for a second, underneath the pimples and patches of facial hair, she saw it. A glimpse of what he'd be. Noah McAllen was right. In a few years he'd break half the hearts in Harmony. He wouldn't even notice by that time that she wouldn't be one of them.

He put on his tattered cowboy hat. "See you, Rea."

"See you, Preacher."

Chapter 8

THURSDAY, 8:30 A.M.

SHERIFF ALEXANDRA MCALLEN CLIPPED A cell phone onto her belt and moved toward her cruiser. She'd rather arrest a drunk or pat down a drug offender than have to play the Grim Reaper.

But there was no way she could pass off this duty to one of her deputies.

She had to drive out to Jeremiah Truman's place and tell him his sister was dead. It was her job but a hell of a way to start the day.

As she backed out of the parking lot, it occurred to her that the old man might have a heart attack and die on the spot at the news. He had to be close to ninety by now; he'd been old all her life.

She swung around to the fire station. Maybe she could talk one of the firemen into going with her. It made more sense than going alone. Most of the men who volunteered at the station had more training in emergency care than she did; Hank had seen to that over the years.

Alex smiled. At least she wouldn't have to worry about Hank being at the firehouse. He always worked his ranch during the week. If he did come into the station, it was usually before dawn to work out or at night for a meeting.

She told herself she could care less about his habits, but it was hard to miss his huge Dodge pickup when it was parked directly across from her office. She pulled into the empty spot marked as his and ran up the steps.

"Morning, Sheriff," Willie Davis yelled from beside the fire truck's engine.

Willie was the youngest volunteer fireman. He was rail thin and had hair that always seemed a month past needing a cut.

Willie had quit school two years ago, but Hank hadn't let him start training until he was eighteen. Then, he couldn't get enough of the station. If Hank had allowed it, Willie would have moved in permanently.

"You missed a spot." She pointed at the dirty bumper.

He sloshed his bucket back a few steps and frowned. "You're right."

Alex didn't step closer, fearing he'd accidentally turn the water hose toward her. "Anyone else around?" Willie would be little help on her mission. At the rate he was learning, he'd be in training for another ten years.

"Hank's in the office. He had to drop his truck off for an oil change, so he said he'd catch up on paperwork till the work was done. You want me to go get him?"

She backed away. "No. Never mind. I don't want to bother him."

Hank stepped out of the office before she could get out of sight. "What do you need, Sheriff?" he asked as if they barely knew each other.

"Nothing really."

He kept staring at her with those dark eyes she swore were more black than brown. He had chameleon eyes, she decided, changing with his moods.

She knew he'd never believe she'd dropped by to visit, so she decided the truth would be the best way not to look like a fool. "I was just headed out to Truman's place to give him some bad news, and I thought there might be one of your men around who'd come along in case the old man takes it hard." She started backing out the door. "But I see everyone is busy."

"I'll go with you." He grabbed his jacket and hat. "Willie, load up one of the medical aid kits in the back of the sheriff's car."

Alex wanted to argue that he didn't need to come, but she wouldn't risk a life just because she hated the thought of being with Hank. They were both professionals. They could ride a few miles out of town and back without yelling or hitting one another. After all, this was Thursday morning, not Saturday night.

Heading out to her car, she tried not to think about what happened at ten every Saturday night. Her life felt like some kind of reverse fairy tale. When the clock struck ten, her mind filled with the memory of her brother lying spread out on the center stripe of a two-lane road. He'd bled so much a river of red had run off the asphalt and into the dirt.

It had been three years ago. She'd just returned to Harmony that night, a week away from graduation and wanting to celebrate. Alex had been waiting in her brother's office for him to get off work when the call came in that he was in trouble. She'd ridden out with one of the patrolmen, thinking her brother must have had a flat or dead battery.

But his patrol car was still running, its lights on bright, shining across his body. She'd watched from the shadows as Hank Matheson and two medics fought for her brother's life . . . Hank had kept fighting even after the others stopped. Finally, he'd held his best friend, her brother, and cried as he said good-bye.

And she'd watched and said nothing . . . done nothing.

Silently, Hank now climbed into her cruiser. Alex pushed her memories aside as she threw the car into reverse before he closed the door.

They were almost out of town before he asked, "What's the bad news for old Jeremiah Truman?"

"Beverly Truman died almost a week ago. It took a few days to find anyone to call who knew her next of kin, and then the morgue in Oklahoma City couldn't get in touch with Jeremiah. Apparently he doesn't have a phone. They overnighted him a letter three days ago, but I wouldn't be surprised if the old guy never bothered to open it."

"So they called you?"

"Right." She glanced over at Hank, who was frowning as usual. "How do you think he'll take the news that his last relative has died?"

"I don't know. He's had two heart attacks that I know of. My aunt checks on him now and then since we're neighbors, but every time she does, she comes back mad and claiming the old guy doesn't have a heart. Last time she took him her Christmas sponge cake, he declared it to be far more sponge than cake, and you know how Aunt Pat feels about her prizewinning cakes." Hank grinned. "Aunt Pat says it's hell being a good Methodist with old Truman for a neighbor."

Alex smiled, finding it hard to imagine Miss Pat ever saying *hell*. The old woman and her sister were in church every time the door was unlocked.

Hank was silent for a minute, then added, "You were right to come get me. The old man may take it hard. He's not the last Truman, though. His great-niece is living with him."

Alex turned off the main road. "What niece?"

"The one we—" Hank stopped. "Never mind, you wouldn't remember. Edith said the girl is Beverly's granddaughter. I don't know where she came from, but she's been out there since Saturday night."

Alex kept her eyes on the road. "How old is she?"

"About fifteen or sixteen, I guess. She'd be in school right now."

"I'll go there next. She may want to come home." Alex turned off Lone Oak Road and into the long tunnel of evergreens that led up to the house. The road was neglected, with steep drop-offs in places where pavement should have been, and trees blocked the sun. "Overgrown," she said to herself as she looked at the tumbleweeds and trash caught in the low branches.

"Fire hazard," Hank added. "One spark and these trees would burn all the way to the house. Half of them are more brown than green."

They pulled to a stop. Hank followed her up to the front door.

Nobody answered when she knocked.

"His truck is here." Hank pointed at an old pickup parked beside the house. "He's probably in the orchard."

"If he were around the house, that dog of his would be barking." Alex looked around. "Last time the old canine chased me all the way back to my car. I don't know if he has enough teeth left to bite anyone, but I didn't want to take a chance."

Alex walked back to her car and reached in. She honked twice and waited. "When I got the news," she said quietly to Hank, who had joined her by the car, "I called Tyler Wright and woke him up. He said he'd take care of the details. The body's already been embalmed so it could be shipped, but Tyler said he'd go get it. He said Miss Beverly would want it that way."

From a distance, they heard the puttering sound of the cart Jeremiah drove around his place. The dog was riding shotgun, growling louder than the motor.

Alex stood straight, waiting, dreading her duty. After more than a hundred years, the three of them represented the original families of Harmony: the McAllens, the Mathesons, and the Trumans. How strange it seemed that two of the families had multiplied many times over but the Trumans were almost all gone.

Beverly had been Jeremiah's only sister. She'd had two children, both already buried in the Harmony Cemetery. The son divorced without children. No one had ever heard of the daughter marrying, though she'd been gone from Harmony for twenty years before she died. She could have had ten husbands and a dozen kids from the time she left until Beverly brought her home to be buried. Apparently she'd had at least the one. Strange that Beverly never mentioned Reagan. Maybe she hadn't approved of her daughter's choices or known about children left abandoned along the way. Maybe her daughter wanted nothing to do with Beverly or the town she grew up in and had kept secrets. Most people leave out details they don't like about their family but it seemed odd that Beverly Truman left out a granddaughter.

The cart came into view from between the trees. The old man leaned over the steering wheel, his body so thin she swore she could see the outline of his bones from a hundred yards away.

Sucking in a breath, she steeled herself for what she had to do. Hank's hand pressed lightly against the middle of her back. "Breathe," he said in a none-too-friendly order.

She pushed his hand away. "I hate doing this."

"I know," he whispered.

"What're you two doing here?" Jeremiah yelled when he was ten feet away. "It's too far away from Halloween for you to be coming dressed up like civil servants."

Alex waited until he came to a stop. Just as he'd always been old to her, she'd probably always be a kid to him, she thought. "Good morning, Mr. Truman."

He unfolded from the cart without offering his hand in greeting. "What do you need? I'm betting you didn't come out to pass the time and since I don't smell smoke, Matheson, it must be the sheriff making an official visit."

"You're right," Hank said. "Why don't we step into the shade on the porch?"

Jeremiah tugged off his hat and let stringy white hair blow in the breeze. "Bad news don't taste better in the shade. I'll take it in the sun, thanks anyway."

Alex cleared her throat and did her job. Efficiently, cleanly, without emotion.

Jeremiah stood in front of them and took the news of the death of his sister with no change of expression. His hard face must have frozen into a frown years ago. Only a nod told Alex he'd even heard her words.

Hank had moved close enough to Truman to be able to catch the old man if he collapsed.

When Alex finished talking, Jeremiah looked out at the orchard and said nothing.

"Would you like me to drive you to town so you can talk to Tyler Wright later about the arrangements?" she finally asked.

"No," he responded. "He'll know more what Beverly would want than I would. Tell him to just do it and send me the bill." He dropped his hat, but didn't seem to notice.

Hank picked it up and tried to hand it to the old man, but Jeremiah just looked at his feet. Hank placed the hat in the back of the cart.

"What about your niece?" Alex wished the old guy would at least look at her. "Hank said she moved in with you last week. I could go get her from school so you wouldn't be alone out here."

"My niece?" Truman huffed as if he'd forgotten he ever had a niece.

"Mr. Truman," Hank said politely. "You remember her. Reagan."

Truman looked at Hank as if he'd just noticed the man was there. "Of course I remember Reagan. She's been helping me for almost a week. Good worker, that one, even if she can down more eggs than a lumberjack."

"I'll go get her." Alex glanced at Hank.

He seemed to read her mind. "I'll stay here until you get back, Sheriff."

Truman grumbled that he didn't need a babysitter, but Alex ignored him. If Truman could forget he had a niece, he didn't need to be left alone.

In her car, she circled back down the tree-lined road to the pavement and headed toward town.

Five minutes later, she walked into the high school office and asked to see Reagan Truman.

Chapter 9

REAGAN WATCHED A STUDENT OFFICE AIDE deliver a note to the worst history teacher in the world. The teacher paused in his dull lecture to read the note and then look directly at her.

She was in trouble. She knew it.

"Reagan Truman," he snapped. "You're wanted in the office."

As she gathered up her books, Reagan heard the aide whisper to one of her friends in the front row, "By the sheriff."

The urge to run bubbled in Reagan's blood. Big trouble. She tried to think of something she'd done lately. She had been in school only four days . . . not long enough even to have skipped a class. She did steal that pint of whiskey she'd paid for her ride from Oklahoma City to Harmony with . . . but surely the law wouldn't track her across the state line for that.

As she walked past Noah McAllen, he winked at her. "Maybe you won the lottery, Rea."

She tried to smile. "I didn't buy a ticket, Preacher."

"Tell me about it at lunch," he offered.

"If I'm still on the loose."

He laughed. Apparently he thought she was kidding.

Just outside the door, the tall woman sheriff was waiting. She was too pretty to be a warden in a B movie, but she was all business just the same. Even if Reagan had thought of an escape plan, she wouldn't have had time. Sheriff McAllen looked totally sober today and perfectly capable of arresting her.

"Reagan Truman?"

"That's me." She thought of adding *Almost*, but saw no need to confess to any new crimes. Besides, swapping out her last name didn't seem like a major crime.

"Mind if we take a walk outside?" the sheriff asked, but Reagan knew it wasn't really a question.

Reagan followed the sheriff out the door. This made sense. By the time the law finished listing her crimes, they'd be at the police car and the sheriff could toss her in the back.

"I got some bad news," the sheriff said. Reagan started, not from the words, but from the sheriff's arm around her shoulders.

"I just came from your uncle's house."

"Did he die?" Reagan pulled away from the sheriff. "Don't tell me he died." If he died, she might as well cut herself up in little pieces and market herself on the Internet as a bite of bad luck.

McAllen mistook panic for caring. "No, honey, he didn't die. He's fine, but I'm real sorry to tell you your grandmother did pass away."

Reagan hid her face in her hands, needing time to figure out her imaginary family tree. Her made-up great-uncle was still alive; good. Her made-up grandmother was dead. No news there. Only the town must just be finding out about Beverly Truman. If the sheriff had told Jeremiah, and now was here calling him her uncle, the old man must know she'd lied to everyone about being his niece. Reagan decided she'd been nuts to think he wouldn't find out, but she had hoped it would be later, not this soon.

The arm of the law came around her again. "I'm so sorry," Sheriff McAllen whispered. "Go ahead and cry if you feel like it, Reagan."

Cry! She wanted to scream nonstop. The old man was just starting to like her . . . well enough to grunt at her over breakfast, at least. He hadn't even paid her yet and she'd worked almost a week. Now, he'd probably have her arrested for impersonating a Truman. One hope flashed through her thoughts: Jeremiah hadn't told the sheriff she wasn't his niece. Maybe he was waiting to expose her in front of others, or maybe, just maybe he also wanted to believe in the lie.

Reagan didn't look at the sheriff as they drove

back to his place. McAllen was saying all the things she figured a sheriff would say. Reagan tried to think of where she could go next. Oklahoma City wasn't an option, and when Jeremiah told the sheriff she wasn't his niece, staying here wouldn't be possible, either. Reagan knew that clinging to the hope he'd go along with her lie now was about as likely as trying to convince herself he liked having her around.

She had two dollars in her pocket and nowhere to go from here.

They got to the farm so fast she swore they must have teleported. Reagan kept her head down as she followed the sheriff up the steps where Jeremiah and the fire chief who'd given her a ride out last week were waiting. There was no telling if Truman was furious. He looked angry on good days.

Hank Matheson nodded at her in greeting, but didn't speak as Reagan passed him and faced the old man. If Hank planned to complain about her not returning his flashlight, he'd have to get in line. A wholesale load of trouble was already headed her direction.

"I'd like to talk to my niece alone." Jeremiah looked over Reagan's head at the sheriff and Hank. "You two can take the cart and go see how the apple trees are doing. Hank, I expect your aunt Pat will want some this year as always. I put in a gate in the fence between your land and mine. She's getting too old to climb over the fence and check on the trees." He waved them on with one bony hand. "You tell her I'm taking good care, and both of you stay out of the mud where I'm irrigating."

Reagan fought down an unexpected smile. Jeremiah was treating the sheriff and the fire chief like they were ten years old.

Jeremiah motioned her into the house as the cart pulled away toward the apple trees. For a second she thought about calling them back, but something inside her knew she had to face the old man alone. She owed him that much. He had a right to have his say after what she'd done.

He went to the first room to the left of the front door. It looked like an old parlor Reagan had seen once in a movie set. She'd never set foot in it and, from the layer of dust, she guessed he hadn't either in years.

He ordered her to open the shutters. "We got some things to straighten out, girl. We might as well do it in the light."

"Yes, sir," Reagan said, giving him a mock salute. If she was going to get kicked out, she'd go her own way.

"Don't get smart with me," he said as he pulled the cover off an old rolltop desk. "We ain't got time."

He sat in an office swivel chair while Reagan fought with the shutters for several minutes. When the room finally flooded with sunlight, she took a seat on the nearest window bench and waited.

About the time she decided he must have slipped into a coma, Jeremiah reached for something.

Reagan stared as he retrieved a roll of bills tied with a rubber band from one of the pigeonhole drawers.

He looked up at her and, for the first time, she saw sadness in his eyes. The kind of sadness that made her heart hurt to look at it. She dropped the attitude and leaned closer, recognizing grief so deep he couldn't speak of it.

No word she could have said would have helped.

Finally, he took a deep breath and cleared his throat. The mask of anger returned to all of his face except his eyes. "I have no desire to go to town and have folks hugging on me just because Beverly died. It won't bring her back. She was a silly woman who should have stayed here with her family."

"She wasn't silly," Reagan corrected. "I think she just liked her privacy."

He glared at her. "So you did know her. That much at least isn't a lie."

"I cleaned her room at the nursing home where I worked after school and read the paper to her. Sometimes I even read her letters to her. We'd talk about Harmony."

"She tell you why she left?"

Reagan shook her head. Miss Beverly had been sad, but not lonely. There's a difference. Even though all her friends were miles away and she only talked to them in letters, Reagan got the feeling she wanted it that way. Beverly had told her once she had a hundred books she'd planned all her life to read. If Reagan had thought about it at all, she probably figured that was why Beverly stayed at a quiet place like the home.

Jeremiah huffed. "She said it was because she couldn't live with the memories of her husband and kids in town and she didn't want to live with me out here."

"I guess you two weren't close."

He was silent for a few moments. "I was in the army by the time she started school. When I came home, she was grown and married. We were never close. A part of me still thinks of her as that little girl I'd swing around. We never had much to say to each other after I came home from the war, but she was my sister and I want to do right by her."

He shoved the money toward Reagan. "You go into town with the sheriff. Buy a new dress for Beverly, a nice one, and order a big bunch of flowers to set on top of the casket. Beverly would like that. Just tell the store to make sure Tyler Wright gets them as soon as possible."

Reagan almost swallowed her gum. "All right," she managed.

He wasn't finished. "While you're there, you might as well get yourself some clothes. Something nice for the funeral and whatever you need for school. I'm tired of looking at those you

71

got on. I've seen refugees fresh off the boat who dress better than you do."

"But . . ." Reagan couldn't argue with his opinion of the clothes. They were hand-me-downs from the thrift store. But the money . . . She'd never held this much money in her hand in her entire life.

"If everybody in town thinks you're my niece, you might as well look like you're not living on the streets." He stared at her. "When the funeral's over, I'll go into town and set up a few accounts for you so you can charge what you need at the drugstore and that Lady Bug store that claims to have everything females need. I'll not tolerate excess, but I am aware a girl needs certain things."

"You're not kicking me out?"

"You got somewhere else you want to go?"

"No." She almost added, nowhere that she *could* go, but she figured he already knew that if she was staying here.

"Spend what you need and put any left over back in this drawer along with the receipts." He pointed at the square little drawer in the middle of the desk. "If you want to air out this room, you can. It's yours to use if you need it." He cleared his throat. "Beverly always liked to read in this room when she was a kid."

Reagan twisted the roll of money in her hand. No one had ever trusted her with a dime. "Thanks for letting me stay . . . Uncle Jeremiah."

She waited for an explosion, but none came.

He moved to the front door. She followed and they watched a battered old pickup pull up behind the sheriff's car. "I'm the last Truman," he whispered, more to himself than her. "If you want to pretend to be family for a while, I don't mind."

Reagan shifted beside him, guessing he wouldn't welcome a hug. "If I go to town with the sheriff, how do I get home?"

"It ain't that far. I've walked it many a time," he said. "But, if you want, I'll drive over about five and pick you up near the post office. We could go to the funeral home and pay our respects. I imagine Beverly will be waiting there by then."

They walked onto the porch just as Noah "Preacher" McAllen reached the first step. The old dog, who barked at everything, including fireflies, was licking Noah's left hand in welcome.

"Who are you?" Jeremiah demanded. "Folks are wearing out my road today."

Preacher removed his hat. "Noah McAllen," he said. "And if you don't mind me saying, there's not much of a road to wear out, sir."

Jeremiah snorted, and Reagan wondered if that was his idea of a laugh.

"I heard about your sister dying, Mr. Truman, and I'm real sorry," Noah said. "I want you to know if there's anything I can do to help . . ."

Jeremiah frowned. "News travels fast."

Noah smiled. "Cell phones. I called my sister

when I heard she'd pulled Rea out of class, and she told me. I came straight over to see what I can do."

The old man stared, taking measure of the kid before him. "You could drive her to town. She'll be making the arrangements. I've got work here that can't wait."

Reagan shoved the money into her pocket, and Noah barely had time to say good-bye before she pulled him toward the truck.

Once they were on the road, an awkward silence rested between them. Preacher looked like he was worried about her breaking into tears. Reagan couldn't tell him that she'd known Miss Beverly was dead for almost a week.

Finally, she broke the silence. "How come old Dog didn't bite you? He still looks at me like I'm a burglar half the time."

Noah shrugged. "I'm good with dogs and babies."

"Try again."

He smiled. "I tossed him the last of yesterday's lunch I'd left in the truck. He ate it, bag and all."

Chapter 10

HANK GRABBED TWO OF THE WALKING STICKS in the back of the cart and handed one to Alexandra.

She followed along behind him, glad to be away from the scene at the house. "Does your aunt

Pat really climb over the fence and steal apples?"

"Yep, and I drive the getaway car. She says they make the best pies in the county. She also considers it her duty to check on the trees now and then to make sure Jeremiah is taking care of things."

Alex pulled on one of the branches, feeling it give in her hand even though it looked dead with winter.

"Now if you'd like to join the thieving come spring," Hank said, "you have to do it right, so listen to the rules. Only get the ones on the ground. Aunt Pat says then it's not stealing, it's retrieving."

Alex laughed at the thought of Hank's eighty-year-old aunt stealing apples. "You know I could arrest her for it whether she's picking or lifting."

"Go ahead," he said as if he meant it. "One less woman at my ranch would suit me fine. I got my mom, two widowed great-aunts, two divorced sisters, and a four-year-old fairy princess. I haven't said a word at the dinner table in five years."

Alex raised an eyebrow. She almost felt sorry for him. No wonder he spent so much time at the fire station. The old family ranch had been his unofficially since he turned eighteen, but his mother had always lived there. When Hank's two great-aunts retired from teaching school years ago, they moved in. Then Hank's sisters came home a few months ago, both broken from divorces. She couldn't imagine how Hank handled them all. Two old women, two divorced women, a mother who thought of herself as an artist, and a four-year-old niece too ill to walk.

When Alex looked up, he was smiling. She'd almost forgotten what he looked like when he smiled.

"Arrest them all," he said. "I could use the silence. Aunt Pat may steal them, but Aunt Fat eats them."

Alex laughed. Hank had always called his two great-aunts Pat and Fat, even though his aunt Fat was thin. She'd known the two old ladies all her life and had no idea what their first names were. When they'd taught they'd both been called Miss Matheson.

"How long have you been helping your aunt in these robberies?" She pointed a finger at him.

"All my life." He held the old walking stick up as if on guard. "Plan on arresting me, too?"

"No. It'd just be a waste of time. Your aunt would recruit another mule to haul her loot. I might as well wait until I catch you all red-handed."

She swung her stick in challenge. He blocked. She swung again, and the fight was on. They moved into the shadows of the trees where the air was still and cold. Something seemed different here. As if they'd stepped out of the real world and into the Sherwood Forest of their childhood dreams.

The aroma of freshly watered soil circled around them. She wondered if Hank felt it, too, but she didn't ask for fear of breaking the spell.

When he raised his hands in surrender, she laughed, remembering how it had always been Hank who let her win when they were children and never her brother Warren.

She looked at him, wondering if he, too, was remembering how the three of them had played in the trees as children. But Hank's eyes were smiling. They were two outlaws now. Old man Truman had chased them off so many times, he'd learned their names.

When they set the sticks in the bed of the cart, he grinned. "Thanks for the memory, Little John."

"You're welcome, Robin," she returned. "But next time, I want to be Sundance and you can be Butch." She rubbed the mud off her boot on the dried grass. "We go for the gold on a train."

He touched two fingers to his hat. "You bet."

They climbed into the cart and drove back to the farmhouse. By the time they'd said good-bye to Jeremiah and were in her car, they were no longer outlaws—just two responsible people doing their jobs.

Chapter 11

≫≪

TYLER WRIGHT LEFT A NOTE FOR WILLAMINA and drove out before dawn. He wanted to get to Oklahoma City and back before two. That was when he liked to send his first e-mail to Kate, his hazel-eyed pen pal. She usually didn't answer until close to five, but it didn't matter; he got a kick out of waiting, checking, anticipating.

When she did e-mail back it had been the same answer for four days. Yes, she'd have dinner with him. He'd fill his plate and stare at the screen while he ate.

He took the back roads so he could speed, knowing that on the way back, he'd stay on the main highway out of respect for dear Miss Beverly. She'd dropped by his office about a month after her husband died and made plans for her own funeral. She had little left besides her Social Security, but she wanted to pay for her funeral so no one would be out anything.

Tyler doubted that her brother, Jeremiah, had any money. He was land rich and money poor, like most folks around. Beverly had said she didn't want to bother anyone. She'd cried when she told him that her husband had borrowed money from almost everyone in town and never offered to pay any of it back. Her husband had thought of it as a game, but she'd been ashamed for years. Ashamed enough to change back to her maiden name after forty years of marriage. She'd paid for her funeral, then given Tyler a slip of paper with all the people in town she owed. She asked him to keep it until Jeremiah died and then ask whoever handled the family farm if they'd pay each one back with her half from the sale of the land.

Frowning, Tyler doubted the slip of paper would hold up in any court. Jeremiah wouldn't sell any of the land, not even to pay his brother-in-law's debts, and now that he'd outlived Beverly, he owned all the land.

As Tyler drove, the sun was coming up. He was forty years younger than old Jeremiah, but in a way they were the same. When they died, so did the family line. When Tyler had been younger, he'd always thought there was plenty of time ahead in which to have children. He had a business to run and his hobby to keep him busy. He was too young to marry in his twenties, not ready in his thirties, and now in his forties he could not think of a single woman he would want to date. Or, to be fair, who would want to date him.

Tyler would never sell the funeral home, not for any amount of money. If he did, he'd have no home, no roots. But he had thought he'd have a wife and children living with him by now.

Three years ago he'd had a blind date with someone's cousin who was visiting Harmony after her divorce. They'd gone out a few times for dinner and managed to keep a conversation going, but when he'd reached for her hand, she'd pulled back. When he walked her to the door, she explained that she couldn't stand the thought of touching a hand that had touched dead people all day.

He hadn't bothered to explain the thousand things about his job that didn't involve touching dead people.

Tyler smiled suddenly. Tonight, when he visited with Kate, he'd ask her what she thought of blind dates. Everything they talked about was interesting. They'd discussed a dozen topics, and she'd never hesitated to tell him her opinion. She loved Mexican food, hated lines at the grocery store, loved her country, hated subways in every town in the world, fought against gun control, and had campaigned for women's rights since she could walk.

He had a feeling Kate was a woman no one would ever talk into anything, but no discussion would ever be dull. He even liked the little codes she had for her favorite swear words.

A little after ten, Tyler picked up Beverly Truman's body, then drove three blocks and pulled around the drive-through at Sonic for a foot-long chili-cheese dog and tater tots, and headed back to Harmony. He'd be home in time to send his e-mail.

Chapter 12

"ARE YOU SURE YOUR UNCLE TOLD YOU TO spend all this money?" Noah asked for the third time.

"All I need, he said." They'd already stopped by the flower shop and were now searching through racks at the Lady Bug for a dress for Miss Beverly. Reagan took her mission as seriously as if it were life or death. Jeremiah trusted her, and she'd decided she would not let him down.

Noah pulled out T-shirts that said things like BORN TO BE WILD and TAKE ME TO YOUR LEADER. "How about buying something like this, Rea?" he asked, holding it up to her as if trying to guess her size.

Reagan closed her eyes and repeated her orders from her new uncle. "Flowers for the casket, a dress for her, and clothes for me." She shoved the T-shirt away. "Nothing else. I can't waste money."

Noah scratched his head. "I don't see anything in this place that looks like dead old lady clothes." He picked up a sundress with tiny pink flamingos on it.

The sales clerk hovering around them must have heard him. "You're looking for a dress for someone who's passed on?"

He nodded and explained everything to this

woman Reagan had never seen before. Then to Reagan's surprise, the lady told them to go to the funeral home. The woman was missing a sale, but was still trying to help them out.

So they drove over to the funeral home, where they found boxed clothes for the dead.

Reagan dug through the boxes while Noah wandered around. "This is great," she said. "I never dreamed they had this kind of thing. Every one of these looks like Miss Beverly. She's probably been buying her clothes here for years."

Noah leaned out from behind an open coffin. "You mean your grandmother?"

"Yes," she said without meeting his eyes. "I didn't really know her." She tried to think of something that wasn't a lie. "The people where she lived just called her Miss Beverly, so I guess that's the way I think of her."

Reagan picked out a pretty blue dress with a white lace collar. She handed it to the woman, who'd followed them from the front desk, who smiled and promised Miss Beverly would be ready for viewing in a few hours. She was so nice Reagan almost wanted to stay around and visit. Almost.

Noah stopped at the Burger Barrel and bought Reagan lunch. She saved half for Jeremiah's old dog. It was time they made friends.

Then Noah drove her to the mall. The center of the mall had two cookie places, a deserted hot dog stand, and a McDonald's with a huge sign that read: LIMITED MENU. The only mall rats were a dozen walkers over eighty.

"How does this place stay in business?" Reagan whispered.

Noah grinned. "You should see it on a slow day."

They went shopping for her clothes. Noah took the work seriously, making fun of half the things she tried on, wiggling his eyebrows when he thought something was wrong, and smiling with all his teeth showing when she tried on western clothes.

In the end, she bought three pairs of jeans, six shirts, one dress, and a cowboy hat she thought looked ridiculous. He promised her it looked cute, and she almost believed him.

"Now you got the hat," he said as they walked out of the store, "you got to come watch me ride this weekend."

"All right. If you'll come to the funeral."

He stopped on the steps and faced her. "Of course I'll come. We're friends, Rea. That's what friends do for each other."

She wondered if he could tell that all this friends stuff was new to her. "I've never been to a funeral," she admitted. "I'm not sure what to do."

"Rea, I don't think anyone really knows what to do at a funeral. I usually just keep my eyes looking down and hug everyone who wants to hug me. Some folks think they have to do that to all the family left behind to suffer the loss."

"You've had family die?"

"Sure, my big brother, Warren, three years ago. I cried all the way through the funeral. I couldn't tell you one thing anyone said."

"How'd he die?"

"He was killed on duty. He was a highway patrolman on his way to becoming a Texas Ranger. A man ran a roadblock and when Warren caught up to him, the guy shot him in the face when he walked up to the car. Strange thing was, the man was only wanted for outstanding speeding tickets. Warren wouldn't have even taken him in that night. He killed my brother for nothing."

"That's really sad."

He straightened as if pushing sadness aside. "You want to hug me?" he asked with a smile that didn't quite reach his eyes.

"No," she answered and smiled back.

"Times like this are like muddy water, Rea, you just got to keep moving through it until you get to the other side."

SHE HAD NO IDEA HOW TRUE HIS WORDS WERE, but she thought of them several times over the next two days. People brought food to the house and hugged her. They went to the funeral home and everyone there hugged her. Jeremiah had a graveside service and it looked like half the town came and most of them hugged her.

Reagan was all hugged out by the time she got

home. Jeremiah must have felt the same, for he went back to his room without a word or a bite to eat and she didn't see him again the rest of the evening.

She went to her room and closed the door. *My room*, Reagan thought. Beverly would never be back to claim it. She could paint the walls or move things around. But she decided, for right now anyway, she'd leave it the same. In a funny way, Reagan thought Miss Beverly would smile if she knew Reagan was sleeping there.

Jeremiah was cooking breakfast in his work clothes when she came downstairs the next morning. All the flowers folks had brought to the house were gone, along with the cards and cakes. He must have thought it was time to get back to normal.

She silently agreed, having no idea what normal was, but it had to be better than the mud of funeral days.

Chapter 13
∽∂〇∾

ALEXANDRA MCALLEN LEANED AGAINST HER patrol car and wiped the sweat from her throat. The morning was warm and her bulletproof vest always made it seem hotter. She'd been standing in the sun for a half hour trying to solve the latest crime in Harmony.

"I'm telling you, Sheriff," Dallas Logan said, not for the first time. "Every night it's not raining or cloudy some fool shoots this light out and I've had enough of it. You got to do something."

The overweight woman huffed, raising her breasts as if she'd use them as battering rams to get something done. At five feet nothing, she might not be intimidating, but she tried to talk everyone she met to death. "I've made a list of who I think it might be. All you got to do is go house to house investigating and you'll find someone who owns a rifle."

Dallas shifted from foot to foot as if playing some kind of senior citizen dodgeball. "You might have to cast a wide net, Sheriff McAllen. Last week, Stella McNabb came to the canasta game at my house and commented twice about how the glare of artificial light didn't seem natural in the night. You ask me, there's something wrong with her. I've seen it in folks who've never lived in town." Dallas wiggled her finger. "They frown at things you and me accept. I know for a fact Stella's never used the ATM. Now tell me that ain't strange. Might be worth a look to check her husband's car for a gun."

Alex guessed everyone within a hundred miles owned a rifle. "I think we'll just replace the bulb."

The round little woman huffed. "That's what you did last week and the week before that."

Alex thought about saying, *You win, Mrs. Logan,*

I'll round up everyone for five blocks around and interrogate them for hours without food or water. We'll get to the bottom of this crime if I have to jail half the town.

"I had to fight to get this light here, you know. It wasn't easy. Ronelle and I went down to the courthouse a dozen times before we finally got them to put it up. This corner was far too dark. All kinds of worthless people could walk right up and look into our windows at night and we'd never know."

Somehow, Alex doubted Ronelle had held up her half of the fight at the courthouse. She'd said good morning to the girl every day since she'd been sheriff, and the postal worker had yet to answer back. If Alex started investigating broken bulbs, the next thing she'd have to do would be to search down the criminal who was working all the crossword puzzles in magazines before they were stuffed into mailboxes. Alex had a pretty good idea who was behind the post office crime, but until someone filed an official complaint, she wouldn't say a word to Ronelle.

Dallas Logan was still complaining about every neighbor around her when Hank Matheson and Willie Davis drove up with a ladder from the firehouse.

They got out and replaced the bulb without a word.

"Well, it's about time," Mrs. Logan said when they were finished.

Alex mouthed a thank-you to Hank.

He smiled. "The city boys were busy with a water leak, so I thought we'd pitch in."

Dallas Logan waddled back to her house mumbling to herself.

Alex watched Willie sweep up the glass, forcing herself not to look at Hank. They hadn't seen each other since the day in the orchard almost a week before.

Hank broke the silence. "Someone said your little brother won a buckle at the rodeo Saturday night."

"Yeah, my dad drove over from Amarillo to watch. We're all real proud of Noah, but I'm not surprised he takes to bull riding; Dad started putting him on sheep when he was four, calves by the time he was seven. I swear, I can still hear the echoes of Mom and Dad's fights over him trying to breed rodeo into his sons' blood. It didn't take with Warren, but Noah claims he was born to ride rough stock."

"Can't blame your dad," Hank said. "He was the best bull rider in the country when he was younger. I remember he took Warren and me with him to the rodeo in San Antonio once. He'd been retired for years by then, but every cowboy in the place paid their respects."

She couldn't argue with that. Her father had always been bigger than life. He had won his first national title before he turned twenty. When he'd finally given it up, everyone in town probably saw the restlessness in him. He'd started a cattle trucking company based out of Amarillo and was gone most nights. Warren took over taking care of the ranch and helping raise Noah while she went away to college. Their dad was always there, somewhere in the background . . . far in the background, but never around when they needed help with homework or just wanted to talk.

When Warren died, their dad lost what little interest he had in the ranch and moved full time to Amarillo. The fighting she'd grown up hearing between her parents now had settled into a polite-stranger kind of talk. They'd never gone to court to end the marriage, but any love they'd ever known had been beaten to death by words long ago.

"Your father stayed over Saturday night, right?" Hank's words broke into her thoughts.

She knew it wasn't a question. Hank was figuring out why he hadn't gotten a call Saturday night to come get her from one of the bars. He figured she'd already had a babysitter for the night—her dad.

Right there on that street corner in the middle of town, she wanted to scream at him that she didn't need him sitting up worrying about her every Saturday night. She didn't have to drink away the memory of what happened to Warren.

"How is Adam McAllen these days?" Hank said, hiding all emotion in his face.

"My dad's fine. Made out of granite, you know."

"All finished," Willie announced, unaware that the sheriff and Hank were doing more than passing the time while he worked. "Who you think keeps doing this, Sheriff?"

"Someone who hates the streetlight, I guess," she answered.

"I know how they feel." Willie folded the ladder. "I used to have a light shining right in my window every night. I finally put up drapes."

Alex turned slowly in a full circle. The street was like most in town, a mixture of different sizes and conditions of homes. Dozens of windows faced the light. It could have been anyone.

Hank helped Willie load the ladder, then turned back to Alex. He frowned before he blurted out, "Any chance you got time to have lunch? My sister flew to Fort Worth to try and sell her paintings of men dying terrible deaths. My mother and aunts went along to go shopping. I've got Saralynn for the day, and she's decided she's a sheriff. I'm sure she'd like to talk to a colleague."

Alex laughed. "Where's your other sister? The one who doesn't paint dying men. Couldn't she watch the kid?"

Hank looked like a criminal about to confess. Miserable. Lost.

"Liz is going to a time management course put on by the library at noon. She thinks it'll help me. I'm sure I'll get the notes and a full lecture tonight."

"You?" Alex bit down a giggle. Hank Matheson did more than most five men in this town. He managed a ranch, ran the fire department, worked out every morning before dawn, corralled all the women in his life, and bullied her on Saturday night.

"Yeah, Liz thinks if I'd manage my time better, I'd have some hours left to date."

"Do you want to date?"

"No," he said. "I just want to have lunch with my niece and let you answer all her questions."

Hank had never been a man she thought she'd feel sorry for, but she took pity on him now. "Twelve thirty, Mexican Plaza?"

"Sounds great." He touched two fingers to the brim of the Stetson she'd bought him and turned away.

Chapter 14

HANK MATHESON HAD JUST CHECKED THE weather report when he noticed his sister Liz pull up in front of the station with Saralynn. He wasn't surprised. Even if she hadn't found a seminar to go to, two hours was about the maximum time Liz could handle babysitting. Thankfully, with all the women in the house, she wasn't asked to keep her niece often.

Liz claimed she didn't have a mothering bone in

her body. Hank wasn't sure, but he had a feeling that might have been the reason her five-year marriage ended. Unlike Claire, Saralynn's mother, who complained constantly about her ex-husband, Liz never said a word about her marriage other than it didn't work out.

"I'm running late!" Liz yelled as she opened the passenger door and unstrapped Saralynn from the car seat.

Hank rushed out in time to lift his niece carefully from the car. The leg braces she always wore clanked against the metal buckle on her child seat. "Maybe after the class you'll be able to manage your time better, Liz?"

"Don't be funny," she said, pulling out the child's bag of books and toys. "Claire called as I was loading the car and told me to make sure I gave the kid her medicine." She shoved the lunch bag of pills that always traveled with the four-year-old. "You'll have to do it. I don't have time to read which pill when."

He held his niece and both bags as Liz jumped back in her sports car and roared toward the First United Methodist Church.

"Good-bye," Saralynn whispered, and made a wave that wasn't answered.

"She just forgot to say good-bye to us," Hank said as he turned into the station. "We'll make her say hello twice when she gets back."

"No," Saralynn answered. "Someone stole her

manners. It's a crime I'll have to investigate." She had a plastic star pinned to her pink jumper and one of his old toy guns strapped around her waist.

"I got a surprise for you." He looked down at his niece, loving the imagination that made up for all she couldn't do. "We're having lunch with another sheriff. I thought you girls could compare notes on how to fight the bad guys."

Saralynn kissed his cheek. "I love you, Deputy Hank."

"I love you, too, Sheriff," he whispered.

An hour from now, the two sheriffs would be sharing stories along with chips at the Mexican Plaza. Hank couldn't stop smiling.

The restaurant was on the south end of town, a round building set far enough off the road that only locals could find it. At one time it had been called the Mexican Hat, but the owner got tired of the wind ripping off the awning that almost made the place look like a sombrero, so he put a fountain in the center of the place, painted every wall a different color, and called it a plaza.

Despite his plan not to, Hank showed up early.

Saralynn ordered the extra-extra-mild hot sauce, which tasted like ketchup to Hank, and watched the fish in the fountain until Alex arrived. All the tables by the fountain were small, made for two, but the owner made room for three chairs just because Saralynn was the first four-year-old sheriff he'd ever met.

Hank stood when Alex sat down across from him. This was as close as they'd come in three years to being friendly, and he didn't want to do anything to shatter the peace between them. He didn't mind that she barely looked at him. She was smiling at Saralynn and giving the girl her full attention.

When she had the child laughing, Alex dipped a chip into Saralynn's special hot sauce and ate it. She looked at Hank and made a face. He slid his bowl of sauce toward her. She dipped again, and this time smiled, waving her hand in front of her mouth. He passed her his glass of water and motioned for the waiter to bring more.

As they ate, Alex talked to Saralynn about the trials of being a sheriff, and Saralynn agreed as if she knew each one personally. Hank ate his chile rellenos and listened.

About the time the second basket of sopapillas was delivered, his knee bumped Alex's leg under the table.

He'd opened his mouth to say sorry, when he realized she'd stretched her long leg out toward him. He bumped it again and heard the slight catch in her voice. She didn't look at him. In fact, she seemed absorbed in the story Saralynn was telling her about how often trolls steal things and hide them in mismatched socks forever circling in the dryer.

He let his leg rest against hers.

She didn't move.

She was playing with him, he thought. He decided to play back. This lunch meeting was about to get far more interesting.

As the girls talked, Hank leaned forward, moved his hand beneath the little table, and slid his fingers along Alex's leg. Her muscles tightened beneath his touch. He heard her breathing grow shallow, but she didn't move away. Didn't look at him.

He shifted in the chair and slid his leg next to hers. All she'd have to do was move a fraction of an inch and they wouldn't be touching. But she didn't. He could feel the heat of her through his jeans. What they were doing made no sense. They couldn't say three sentences to each other without getting into an argument. She'd threatened to kill him a dozen times and tried to a few.

But something drew her to him. Something she probably didn't understand any better than he did. He liked the feel of her next to him, and he guessed she also did. He bumped her leg lightly, and she bumped his leg back.

He smiled, wishing she'd look at him. He had a feeling those stormy blue eyes of hers might be filled with something besides anger.

Alex's phone sounded and she moved her leg away. She took the call, then stood. "I have to leave, Sheriff Saralynn, but I've enjoyed having lunch with you."

"Me, too," Saralynn said. "Are you leaving because there's been a bank robbery?"

"No," Alex brushed her hand over the girl's cheek. "State investigators up from Austin want to talk to me about an old case that may come up for retrial soon. I didn't expect them until two. They're early."

Hank stood, studying her. "Maybe we can do this again."

Alex continued to look at Saralynn, who was busy feeding the fish the rest of her sopapilla.

"I don't think so," she said, and finally looked at Hank.

The old sadness was back. She was looking at him, but she was remembering her big brother. If Saralynn hadn't been there, he might have said something he would regret. Warren had been dead for three years. They'd both seen his body on the road that night. They'd both grieved. It was time Warren's memory stopped haunting them both.

She was gone before he could come up with a response.

AFTER LUNCH, HANK WENT BACK TO THE FIRE station. The wind had kicked up to about thirty miles an hour. With the lack of rain, he was starting to worry. The land was ripe for a fire. It was only a matter of time, and he had to get everything ready while he prayed nothing would happen. He made a mental note to call Bob McNabb. The guy was far too old to be active as a volunteer, but he knew more about grass fires than anyone around.

Saralynn sat in the only comfortable chair in his office, her braced legs covered with one of the extra blankets from the station, while he worked at his desk. After worrying over a training schedule for a while, he looked up and smiled at the sight of her concentration on her coloring book. The tip of her tongue stuck out of the corner of her mouth. She was so cute, she had to be an angel.

"I love you, kid."

She looked up. "I love you, too, Uncle Hank. Mom says you're the only good man left on the planet."

He grinned. "I'm sure you'll find another one, better than me, one day. Then you'll get married."

She shook her head. "I'm going to live with you and Grandma and Momma and Great-Aunt Fat and Great-Aunt Pat and Liz all my life."

"Liz is your aunt, too, you know."

She nodded. "I know, but she told me to call her just *Liz* because *Aunt Liz* dulls her down." Saralynn frowned. "Have any idea what she means, Uncle Hank?"

He hadn't understood either of his sisters since they were born. When they hit puberty and got their periods about the same time each month, it was like living with a serial killer and a suicidal manic. His mother used to say they'd grow out of it, but they were now twenty-seven and twenty-eight. He saw no sign of it yet.

Saralynn went back to her coloring, and he went

back to his paperwork and tried not to think of how good it had felt to slide his hand along Alex's leg. He wouldn't mind doing it sometime when she wasn't wearing trousers. And a gun, he thought.

A few minutes later he looked out the window and saw his mother's battered old Suburban pull up. The green truck was like a fixture in town. If she kept it much longer someone would stick a historical marker sign on the thing. Everyone knew where she and the old aunts were by where the van was parked.

Hank watched Claire, his redheaded, fiery sister, climb out of the Suburban and run toward the fire station. She hit his office door laughing.

She hugged Saralynn wildly and shouted, "They loved my paintings, baby! They loved Mommy's work."

"They did?" Hank and Saralynn said at the same time. Hank couldn't imagine anyone even giving them more than a blink of a glance. He'd seen one with a man spread out on a linen dining table. He'd been sliced apart about every inch down from his head to his toes. Claire had named the painting *Last Guest for Dinner*. He'd seen another one of a man's head with every tool he could think of implanted in his skull. She'd titled that one *The Perfect Tool*.

"Yes, they loved me." Claire circled around the room, dancing with an invisible partner. "They want me to do a show this spring. Imagine. My own show in Fort Worth. The walls of a gallery completely covered with my work."

Hank hoped the gallery didn't serve food at the opening. "That's great, Sis," he said. "I'm proud of you."

She lifted Saralynn. "We're celebrating tonight," she said to Hank. "Be home for supper by seven if you can."

"I wouldn't miss it." He picked up Saralynn's books and medicine bag and followed Claire out to the truck.

His two old aunts were on the third seat completely surrounded by shopping bags. "I see the hunt was successful." He grinned at them.

They both giggled. "We found Victoria's Secret," Aunt Fat whispered. "We went a little crazy, I'm afraid."

For a moment he pictured his bowling-ball shaped Aunt Pat walking the runway wearing one of the Victoria's Secret outfits of lace and feathers, or his aunt Fat in her thin frame wearing only underwear. The image made him want to grab the fire hose and screw it into his ear to blast the thought from his mind.

He closed the truck door and jogged back to his office in time to catch his phone before the answering machine picked up.

Chapter 15

≈≈

REAGAN STOOD IN THE SPOTLESS KITCHEN AND stared at Jeremiah. "It's not a date," she said, fighting down a scream.

"You're going out. He's picking you up." Jeremiah cut himself another slice of coconut pie. "If it walks like a duck and talks like a duck . . ."

She leaned closer and pointed her finger at his nose. "Don't start that duck logic with me again."

He shoved her finger away with his fork. "You're full of spitfire and vinegar, girl. I can't believe any boy'd want to take you out. You sure he's right in the head? If he's riding rough stock like his old man used to, he's probably got mush for brains. I don't think it'd be wise to date some fellow like that."

"It's not a date and if I'm hard to get along with, it only proves I'm related to you. As for brains, I'm not too sure. Maybe I'm the one with brain damage, going to a rodeo when I don't even know anything about it."

Old Jeremiah snorted. "Don't change the subject. You got brains. I ain't worried about that. Which reminds me, don't think for one minute I don't know you made this pie in hopes of sweetening me up."

"Did it work? I used an old recipe from the box

that looked like it was in Beverly's handwriting."

"No, it didn't work, but I will admit you make a fine pie." He carried the dessert to the table where his coffee waited. "And you can tell that boy who you're not having a date with that he'd better get you home early 'cause we got a full day of work tomorrow."

Reagan grabbed her hat. "I'll be ready to work at eight."

He stared at her. "You got money in your pocket? Never go nowhere without enough to get you home."

"I got money and I know my way home." She hurried out the door, almost choking on her last words. If he could call it her home, she could, too.

They'd work hard tomorrow and he'd complain about everything, but it didn't matter. For the first week she'd been at the most dilapidated place on Lone Oak Road, she'd counted the days, wondering how long it would be before he kicked her out. The second week, she'd been afraid to breathe. He'd known the truth about her, or at least some of it, and she thought any minute he'd tell everyone she'd lied about being a Truman. Then the state would come in and take her away even if she didn't want to go . . . even if he wanted her to stay.

Now, they'd made it two weeks. He was still griping about the chickens laying too many eggs, but he hadn't said a word about the things she'd bought in town. She'd been careful not to spend too much, but wondered if the old man had any idea how great it felt to have her own shampoo and soap and a hair dryer she didn't have to share. She had a dozen hangers in her closet with new clothes no one else had ever worn.

It couldn't last. Nothing lasted. But when it ended, she'd have something good to remember. She could look back and think of Harmony and the old house as home. And she'd feel, even if it were only for a little while, that she was with family.

Noah's truck bounced down the dirt road. "Ready?" he yelled when he saw her jump off the porch.

"Ready." She ran toward the truck as he leaned over and opened her door.

He never came to a complete stop as he circled the yard and headed back up the dirt road. "Hang on, Rea," he grinned at her. "We've got to make the forty miles to Bailee in thirty minutes."

"Does this thing go that fast?" She was so excited, she had to fight down squealing. She'd hung out with boys before. Not dates really, just group things where no one paired off until late. This was different. It might not be exactly a date, but it was the closest thing she'd ever had.

Deep down in her gut she wondered about what he'd do when it got late. From the few times she'd been around boys, she'd learned fast that they were like werewolves, changing into something different after midnight. She glanced at Noah, wondering if he would, too, and hating the thought that he might.

"Don't worry about this truck." He patted the steering wheel. "We'll make it. I thought we'd get to Bailee early and stop in town for a hamburger, but looks like I'll have to buy you dinner at the chuck wagon."

"You don't have to buy me dinner. I brought money."

He pulled onto the farm-to-market road and gunned the engine. "If you're with me, Rea, I pay. We may only be eating burritos out of the back of a truck, but I pay. That's the way it is."

She thought of telling him he was living in the past, but she didn't want to start the almost-date out with an argument. "But you have no idea how much I can eat."

He glanced at her. "I got twenty dollars in my pocket. If you eat more than that I'll borrow money from you and feed you, then I'll pay you back come Monday."

"Fair enough."

"I like that new shirt, Rea. It's not western, but it'll do."

She smiled her thanks. She'd been wearing T-shirts and jeans to school, but she wanted something different tonight. She'd found the plain blue shirt on sale in the boys' department.

Tucked in, with a white T-shirt underneath, she didn't think it looked bad.

They talked about school until they reached the small rodeo grounds just outside Bailee. Noah left her at the stands while he ran to register, and then they bought dinner at the food wagon parked beside the stands.

When men on horses began lining up at the far end of the arena, he stood, tugged off his coat, and dropped it over her shoulders. "Keep this on," he said.

"But I'm not cold."

"No one will bother you if you're wearing it. I'll be back after I ride."

There was something in his eyes she hadn't seen before. A warning. Looking around, she saw no one sinister, but she didn't argue with Noah. This wasn't the streets of the city. She doubted there were a hundred people in the stands, and they appeared to be high school kids or parents. Noah was gone before she could ask what it was she was supposed to be worried about.

The coat did feel good; it still had the warmth of him inside. Reagan pushed her hands through the arms and shoved up the sleeves. The patches on the jacket marked Noah as part of the rodeo team, and his giving it to her seemed to make her a part of the team. Almost.

As the sun set, she leaned back against the bleachers and watched her first rodeo. There was a way of life here, a whole subculture she'd never imagined. She watched it all, fascinated. There was almost a dance about it, the way the horses stomped in the soft dirt, the flash of fringe on the chaps, the flow of riders and ropes.

Noah rode saddle broncs first. He fell off almost before he was out of the chute. But the announcer yelled that they should all give "Preacher" a hand, and Reagan clapped as loud as she could as she watched him dust off his bottom and collect his hat from the dirt.

When they switched to team roping, her heart slowed down a little. She'd never been interested in any sport, but this was different. This was one-on-one with the challenge, and the men were helping and rooting for one another. Again and again she saw them pick up another rider's gear or jump off the gate to guard a downed cowboy from the wild spins of a bull. One man in baggy pants and a red shirt looked like a clown, but the announcer kept calling him the bullfighter. It didn't take long before she realized he was there not to entertain the crowd, but to help out when needed.

A body plopped down beside her on the bench, and Reagan knew it wasn't Noah before she turned her head.

"You here all by yourself?" a voice whispered so close she fought the urge to swat it away like a buzzing fly.

"No." Reagan turned to look at the overweight boy about her age who was sitting next to her. He wasn't dressed western but wore baggy pants and a black T-shirt with holes in it.

"I'm Brandon Biggs," he said, as if she cared. "I looked around and I noticed only one girl I didn't know. So this is your lucky night. I'm going to sit with you."

He seemed to notice the jacket she wore for the first time. "Who's that belong to? It's not yours, for sure. Way too big."

She didn't want to talk to this guy. Reagan had met creeps like him in every place she'd lived. He thought he ran the world. "It belongs to Preacher McAllen and I really wish you'd leave."

Brandon laughed. "It's a free country. I can sit here if I want to. Besides, I know who Preacher is. Saw him almost ride."

"Leave, or I'll leave."

She stood and moved one step sideways before he caught her hand.

"Don't go away. Preacher and me are tight. He wouldn't mind us hanging out." Brandon wiggled his eyebrows. "Besides, pestering you is far more interesting than this dumb old rodeo."

"But *I* mind. I'd rather sit somewhere else because I *am* interested in the rodeo." She didn't want to attract attention. "Let go of my arm."

Brandon opened his mouth to say something,

then looked past her and seemed to think better of it. He pulled his hand away and huffed. "Prickly little girl, aren't you? I was just trying to be friendly."

When she tried to move around him, he shifted his leg so she'd have to brush it to get past him on the narrow space.

Reagan *brushed* his leg hard with the heel of her shoe, a few inches below his shin.

He smiled for a second before her heel dug in, sliding down his leg, scraping skin as if it were the top layer of tree bark.

From the expression on his face it was obvious he was bleeding beneath his black jeans.

Pulling away, he let her pass, then yelled for some kid walking by to wait up. He limped down the steps, shoving people aside as he moved.

She expected to see Noah standing behind her, but when Reagan turned, no one was there. It was as if Brandon had been frightened by a ghost. No one was even looking at her.

Then she saw them. Blue jackets, just like the one over her shoulders, had moved in around her. Not so close that she'd noticed them, but close enough to make a point. She sat down as the barrel races started, aware of the blue jackets slowly moving away. Reagan had a feeling that if Brandon or someone like him returned, they'd be back.

It was a strange feeling, being protected. She'd

thought she was alone watching while Preacher rode, but all along they must have been watching over her.

A few minutes later, Noah climbed the bleachers two at a time and plopped down next to her. He looped his arm lightly over her shoulders. "How'd you like my ride, Rea?"

"What ride? You fell off."

He laughed. "I stayed on four seconds. I was halfway there. Wait until I ride the bull. I'll make the buzzer."

"Before you fall off?"

He nodded. "Before I fall off."

She poked him in the ribs. "So this falling off is part of it, win or lose. Noah, doesn't that seem strange to you? Seems like if you make the time, they should train the bulls to stop at the bell and let you get off."

"I'll put that in the suggestion box." He laughed.

Thirty minutes later, he lasted five seconds on the bull before he was bucked off and rolled in the dirt and mud. She clapped, figuring he was making progress.

As the last few events wound down, the wind seemed to kick up as if pushing the crowd toward their cars. Families bundled up the kids and headed for home.

One of the blue jackets behind her walked past, his girlfriend right behind him with her hand on his shoulder to steady her.

"Wanta go down by the chutes?" the boy asked Reagan. "You can meet up with Preacher there."

His girlfriend nodded once, as if to reassure her.

"Sure," Reagan said, not wanting to be the last one left in the stands.

She found Noah behind the fence. He was dusting the dirt from his jeans. When he straightened, the light reflected off something wet on his shirt.

"What's that?" Reagan moved closer, touching the sticky liquid.

"Bull snot," he said.

"Oh." She wiped her finger on her jeans.

"It'll dry"—he slapped at his leg—"but this shit I fell in is all over me."

"Nice ride," she managed, trying not to think about what he was covered in.

"Yeah, I almost made the time."

She was beginning to think maybe he did have mush for brains. He didn't seem the least upset that he'd failed at everything he'd tried tonight.

He offered her the hand he'd been using to dust off his jeans. "Want to go to the dance?"

She swallowed and took his hand. "Sure." If it didn't bother him that he was covered in snot and shit, she guessed it didn't bother her. "But I don't know how to dance."

"Me neither."

They listened to the music and watched the

dancers for an hour, and then he drove her home, explaining all the rules of the rodeo. She asked questions more because it was fun to listen to him talk, all excited and happy, about something he obviously loved.

When he pulled into the yard, she saw Jeremiah sitting on the front porch.

"Your uncle waited up," Noah whispered as he accepted his jacket back.

"He's probably asleep in the chair."

"He was worried about you," Noah added.

Reagan doubted that, but she said, "I'd better go in before this pickup turns into a pumpkin."

Noah grinned. "You had fun?"

"I did." She thought of telling him that this was very nearly the best night of her life. She'd laughed more than she had in months, and she'd felt protected. For her, both were too new to be taken for granted.

"You want to go with me again next week?"

"Don't your folks come?"

"No, my mom's never cared for rodeo. My dad lives in Amarillo and only comes over to one now and then. My sister is usually too busy being sheriff to worry about me. It was kind of nice having someone in the stands watching me almost make the ride."

"I'd like to come." She thought of being hesitant, playing it cool, but she couldn't. "Only I bring the food next week." She'd seen a few picnic baskets and buckets of chicken. She wasn't sure she could face another burrito that tasted like it had been made from the oldest bull.

"Fair enough," he said as she opened the door. "See you Monday at school, Rea."

"See you," she answered, and hopped out of the cab. "Thanks for not turning into a werewolf."

"What—"

She slammed the door and ran toward the house.

Chapter 16

HANK ROLLED OUT OF BED AND PULLED ON A worn pair of Levi's as he walked across the room to answer his cell.

"Chief." Willie's voice was high with excitement. "We're pulling out now. You said to call you no matter how small the fire if we took the truck out."

Hank could hear the siren in the background. "What is it, Willie?"

"Highway patrol called in a trash fire out at the north rest stop."

Willie had been sleeping at the fire station since he turned eighteen and his stepfather kicked him out. Brad Rister would be there tonight also. He slept there every time his wife kicked him out. Andy Daily, one of the night dispatchers across the street, would have caught a ride as well. Andy wasn't much of a fireman, but he was an adrenaline junkie and about to starve to death in a town the size of Harmony.

"I'll meet you there," Hank said, and closed up his phone.

Andy and Brad were levelheaded, and Willie could follow orders. They didn't need him to put out a trash fire. But Hank had been restless all night. He might as well go check everything out himself rather than lie in bed worrying about it. With a trash fire, there was always the chance it could spark a grass fire.

Glancing at his watch, he realized in an hour he would have been up anyway. He liked to get up and be at work before dawn when he was at the ranch. He'd work a few hours before coming in for breakfast with his mother and Saralynn. His sisters usually slept late, and his old aunts had their morning tea and bakery scones in their quarters.

As he took the side stairs outside his room, he hoped he made it back for breakfast. Tuesdays, his mother left early to visit the gallery in Wichita Falls that handled her pots, but every other morning, the three of them laughed and talked over pancakes and eggs before they started their day. Sometimes he thought his family circled around him in endless rings, but at the core were Saralynn and his mother.

When Hank pulled up to the north roadside park, he could see smoke rising gray against the night sky. The huge Dumpster was still popping with the heat, but the fire inside had been put out.

His men had sprayed the dried grass around the site to ensure that no spark would start something far worse than a Dumpster fire.

"What do you think happened?" Willie asked.

"Some traveler tossing his trash along with an ashtray, maybe," Hank guessed. Dumpster fires weren't all that unusual. An odd smell drifted with the smoke, making Hank wonder if some animal had been trapped in the Dumpster. Or maybe road-kill had been tossed in.

He noticed one of the sheriff's cars pull up beside the highway patrolman's vehicle, but Hank didn't move out of the dark. If Alex was here, she was on duty and probably didn't want to talk to him. For the second Saturday in a row he hadn't gotten a call from the bar. She'd stayed out of trouble. Part of him was proud of her, and part wondered if she was staying away from him.

Flashlight beams floated around an old station wagon parked near one of the picnic tables. The crack of a police radio crackled across the cold air.

Brad Rister approached Hank. "Should we try to determine the cause, or just wait and come back in a few hours when it's light? Both lids were down when we got here, so the fire had pretty much choked itself out. All we got was smoke; no flame when we popped the latch."

"Go on back and try to get a few more hours of

113

sleep." Hank turned his collar up. "I'll stick around for a while."

Brad motioned for Willie and Andy to pack up.

Hank noticed the beam of a light moving toward him. He didn't move as Alex's tall, lean shadow materialized from behind the light.

"Fire out?" she asked.

"It's out."

"Mind if we have a look inside?"

"The Dumpster's probably still hot and smoking, but knock yourself out." He followed her and two highway patrolmen. "Any reason this can't wait until dawn?"

Alex didn't answer, but the patrolman said, "We found drugs in the station wagon. There is a possibility that the driver climbed out of his car for some reason and decided to light up in the Dumpster."

Hank frowned. "You think he caught himself on fire?"

"I've seen it before. In the car, out where we could see him if we passed by, wouldn't seem near as safe as inside the Dumpster. Only problem was he might have closed the lid."

Hank could fill in the blanks from there. A few years ago, the parks department had put on latches to keep animals out of the trash. A five-year-old could open the lid from the outside, but there was no way to open it from the inside. A few park workers had complained about almost having a heart attack when they opened the lid and an angry raccoon shot out.

Hank stood behind Alex as she leaned over and shone her flashlight in. One of the patrolmen did the same.

Hank didn't have to look. He had a feeling they'd find something dead inside.

Alex stepped back and, in the dark, no one else noticed Hank steady her.

"We'll need a crime unit," she said, fighting to keep her voice calm. "He's burned, but the cause of death may be asphyxiation."

"Or drugs," Hank added. "Does it really matter? He's dead."

No one heard him. They began talking about what had to be done. Hank walked back to his truck just as the sky started to lighten. With the door open, he sat in his Dodge and watched the show. Usually, he loved sunrise on the prairie, but the smoky haze in the air and the stench took the joy out of it.

He barely noticed most of the cars leaving. The sky was rose-colored when he heard someone come around the side to the open door of his truck.

"You can go," Alex said, then added, "Thank your team for coming out. Thank you for coming."

He didn't move or look at her. "I wasn't asleep." He almost added that he'd been thinking of her, or, more accurately, thinking of her in bed beside him.

She came closer. "I'm staying until the crime

boys get here. There's no reason for you to have to stay."

He turned his head and found her only a foot away. The dawn reflected in her eyes. She stared; an ocean of words that needed to be said flowed between them, but neither had any idea how to begin. The memory of the way she'd felt in the restaurant with her leg pressed against his filled his tired mind, blocking out all else.

"You need something, Hank?" She raised one eyebrow slightly.

"Yeah, come closer." He was just tired enough not to be able to act like he didn't want her anymore.

She took a step closer, almost touching him, her eyes daring him.

Hank slowly lifted his hand and slid his finger around the back of her neck. He didn't tug her forward, but leaned out of the truck and kissed her lightly on the mouth.

When she stiffened, he moved away. "You can shoot me out here if you want to, Alexandra, but I've been wanting to do that for a while." He had no idea what she'd do or say. He didn't care.

She braced her hands on either side of the open door frame and leaned in, kissing him full on the mouth hard.

His arm circled around her and tugged her in beside him as her mouth opened and the kiss deepened.

She broke the kiss, but she couldn't pull away. Her back was pressed against the steering wheel, and her front was pressed against him. "This doesn't mean anything," she whispered, as if to herself, not him. "Don't think we're even friends."

"Fine with me," he answered as his arm tightened, pulling her hard against him and covering her mouth once more.

He wanted to feel her heart pounding as she kissed him back, but all he felt was her bulletproof vest. The knowledge of where they were and who they were must have registered with her a second after it did with Hank.

He broke the kiss as she slid away. Neither of them looked at the other.

Hank started his pickup. She closed his door with a slam. He didn't trust himself to look at her until he'd backed out and thrown the truck into gear.

He wasn't surprised to see her standing, legs wide apart, fists on her gun belt and glaring at him like she hated his guts. She deserved better than to be kissed in a roadside park crime scene. "Smooth," he mumbled, "really smooth." He could have at least said something. Women need words; men only need women.

After he'd used every swear word he could think of, it dawned on him that she'd kissed him with the same hunger he'd kissed her.

By the time he pulled up to the ranch house, Hank was smiling. Apparently neither one of them had a romantic bone in their bodies. A roadside park with a body forty feet away wasn't exactly a romantic spot. There had been no words of love, or even caring. They reminded him of wild mustangs mating. If they ever did make it to bed, their pillow talk would probably be cuss words whispered to each other.

He shook his head. He didn't care. She'd kissed him back; that was all that mattered. They might never sit down to a candlelight dinner, or go to a movie, or waltz in the moonlight, but the next time they touched, she wouldn't be wearing that damn vest and they wouldn't be in a public place.

When he walked in the kitchen, Saralynn and his mother were sitting down to breakfast in the kitchen.

"Everything all right, son?" his mother asked.

"Everything is fine," he answered as he crossed to the sink and washed his hands.

"Perfect," he grumbled beneath his breath, "but way too public." He could still taste Alexandra's lips on his mouth.

Chapter 17

THERE WAS A CHAIN OF COMMAND IN MATTERS of death, and Tyler Wright knew he was at the bottom. When people killed themselves or died under unusual circumstances, he was always the last one to get the body. Tyler had a staff of five. Two men who did the embalming and helped with funerals. One bookkeeper, one secretary, and one night host who worked after hours when needed. The Wright Funeral Home had a standing rule that whenever a body was resting in state, the night host, or Tyler himself, was there if the family wanted to come in, no matter the hour.

In all his years he'd never had to open the doors after ten P.M. more than a dozen times. Once a son drove in at two A.M. insisting on seeing his father before he was buried at dawn, and a few times widows wanted to sit up all night with their mate. But for the most part, the host worked a few days a week from five to nine P.M.

Since the beginning, the host had always been a man, usually a retired member of the staff. But for the past eight years the host had been Stella McNabb, a retired home economics teacher who knew everyone in town and, more important, remembered each of their names. Those she hadn't taught, she'd made home visits to when their children were in school. The U.S. census takers could have saved themselves days by just visiting Stella. She was sixty-three and pleasantly fluffy, and she cried with the mourners at every viewing. The perfect host for a funeral home.

Tyler liked Stella. He'd hired her on the spot when she'd answered his ad. The fact that she'd been the only one who answered might have been a factor, but Tyler liked to believe he'd hired her because she was the opposite of him. He'd start a sentence with something like, "You know that family that lives out by . . ." and Stella would give him the names, ages, and sometimes ailments of everyone who lived under the roof before he finished his sentence.

Tyler swiveled in his chair and looked out his office window. He'd called Stella an hour ago to come in and sit with a family tonight. The old teacher was never late.

Sure enough, Bob McNabb pulled up as Tyler watched. The weekend farmer let his wife out and drove away. He'd drive over to the fire station and spend his time, then be back for her at nine. Tyler often wondered why he didn't just drive the five miles home and come back, but then farm folks thought of coming to town as an event and made the most of every trip.

Stella was carrying a big plastic container. Cookies, probably. The woman could turn sugar, white flour, and shortening into heaven.

Tyler sucked in his stomach. He'd lost ten pounds the past three weeks, but avoiding Stella's cooking wouldn't be easy.

He stood and walked out to the lobby.

Stella had set the cookie tin down and was working on the knot of her head scarf. "Evening, Tyler," she said in her sweet way.

"Evening, Mrs. McNabb." He might be more

than twenty years out of high school, but he would never be comfortable calling her anything else. "Glad you could come in. The Trudeaus are having a family visitation at six. You think you can handle them all? There could be forty or fifty coming."

She smiled. "I can handle them. There's not a one of them I'd hesitate to thump on the ear if he got out of line."

Tyler grinned. He wouldn't have put it past her. "I've got work to do in the office tonight. I'll check in a few times." He'd already been out to the house to deliver a funeral wreath for the Trudeaus' door. The place looked like a bus terminal that had never been cleaned. Chairs and trash everywhere. It made sense to use the funeral parlor to welcome folks who wanted to pay their respects.

Stella finally got her scarf off, but her hair looked worse than if the wind had blown it. "I always felt so sorry for Mary Trudeau. By the time she stopped nursing kids, she was taking care of Martin. I'll say one thing for him, though. He fought that cancer." She patted her hair, trying to make it look like it did when she'd had it back-combed and sprayed several days ago.

She moved down the hall to where it widened into an area with coffee and bottled water. She set the cookies out on a plate and stored her container with a dozen others beneath the counter. "I'd better make the coffee early tonight. I may need some myself to stay awake. I've been having this dream over and over last night, and I swear I found no rest even if I was asleep. It's a vision, really, about a terrible storm coming. Last night, I saw a coffin coming out of the storm and we all know what that means."

"What?" Tyler asked as he finally broke down and picked up one cookie. Peanut butter, his least favorite. He'd eat only two.

Stella frowned. "When you see a coffin, it means someone's going to die."

He almost choked on the cookie fighting down a laugh. Finally he managed to say, "I've found that very true."

She didn't notice his distress. "My Bob don't believe in my visions, but I've traced my family tree and I've got Gypsy blood. It may not make sense even to me, but there's something to be said for dreams."

Tyler nodded without having any idea what she meant. He was always dreaming some version of a dream in which he woke up late and ran to the cemetery to do a graveside service and somehow he couldn't find the grave or, when he did, all the people were waiting and he noticed, too late, that he'd run into the crowd naked.

Wonder how Stella would interpret that dream? She'd probably think he was on drugs, or worse, that he was some kind of sleepwalking exhibitionist.

He said good-bye and rushed back to his office.

He wanted to jot down notes and search the Internet before he e-mailed Kate tonight. They could talk about the meaning of dreams. That would be something new and fun.

Willamina, his housekeeper, had brought his supper on a tray and left it in the office. Pork chops with gravy, cheesy potatoes with gravy, and sweet corn with butter melting on top. He covered the meal and left it by the door while he ate two diet meal bars. He knew one was a meal, but he always had another for dessert.

It was seven thirty when Kate's first e-mail came through. *Evening, Ty, how was your day?*

He smiled. No one had ever called him Ty. *Evening, Katherine.* He was guessing Kate would be short for Katherine. If she could shorten his, he could lengthen hers. *My day's perfect now I can talk to you.* He'd been thinking about saying that for two weeks. *I had a dream last night that you were walking out of a storm toward me.*

Do you believe in dreams? she came back before he had time to pat himself on the back for being such an interesting person.

Do you? He didn't want to commit before she did.

As always, she didn't hesitate to tell him what she thought. *Sometimes I wonder if you're not more dream than real.*

I wonder the same thing. He thought for a moment and added, *Sometimes I wonder if you're not the only real thing in my life, my hazel-eyed dinner partner.*

She wrote that she was laughing, and he swore he could almost hear her.

They talked of crazy dreams they'd had over the years. Tyler hated to end the evening, but he had to check on the Trudeau family.

Until tomorrow night, he typed.

Dream of me tonight, she answered back.

I'll do that. He signed off, leaned back in his chair, and smiled. When he talked to Kate, he wasn't the overweight undertaker, he was someone special. He closed his eyes and tried to remember what she looked like, then realized it didn't matter. She was beautiful to him.

Chapter 18

SATURDAY AFTERNOON

SHERIFF ALEXANDRA MCALLEN WALKED through the old mission-style home on her family ranch. The place was covered in dust and smelled faintly of decay. Even though her brothers had fought leaving and her father had hated to move from the ranch, their mother had relocated the family to town years ago.

Both of the boys came back as soon as they could drive. First Warren, and now Noah. It was as if they belonged to the land, more than the land belonged to them. Their father helped Warren get started, but after his oldest son was shot, Adam McAllen lost all interest in a ranch that had been in his family for generations.

Alex walked through the empty rooms, remembering how her mother had never liked living out here alone where she couldn't see a sign of civilization in any direction. Living on the ranch had been just one more thing her parents had argued about. Her mother had always claimed the land was worthless. Adam McAllen used this home only as his base camp between rodeos. He wasn't there enough to keep the place as a working ranch. Finally he'd given in, and the family moved to town. The fighting eased, but the scars were still there. They'd married young, then spent years having kids and fighting. Now, Alex thought, Dad lived in Amarillo and rarely returned and Mom lived bitter.

Alex looked at the blank wall that had once held a dozen family pictures. Almost all her memories of her father were the same. He'd come home after being gone on the rodeo circuit for months. There would be hugs and presents all around, and then that night she'd hear the arguments after her mother and father thought the kids were asleep.

Adam McAllen seemed to come home less and less. He must have lost at least one argument, though, because her mother never moved back to the ranch. At some point, Alex started calling her father Adam. When he did come back, he stayed on the ranch until the place got too dirty to use even for a night.

"Alex!" Noah yelled from the front entry. "You in here?"

Her kid brother's voice had changed, lowered, and for a second she thought it was her big brother yelling. Alex swallowed hard and answered, "I'm in the den, Noah."

He rushed in. "Thanks for coming. I want to show you the horses I'm getting today. The first of a future herd I'll have running over this ranch. Michael says, as long as he and Maria are still living on the place, he'll watch over them if something happens and I can't get out. He and Maria planted a garden out back of the foreman's house, so I guess that means they're planning on staying." Noah finally took a breath. "What you doing in the house?"

She ran her hand over the fireplace mantel. "I was just looking around."

"I know you remember this place a lot better than I do."

She smiled. "You were little when we left. Warren was fifteen. He threw a fit, cussing like I'd never seen, and I cried so hard I made myself sick. Mom said you joined in yelling with the pack. She claimed we all sounded like coyotes and she thought of just leaving us here."

"I wish she had," Noah said. "I love this place. I've already told Mom as soon as I turn eighteen, I'm moving out here."

Alex felt sorry for him. If ever a kid belonged on the open range, it was Noah. Growing up in town wasn't for boys like him. "What'd she say?"

"She said that it's probably in my blood, and the next time around she's going to marry a banker and raise kids who love the smell of vaults."

Alex put her hand on his shoulder. "She shouldn't be too worried. I'm only a half mile away at the cabin. If you get into trouble or start to starve, you can always make it to my place."

"You've got food?"

"Cheerios," she said with pride. "And, once in a while, milk."

They walked out of the house and down to the barn, laughing about how bad a cook their mother was and how it was no wonder they were both so thin. Last Christmas she'd made cookies out of artificial sweeteners and wheat germ. Even the birds wouldn't eat them.

The first thing Alex saw when they stepped into the barn was a beautiful Appaloosa mare and her colt. They were both chestnut brown with markings in white over their backs. The mare had a blaze of white down her face and the colt bore a star between his eyes.

"They're wonderful!" Alex bent down to touch the foal, who looked to be about five weeks old.

He resembled a giant stuffed toy with his woolly coat called milk hair and big brown eyes. He stood upright, with his legs straight and far apart like a tripod.

Noah bushed his hand along the mare's neck. "It's time I started raising horses, Alex. Mom says I have to go to college, but by the time I get out, I could have a real herd of these beauties. Michael says we can run horses on this place as well as cattle, so the only upkeep will be vet bills and grain in the winter. He said he'd keep an eye on them if Mom makes me go away to school."

"And who will put in the hours of mucking out this barn?" she said, thinking they were lucky to have Michael and Maria on the place. Free housing in exchange for watching over the land seemed a fair exchange.

The mare nudged her shoulder, wanting attention. Alex laughed. "Where'd these beauties come from? They remind me of a horse Warren used to have."

"They came from my place," Hank Matheson said calmly as he stepped out of the tack room.

Alex did her best not to show how startled she was. It made sense that he was here. Someone had to have brought the animals in, and she hadn't seen a trailer parked out front. All Hank would have had to do was ride the fence line of his place, cross over Lone Oak Road, and bring them in using the back trail to the barn. All he'd need was a lead over the mare. The baby would follow.

Noah caught the brush Hank tossed him.

"The mare should look like Warren's horse," Hank said without looking at Alex. "She's the granddaughter of his mare."

"Remember that filly Warren gave to Hank six years ago?" Noah brushed the horse. He patted her neck. "She sure did grow into a beauty, and this is her first foal."

"I sold Noah the mare," Hank said to Alex, "but I gave him the colt."

"That was nice of you," she managed.

"It's time," Hank answered. "He can handle them." Hank winked at Noah. "Can't you, Preacher?"

"You bet. This is the start I needed."

She smiled at her little brother. "I hope so. Mostly all he knows about horses is how to fall off."

After they played with the colt for a while, Alex decided it was time to head back to her cabin. She'd had a long day, a long week. Once home, she decided to take a quick shower and go into town for a meal and a drink. One drink, she told herself, maybe two and that was it. Her days of having Hank drag her out of the bar were over.

In the shower, she thought about Hank touching her leg in the restaurant. It hadn't been an accidental touch or a casual brush. He'd moved his hand under the table and slid his fingers down the side of her leg. She should have said something right then. Or maybe stormed out, embarrassing him, letting him explain to his niece why she had left.

If she'd taken action when he'd touched her, he wouldn't have kissed her at a crime scene and, more important, she wouldn't have kissed him back.

What did he think he was doing, flirting? Proving a point of some kind? Being funny?

She stepped out of the shower, dried off, tied on a wrap, and began drying her hair. If Hank Matheson was flirting, he was doing a terrible job. If he thought he was proving a point, he hadn't, and if he was being funny, near as she could tell neither of them were laughing.

Alex tried to keep the kiss they'd shared at dawn last Wednesday out of her mind. She couldn't blame that on him. Well maybe the first one, but not the second. She crossed to her bedroom and slipped into a pair of jeans and a shirt. There was no need to dress up; she wasn't planning to pick anyone up. She just wanted a meal and a few drinks tonight.

As she walked into the living room, the sun was low in the sky. The view out her huge windows was breathtaking, except for one thing: Hank sat on her front porch.

She stormed out. "What do you think you're doing here?"

He'd tied his horse to the railing. He looked different than he did in town. The Stetson was still there, but his long legs were strapped into chaps. The spurs buckled across his boots reminded her that he was a working rancher, not one who dressed for show. The dried bloodstains on his plain chaps left no doubt about that. The cuffs of his shirt were rolled to his elbow, revealing strong, tanned forearms.

"I haven't been in from work to clean up yet," he said, slow and low as if he thought he might frighten her. "But I wanted to stop by here first on my way home."

"You smell of sweat and horses." She leaned against the porch railing, waiting to hear what he had to say.

He stared out at the sunset. "You hate ranching like your mother did?"

Fighting to control her anger, she said, "That's none of your business, but no, I don't hate ranching."

She wanted to add that what she hated was that everyone in town knew about her parents' troubles. It occurred to her that he might be worrying about her little brother. If the kid tried to work the ranch, he'd be stepping right in between her parents. "If Noah wants to make a go of the ranch, I'm all for it. I'll even help when I can."

She stood, arms folded, waiting for him to leave. He just stood there.

Finally, he turned and looked at her as if just

noticing she was standing next to him. "You hungry, Alexandra?"

Alex hadn't expected the question. She didn't have time to lie. "I could eat."

He stepped off the porch and put on his hat as he tugged the reins free of the railing. "How about a steak over in Bailee?" He swung onto the saddle. "I'll clean up and be back in a half hour."

He kicked his horse and was gone before Alex thought to close her mouth. After all these years of knowing Hank Matheson to be one of the most predictable people in town, he'd surprised her. First touching her leg, then kissing her, and now . . . now what?

She was way out of practice, but she could swear the man had just asked her for a date.

Alex put on a little makeup and combed her hair as she tried to think of how to tell him they couldn't go out. He was over thirty. If he had decided it was high time he started dating, he'd have to look somewhere else. She knew she could never look at him without remembering he'd been her older brother's best friend.

Maybe she shouldn't have allowed him to kiss her. She must have sent the wrong signal. Of course, there was also the possibility he was just trying to be nice.

Thirty minutes came and went. Alex reached for her keys. He wasn't coming. Maybe this was all just a plan to keep her on the ranch. He probably thought she'd wait an hour or two, and then it would be too late to go into town.

Well, she'd fool him. Alex grabbed her coat and was out the door before she could change her mind.

Halfway down the steps, she saw his truck flying up the road. He cut the engine and was out of the cab before she could come up with a strategy.

"You were leaving?" he asked as he met her on the steps. Even in the shadows she could see the anger in his face. "You were walking out?"

"I thought you weren't coming." She took a step backward, ashamed of herself for not believing him. Hank might drive her crazy, but he wasn't a man who lied. They'd both be better off if she'd just tell him that she doubted they could talk to one another for five minutes without getting into a fight. They were fooling themselves if they thought they could have a conversation over dinner.

"Alexandra." He said her full name slowly. "I may be a lot of things in this life, but a liar isn't one of them."

She backed to her door and grabbed the handle, knowing she had to be honest. Whatever his reasons for asking her, this ploy wouldn't work. "Dinner was a bad idea, Hank. A real bad idea."

He was so close she could feel his breath on her cheek. "You're right," he said. "I'm not interested in food."

With only a slight movement, he leaned down and kissed her. When she didn't protest, he closed the space between them, pressing her against the door.

He felt so right next to her that for a few minutes she just let feelings wash over her. It had been so long since she'd felt . . . a lifetime since she'd thought of anything but family and work. She couldn't count the Saturday nights in the bar when she'd gone in to drink and forget about all feelings.

Hank wasn't flirting with her; he was showing her exactly what he wanted.

His hands slid up the sides of her body, boldly feeling her. His mouth moved from her mouth to her neck, tasting her flesh. He was so close she felt his chest press against her each time he breathed.

This was Hank. She closed her eyes. She'd known him all her life. He'd spent years teasing her when she'd tried to tag along with him and Warren. He'd bossed her around when she was in her teens and he was in college, always accusing her of going wild. He'd held her brother's body in the middle of a road while she'd stood in the dark and stared. This was Hank.

If she kept her eyes closed, maybe she could forget everything but the feel of him molding her body, turning her on, warming her blood. God, it felt so good to just relax and let someone pull her to him. But this was Hank.

Slowly her body stiffened. "Stop," she whispered. "Stop."

He held her tighter for a moment as if fighting, and then he stepped away. "You want this, Alex. You want it as much as I do."

She held her head up. "I want it, but not with you. Never with you."

Bracing, she wouldn't have been surprised if he'd hit her. But he didn't. He simply swore under his breath and walked away. She stood, staring at the taillights until they vanished.

She'd hurt him worse than she'd ever hurt him in the hundred fights they'd had since Warren died. Alex knew it deep down, just as she knew him. He hadn't been offering a one-night stand. He'd been offering himself.

She had to stop this now, no matter how much it hurt them both. She couldn't let him make love to her and then find out sometime later that she had been the reason Warren died. And she couldn't live with herself if she slept with Hank without being honest.

Alex crumbled on the porch and cried like she hadn't cried in months. The kind of sobbing that made her guts hurt. The night three years ago came back to her as if it were yesterday.

She'd just gotten her master's and come home to celebrate. Everyone knew she'd been waiting that night at Warren's office. But no one knew that she'd talked Warren's partner into skipping the patrol he should have been making with Warren so he could entertain her.

She'd been having sex in her brother's office when he was shot on a country road without anyone to cover his back. The image of Hank fighting to save her brother as Warren's blood ran across the road flooded her thoughts.

Finally, as she knew they would, the tears no longer came. Alex curled up in a ball, feeling cold and drained but refusing to go inside. If Warren's partner had been with him, he might still be alive. She'd wanted to celebrate that night, a walking wild, half-drunk woman party looking for excitement. It had cost her brother's life, and she couldn't even remember the partner's name. He'd blamed himself and quit the force. But Alex knew who was at fault. She was. She'd come on to the guy. She'd begged Warren to let him stay at the office when the late call came in. She was the reason her big brother died on that back road three years ago.

Two months after the funeral, she'd run for sheriff and been elected. She'd turned her life completely around, but it took her a year before she could look at Hank and not see the tears she'd seen that night running down his face.

He'd fought to save her brother, even refusing to stop when the doctor said it was hopeless.

And she'd stayed in the darkness and watched. Frozen.

Chapter 19

REAGAN WAS CONCENTRATING ON HER MATH when Jeremiah passed through the kitchen. "It's almost sunset," he said and walked out the side door.

"He's worse than a freaking grandfather clock," she mumbled as she closed her book and followed him.

They had a routine. At sunset they always sat in the two west-facing chairs and watched. The only thing that had changed in the yard since she'd arrived six weeks ago was that now a pair of chairs faced all four directions. Jeremiah watched the sun rise and set every day. He watched the clouds. He watched the birds. He watched the dust blow. She had a feeling that if it ever rained, he'd sit outside and watch that, too.

Reagan decided nature was his TV.

She curled up in the blanket he'd left on what was now her chair and studied the sky. She'd never lived in a place where folks were so aware of the weather, but she liked this time of day. Watching the sunset was a routine, and she'd decided the third night she was in Harmony that she liked routine.

If Jeremiah had anything to say to her, he usually said it now. He wasn't one to waste time talking at the table when he could be eating.

"You passing in school?" he asked without looking at her.

"Yep," she answered. "Signed your name on my report card last week. I got all Bs."

"Good." He didn't sound like he cared one way or the other. "I was thinking maybe you should drive the truck in a few days a week and then you could get supplies on your way home, saving me a trip."

"I don't have a license." She tried not to let her excitement show. She'd been driving the truck around the farm and once to town to get a saw fixed, but she never thought she'd be able to drive it to school.

"You got a birth certificate?"

"Yep."

"That's all you need. Turn it in, take the test. If you have to do anything else, find out. If you're not smart enough to figure it out, you're too dumb to drive."

"You think I might be too dumb to drive?" She didn't want to tell him that her name wasn't Truman on the birth certificate.

"You're smart enough. I think you'll do just fine." He stood. "I'm going out to the shed. I'll be back in an hour or so for supper. Remember, you're cooking tonight."

"I remember."

She watched him fold himself into his little cart and head down the path to what he called the shed.

In truth, it was a large metal storage building back behind a forest of aspen. It looked like it would easily hold a dozen cars.

She'd looked inside a few times for a glimpse of his collection. Of all the things she'd thought he would have collected, tractors weren't even on the list. These weren't the huge tractors she saw moving up and down the back roads; these were old tractors. The kind that looked like they should be in a museum. She had no idea why he had them—not a spot on the farm appeared to have ever seen a plow—but almost every night he spent an hour or so working on the engines and polishing. He'd never invited her in for a close look, but he didn't bother closing the door most nights, so she knew he wasn't keeping them a secret.

She'd found other collections in the house. One wall in what could have been called his office was covered with clippings of World War II. He'd framed each clipping and printed dates on the glass. None of them, as far as she'd read, mentioned Jeremiah, but she had a feeling they were battles he'd been in.

She also found a box of what had to be every card he'd ever been sent in his life. Old Beverly might have not wanted to live with him, but she'd sent her brother a birthday card and a Christmas card every year. He'd saved them all. Reagan guessed he'd never sent one in return.

There were probably other collections in the

rooms she hadn't ventured into yet. She had her room, they always used the kitchen, and she'd made a place in the front room where he kept the rolltop desk with his money tucked away. She'd made up her mind the day he handed her his roll of bills that she'd never take a dime without leaving a receipt.

On Sundays, she liked to curl up on the couch in the front room and read. The light was good and she could almost feel the ghosts of all the dead Trumans around her. They weren't frightening, just sad, and the longer she lived in the house, the more she felt like they were her relatives. She'd learned the names of all the people in the old portraits. Jeremiah didn't seem to mind telling her about his ancestors. They'd talk about them after dinner sometimes as if they were still alive.

Jeremiah would say things like, "Wilbur wasn't worth a dime from the day he was born in 1890." Or "Agnes didn't know her directions. Half the school days, her pa would have to hitch up the wagon and go find her, knowing she'd taken the wrong way home. Worst wrong turn she ever made was marrying a railroad man. He'd leave every spring about plowing time and not come back until it was too cold to work outside."

Once, the old man made Reagan laugh so hard she cried when he told her that his father's brother, Mac, got kicked in the head by a mule one summer and hopped around like a rabbit for a month. "He was just plain dumb," Jeremiah admitted. "Drowned in water he could have stood up in and walked out."

Reagan smiled at the story, feeling like she knew all the people who'd lived in this place. She made her way back inside as the last sunlight faded. She wanted time to try out another one of the recipes in Miss Beverly's handwriting. She loved the way Beverly added little hints at the bottom of each one, the little secrets that turned a pie from ordinary to wonderful. Reagan felt like the old woman was teaching her, one step at a time, to cook.

As she collected the ingredients, she noticed they were low on cocoa. The keys to the old truck were on a nail by the door. Reagan grabbed them, made sure she had enough money, and decided to drive the two miles to the gas station store. She could be back in five minutes. Uncle Jeremiah would never miss her.

The old truck started with a hum. She circled the yard and bumped her way down the dirt road to the pavement. Night had moved in, and the big old trees lining the road hugged in around her.

Reagan kept her eyes fixed on the beams of light in front of her and told herself trees were not something she needed to be afraid of in this world. Not even huge old bushy ones whose tops pointed like aging fingers. On cold nights, when the wind whipped around, the tops seemed to shake their bony fingers at her.

She stepped on the gas and was going at least thirty when she swung onto the pavement and headed toward town.

Four minutes later she pulled into the tiny grocery store and ran in. It took another minute to find the cocoa and pay. Only one person was in the store besides the clerk, who had the bored expression of one who'd left mentally on break and forgot to take his body.

He gave Reagan the wrong change and turned to a woman of about twenty-five buying a crossword puzzle book.

Reagan smiled at the sad-looking woman and said, "Hi."

The woman's expression didn't change. In fact, Reagan wasn't sure either of them even noticed her passing through the store. She probably could have shoplifted the cocoa and no one would have noticed.

Reagan climbed back in the pickup, deciding that if the invasion of the body snatchers passed by here, they'd skip the two at the gas station. Aliens would have better luck with mind control over geraniums.

Backing out of the drive, she noticed one car half a block away coming toward her, so she gunned the engine and headed home.

Halfway there, the car caught up to her and flashed red and blue lights.

For a second, Reagan thought of making a run

for it, but in this old bucket she'd be lucky to make it to the spooky old trees.

She pulled over and waited as the lady sheriff walked to her window.

"You got some kind of trouble, Reagan?" Sheriff McAllen asked.

"No," Reagan answered. "I was just out of cocoa."

The sheriff laughed. "So you're cooking."

"Every other night." Reagan tried to sit up straight. The sheriff didn't have a ticket book in her hand, or handcuffs. That had to be a good sign. "I'm trying out some of my grandmother's old pie recipes. Uncle Jeremiah seems to think they're edible."

Alex McAllen put her elbow on the window rim. "Really. I remember her pies. If you can make them as good as she did, I bet Cass at the Blue Moon would buy them from you."

"Really?"

Alex backed away. "I don't want to keep you if you're baking, but you tell Jeremiah that he needs to get you signed up for driver's ed. Till then, stay off paved roads."

Reagan put the car in gear. "I'll do that." She couldn't believe she wasn't at least getting a ticket. "Tell your brother I finished the math homework."

Alex smiled. "You two competing?"

"Not much. I beat him almost every time."

"That's because he can only count to eight." The

sheriff waved. "You keep making him work, Rea, will you?"

"I'll try." Reagan drove away smiling. In her whole life she never thought she'd have an officer of the law call her Rea like they were friends or something.

Chapter 20

⚬⚬

TUESDAY

HANK DROPPED HIS NIECE OFF AT PRESCHOOL and headed straight for the sheriff's office. It had been a few weeks since he'd almost attacked Alexandra on her front porch. He'd seen her from a distance a few times and she hadn't shot at him, but he had no illusion she was over being mad at him.

He walked in past the dispatchers and clerks. "Morning," he said to Andy Daily.

Andy looked tired. Hank guessed he was just finishing his night shift as dispatch. Between manning the phones here four nights a week and staying at the fire station three, Hank wondered when the man slept. During the day he owned the town's two Laundromats, one in a run-down apartment building and the other a block from the mall. He didn't do much to keep the places up, but he kept enough machines running to make sure people came back.

Hank had noticed that Andy's pockets always jingled, and he wondered if the man dropped by one of his places every day and cleared a box of coins to use for coffee money.

Andy downed the last of his cup of coffee and hurried after Hank. "You here about what we were talking about last night?"

"I am," Hank, said trying to get his thoughts off Alex's porch and on to the problem at hand. "I'm filing a report with the sheriff this morning."

Andy nodded. "Like you say, it might be nothing, but better safe than sorry."

"I'll let you know what, if anything, we decide to do at this time. I like your suggestion that we go on full alert at least until it rains."

Andy smiled. He liked being included.

Hank reached Alex's door and turned. "There's coffee at the station if you want to keep Willie company for a while. I'll be back as soon as I'm finished here."

"I'll do that." Andy nodded one sharp nod and turned on his heel.

Hank took a long breath and walked into the sheriff's office.

Alex's secretary, Irene, was on the phone. She waved him past her desk, leaving no doubt that Alex was expecting him.

When he stepped into the sheriff's office, he was surprised to see the highway patrolman from the night they'd found the body in the Dumpster and one of Alex's deputies.

The thought crossed his mind that she'd planned it so they wouldn't be alone, even though this was official business. He nodded at the two men and took his seat at the round table Alex had in the corner of her big office.

"Thank you for seeing me, Sheriff," he said formally. "Trooper Davis. Deputy Gentry. Glad you could join us."

Alex stepped around her desk and took the last chair at the table. "Let's get right to business, Chief."

Hank fought down a smile. She'd never called him Chief before.

"All right." He forced himself to look at her without emotion. He could play this game just as well as she could. "The boys at the fire station have been keeping a record of the fires we've had since the burn ban went into effect a few months ago. We've been lucky; none of the grass fires have happened around any homes, and most were small enough to be contained within a few hours.

"Leaving out cooking fires in town and a few boys playing with matches, I've marked all others." Hank spread a map out on the table, forcing Alex to lean closer. "All this is of little interest to law enforcement, unless you consider when and where the fires happened." He pointed at the first red X on his map. "This was the first one.

Since then, the fires chart counterclockwise in a circle." He moved his finger. "Six fires in two months. All seemingly accidents. All sparking on relatively calm nights. All moving until they've completed three fourths of a circle with Harmony smack-dab in the center."

The highway patrolman stood and leaned over the map, and so did the deputy. Alex continued to make notes.

Hank moved his finger slowly. "This first one we thought might have been a cigarette tossed. The second one wasn't near a road, so we guessed dry lightning sparked it. We found no cause evident on the third and fourth. The fifth looked like it might have been a camper who didn't put out his camp-fire. The sixth was our Dumpster druggie."

Alex's deputy whistled. "Holy shit. If these are really being set, that means our druggie may have been murdered. Someone could have seen him crawl in the Dumpster to smoke and tossed something burning in before closing the lid."

Trooper Davis frowned. "We've no proof it happened that way. The crime report won't be in for another week or more."

"We've no proof it didn't," Gentry added.

"Six accidental fires in two months?" Alex raised an eyebrow at Hank.

"Not likely," he said. "But not impossible."

"And all forming a circle at what looks like about five miles from town."

"Impossible," Hank whispered knowing she was following his logic.

"And the next one?"

"If it follows the pattern, it's due to hit toward the end of the week, right about here." He touched a place on the map just southwest of town. "Only our luck may have run out. The weatherman tells me there's a strong chance of winds over thirty every night this week and no hope of rain. If someone sets a fire on a windy night, we don't have the manpower to contain it. Even calling in every county volunteer fire department, around thousands of acres could burn before we could stop it. With all the grass around here in the government's Conservation Reserve Program, a lot of the grass is long and thick. That kind of fire could jump a road."

"We have to keep this quiet," Alex reasoned. "And we have to prepare."

Hank smiled. Despite hating his guts, she believed him. The four of them began to work on what could be done. The highway patrols could concentrate southwest of town. They might not be able to stop everyone, but they could keep an eye out for trouble. The deputy said he'd station men at high points to watch for smoke, and Hank planned to have a full team sleeping at the fire station. Alex remained silent.

He had his doubts about the location. The circle wasn't exactly even. Some of the fires were closer to seven miles out, some only four. And if they were set, the guy wasn't always moving the same distance around his imaginary circle. Two of the fires were within sight of one another. Then there was the slim chance this was just coincidence, nothing more. Fighting grass fires was their most common problem. They were a curse to dry land. Between lightning and careless folks burning off trash, grass fires kept them busy. Spring was on the way and with the wind and storms, their busy season was about to begin.

But this time it didn't feel like coincidence. Some-one was playing a game with them. Hank felt it.

If he was wrong, all he'd wasted was time. If he was right, he just might save lives. He didn't care whether he was a fool or a hero. He had to follow his gut.

When he stood, Alex finally spoke. "If you have no objection, I think I'll investigate each one of these fires."

"I've no objection." He looked at her, but she didn't meet his eyes. "My files are open, and I'll even go with you to talk to anyone."

"That won't be necessary," she said. "If I get lucky, I might find a small clue that your firemen overlooked."

Hank walked out with the other men, wishing he'd had a moment to talk to her alone. But . . . what would he say—that he was sorry about that Saturday night? Not likely.

He spent the day doing all he could to be ready if another grass fire sparked. When he left to pick up Saralynn, he had a headache bigger than Texas and he had to act like nothing was wrong.

Saralynn waited for him in her classroom as always. She could have used her crutches and made it to the front of the building, but he knew school always wore her out. Plus, she had to be very careful around other children and most animals. One bump, one fall could send her back to the hospital with another broken bone.

He always waited until the other children were gone before he picked her up. He knew she wouldn't have liked them to see her being carried in and out.

She was waiting for him with a pirate hat on and beads made of macaroni.

"You a pirate today?" he asked as he lifted her.

"No. I'm one of the lost boys and we're only pretending to be pirates."

Hank nodded at the teacher, who was busy gathering up all the scarves and cardboard swords that helped fuel Saralynn's imagination. "Mind if I take one of your pretend pirates home?"

"Go ahead and smooth sailing." The teacher winked.

Driving home, they stopped, as they always did on Tuesdays, at the Dairy Queen for a chocolate-dipped ice cream. His mind was full of worries, but he listened to every word his niece said, figuring that today his mother wouldn't be home to listen and his sister Claire would be too busy painting and his other sister, Liz, would just be too busy.

Sure enough, when they got home, Claire had locked herself in her studio to work on her new masterpiece called *Man on a Hook*. Hank didn't even want to think about the finished product. Last week she'd frightened him with a pencil sketch of a work in progress called *Mr. Dismemberment*.

He carried Saralynn all the way to the back of the house, where his two great-aunts lived. They had separate bedrooms and shared a bath and a sunny sitting room. They welcomed him but didn't stop their gin game. They played gin every afternoon, and at last count he noticed Aunt Pat owed Aunt Fat twenty-three hundred dollars.

He sat Saralynn in the sunny window seat and helped her pull out her coloring books. The aunts would take care of her, spoil her with sweets, and keep her occupied until Claire finished her latest mutilation of man on canvas or his mother got home.

Hank stood. "I got to go back to town," he said. "I will not be back for supper tonight."

They both nodded absently.

Saralynn said reassuringly, "I'll remember to tell Grandma."

He looked at her framed in the afternoon sun. Her blond hair almost looked like it was on fire, and the thought that someone was out there setting fires made him sick to his stomach.

Hank was at a full run by the time he left the house to get back to the fire station.

Chapter 21

~~~

REAGAN CUDDLED INTO NOAH MCALLEN'S jacket and shivered as she watched one bull rider after another fall off. This Friday night was nothing like the last few rodeos. No families, no snack truck parked nearby with hot chocolate and hard, barely edible burritos. No friendly atmosphere.

Tonight, the wind howled out of the north and the air seemed thick with dust. She fought to keep her curly hair out of her face and stuffed it back into the hood of the wind jacket she had on underneath his coat. She should have brought something to tie her wild mop back because she'd never get a comb through it when she got home.

She'd taken to thinking of her hair as tumbleweed styled. The new hair products made it shine with health, but nothing seemed to tame it. In foster care, she'd always kept it short, like a fuzzy red football helmet on her head, but she hadn't cut it since she'd been in Harmony. It almost touched her shoulders now.

Reagan swung her legs, trying to keep warm on

the hard, splintery wooden bleachers. She couldn't even remember the name of the town they'd passed through before they reached the rodeo grounds. A few of the same kids she'd seen last week, at the Guyman rodeo, were in the stands. She'd noticed Brandon Biggs smoking at the end of the rickety bleachers. He didn't look in her direction, but she was sure he'd seen her. The crowd was so small it would be hard to miss anyone.

Most of the kids from Harmony hadn't made the three-hour drive tonight. Noah said several of the guys thought the prize wasn't worth the gas to come so far, but he took every chance to ride he could get.

He had tried to talk her out of coming, warning her that it was the worst school district in the state, and that half the time a fight broke out at the end.

Reagan had set her books on the hood of his pickup and faced him, or rather his chest. "Then you'll need someone to cover your back, Preacher," she said, her hands on her hips as if she'd fight him if he didn't stop arguing.

Noah had laughed, bending down until they were eye-to-eye. "You're right, Rea, I can think of no one else I'd rather have on my side in a fight than little old you. Come on along if you're brave enough."

That had settled it. They'd climbed into his truck and hit the road. She'd already told Uncle

Jeremiah she would be late because it was Friday night, so he wouldn't be expecting her.

Now, as she watched the sun set against a brown sky, she wished she were home. Noah was busy at rodeoing and spent little time sitting beside her. When he wasn't riding, he was helping out in the chutes or talking to the other riders.

The announcer yelled that Preacher McAllen was up next, riding a bronc named Blue Thunder. Reagan turned to watch just as the gate swung wide.

Noah's long body jerked and popped as the horse whirled. With one hand in the air and his hat crammed down, his body bowed as if boneless in the saddle. Reagan felt the pain with him as she clicked off the seconds in her mind. Five. Six. Seven. Another hard buck. His hat flew, but he held on.

She was on her feet when she yelled, "Eight," just as the buzzer sounded and Noah dropped his arm and leaned forward on the powerful animal.

Pickup men moved in on either side of the still-bucking bronc. Their horses were big, well-trained animals, and despite the condition of the arena, the two seemed skilled at their jobs tonight.

Noah grabbed one man's waist and hung on long enough to be out of stomping distance before he slid to the ground, stumbled backward, but stayed on his feet. The riders shooed the horse toward the open corral gate.

Reagan ran toward him as he picked up his hat and moved to the fence. "You made it!" she yelled. "You made the full time."

He grinned down at her through the fence. "I do now and then, you know, Rea. Don't look so surprised." He stepped on the bottom board of the arena fence and swung himself over to stand next to her. "If I'm going to go pro someday, I got to start staying on. That's my plan. Besides, I didn't want to hit that ground. I've seen blacktop softer."

Reagan laughed. "It was worth coming and waiting out in the cold to see that ride. You looked great. I was so worried I swear I could feel my heart pounding in my throat."

Noah looked at the almost-empty stands. "I'm glad you were here. Nobody else was. Now I've got someone to back me up when I brag and tell what happened." He messed up her unruly curls with his big hand. "I'm glad I let you talk me into you coming along."

The rodeo came to an end and Noah collected the buckle, and then they piled into the truck and headed home.

As they passed back through the little no-name town, Noah asked, "Want to stop for an ice cream? I feel like celebrating."

"Sounds good," she said, still shivering. "As long as we can run the heater on the way home."

They pulled into a hamburger place, and he was

still explaining how he'd planned his ride tonight as they took the back booth.

"What are you going to do when school's out?" Reagan asked after the waitress took their order.

"I got it all planned out. Hank said I would work part time at his place. With the money I make, I'm going to start buying stock for the ranch. When my brother was alive, he ran a hundred head on our land and had dreams of twice that. Mom says the ranch isn't worth the taxes on the place, but I think if I had a stake I could make it work. We have a couple, Michael and Maria, living next to the main house in a place that used to be the foreman's quarters. They stay rent free for watching over the ranch. Michael said he'd keep an eye on any stock I had grazing."

"Why does your mother hate it so much?" Reagan didn't care about the cattle; people interested her more.

"Dad told me once she hated the land more than she loved him. Whatever that means." He shrugged. "Sometimes I think they just got married to fight. Everything about them is polar opposite. She's from Dallas, never rode a horse till she met Dad. He said she thought the only cowboys left played football. I asked my brother once a few years before he died why he thought a rodeo cowboy and a Dallas cheerleader would marry, and he said he'd explain it to me when I was older." Noah frowned. "I'm older now, but he's gone."

"Are your folks divorced?"

Noah laughed. "Hell, no. I guess they figure if they divorced and married someone else, they'd just make two more people miserable. Alex says Dad pays the bills on Mom's house in town, and he sent checks regularly for her schooling. Mom works at the Lady Bug in busy seasons to make a little extra money, but she's got a small trust fund that's enough to keep her in new cars every few years."

"Why didn't your dad move back to the ranch after she left?"

"He's got his life in Amarillo, I guess. He was from ranching folks, but I think the only part of it he really loved was the competition. Now, folks say he's a workaholic. To tell you the truth, I don't know him very well. I know he loved the rodeo, but he didn't really teach me. I think it was just in my blood. I don't remember him being around much."

Reagan smiled. "He must have come home at least three times."

It took Noah a second to figure out what she was implying. He looked down. "Yeah. I guess he thought he wasn't needed after Mom had us kids. You should meet her; she turned into a supermom when it came to raising kids. Dad probably thought with all the relatives in town, he wasn't much needed. I think of him as kind of a jack-in-the-box father. He pops up now and then."

"You like him?"

Noah smiled. "I respect him. Since he's never been around, I can't say as I miss him." He leaned back. "What about your dad?"

Reagan was saved from lying by the arrival of banana splits in tiny red boats.

As they ate, the place filled with high school kids, loud and traveling in small packs. While Reagan watched them, Noah stole every other bite of her ice cream.

"We'd better get out of here," he said in a whisper. "Too many people around bothers me. I see a few of the guys I rode against tonight, and they weren't happy about me winning the buckle."

"I'm still hungry," she whispered back.

"I'll buy you a malt on the way out."

She grabbed his jacket and folded it over her arm, holding it tightly as they moved through the crowd. Noah looked back and offered his hand.

Reagan didn't take it. She wasn't into holding hands. He didn't seem to mind. He just ordered the malt, and by the time he'd dug the money out, it was ready.

They made it almost to his truck before a shout stopped them.

"Preacher!"

"Get in the truck," Noah ordered her as he turned to face trouble.

Three shadows moved toward them, kicking up the white dust of the parking lot as they rushed.

Reagan, making no move toward the cab of the truck, tried to see around Noah as he widened his stance.

The local boys had been at the rodeo, but all three wore leather football letter jackets, not denim. They weren't part of the rodeo, they were just locals. Boys a few years past high school but still refusing to grow up, she guessed.

All three were older than Noah.

She couldn't make out their faces, but the way they spread out told her this probably wasn't the no-name town's welcoming committee.

"You came a long way to take our prize," one said. "My little brother was riding tonight, and he was hands-down the pick to win until you showed up."

"Look." Noah stood his ground. "Your brother is more than welcome to come down to Harmony's rodeo and compete for our buckles."

They'd spread out enough so that Reagan could see one of the guys clearly. He wasn't tall, but had a hard kind of beefiness about him.

Noah could no longer keep an eye on all three, so he spoke to the one in the center, who seemed to be the leader. His voice was low and calm, but not friendly.

It crossed her mind that these three were the most incompetent thugs she'd ever seen. They were trying to frighten Noah and her, but they didn't look like they knew what to say. These boys should have stopped by some of the foster homes she'd been in for a course in bullying.

Finally, the one nearest her laughed. "Is this your girl, Preacher, or your little sister?"

Reagan glared at him. She hated not looking her age, and she despised it when others mentioned it.

"She don't look old enough to be out this late, Preacher. Maybe we should turn you in for pestering a kid?"

"Yeah, maybe you're some kind of child molester," another one shouted.

Reagan sensed it now. Noah might not have been angry when they tried to bully him, but he didn't like them picking on her.

"Lay off," he said. "She's a friend."

"Cute." The guy moved closer, puffed up like a horned toad. "Reminds me of those Ewoks in *Star Wars*. She's got the wildest hair. What color is it, anyway?"

As his big hand reached out toward her, Reagan decided she'd had enough. She threw her malt directly at his chest.

The paper cup exploded, sending the cold cream from his face to his boots.

Out of the corner of her eye, she saw the other two moving on Noah. All Reagan could do was think about keeping the one before her from joining his friends. She began kicking the beefy guy as he swore and screamed and backed away, trying to wipe malt out of his eyes.

She doubled her kicks, landing several against the back of his knees, making him almost fall as he twisted and turned to avoid her assault.

He finally stormed away, calling her every name he could come up with.

When Reagan turned, she was expecting to see the other two beating Noah, but they were just standing five feet in front of him, frozen.

It took her a moment to realize what had stopped them.

Standing on the bed of Noah's truck was Brandon Biggs with a pipe in his fists long enough to do some serious brain damage.

Noah slowly turned until he also saw what had stopped them. "I don't need your help, Brandon," he said. "Get out of my truck."

Brandon smiled. "I ain't here to help you, Preacher. I'm here to save these fools before they get too close to that girl of yours. I'm still doctoring the scabs on my leg from the last time I talked to her."

Brandon swung out of the truck bed without turning loose his pipe. "Why don't you take her home while I finish talking to the Fraser boys? We've been waiting for weeks to discuss a problem we had the last time they visited Bailee. I figure tonight is as good a time as any to settle things, and I'd appreciate you butting out of my business."

The Fraser boys were already backing away when Noah pulled Reagan toward the truck. He opened the driver's-side door, pushed her inside, then climbed in behind her.

"Should we leave Brandon? Those guys are older and there are three of them." Reagan couldn't believe she was worried about the troublemaker.

"Brandon can take care of himself. Trust me, he lives for this kind of stuff."

"Are you two friends?"

"No." Noah backed the truck into the road. "But I don't hate the guy like a lot of kids do, so I guess that makes me as close to a friend as Brandon's ever had."

"I'm sorry I hurt him now."

Noah laughed. "You got his attention. Sounds to me like he respects you, Rea. It appears my girl is tough."

"I'm not your girl," she snapped. The last thing she wanted in the world was to be someone's girl. She knew what that meant, and little of it was good, from what she'd seen. "And stop acting like that creep has a crush on me."

He looked at her as if trying to read her in the low glow of the dash lights. "What's bothering you, Rea?"

She waited a minute, then decided to be honest. If it ended the friendship, so be it. She'd been fine before she met Noah McAllen, and she'd be fine if he walked away and never spoke to her again. "I think we need to get a few things straight."

"About me turning into a werewolf?" he asked. "I've been trying to figure out what you meant."

"No, not that. Well, partly, but not all." She wasn't making any sense. "Rule one," she started over. "I don't like people touching me. Not you. Not anyone."

"I kind of noticed that," he answered.

"And I don't want to be called some guy's girlfriend like I belong to him or something."

"All right. We stay just friends. Fine with me."

She thought for a moment, then added, "And you be straight with me. Don't ever try to play me."

"Agreed," he answered. "I try to be straight with everyone. I don't have the brains to remember lies."

"Okay, tell me. Why do you want to be my friend?"

Noah shoved his hat back. "I don't know, really. I just saw you out on that bench one day eating lunch all by yourself, and I wanted to get to know you."

"Because you felt sorry for me?"

"Because I already know everybody else in the school, but I didn't know you. Because you didn't look busy." He laughed. "And you didn't look like you'd make it easy."

She smiled. "And you don't like doing things easy."

"You guessed it."

They spent the rest of the way home reliving the

almost-fight, making it longer and more exciting with each telling. They talked.

She waved good-bye from the porch as he pulled away, even though she knew he couldn't see her in the dark. Uncle Jeremiah would never waste electricity by leaving on a light.

After the pickup had disappeared, she stood looking at the moon and thinking that for the first time she could remember, she felt peaceful.

It couldn't last, she reminded herself. Nothing ever lasted. The only thing she knew for sure about people was that eventually, they'd let you down.

Chapter 22

TYLER WRIGHT WENT INTO THE POST OFFICE to make his weekly complaint that someone was working all the crossword puzzles in his magazines before they reached his mailbox. But in truth, his heart wasn't into complaining today. For weeks he hadn't had time to do more than flip through the magazines, and then it was for discussion topics, not the puzzles. He had other things on his mind.

Correction, he had one thing on his mind . . . talking to Katherine. He'd decided his mystery lady was more a Katherine than a Kate, though if he ever did meet her again, he thought he'd call her both. Katherine when they discussed interests they had in common, Kate when he teased her.

As he waited his turn, then stepped up to the counter, Johnny Donavan, the postmaster of Harmony, was ready for him. "I know. I know, Mr. Wright. Someone is reading your mail."

"Not reading it. Writing in it," Tyler answered. "I buy those magazines for the foyer of the funeral home, and they look used the day I get them."

Johnny pressed his lips together and smiled, making wrinkles wave across his cheeks all the way to his ever-growing ears. "Well, Mr. Wright. It's not as though your customers are going to read the magazines. Or, for that matter, complain."

Tyler hated funeral home humor. He hated it when people introduced him as "the last to let them down" or "apt to give you grief."

He tried another tactic. "Who sorts the mail, Johnny?"

"You know as well as I do that Ronelle Logan does the downtown mail. She has since her daddy got her the job four years ago."

"Could I talk to her?"

"No." Johnny shook his head. Not all of his chins kept up with his face. "Last time you tried that, she was sick for two days and her mother came in to give me a piece of her mind. And believe me, Mr. Wright, you don't want a piece of that woman's mind."

"I don't want to upset Ronelle." Tyler smiled. "I just want to give her this. I picked it up in Lubbock the last time I was there."

Johnny frowned. People were always bringing in little gifts for him at Christmas. Cookies, cards, even gloves now and then. But no one had ever given Ronelle anything. It looked downright suspicious even if he didn't know why.

"Just tell her it's from a friend," Tyler said. "I don't even want her to know it's from me."

"Well, I guess it would be all right." He took the envelope, moving it slightly as if guessing the weight. "I'll have to look at it first."

"I didn't seal the envelope," Tyler answered, wondering if he'd have to put postage on the package before Johnny would deliver it to the back room.

The postmaster opened the flap and tugged out a large crossword puzzle book. *"The Best Crossword Puzzles of 2005 from the Country's Top Newspapers,"* he read.

"I'll look for 2006 when it comes out."

Johnny nodded and shoved the book back inside the envelope. "I've never seen one so big. She usually brings in those little ones she gets at the gas stations."

"Neither had I. They sell them at the big truck stops." Tyler smiled. "I'm hoping it'll last her a while."

"It might, but she considers crosswords a timed event. If it ever makes it into the Olympics, we'll lose her to the glory, I'm afraid."

"It'd be Harmony's loss." Tyler tried to look like he meant the lie.

Back in his car, he picked up the copy of a hand-drawn map of an old cattle trail. A librarian at the state capital had sent it to him, guessing he'd love to study the details marked down more than a hundred years ago.

Friday afternoon, the sun was shining, and he had no funerals pending. Life didn't get much better, he thought. He'd decided over breakfast to take the afternoon off and wander the back roads. If he got lucky, very lucky, he'd see an indentation in the earth where thousands, maybe hundreds of thousands of cattle crossed this land before fences barred their way to the railheads in Kansas.

Just thinking about walking on the exact spot where early settlers had walked always made Tyler smile. His father had loved history and made bedtime stories out of the legends of this part of the country. After his father died, Tyler spent months writing down all the stories he remembered, but in the end they only made him sad when he realized he'd never have children to pass them on to.

Tyler checked his watch. If he planned it right, he'd miss dinner but still get back in time to e-mail Katherine. As he drove out of town he thought of how much he knew about his Kate, and how little at the same time.

He knew she was allergic to shellfish and liked to eat barbecue with her fingers even though it was messy. She'd said she loved rainy days when the earth was sleepy. She thought she was fat. She'd read *Gone With the Wind* every summer since she was fifteen and had never seen any of the Harry Potter movies. She collected crystal snowflakes for a Christmas tree she said she never had time to put up.

Tyler waved to a farmer mending fence as he turned off one farm-to-market road and onto another.

There were so many important things he didn't know about Kate. He didn't know how old she was. He knew she rented a two-bedroom apartment and she could hear planes flying over, but he didn't know the town. He knew her favorite movies and TV shows, but he had no idea what she did for a living.

Something important, he bet. She was a worker, he sensed that. And, as much as she dreaded work, sometimes she was dedicated to it. The few times she'd had to leave, or been late e-mailing, she'd said that it couldn't be avoided. Once she'd said she was in D.C., but she hadn't told him why. They'd talked of the capital but never of her career.

He knew if he asked, he'd open the door for her to do the same, and he didn't want to tell her he owned a funeral home in a small town she'd probably never heard of.

Tyler passed a highway patrolman parked near the crossroads and decided he'd better pay more attention to how fast he was going and stop thinking about Katherine. But he knew that was impossible. She was in the back of his mind all the time.

She was like honeysuckle in a garden. Most of the time you didn't even notice it among all the flowers, but the smell was always there, welcoming. Katherine was like that in his head. Tyler laughed and hit the steering wheel with the palm of his hand. He couldn't believe his thoughts. If he wasn't careful, he'd be writing poetry.

As he passed the McNabb place, he thought about Stella and Bob, who'd been married for forty years. Some folks thought it strange that Stella, an educated woman, being the high school home economics teacher, had married Bob, who had barely made it out of high school. But they fit together. More important, they seemed to really like each other. Bob waited outside in the car for her every time she kept the funeral home open at night. Tyler had never heard either one of them say a cross word to the other. Stella knew and talked to everyone in town. Bob waved, and that seemed enough.

Tyler wished not for what they had, but that he and Katherine could continue to have what little they had for a few years.

If he could just have that much, it would be enough.

Chapter 23

SATURDAY MORNING

HANK MATHESON WALKED INTO THE BLUE Moon Diner with no illusions that Alexandra had called him to have breakfast. She'd been all business when she'd said, "Seven, tomorrow morning at the diner." The only question in his mind was why not one of their offices?

The place was deserted. The usual old guys who had breakfast every morning during the week weren't here because on Saturdays the senior citizens served a free pancake breakfast and Sunday they'd all have coffee and doughnuts at the church before Sunday school. The two days away from the diner gave the old men new stories to tell Monday.

With the regulars gone and no one in the downtown offices grabbing a meal before the start of a workday, the place looked closed. If Ronelle hadn't been at her usual tiny table at the door, Hank would have thought Cass, the owner of the place, had simply left without turning off the lights or locking the door.

"Morning, Ronelle," he said as he passed by.

She didn't look up from her crossword puzzle book.

When Hank took a seat in the back booth by the windows, Cass yelled to him through the pass-through window, "What'll you have? Ain't got no waitress this morning, so you'll have to fend for yourself."

"Just coffee for now," Hank yelled back. "I'll get it."

He stepped behind the counter and poured himself a cup. He could see through the window that Alex was pulling up her Jeep beside his truck, so he poured her a cup as well.

She hit the door moving fast. Ever since he could remember, Alex was like a storm. Warren used to complain about his kid sister, but Hank had always been fascinated by her. She was a woman who took life at full speed. Warren and he used to laugh that boyfriends had the half-life of Kleenex around her. She changed majors twice a year until Warren talked her into settling on criminal justice, and then she'd gone all-out straight through to the terminal degree, a master's. Just like her big brother. Only for Warren, the career path had proven terminal.

Hank shoved the memories aside as Alex slid into the seat across from him and unzipped her jacket.

"The boys from the crime lab found a few things that point to the possibility that you're right about the fires being set. They also said whoever did it had some knowledge of fires and a good sense of place. The guy's exact words were, 'Our arsonist knows the lay of the land.' " She met Hank's stare. "There's a good chance he's either in law enforcement or one of your volunteers at the station."

"Shit," Hank said under his breath.

Alex took a sip of the coffee, then added sugar, giving him time to think. "I'm starving," she murmured, more to herself than him.

Hank stood and walked to the pass-through. "Two specials, Cass."

"Ain't got no specials on Saturday," he yelled back. "I can make you up two breakfasts, but you'll have to take what you get."

"Two surprises," Hank agreed, knowing that he'd eaten everything on the menu in this place, so nothing would be too shocking. "With whole wheat, scrambled, well done, and dry," in case any of those words applied.

"You got it," Cass answered. "I'll ding the bell when your order's ready. Pick it up fast if you want it hot."

Back at the table, Alex smiled up at him, but the smile didn't reach her eyes. He wanted to pull her close and tell her everything was going to be all right. They'd make it through this trouble. But he knew she wouldn't welcome sympathy. She needed someone she trusted to talk things out with, and he guessed he should be thankful that she considered him that. They might fight about pretty near everything, but they'd never lied to one another.

"There's more, isn't there?" Hank asked.

She nodded and waited until he sat down before she said softly, "The highway patrol has one suspect who isn't either one of my men or one of yours. Right now they're calling him a person of interest."

Hank relaxed. "That's good news, I guess." He didn't want to think that one of his men could be setting fires, even though he'd heard about it happening a few times over the years.

"No," she answered. "Not good news. Their person of interest is Tyler Wright."

Hank shook his head. "That's not possible."

"I feel the same way, but they've got records of people seeing him driving by at least three of the fire sites just before the fires."

Hank leaned forward, staring right at her. "I'm not buying any of this."

"You'd rather believe it's one of your men, or mine?"

Hank downed the bitter news along with his coffee and stared at the scarred wooden table between them. "Maybe my theory is just that, a theory. Maybe all these fires aren't related. We've had six grass fires before in two months. Even the results on the Dumpster fire couldn't prove that it had been set by someone other than the druggie. Maybe . . ."

She leaned closer. "I know Tyler is your friend, Hank, and you stand with your friends to the end."

His head shot up, and he knew she was thinking the same thing he was at that moment. He'd been the first to the scene that night Warren was shot, and the EMTs had had to pry his friend's body away from him. Hank had been a full-grown man, educated and trained to deal with anything, but he couldn't, wouldn't let his best friend go. In those moments, he'd believed with everything he had that if he could just hold on tight enough, fight hard enough, he could keep Warren from dying.

Hank saw the sadness in her eyes. The heartache he'd seen since that night. It had been three years, but now and then the pain twisted like an embedded spur.

Cass broke their silent standoff by clanking two plates on the table. "I got tired of ringing the bell. Eat up, folks," he said, then walked away.

Alex looked down at the mound of food. "I'm not hungry anymore," she said.

"Me, either."

"I'll want a list of all your volunteers dating back ten years."

Hank nodded. "You'll have it in an hour."

"You staying at the station today?" She zipped her jacket. "You still got that feeling another fire's coming?"

"Yes to both."

She slid to the edge of the booth. "I'm staying close today, too. I'll be working in my office if a call comes in."

"Dinner tonight, here," Hank said in a flat voice. "We'll go over any detail we find in a file. With our phones transferred to our cells, we'll get any calls."

"Fine." She looked at her plate of food. "With our luck, Cass will warm all this over and make us eat it for dinner."

Hank stood, dropping a twenty on the table. "Call me when you're ready."

She climbed out of the booth, and for a moment they were standing so close they would have touched if one had shifted. Neither moved.

A river of unsaid words flowed between them, and neither knew how to cross. Hank had sworn after last week that he wouldn't be the one to try again. He stepped back, reaching for his hat.

"It's not Tyler," he said. "I'd stake my life on it."

"I'll still check him out."

"You do that, Sheriff." Hank tried to keep the anger from his voice. It wasn't fair to be mad at her for doing her job. But he knew it would be a waste of time. A man who kept a quarter in his vest pocket just in case he ran into a four-year-old princess wasn't the kind of man who set fires.

They walked past Ronelle, bidding her good day. She ignored them both.

Chapter 24

SATURDAY EVENING

BOB MCNABB HAD NEVER CONSIDERED HIM-self much of a farmer, but he leased ten acres five miles outside Harmony because Stella wanted to live in the country. He drove back and forth to wherever the Texas Department of Highways and Public Transportation sent him every day for thirty years to do highway maintenance, and then he retired and drove Stella around. When he was alone in the car, he liked listening to western novels on tape. He'd probably checked out every one the library stocked at least twice.

When Stella retired from teaching, she began practicing what she'd preached all those years. She canned and made jams in the fall, quilted all winter, and gardened in the spring. She belonged to every ladies' club in town and served as queen of the biggest Red Hat Society in the panhandle. She taught the youth classes at the Baptist church on Sunday nights, worked part-time at the funeral home when Tyler Wright needed her, and volunteered at the Pioneer Museum on the Square.

Bob took on only one hobby: raising long-eared rabbits for the tristate fair every year. Stella, having been a professional, wasn't allowed to enter her quilts or canned goods or even vegetables, but Bob could enter his rabbits. He had ribbons all over one wall of his small barn. Stella's favorite joke was to introduce him as a rabbit wrangler.

Tonight, he could hear Stella singing with the radio as he walked outside to smoke his one cigarette of the day. They made a pact years ago. He'd cut his smoking down to once a day, except after making love, and she'd stop bothering him about the habit. He'd thought it was a good rule, but to be honest there were a few times he'd have sex just to get to the cigarette afterward. Stella must have figured it out, though; about two years ago she stopped being in the mood. Bob didn't know if she was no longer attracted to him in that way, or if she thought she was improving his health.

He lit up and walked out by the barn. The land next to their few acres was leased for grazing, but it had been so dry lately he hadn't seen cattle on it.

Bob strolled all the way to the fence post watching the evening sky, wishing he'd see a cloud. Without rain, the warmer days coming would be even hotter. Even with the sides of the barn open, the rabbits would suffer, and Bob couldn't afford to buy air conditioning for pets. A few days last year when it had been well over a hundred, he and Stella had brought in the rabbit cages. They'd stacked them in the kitchen and bathroom tub, but it had been a mess.

He looked up, smelling something in the wind.

Someone burning trash, he thought, then remembered the burn ban. Anyone would be a fool to burn, knowing the fine.

Then he saw something black moving across the short grassland a few hundred yards beyond his fence. It moved like the shadow of a black cloud, shifting unevenly as it crawled toward him.

"Fire," he whispered with an intake of breath.

He stared hard. The dry stubby grass burned so quickly, he could barely make out the flame between the smoke and the earth.

Fire!

Bob crushed his cigarette with his foot as he turned and ran back toward the house. "Stella!" he yelled. "Call the fire department."

She came to the door and stared at him. Then, behind him, she must have noticed the smoke. Her face seemed to go pale as the moon in the evening light. She put one hand over her heart, then took a quick breath and disappeared.

Bob ran to the barn and began loading up the cages as fast as he could. He had his van full by the time she came around the house with the garden hose. A gray fog of smoke drifted between them. The black ground cloud had moved twenty yards closer.

He took the hose from her hand, wishing it would stretch past the fence. "Get in the van and drive across the road with the rabbits. I'll wet the fence line down."

Stella had never taken orders well, but for once she didn't discuss his plan. She climbed in and gunned the engine. For a woman who never liked to drive, she looked like a racer flying down the road.

Before she was out of sight, a pickup turned down his drive. The McAllen kid, Bob thought. He'd seen the boy pass by on his way to the old worthless McAllen ranch ever since the kid could see over the steering wheel. Everyone said he was a good boy despite being as crazy as his old man about the rodeo.

Noah McAllen jumped from the truck before it stopped moving. "How can I help?"

Bob motioned to the old washtub he used to clean up the rabbits for show. "Grab that and bring it to me, then get all the feed sacks you can find in the barn."

By the time Noah found a half dozen sacks, the tub was full of water and two more neighbors had arrived. They knew what to do. Noah might be only a kid, but he learned fast and did twice the work of the others.

One man cut the fence with pliers he kept on his belt, and they all stepped into the field beyond Bob's property. Barbed wire wouldn't stop the fire; only a road would, and Bob and Stella's home lay between the fire and the road.

The four men took wet sacks and formed a line about twenty feet apart. Each man had to hold the fire line so that it didn't reach the thick grass of the yards and flower beds or beyond to the house and barn.

Bob worked as fast as he could, knowing that even if they held the fire, it would eventually bend and come up the sides. There wouldn't be enough men to stop it then. Four men could hold one side of his property line, but it'd take a dozen or more to save the place.

The black smoke burned into his lungs and his face, and Bob's hands felt sunburned in the heat.

He was aware of Stella even in the smoke. He'd hoped she would stay with the van, but he knew it was in her nature to come back and join the fight. She was passing out soaked sacks and tossing burned ones into the tub. She moved with the hose, spraying the men down as well as the ground when they came near enough for her to reach them. The fire constantly pushed them backward. Before long they'd be at the fence line. Bob tried not to breathe deeply as he fought harder.

The sound of sirens filled the air moments later. Bob felt like it had been an hour since he'd first seen the fire, but it couldn't have been more than ten minutes. The sheriff's car pulled in first, and then the fire truck crossed the grass and headed toward the open spot in the fence.

Another pickup, loaded down with men with shovels, pulled up near the house. The men jumped out and ran toward the fire line, holding their shovels high like ancient Scots going to battle.

Bob stepped back as the fire hose came to life, spraying water over the grass in a twenty-foot sweep.

Men with shovels dug a ditch in the ground between the barn and the grass. If fire came again, it would have to jump the line to reach the barn.

He stared and watched, knowing how close he'd come to losing his home, Stella's quilts, the rabbits. If he hadn't seen it coming when he did . . . he couldn't think about what would have happened.

"You all right?" someone whispered as Bob felt a hand rest on his shoulder.

He turned and smiled at the sheriff. He had no words. *Thank you* seemed an empty bucket, considering what they'd all done.

She seemed to understand. "Your wife went in the house to wash up. The boys will take care of making sure it's out. You look a sight."

When he didn't move, she added, "It's over, Mr. McNabb. You can rest now. It's over." She put her arm around him and tugged him toward the porch.

"Your little brother was here when I needed him," Bob managed. "Without him . . ."

Alexandra smiled. "I know. I'm proud of him. He's a good kid."

Bob nodded. "The best, if you ask me. Tell him I said so."

"I sent him inside to wash. You can tell him yourself."

Bob took a few steps toward the house and

stopped. He stared at the open door, with Stella moving around the kitchen. They didn't have much. Didn't even own the house they'd lived in for half their marriage. But when he thought about losing everything, he realized just how rich he was.

He walked in, his face and clothes black with smoke. Walked right up to Stella and kissed her on the mouth like he hadn't done in years.

As always, she understood him and moved into his arms. They were alive.

When she tugged away, he asked, "How are the rabbits?"

"They're fine."

"I meant for you to park the van across the road and stay there."

She shrugged. "I know, but I couldn't see sitting with the rabbits while you were just down the road fighting to save the house. If those rabbits had died, we'd have dinner, but if you'd . . ." She couldn't finish for crying.

He held her tightly and smiled. He felt the same.

People were moving all around now, washing up, doctoring burns on their hands and faces, rolling up the fire hose, but he didn't care. Bob leaned close against her ear and whispered, "I think tonight, when we're alone, I'd like to make love to my wife."

She giggled just as she had when he'd first mentioned the idea forty years ago.

"And," he added, "I don't think I'll smoke a cigarette afterward, if you've no objection."

Chapter 25

⚜

ALEX CHECKED THE SECOND-DEGREE BURNS on her little brother's hands and face. "You got too close without gear."

Several of the firefighters in the country kitchen agreed with her.

Noah tried to pull away. "I didn't exactly have time to go shopping for the crisis." Immediately he looked like he regretted snapping back. Unlike her, Noah was usually even-tempered. "When I drove up and saw the smoke coming toward the McNabb house, I only thought about helping."

"Next time," said Hank, who had joined them, "wet a bandanna and tie it around your face. Dunk your hat, too, if you get a chance."

"And wear gloves," Alex ordered. "Mom's going to have a fit about you getting singed."

"I'm not hurt," Noah insisted, glaring at his bossy sister. "I've had sunburns worse than this."

Alex chose not to argue with him in front of everyone. They could both see the blisters rising on the backs of his hands.

She nodded a thank-you as Stella passed, offering everyone iced tea in mason jars. When Noah joined the other men, Alex walked out into the night, where the smell of smoke was still thick in the air. Usually, this time of night was her favorite part of the day, but now danger drifted in the wind as if whispering of more trouble to come.

When she reached the fence, she heard Noah's truck and knew he must be leaving. The fire truck started backing through the mud toward the house. It was over. In a few minutes the night would be still and quiet again. And, thanks to the breeze, free of fire.

Alex knew it was Hank who walked up behind her. She didn't turn but whispered into the smoky stillness, "You were right. You warned of a fire tonight."

"Yeah, and I hate that I was," he answered, resting his arm on the fence post. "If we'd been five minutes later, the McNabbs would have lost their home."

"McNabb told me he knew you'd come." She smiled. "He thinks you hung the moon, Hank. Told me you were like a son to him."

Hank shifted. "He never told me that. I think a lot of him and Stella, too, good people. If he were twenty years younger, I'd give him this job and stay on my ranch long enough to make some money."

Alex shook her head. "No, you wouldn't. You'd find something else to keep you busy. You're nothing but a Boy Scout, Matheson. Always trying to help people."

He didn't deny it. "You're nothing but a wild child, McAllen. If you hadn't been sheriff, you'd probably been an outlaw."

She didn't argue. She'd made her share of dumb choices.

They were both silent for a while, and then he added, "I hate the thought that someone is out there starting these fires. We have all we can handle with the accidental ones started by lightning or backfiring cars, or downed transformers. We don't need a nut running around setting them on purpose."

"If the wind had been stronger tonight . . ." she began.

"We'd be standing beside ashes," he finished.

On impulse, she gripped his forearm and closed her fingers around the solid muscles a few inches above his wrist. "You're not in this alone, you know; we'll fight this, Hank. We'll fight it together." All the problems they had between them—all the past that haunted them—didn't matter. All that mattered was stopping whoever was setting the fires before someone was killed.

His hand closed around hers. "There's nothing else we can do here tonight. I'll call in help first thing tomorrow morning and we'll find the point of origin. Maybe our firebug got careless and left a clue."

"Until then," she said, wishing she could see his face in the darkness, "I'll have a patrol out here making sure no one sets foot on the land. As far as I'm concerned, this entire burn is a crime scene and I'm treating it like one."

Someone yelled, "Chief!"

Hank turned, pulling away from her touch. "Tomorrow," he whispered, as if someone might be close enough to hear.

She nodded, then realized he couldn't see her any better than she could see him. "Name the time?"

"Seven, your office for coffee. The team should be here by eight and we'll find out where this fire started."

He walked toward the house, but she stayed in the shadows. She wanted to stand there and listen to the wind, feel the heat still in the earth, smell the smoke. Somewhere near was a criminal who was trying to destroy her town, and she planned to get to him first.

Chapter 26

REAGAN SAT DOWN BESIDE JEREMIAH IN WHAT she thought of as her chair. The darkening sky seemed muddy tonight, but the air was far too dry for it to be fog. She swore this part of Texas sometimes had negative humidity. The air just sucked what little moisture there was out and turned it into dust mites.

"There's a fire northwest of here," Jeremiah said to himself. "I can smell it."

"Any idea what's burning?" She'd learned he

could read the atmosphere better than a crossbreed of a weatherman and mystic.

"Grass, I think, just grass. When trees burn, they leave the smell of heartbreak in the air."

"Oh." She tugged her blanket around her, thinking she'd always wondered what heartbreak smelled like. "How far away do you think the fire is?"

"It's out by now. All we're getting is a drift of the smoke in the wind."

She looked at the silhouette of him a few feet away. Even in the night she could see his bent, crippled-up frame. Like an old tree root, he seemed to draw life from the earth. There was not one ounce of doubt in her mind that he loved his apple trees more than he'd ever love any human.

"You ever have your heart broke?" she asked, just for something to say.

He was so quiet, she wasn't sure he planned to answer, and then he surprised her and said, "Once."

Reagan waited. For Jeremiah, the flow of conversation was more like a drip.

"I was engaged to a Matheson girl before I left for the war. I thought she was about the prettiest gal in the state. She called me Dimples and giggled every time she said the word. I suspect that would have gotten irritating in time, but when I was eighteen I remember thinking it was cute."

"Really." Reagan leaned over the arm of her

chair and looked at him upside down. "Was this girl any kin to the Mathesons in town?"

He didn't answer, but she could feel the look he was giving her even in the dark. It was the one that silently said she was dumber than a chipped rock.

"Oh, of course. You grew up around Mathesons with their ranch bordering us near the apple trees." It occurred to her that if he'd married the girl, the Truman name wouldn't be down to two. Now, when he died and the town figured out she wasn't a Truman, one of the founding families would be gone. Completely gone. The thought hurt Reagan's heart. How would she tell people that her family was extinct?

"So, what happened to the giggling Matheson girl?" she asked him as she shoved aside her thoughts of being alone again.

"When I got back from the war, she said she was more interested in a career than me. Became a grade-school teacher and lived with her sister in town until they both retired and moved out to Hank's ranch where they grew up."

Reagan had heard Noah say once that Hank lived with a houseful of women, but she never thought one of them might be Jeremiah's old flame. "Did you ever go over and say hi?" Hank's ranch was within walking distance.

Jeremiah didn't answer, but she thought she saw him shake his head.

Finally, he said, "I didn't have nothing to offer

her. My land ain't hardly fit for farming, and I never wanted to nurse a bunch of cattle. If it weren't for those apple trees my father planted a hundred years ago, I would have starved by now. The government pays me to let all my grass go back to nature. Even sent me seeds years ago." He looked out in the darkness as if he could see his land. "I like the idea that the native grasses are growing up, making my place look like no one ever settled here."

"If you like the natural land so much, why have all those tractors?"

He laughed. "Do you wake up ever' morning with a certain number of questions you have to ask?"

"No. What about the tractors?"

"I fixed trucks in the army; never carried a rifle all my time in the war. I got so good at it I could tell what was wrong with a motor when they pulled a truck into the garage. When I got home, old tractors were about the only thing around to work on. Working on them was easy, and it passed the time. I used to do work for everyone around, even bought all kinds of old farm equipment and fixed them up to sell, but when newer models came along, they weren't so much fun, so I quit and just kept the old ones I liked."

Reagan almost giggled. Jeremiah had just said more words than she'd heard him utter in weeks. "Would you show me them?"

"Sure." He patted the dog's head and the dog stood. "Maybe tomorrow before supper. I think we'll turn in now."

The old dog and the elderly man moved silently toward the house. The dog that had no name but Dog was never far from Jeremiah's side. The few times she'd gotten up earlier than Jeremiah, she'd seen the dog on a rug just outside the old man's door.

Reagan curled into her blanket. She loved it here. Each day a piece of her soul dug deeper into the soil of this land along Lone Oak Road. She wasn't sure if it became more of her, or she was slowly becoming a part of it, but she knew she'd never leave this place completely no matter what happened. A part of her would always be here.

She watched a pickup turn off the main road and recognized the sound of Noah's truck.

Jeremiah moved up the steps. "Tell that boy to change his spark plugs. Engine's missing."

"I will."

"And tell him he's welcome to a slice of leftover pie. He gets any thinner I'll mistake him for a sapling."

"I will." Reagan smiled as she stood. Jeremiah liked Noah McAllen even if he did complain.

"Don't let him talk your ear off, girl. We've got work in the orchard tomorrow."

"I won't."

Noah's pickup pulled to a stop just as she heard

the kitchen door close. Jeremiah might like Noah, but that didn't mean he planned to be sociable.

She saw the white of the bandage on his left hand as he walked toward her.

"Are you hurt?" As he approached, she tried to see his face beneath the shadows of his battered cowboy hat. "Did something happen?"

He stopped several feet away. "Now don't start babying me, Rea, or I swear I'll leave. I just got a little burn. It's not even blistered in but a few spots. Between my sister and my mother I've had all I can take of being pampered. I came over to tell you about the fire at the McNabbs' place tonight."

"I know about it."

"You know?"

"Sure, Uncle Jeremiah said he smelled smoke. Grass fire, right?"

"Right. What else did the old man say?"

Reagan smiled. "He said you could have some pie if you wanted."

They moved toward the kitchen door. "You know something," he said as he held the door with his good hand and let her pass under his arm. "Food seems to come with being hurt. I never noticed it before."

She slid the pie tin toward him, sat down on the seat next to him, and handed him one of the forks.

The kitchen was still and silent, like the night. With no TV and a radio that got only three stations, she was glad for the company.

He told her all about the fire while they finished off half a chocolate pie.

He moved his bandaged hand to rest on the back of her chair, just above her shoulder, and she didn't mind. Maybe she was getting used to his nearness. Maybe she knew he meant nothing when he drew closer.

"I did something good tonight, Rea, and it felt really great."

"I wish I could have been there."

"Me, too." He stared at her for a few seconds and added, "Want to go with me to Dallas next week? There's a PRCA rodeo and for once, I'd be going just to watch. Several of us are skipping school after lunch and heading down, but it'll run too late to drive back on Friday. There's a church that opens their doors and lets us sleep on bedrolls in their fellowship hall. Last year there were kids from all over the state sacked out on bedrolls. The rules are strict, but you'll—"

"No," Reagan said without hesitation.

"But—"

She didn't give him time to try to talk her into anything. "Uncle Jeremiah is feeling bad. He's got a cough. I'd better stay close."

Noah nodded, but the look in his eyes was skeptical. "You're still afraid I'm going to turn into a werewolf or some other kind of monster, aren't you?"

"No." The word came too fast to be complete

truth. "I just don't want to be that far away from home."

She hated it when he got that kind of smile that said he'd read her mind. He couldn't read her thoughts. He couldn't know . . . he didn't know anything about her. Yet he understood.

"All right, stay home, but you're missing a good time."

She'd heard those words before in another place, another time . . . and they'd been wrong.

"Well"—he tapped her shoulder—"how about watching me ride in two weeks? The rodeo is right here in Harmony, close enough for you to walk home."

"I'll be there."

When she stood to wash the pie pan, she noticed him looking at a calendar on the wall by the door. "You marking off the days to something?"

"Not me, Uncle Jeremiah. Every morning he crosses one more day off."

"It's a long time before Christmas. What do you think he's marking?"

"I have no idea. He hates talking at breakfast and by evening I've forgotten about it." She frowned. "If I were guessing, I'd say he's marking off the days until I leave. I don't think he's really gotten used to the fact that I might stay."

She tugged Noah out of the chair by his unbandaged hand and walked him to the porch.

Just before he headed down the steps, he turned,

shoved his hat back, and leaned close as if to kiss her on the cheek.

She moved away, looking down, not wanting to see his face.

Neither of them said good night. He just walked to his truck and drove away while she watched.

"Don't get close," she whispered to the night. "Never let anyone close." She watched at the tail-lights faded. "Not even Noah."

Chapter 27

HANK WENT BY THE FIRE STATION WHEN HE came back from the McNabb place. He showered, then made sure all was in order.

Willie Davis was so pumped Hank almost had to peel the kid off the ceiling. He'd been around a year, but this was the first real firefight he'd been in. Luckily, Andy Daily was still at the station running off copies of pictures he'd taken when they were fighting the fire. He seemed to enjoy rehashing the details as much as Willie did. He finally had to leave to walk across the street to the city dispatcher's desk. Hank had a feeling Andy would have no problem staying awake tonight.

Adrenaline still pounded in Hank's blood, too, so instead of going home, he headed down North Street for no reason. The fires, or rather the fact that someone was setting them on purpose, ate away at his gut. He took the crimes personally, as though each were committed against him.

Since his father died when he was a kid, Hank had always thought he had to take care of things. His branch of the Matheson family didn't have much money, but Hank had the original land old Harmon Ely had given his great-granddad. Somewhere a few generations back, his ancestor had managed to buy out the others. Every other relative moved to town or away except his branch of the family tree.

He had cousins who worked in the bank and one who owned the Ford dealership. Cousins taught school at every level. One second cousin was a lawyer, one the youth minister at the Hilltop Baptist Church. Almost everywhere he looked in town, he had a relative who worked there, but none wanted to ranch, except him. Hank's father must have handed over the last gene for ranching before he died. Maybe that's why Hank understood Alex's brother Noah so well; he knew how the kid felt about the land.

The day Hank graduated from college, his mother signed the ranch over to him with the understanding that the big rambling house would always be home to family. His two sisters would always have a place to come home to, but Hank held the title to the land. Which, as it turned out, was very smart, otherwise some ex-brother-in-law would now own a slice of the Matheson ranch.

His mother had been selling her pottery for as long as he could remember, but she never mixed that money with ranch funds, except once to build on to the house. Which, considering his two great-aunts and two sisters who all came home to roost, hadn't been a bad idea. She had her studio, a low adobe-style building off the garden, and Hank had his barn out back, far enough away that the ladies didn't smell his horses.

He'd also closed off one upstairs wing for his bedroom and study. All the women said they understood, but Hank had the feeling that if he ever left the door to his wing unlocked they'd have his socks matched and underwear folded before he was out of sight of the house.

Some years the money from the ranch barely kept the taxes and utilities paid, but Hank knew he'd never sell. In good years he'd buy a new truck, repaint the barn, and improve the stock. In bad years, he'd hang on and hope.

His mother had her business but when Hank got home from college, the ranch was all his. She took care of the house. The aunts managed the flower beds, which grew larger every year. Claire, Saralynn's mother, painted in the attic, and no one was quite sure what Liz, his younger sister, did. She had two college degrees and had been telling people she was studying to take the bar exam, though Hank had yet to see a law book around the place.

As Hank turned around at the end of town, his thoughts turned dark. Hank liked order. He liked everything to make sense in his life. He liked reason, but this time reason told him that if the arson followed around, closing the circle, his ranch or one close might be the next target.

He laughed without humor. Right now nothing made sense; why should the arson? Hank was crazy about a woman who hated him. His two divorced sisters were settling in, planning to never leave. His niece grew weaker every day. The police thought his good friend was a person of interest.

For a man who liked order, Hank was batting zero.

When he passed the Blue Moon Diner, he noticed Alex's Jeep parked across the street on the back row of the Buffalo Bar and Grill parking lot. She'd almost hidden it in the trees that lined the alley, but he knew it was hers.

Hank swore and pulled in beside the Jeep. Alex seemed to be determined to make his long day endless. He thought that a minute ago everything that could go wrong already had, but he'd forgotten it was Saturday night.

He walked in the smoky bar and looked around. He was hoping she'd ended her habit of coming here on Saturday nights, but that would be too much to ask. If she was drunk, she'd be wild and hard to handle, but he'd do it. He'd get her home safe, sober enough that he could leave her, and then walk away, cussing himself for caring one way or the other what happened to her.

Saturday night Buffalo's always had a band playing, and the place was usually packed. Tonight was no exception. The bar smelled of sawdust, sweat, and beer. Lights blinked along the dance floor, offering only flashes of light. The low rattle of conversations blended amid laughter and the sound of bottles clanking.

Alexandra wasn't at her usual place at the far corner of the bar. In fact, she wasn't anywhere. When he finished his second lap around the place, Hank wondered if he'd been wrong about the Jeep being hers. A tall blonde wearing a sheriff's badge wasn't an easy person to miss.

The thought crossed his mind that she might already have left with someone. He checked his watch. Even if she'd come straight from the McNabb place, he didn't think she'd had time to get drunk enough to go home with someone yet. Besides, one of the bartenders would have called him if she was acting out, not because they owed him any favors, but because they all respected Alex and didn't want to see her make a fool of herself.

He spotted her walking out of the ladies' room. She hadn't noticed him yet. She walked toward the dance floor, stopping only long enough to gulp down the last half of a beer, and then she stepped into some cowboy's arms. They began to two-step across the floor. He was dressed western, but not with clothes that had ever seen a day's work on a ranch. He also seemed far more interested in showing off his dancing moves than in his partner.

Hank watched her for a while. She seemed to be enjoying the dancing, but she wasn't talking to the guy whirling her around. She wasn't even looking at him. Her eyes were closed as she moved to the music.

When the song ended and the cowboy stepped away, pointing toward the bar, she shook her head and turned her back to her partner.

Hank's boot hit the dance floor wood hard as he moved forward.

He saw the anger in her eyes the second she spotted him, but he kept walking straight to her.

"Are you checking up on me again?" she snapped when he was close enough for her words to be private.

"No." He tried to smile, but couldn't pull off casual when she was glaring at him. "I came to dance."

Without giving her time to comment, he circled her waist as the music started.

She didn't move. "I don't want to dance with you."

He tugged her against him and moved her as if she were a mannequin. "Just close your eyes again, Alexandra, and pretend I'm the nobody you've been dancing with all night."

To his surprise she took his suggestion. Her body began to move with his, her hands rested on his shoulders, and they danced.

First one, then another, then another. Hank hadn't danced except at a few weddings since college, but the good thing about country music was that the dances he'd learned in bars near campus seemed to still fit. As with all bands toward the end of the night, the music got slower.

Alex slid her hands down his back and hooked her thumbs into the waist of his jeans.

When she rested her head on his shoulder and breathed against his throat, Hank drew her closer and she melted into him like warm butter.

He pushed her hair away from her face with his chin. "How about we take a night off from hating each other and just relax? I'm too tired to fight. Why don't we just pretend we're strangers?"

"I don't want to fight anymore," she whispered. "And I don't hate you, Hank, I just don't . . ."

"I know, baby, I've heard it all before. All I want to do tonight is dance with you."

He felt her nod of agreement and moved his hand slowly down her back. He didn't want to dance at all, but if she'd stay in his arms, he'd give it his best shot.

She felt so good against him. Without the vest he could feel her chest rising and falling against his. She fit perfectly in his arms, just as he knew she would. He rested his hands at her waist and moved his thumbs over her last few ribs. He thought of teasing her about being too thin as he'd done a hundred times when they were growing up, but he didn't want to tease her tonight. He just wanted to hold her against him.

She was tall and lean and stronger than most men he knew, but right now, in his arms, she was all woman. No gun. No badge. No smart mouth. Just pure woman, leaning into a man.

What he wanted to do with her would probably shock even wild Alexandra. When she'd been sixteen, he'd reminded himself he was four years older and she'd think he was a pervert if he flirted with her. When she'd been twenty and having her fun with every man she liked, he'd reminded himself he was her brother's best friend. Hank felt like he'd been watching over her and wanting her all his life.

When the band took a break, he closed his hand over hers. "How about I buy you a beer and we split some wings?"

She shook her head. "I want my own basket of wings."

He smiled, tugging her off the dance floor. "You got it. Find us a table and I'll order the wings at the bar."

She looked up at him, her grip tight on his hand. "Before I forget or reality comes crashing in, thanks for the dance. It was nice."

Before he could react, he tasted the touch of her

lips on his mouth, and then she was gone, vanishing into the crowd.

It took all his self-control to head toward the bar. He ordered the wings, grabbed two beers, and went to find her.

The third time he circled the bar, he accepted the fact the she'd ditched him.

Frustrated, he walked outside to clear his head. He expected to see the empty spot next to his Dodge where her Jeep had been parked. But the Jeep was there.

Letting his eyes adjust to the night, he looked around. The noise of the band tuning up for another set drifted from behind him. It crossed his mind that Alex might be playing a trick, or worse, teasing him, but that wasn't like her. She hadn't been drunk enough to pass out in the restroom or think she could walk home, so she had to be somewhere near.

He set the beers on the railing and walked toward her Jeep.

He'd guessed right. She was sitting in the front seat with the door open.

Hank thought he knew women, but Alex was from a planet all of her own. She didn't get her hair done or her nails painted. Half the time he couldn't tell whether she wore makeup, but to him she was sexy as hell.

"You trying to run out on your wing order?" he asked as he rested an elbow on her Jeep's door. "Or maybe me?"

"Neither," she answered. "I couldn't find a table so I thought I'd come out here to think."

"About what?"

She looked up at him with those less-than-innocent blue eyes. "About how we might as well do it and get it over with."

"What?"

"You know what, Hank. The tension between us is so strong I swear I can see it in the air sometimes." She stood and tugged her T-shirt free from her pants. "Right here, right now. You've got more room in your Dodge than I do in the Jeep, so let's go there."

When he didn't speak or move, she added, "Or we can do it standing. It's dark enough between the cars."

She was so close when he inhaled, he breathed her in. He felt her hands brush his middle and move to his belt. She began tugging the buckle loose.

He leaned to kiss her, but she turned away. "Don't waste time. Let's get this over with."

Hank had wanted her so long his brain couldn't function. After all this time, suddenly, she wanted him, right here, right now.

He dug his fingers into her hair and twisted his hand into a fist, then tugged hard until her face lifted and she met his stare. "Stop it, Alexandra. Stop it right now."

She raised an eyebrow. "You don't want me, Matheson?"

"You know I do, but not like this." He realized that *like this* might have been the only way she'd ever had it.

She pushed away. "Well, if you're waiting for me to wear a strapless dress and a pushup bra and bat my eyes all evening before I finally surrender, you're out of luck. I'm not that kind of woman."

Hank remembered once Warren had slugged a guy in a bar for commenting about Alex. The drunk had said he could tell she was from rodeo people. She wouldn't let a man stay on her longer than eight seconds.

Hank pulled her head toward him, ignoring her protests, and kissed her hard, then whispered against her lips, "You're not any kind of woman, Alex; you're an original, and I wouldn't want you to be any other way than just how you are." He kissed her softer, then moved to her ear and added, "We're not making love for the first time in my truck."

She pushed on his chest, and he let her go. "What makes you think there will ever be a second time, or a second offer?"

"I'm betting on it." He buckled his belt, wondering if he wasn't a fool for turning her down. Half the men he knew had an any-woman-any-time-offered rule they followed, but Hank knew he wanted far more from Alexandra. "Tuck that shirt in and let's go eat our hot wings and warm beer."

"You're not my big brother," she snapped.

"Damn right about that." He grabbed her shoulders and pushed her against the Jeep. While she protested, he kissed her again. He tasted when passion sparked once more in her and felt her move against him, trying to be even closer than they had been on the dance floor.

He slid his hand inside her T-shirt and cupped her breast, then broke the kiss and listened to her rapid breathing as he pressed his palm against her soft flesh. He liked the little sounds of pleasure she made as he molded her in his grip.

With his last ounce of control, he pulled away and said in a voice that came out more harsh than tender, "I'm not your brother, Alexandra, and there *is* going to be a second time, but not here."

He stepped back from her. "We're going inside and having a drink like old friends, or half the town will be talking about us tomorrow."

Alex straightened and said in a low voice, "Have I mentioned lately that I hate you?"

"No, but it's about time. I thought for tonight we were calling off the war."

She looked like she might argue, then turned and followed him into the bar. He had no idea if it was the food or the drink that made her return, but he had a strong feeling it wasn't him.

Just before they reached the door, Hank realized he'd been talking to Alex all her life, but he'd never talked to her like a lover. He risked looping his arm around her neck. "One more thing,

Alexandra, I think you're about the sexiest woman alive just the way you are. If you ever did consider that strapless dress and pushup bra, my heart probably won't be able to take it."

She jabbed him in the ribs. "You missed your chance. Now all I want is a meal. And you'd better not drink too much, Chief; you're due in my office at seven."

She was letting him know everything was back to normal.

He followed her inside, letting her set the ground rules. They talked about the fire as they ate, and then she walked to her Jeep with her cell phone to her ear. He had no idea who she was talking to, probably dispatch. She climbed in her Jeep, closed the door, and waved as she drove away.

Chapter 28

~~≈≈~~

TYLER WRIGHT PACED THE HALLWAYS OF THE funeral home. He had to try and find a reason that he could accept for his Katherine not answering any of his e-mails in three days.

He could think of none. Depression followed him like a shadow.

He turned the corner and passed down the hall with empty viewing rooms on either side. If he didn't come up with an answer he could live with, he'd wear out the carpet.

Turning right again, he walked past the offices and copy room, thankful that his grandfather had built Wright Funeral Home in a square. At least he didn't have to decide which way to go. The brothers who'd built the place had actually been wise: By making the hallways run along the outside frame, they could easily put in private sliding pocket doors between the rooms, allowing them to move anywhere in the building without being noticed. The last thing a grieving family wanted was to have a casket pass by.

On each corner, the hallway widened into a seating area large enough to hold twenty visitors waiting to pay their respects. Tyler now stopped at each corner to catch his breath before storming off down the next hallway.

After he'd passed his office the third time, he gave in and decided to check his e-mail once more. It was almost midnight. He had little hope she'd answer this late, but tomorrow seemed a lifetime away.

He stared as the latest e-mail came up. The subject line read, *Sorry.*

He hesitated, then clicked.

Sorry, Ty, things are crazy here at work.

He wrote back, *I've missed you.*

I've missed you, too. More than you know.

He read the words several times before answering, *These last few days have made me realize how thin the thread is between us. If for some reason you didn't write, I'd have no other way of reaching you. I could lose you forever.*

He waited, staring at the screen, wondering if he'd already said too much, been too bold. Lost her. All she'd have to do was click Erase a few times and everything they had would be gone.

I understand, she wrote. Nothing moved for a minute, and then she sent, *I suggest a plan. If for any reason one of us disappears and doesn't answer back, the other agrees to go to Quartz Mountain on the first Monday of the month for three months and have dinner. If the other never e-mails or shows up to dinner, the one at the dinner table will order a drink and toast what we had with a smile and promise never to try and find the other.*

Tyler wanted her to tell him who she was, where she was, any other way to contact her, but he knew if he did, somehow what they had would change, and he couldn't risk losing her.

You have my word. If you disappear, I'll go for three first Mondays and have dinner on the mountain. I'll toast our friendship.

What if it's you who breaks this off, Ty?

It won't be.

She didn't respond. After a minute, he added, *Hope all at work is better.*

It's a mess, she answered. *Sometimes I wish I could just dig a hole and bury my job.*

I know how you feel. He laughed so loud in his study he was glad no one, not even the dead, could hear him.

He then settled back in his chair and told her of a woman he'd met who had a collection of a hundred clothespin dolls with faces all painted and dresses made to fit the wooden clothespin.

She laughed.

He didn't tell Katherine that the lady's family decided her collection should be buried with her. Tyler strongly suspected not one relative wanted to continue the hobby.

Katherine told him about having car trouble and having to deal with a mechanic who suggested changes she knew she didn't need. She described growing up with a father who made her change her own oil and rotate her tires. He ran their house like it was a boot camp. She told of being able to make a bed a quarter would bounce on by the time she started school.

Tyler was impressed. He'd always considered himself being very mechanical when he refilled the wiper fluid, and he'd never made a bed in his life.

They talked for an hour before she wrote, *After midnight, have to get some sleep.*

Me, too, he answered.

Tomorrow. Good night, dear one. If I ever disappear for a few days, trust that it will not be by choice on my part.

I feel the same. Good night, my Kate.

He stared at the screen for a while. He was someone's dear one.

Chapter 29

ALEX REFILLED HER COFFEE CUP AND SAT back down at the table across from her deputy, Phil Gentry, and Trooper Davis from the highway patrol. They were both men with experience, trusted men. Davis followed his gut feelings and now and then stepped on a few toes, but he'd asked for this assignment, so she knew it mattered to him. Phil Gentry had been with the department in Harmony for more than twenty years and always thought out every possibility.

Trying to concentrate, Alex figured she was the weak link in the team. She couldn't remember what they'd been talking about before she went for coffee. Translation, the only man she truly saw in the room this morning was Hank Matheson. He seemed all professional and distant, as if nothing had happened between them in the parking lot of a bar last night.

For once she wished she'd had enough to drink the night before to have trouble remembering what she'd done. Unfortunately, she remembered every word, and worse, she remembered every touch. It had all started with the way Hank gently handled her on the dance floor. No one had ever driven her so crazy with such an easy touch. He'd brushed her, pressed against her, moved with her through song after song, but he'd never taken it beyond the limit. If he had, she could have stepped away. She might even have slapped him and stormed off the dance floor. As it was, she'd been the one making a fool of herself.

"If our arsonist follows the pattern," Hank said, tapping the map on the table without looking at her. In fact, he hadn't really looked at her since he'd arrived exactly at seven. "I figure he'll strike in about ten days, maybe two weeks."

The others agreed with his assessment. Alex downed a big gulp of hot coffee, knowing her concentration was off. Hank had been ready to work this morning and so had she—in theory. She couldn't help wondering if last night lingered in his thoughts the way it did in hers. She remembered the way he'd touched her breast, not like a man exploring, but more like a man who knew exactly what he wanted. The man before her now was nothing like the man who'd kissed her last night.

Hank circled a spot on the map with a highlighter as he said, "I'm guessing right about here. I could be a mile or two off in any direction, but this guy is playing some kind of game, and it looks like Harmony is in the center of his target. When he finishes roping us in, he'll head for town."

Alex leaned forward. The area he thought would be hit next took in one corner of the McAllen ranch, half of Hank's land, and part of the old

Truman place on Lone Oak Road, along with four other small places scattered in between.

"What do we do that we're not already doing?" Trooper Davis asked.

"We could ask the farmers to plow a fire break between the farms. That, and the roads will keep most fires from spreading." Hank frowned. "If flames reach the CRP grass here, and here, it's tall and thick. That kind of fire might jump, even a road or a plowed line."

"I could get county crews to mow anything along the roads," Alex suggested.

"That'll help, but we don't want to cause our arsonist to get suspicious. He might move somewhere else, and we can't watch every mile of road. I'm thinking right now he has no idea we're on to him."

"We don't know much," Alex admitted. "We don't know what he'll do once he's made his circle."

"And," Hank added, "if he panics, he could set more than one fire at a time."

"We need rain," the deputy said.

Hank straightened. "We can pray for rain, but we plan for fire."

They all agreed.

"One last thing." Hank finally glanced at her, but she saw no emotion in his stare. "On the outside of this circle, a mile or so farther out from Harmony than he's ever set a fire, there's a small branch of the Palo Duro." Hank hesitated, pointing to what looked like a root running across the map. The Palo Duro Canyon ran for hundreds of miles across the flat land of upper Texas. The canyons grew shallow and small, branching out in thin veins cutting into flat land. There were long stretches of miles where no roads had ever been cut.

"If our firebug sets a fire at this rim of the canyon, there are no farms close and no roads to get the trucks into the area fast. A grass fire could burn wide before we could get to it. I've got two trucks at the station, but we can't battle a fire line miles long and have any chance of putting it out before it reaches a fence, much less a road."

Deputy Gentry leaned forward. "What if we had Wild Derwood fly over those sections a few times a day?"

Hank shrugged. "Who'd pay for it? The fire department runs on volunteers, and last I checked the city and county budgets had no extra funds."

"If we requisition money, everyone in town would know about it," Alex added. "Whoever is setting these fires would love all the talk. This kind of guy lives off the excitement. He could be right in the middle of us and we'd never know."

"Right," Hank agreed.

Phil Gentry smiled that fake smile he always used in poker games. "Wild Derwood would love to be on the volunteer fire department, Chief."

Hank frowned. "Derwood's crazy. Everyone knows that. He stole his dad's Cessna and went joy riding when he was twelve. He flies over the cemetery every Sunday to wave at his mom, and his favorite topic of conversation is clouds. A few years back he told me he was born with cloudaphobia and had to fight like hell to overcome it. I think he may have gone too far in the other direction."

"He brought the plane back safe that day he was twelve, so we know he's a good pilot. And good pilots always watch clouds," Gentry said, "and you can't fault a man for loving his mother."

"That doesn't make him sane." Hank folded his arms. Everyone at the table knew Derwood also occasionally smoked the weeds he grew in his backyard, but no one mentioned it or they'd have to deal with the problem and in so doing lose the town's only good pilot.

"So, if his only flaw is insanity"—Alex looked from Phil Gentry to Hank—"what does that make him?"

Hank frowned.

Phil smiled. "A firefighting volunteer."

Alex choked down a laugh. Hank looked like he'd swallowed a horned toad. She knew he didn't want Derwood around the fire station, but he also saw Phil's point. One plane could do more good at spotting a fire than twenty men.

She watched Hank fold up the map and shake

hands with the other men as they moved to the door. He didn't say a word to her. She told herself everything was back to normal. Last night had been a lapse into a place neither of them planned to go.

If and when she was ready to get involved with a man, it wouldn't be Hank Matheson. He'd always seemed so much older than she was. When she was sixteen, going to her first dress-up dance, he and Warren had been like two fathers, questioning the boy, taking pictures on the porch. Half the conversations she'd had with Hank in her life had been when he was telling her what she should do or ordering her to listen to her brother or telling her to grow up and act like a lady.

Alex frowned as she took a seat behind her desk. She hadn't acted like much of a lady last night. But then, he wasn't exactly acting like a big brother.

She knew they should put this attraction for each other aside, but when this was over she had a feeling a different kind of sparks were going to fly.

"Alex." Hank's voice snapped her back from her thoughts.

"Yes." She grabbed a pen and spent a few seconds looking busy before she glanced at the door. She couldn't help but notice he looked a little hesitant. "What is it?"

He took one step into her office and stopped. "I told Noah he could come over to the station this afternoon and I'd start his training. I want him more aware of safety before he stops to help out at another site, if that's all right with you?"

"It's a good idea." She knew no one in her family could stop Noah. She'd been a wild child, but her little brother was both wild and brave, a far more dangerous combination. "Thank you, Hank."

"No problem." He leaned against the wall. "You know, when he learns enough to go on a call, I'll do my best to keep him out of harm's way."

"I know." She smiled. "He's stubborn."

Hank gave her a pointed look. "It must run in the family."

He was five feet away and she swore she could feel his hand on her breast. This man drove her mad. He wasn't her type. He knew every fault she had, every wild thing she'd ever done. She wasn't looking for a man, and if she were, it wouldn't be him.

She liked her men reckless and out of control with the taste of danger on their lips. Hank was steady and solid. How reckless can a man be who lives with his mother, two sisters, two great-aunts, and a four-year-old? The man had so much baggage he needed his own U-Haul.

Last night in the parking lot was probably as close as he'd ever come to being out of control. And even then, he'd been the one to stop, to think of what a scene they'd make, to think of her.

The memory of how he'd handled her in the dark flooded back, and she felt fire in her cheeks.

She looked up and saw that he was still standing by the door staring at her. "What are you looking at?" she snapped.

"You," he said, and his slow smile told her he had guessed what she was thinking.

He turned and walked out of the office.

Alex put her elbows on her desk and held her forehead in her palms. "That's it," she whispered. "When this is all over I'm going to check myself in for observation. I'm losing my mind." She slapped her forehead. "Or, maybe I'll go flying with Wild Derwood and let him tell me about clouds while we fly over the cemetery and wave at his mom."

Chapter 30

REAGAN SAT IN THE PACKED STANDS OF THE Harmony rodeo waiting for the bull riding to begin. Everyone in town was at the rodeo grounds tonight, and most had come to see Noah "Preacher" McAllen ride. She'd heard talk that many thought he might just be a better rider than his father, Adam, had been. Adam McAllen had put Harmony on the map in his youth. When he'd ridden in the national finals, it was said that more than a hundred folks went to Las Vegas to see him win.

Adam McAllen was a legend. Even when he moved to Amarillo three years ago and separated from his wife, he still told reporters in interviews that he was from Harmony.

Reagan didn't care about Adam McAllen. All she cared about was his son. She hadn't seen Noah except at school for almost two weeks. Since the night of the fire at the McNabb place, Noah had been hanging out at the fire station when he wasn't training for this one eight-second ride tonight.

At lunch, he'd told her all about it, until she felt she knew as much as he did about how to fight fires. She also learned that both his sister, Alex, and Hank Matheson were worried that there would be more fires. Hot, dry weather warned of it, and spring seemed to have nothing but hot, dry days coming one after the other.

She and Noah had sat on the tailgate of his pickup one afternoon and planned what would have to be done on Jeremiah's place if fire came. Reagan hated the thought of it. She didn't mind that the spooky old trees to the main road might have to be cut down, but she didn't like the idea of scarring the earth with a plow. Jeremiah loved looking out over his land and it wouldn't be the same if they plowed a fire line.

She pulled her thoughts away from the threat of trouble and watched people wandering around the grounds. Some of the middle school kids in front of her hadn't seen any of the rodeo. They were too busy walking from one end of the stands to the other, or talking, or hopping from bench to bench.

Three blond girls about fourteen were dressed like they thought they were going to a beach party and had gotten off at the wrong stop. Even though it was after dark, they still wore their sunglasses.

Little kids played under the bleachers, and a group of men were taking a smoke break over by the parked cars. Reagan almost preferred the "no name" rodeo to this one. Too many people. She recognized most of their faces, and most smiled or waved at her, but she really didn't know them.

Speaking of too many people, Brandon Biggs stepped on the empty seat next to her with a hard pound that wiggled the entire bleacher. He had on army-style boots and a jacket the local giant must have lent him. Brandon could have wrapped it twice around his stocky frame.

"Mind if I sit down?" he asked.

"If you'll behave yourself," she answered.

"If I accidentally forgot, the scar on my leg from the heel of your shoe would remind me."

"How did things go the other night after we left?"

"Me and the Fraser boys had a real nice visit." He leaned over. "They're nothing but trash, you know."

She snorted. Whatever.

As the announcer introduced the next rider, two of the three middle school blondes stood up. Brandon yelled for them to sit down or they'd be needing the dark glasses to hide a black eye.

The girls squealed indignantly, but sat down.

The first bull rider managed to hang on to the count of seven.

When the cowboy hit the dirt, Brandon stood.

"I better move on. Everyone knows you're Noah's girl."

She thought better of correcting him. "Brandon," she smiled, "before I get mad at you and forget it, thanks for what you did the other night."

He stood just a bit straighter. "You're welcome."

She watched him push his way down, pestering a few of the middle school kids just for the hell of it.

The announcer yelled that Preacher McAllen was the next rider. Reagan stood up.

Noah came out of the chute spinning on a bull that looked like he'd breathed in smoke and couldn't wait to blow it out. She'd never seen one buck so high. Noah's free hand reached for the sky as he gripped tight, and the battle between man and bull went full force.

With snot flying, the bull turned left toward the gates, snorting and heaving, and then suddenly twisted right.

Noah tumbled as if snapped off as quick as an icicle breaks.

He rolled, but the bull was still kicking in a tight circle.

Reagan screamed as Noah's body curled and twisted beneath the animal.

Noah was on the ground, fighting to crawl free, but the bull kept turning like a mixer, catching him with every turn. The clowns she'd watched and laughed at took on their real job, bullfighters. They moved in, trying to get the bull's attention. The first caught a horn in his side and slammed into the chute gate; the second tumbled backward on the uneven ground.

For one heartbeat there was no one near to help Noah.

The pickup men couldn't get close and the bull paid no attention to the last rodeo clown, a kid in training, as he waved and danced like a medicine man around a fire.

Reagan couldn't breathe. She counted seconds in her head as if at some point there would be a bell and the round would be over.

"Don't let him die," she whispered.

As if in answer, a tall man jumped down from the back fence and swung his hat at the bull. When that didn't work, the man spread his arms wide and rushed forward with his chest.

The animal charged the stranger, his horns pointed straight at the red shirt beneath the man's western suit.

Like a matador in the movies, the stranger jumped out of the way a second before the bull reached him. A heartbeat later, the riders had their ropes, swinging them like whips as they turned the bull toward the corral.

It had all happened so fast, yet the seconds had seemed endless. Reagan began to shake as the bull charged into the corral. Nothing had prepared her for such panic, such violence, such fear. For those few seconds with Noah under the bull, the entire world seemed to be holding its breath.

She watched Noah, expecting him to stand and wave that he was all right, as all the others had done.

But Noah lay curled in the dirt like a broken toy cowboy. His hat was gone. Dark hair mixed with shiny red blood covered part of his face.

The stranger who'd saved him knelt at Noah's side. The crowd fell silent. Everyone watched as the doctor ran out with his bag. A circle of men all knelt around Noah, blocking any view from spectators. Behind the chutes, emergency lights flashed through silent air and an EMT van pulled to the edge of the arena. The announcer's voice seem to whisper in the air, "Preacher may need your prayers tonight, folks."

Reagan pushed her way from the stands and headed toward him. By the time the stretcher was brought onto the grounds, she'd crawled through the fence and was almost to Noah.

She saw his face, gray-white as they lifted him carefully and began to carry him out. She tried to see him as they put him in the ambulance, but there were too many men, all taller than she was.

The sirens sounded as she screamed his name,

but Noah couldn't hear her. For a moment in the chaos, she couldn't hear herself.

The door closed and red lights flashed. She heard someone yell to call the sheriff and let her know her brother was heading to the hospital.

Reagan backed away to the shadows of the bleachers. She shoved hot tears off her cheek. Noah was all right, she thought. He had to be.

The rodeo went on, but people had lost interest. She waited in the darkness, not wanting to talk to anyone or see anyone.

She wanted to be with Noah. She wanted to know what was going on. She crossed her arms around her and wished she could hug away the pain she felt inside. If this was what it felt like to care about someone, it hurt too much.

"You all right?" A voice came out of nowhere.

She turned and saw Brandon. "No," she said. "Where's the hospital?"

"It's all the way north on North. I pass it every time I come in from Bailee. You sure you're all right?"

Reagan shoved her fingers into the pocket of Noah's jacket. She felt his truck keys, as she knew she would. "I'm fine. I'm going to check on him."

Brandon opened his mouth to say something, then changed his mind.

She circled beneath the bleachers and crossed the darkness to where Noah had parked his pickup.

"Eight," she whispered to herself. "He was only on the ground eight seconds."

Chapter 31

⚞⚟

ALEX WISHED SHE WERE AT THE RODEO instead of driving the back roads looking for any sign of a spark. It had been two weeks since the last fire. If trouble was going to flame, it would be soon. The guy they were looking for had set maybe as many as seven fires in the past three months. Either he was hooked on the adrenaline of what damage each new one might cause, or he loved to watch the flames build and grow. She could almost see him in her mind, planning, waiting maybe for more wind or a time when he thought no one was watching.

Waiting for her to blink.

She had no intention of blinking. This was her town, by blood and by occupation. She wouldn't let someone destroy it. She glanced at the man beside her and knew Hank felt the same.

In the past dozen days, she'd seen Matheson about ten times and talked to him on the phone at least twice a day. Neither had mentioned the parking lot episode. She had no idea if he thought about it as much as she did. Hell, it had become her favorite bedtime story on those nights she didn't fall asleep before her head hit the pillow.

Alex stopped her cruiser at the crossroads of Lone Oak Road and the county highway. Hank got out with his binoculars while she stepped to the front of the car and searched the horizon. They'd been riding together for two hours, both constantly checking in with all other spotters. They'd had a feeling it would be tonight, but now she had her doubts.

Hank wanted them to go together over what he called the eye of the circle. He was guessing they'd be able to spot something first, and if they did, both could be in contact with their people at once. With luck, if a fire started, the police could cut off all exits out of the area and the fire department could move in fast. Putting out the fire would be first priority, but catching the criminal would run a close second.

"Nothing," Alex said for the tenth time in an hour.

"Nothing," Hank echoed.

They both knew that all the other fires had been set before nightfall. It was almost an hour after dark. If someone had set a fire, it would be burning bright enough to be seen for miles on a clear night like tonight.

"I'll check and see if Derwood's called in yet." He lifted his cell and nodded toward her radio.

She understood. She picked up the receiver to call dispatch.

She could hear Hank talking as she waited for dispatch to answer. One ring. Two. Three.

"Derwood called in ten minutes ago," Hank

reported as he snapped his phone closed and circled to her side of the car. "Nothing. He's making another flyover, then I told him to call it a night." Hank sounded tired. They'd been chasing a ghost every night since the last fire. Both were exhausted.

She'd thought tonight would be the night, almost wished for it, so they could catch the criminal and this all would be over. Even going back to changing the lightbulb outside Dallas Logan's house looked good compared to what she had been doing.

Fourth ring, then just as the fifth one dinged, someone picked up at dispatch.

"Alex," Andy's voice scratched across the radio. "Sheriff McAllen!"

"Here," she answered as she reached into the car to turn up the speaker so Hank could also hear. "What's the problem? Any fire?"

"No fire," Andy was almost screaming at her. "All quiet in that area, but, Sheriff, your brother, Noah, is on his way to the hospital. He was hurt at the rodeo."

Alex dropped the radio and grabbed her binoculars resting on the hood.

When she turned back to her door, Hank was already there, shoving her aside. "I'll drive. You call in and see if you can find out anything."

She ran to the passenger side. Andy had patched her through to the ambulance by the time Hank hit eighty miles per hour.

"He's breathing," she echoed what the EMT said. "Looks like a blow to the head and multiple wounds on his arms and legs." Alex paused, then added, "I heard."

"What?" Hank glanced over at her. "Alex, what else?"

She looked at him, but didn't really see him as she repeated the driver's words. "My dad's riding in the ambulance with Noah. Adam was at the rodeo."

Five minutes later, they were pulling up to the county hospital. They jumped out and headed inside at a full run. The ambulance had emptied its load, and everyone had disappeared behind the emergency room doors.

The waiting room and desk were deserted. The place looked old and tired. Alex felt she was walking through death's parlor; she kept moving.

They ignored the sign that read AUTHORIZED PERSONNEL ONLY at the next set of swinging doors.

Adam McAllen, tall, thin, and gray-haired, stood alone at the end of the hallway that was marked NO ENTRY. He looked strong as a statue, but she didn't miss the worry in his deep blue eyes. He was dressed like the successful businessman he was, except for the blood that was spattered across his jacket and the dirt-stained knees of his trousers.

Alex didn't move into her father's arms. There had been too many times he hadn't been there for her. Her brothers might have come to terms with their father leaving their mother, but Alex never had.

Adam held his daughter in his stare but made no move to touch her. "They took him straight to the operating room to do the examination. Both doctors on duty are with him."

"What . . ." Alex wasn't even sure which questions to ask.

"I don't know anything," he admitted. "But I think it would be wise to call your mother."

Alex wanted to scream that he should call his own wife. After all, they were still married even though he never called her anything but *your mother*, and they hadn't seen each other more than a dozen times since Warren's funeral three years ago.

But there was no time for that. Noah was all that mattered right now.

Alex walked to the windows and dialed her mother.

IN A MATTER OF MINUTES, THE LITTLE WAITING area was filled with friends, family and high school kids. If anyone in town had need of the emergency room tonight, they'd have to fight their way in.

The crowd parted as Frances McAllen rushed in. She was wearing a peach jogging suit and looked fit enough to step out on the fifty-yard line and cheer at the Dallas Cowboys football games. Thirty years of being a mother might have turned her hair silver-blond and carved tiny wrinkles around her eyes and mouth, but she was still a beauty.

Frances went straight to her husband.

To Alex's surprise, her father put his hand on her mother's shoulder and talked to her softly.

The room went silent and Adam's words drifted like smoke through the air. "He took a blow to the head, Fran; I think that's what concerned the doc most. The other injuries look like they'll heal."

Fran leaned against Adam's shoulder and began to cry. A river of ice set Alex's spine. It was a scene she'd seen once before three years ago. Warren had been dead when they lifted him from the road, but they'd still loaded him into the ambulance and brought him here. Her parents had stood just as they were now, her father talking softly, her mother crying. Two people who never got along in the calm of life clung to one another in crisis.

Alex pushed her way through the crowd. There wasn't enough air in the world for her to breathe. She made it outside and away from all the bright lights. She couldn't watch her parents. Not again. She couldn't look for Hank, either. If she saw Hank now, all the memories of Warren's death would flood back and she couldn't deal with it, not with Noah hurt.

Once she passed the doors, the only dark place

she spotted was a shadowy drive leading to a back parking lot behind the hospital. Alex almost ran to it.

One person stood in the center of the drive. She saw him too late to choose another direction. Hank. He'd found the darkness before her.

Part of her wanted to turn and run. Part of her knew this one man would be the only one to understand. He'd walked the nightmare once before. He'd hear the echoes of it again.

He turned to her and opened his arms. She stepped into his embrace, needing the strong hug her father had never given her.

He pulled her close. Holding her to earth as he always had.

They stood for a while. When she felt the silent tears running unchecked down her face, she pulled back. "It's too much like . . ."

"I know," he answered.

He pushed her hair out of her face. "Noah isn't Warren. We don't know much, but we know one thing: Noah's alive."

She nodded. "Promise you'll stay until we know more?"

He smiled. "Of course."

They moved apart and walked back into the waiting room, where she joined her parents. Everyone else in the room was talking, but she felt she was floating in a silent bubble with her parents. The only thing keeping her sane was Hank ten feet away, keeping an eye on her. She had a feeling if she bolted again, he'd be right there to meet her in the shadows.

Finally, the doctor emerged with a status report. Noah seemed to be out of danger. He had two cracked ribs, multiple bruising, and a concussion. They were keeping him for a few days to run more tests.

Alex closed her eyes and breathed.

Her parents went in to see Noah, and Alex encouraged the friends and relatives to go home. The doctor had insisted on no visitors.

When the last one left, she turned to Hank. "Thank you. For being here."

"You're welcome," he responded, his hands in his pockets. After a moment, he added, "I called in ten minutes ago. Still no sign of fire."

She'd forgotten about the fire. "Good," she managed. "I think I'll ask if I can go in and say good night to Noah."

Hank moved toward the parking lot. "I'll be here when you get finished. Take your time."

"You don't have to wait." She frowned. She'd appreciated his presence tonight, but that didn't make them a couple.

He smiled. "Yes, I do. You're my ride back to my truck."

"Oh." She felt stupid. "Of course. I'll be out in a few minutes."

In Noah's room, her parents were on either side

of the bed. Her mother clutched Noah's hand in both of hers. Her father stared at his sleeping son with tubes taped to his arm.

"I can't stand seeing him like this," Frances whispered. "His riding days are ended."

"We'll talk," Adam also whispered in his gruff tone. "He'll wear a helmet and a vest from now on. He should have had one on tonight."

Alex let them leave without her, knowing they'd be arguing as soon as they stepped outside the door.

"Hold on, little brother," she whispered to Noah, as she must have a thousand times when they were growing up. She threaded her fingers through his. "Hold on tight."

Chapter 32

~~~

"I KNOW YOU'RE THERE." NOAH SOUNDED like he had a sore throat. "You might as well come on out."

Reagan thought of staying in the corner between the blinds and the shelving filled with supplies. Maybe he'd go back to sleep and when he woke again he'd think he'd dreamed he had seen her hiding.

"Rea, come on out."

She looked at the door. A nurse wandered in now and then, but she'd heard a racket in the hallway and knew that another round of customers had arrived at the emergency room. Slowly, Reagan slipped from concealment and approached Noah's hospital bed.

"You look terrible," she whispered.

He raised his left hand. The back was blue from where it had been stomped on, and the fingers were swollen double in size. Three or four stitches laced across a cut at his wrist.

"I probably look better than I feel," he said. "My side is killing me and I feel like one of the doctors, the fat one, is sitting on top of my head."

Reagan smiled. "He is. You want me to tell him to get off?"

The corner of Noah's mouth twitched. "Any chance you want to hug me, Rea?"

"No, and even if I did, I'd have trouble finding a place on you that's not bruised, bleeding, or bandaged. They could use your body for the model in a new Operation game."

Noah lifted his right arm. There was a bandage from his elbow to his shoulder, and his hand had tubes taped to it. "I don't like this."

"Me, either." She scrubbed at her cheek. In fact, she hated seeing him like this, all broken and pale.

"Have you been crying?"

"No," she lied. She'd waited until everyone left, not knowing what else to do. When a dozen people from a bar fight stormed in, all the hospital staff had their hands full. It hadn't been that hard to slip between the doors and find Noah. She'd planned to just talk to him a minute, but she'd waited an hour for him to open his eyes.

His cracked lip twitched again. "You were worried about me."

"No, I wasn't." Reagan ducked into the shadows as the door opened.

Noah closed his eyes.

A nurse whose name tag identified her as Georgia Veasey looked at the monitors, adjusted a few bags, and left. Before the door closed, they heard someone down the hall yell that someone had thrown up in room three.

Reagan reappeared and finished her sentence. "I wasn't worried about you, I was just worried I wouldn't have anyone to eat lunch with. I've kind of gotten used to you bothering me."

"You should go on home. I'll be all right." His words came slow, like someone who hadn't slept in days.

"No," she said simply.

"You think I'm lying? I'm just waiting until you're gone so I can die."

She bit her lip. "I wouldn't put it past you."

He smiled weakly. "You're staying then? No matter what I say?"

"Until they kick me out. You're not much in the way of a friend, but you're all I got."

He moved his left hand away from his body, making room on the bed. "You may not like any touching, Rea, but I could sure use someone next to me about now. You look tired enough to drop, plus you're the only one left around."

She hesitated, glancing at the door.

"What are they going to do," he asked, "kick you out five minutes earlier? They'll do it anyway; you might as well rest until she comes back."

She crawled carefully up beside him and stretched out next to him, her hand gently crossing below the bandages on his ribs.

He sighed and kissed the top of her head. "It's over, Rea. You don't have to cry. I'll be around to bug you tomorrow."

She closed her eyes, and they both fell asleep to the rhythm of the machines.

Fifteen minutes later, Nurse Veasey opened the door to check Noah's bags. She froze at the sight before her. A Truman was curled up against a McAllen.

Everyone born in Harmony knew that the youngest, and soon to be the last, Truman had come to live with her great-uncle out on Lone Oak Road. Georgia hadn't seen the girl up close, but there was no mistaking that wild red hair.

Georgia smiled. The kids were close in age, about sixteen or seventeen, but he looked double her size. The girl was curled close, barely touching him with her hand resting on one of the few spots on his chest not bandaged. They were both sound asleep.

As a nurse, she should wake the girl and tell her to get out, but Georgia couldn't. Everyone knew Trumans and McAllens never spoke, not for years and years. Yet here they were, curled up together like a lion and a lamb. Only from what she'd heard from her husband, who taught English at Harmony High, the girl was the lion.

Georgia slowly closed the door, knowing it would be an hour or more before she got all the drunks now piling into emergency sorted out, doctored, and sent home to sober up. Let the kids sleep until then. She'd see they weren't disturbed.

The feud, if there still was one, could wait for another day.

Chapter 33

UNCLE JEREMIAH WALKED THROUGH THE back door and into the kitchen. He crossed to the sink and washed his hands, then sat down to breakfast.

Reagan had made French toast, which he ate without comment.

"Where's the McAllen kid?" he asked between bites with the same disinterest with which he asked everything.

"Maybe he spent the night here," she answered, just to see if Jeremiah would bother to look up from his food.

"He didn't." The old man kept eating. "If he had, you'd have set another place."

Reagan smiled, guessing that if Noah walked into the room in his underwear, Jeremiah would simply tell him to pour himself a coffee and keep eating.

"Noah was hurt last night at the rodeo." She whispered the words, hoping that would make them sound not so frightening.

Now Jeremiah looked up. "He all right?"

"He will be. I stayed with him until midnight just to make sure he didn't die, then I drove his pickup home."

"I thought you two might be planning to leave for parts unknown in that old junker of his."

"Nope." She passed him the syrup. "I think I'll just go to see him as soon as the dishes are done. I won't be long and I'll work extra fast to make up the time I'm missing in the orchard."

Jeremiah nodded as he refilled his cup. "The sheriff told you not to drive until you passed your driving test."

"I know, and since Noah's her brother, she's bound to notice when I drive his truck back into town to check on him this morning." She stopped and waited.

Like a slow cooker, he stewed on what she'd said a while before he asked, "You want me to drive you in?"

"Would you?"

He nodded. "But I'm not going in. I don't like hospitals. I went in one back in eighty-seven with one problem and came out with two." He reached for the calendar on the wall behind the door and marked off the date. "Month is sure going by," he mumbled, and put the calendar back on its nail.

Reagan hurried to finish as she added between bites, "If you drive me, we can stop at the bookstore and I'll go in and get you a new copy of the Dallas paper. That one you got in the front room is two months old."

"Fair enough," he echoed. "I can start reading it while you visit."

A half hour later she walked into Noah's room.

He was sitting up in bed talking to several girls from the cheerleading squad. They all had their uniforms on and giggled at everything he said.

Reagan made no attempt to announce her presence; she just stood at the door and watched.

"That last hug made me feel a lot better, Arlee." Noah smiled at the girl in a goofy way she'd never seen him smile.

"You want another one?" She laughed. "We're all happy to do whatever we can to help out the sick."

"And brave," one of the other girls said. "That was so brave."

"No." A blonde beside Arlee pushed closer to the bed. "It's my turn to give him a hug."

Reagan wanted to throw up. They giggled and

talked on for five minutes. Most hadn't been at the rodeo last night, but apparently visiting someone in the hospital was a free pass out of church, so they'd all decided to put on their uniforms and cheer him up.

Reagan knew there was no substance to the group. Not a redhead among them. But Noah didn't seem to notice. She slipped down the hall to the restroom, not wanting to see or hear Harmony's boob trust in action.

She stepped into a stall and leaned against the wall, wishing she'd taken up smoking once when she'd been offered a cigarette. If she had, she'd have something to do right now besides wait.

The restroom door popped open, and giggling came from just beyond the stall door. Reagan had no trouble guessing who had come in. From the voices, three cheerleaders were now far too close to her.

She didn't have anything against cheerleaders. The last two schools she'd been in, none of them had bothered her. In fact, Reagan—and girls like her, she guessed—were invisible to the popular girls. They weren't boys to flirt with or cheer on. They were no competition. Reagan and her kind didn't matter.

Reagan closed her eyes and wished she could close her ears. The girls were talking about Noah. One said he had bedroom brown eyes. Another said he was too thin. Two out of the three claimed he'd be worth having a few nights' fun with, and then they giggled. The third said not to bother; she wouldn't be caught dead in his old truck, plus he had no butt.

After they left, Reagan stood in the stall for a long time. She hated that they talked about him like he was some kind of toy they'd just noticed. She hated what they said, and she hated even more that she cared.

When she stepped back into Noah's doorway, he was alone. For a moment, he didn't notice her, and she saw how tired his eyes looked and the pain in his face as he tried to shift in the bed.

Then he looked up. A smile came just a bit slower than usual to his lips.

"Morning, Rea," he said. The bruising on him looked even darker than it had last night, but his color was better.

"How are you?" she asked, feeling angry for no reason.

"Better. The doc came in and said I can go home in a few hours, but he wants me to take it easy for a week or so."

"You were lucky." She crossed her arms and didn't move closer.

"I know, but it feels like maybe I'd have been luckier if I'd drawn another bull. One of the guys who dropped by told me this morning that it was my dad who jumped in to get the bull to quit dancing on me. He said it was a sight; everyone was screaming and yelling. They all thought I was dead for sure."

"What else did he say?" That every girl in town seemed to have noticed him? That they all thought he was a hero? That two-thirds thought it would be fun to go out with him?

Noah raised an eyebrow. "What's wrong with you, Rea?"

It had taken him a while, but it finally seemed to dawn on the brain-dead cowboy that she wasn't happy.

"Nothing," she lied.

"Why are you standing at the door? What's happened? Did they tell you something about me that they didn't tell *me*?" He looked worried. "Hell, I'm probably dying and the doc's not telling me 'cause I'm not eighteen yet. Or maybe they just found out I'm contagious and that's as close as you're allowed to come?"

Rea resisted smiling. "You're not dying, at least not that I know of, and I don't think being dumb enough to climb on sixteen hundred pounds of fury is contagious."

He relaxed back on his pillow. "Thank God. I'd hate to die and not know it."

She laughed now and moved to his bedside. "Shouldn't joke about it."

"S'pose not," he said, turning his hand palm up to her.

She didn't take his hand.

Without taking offense, he lowered his offer. "So, how about telling me what's got you so upset this morning, other than seeing that I'm better?"

"I heard them talking about you in the restroom."

"The nurses?"

"No." She laughed. "Worse. The cheerleaders. One said you had bedroom eyes, whatever that means."

"Which one?"

She glared at him. "I don't know; they all sound alike to me. They all *are* alike. I swear there's probably a factory in China that turns them out by the thousands every year and ships them all over, pom-poms in hand."

He didn't seem to be listening. "Did they say anything else?"

"One said you didn't have a butt."

He frowned, and she almost felt sorry for him. Then he said he'd noticed none of them had that problem, and she wanted to hit him on one of the few spots available to her.

"You're mad because they came up," Noah said. She could almost see his brain working it out. "You're jealous."

"I am not. I couldn't care less if they hug you and make a fuss over you and talk about how they wouldn't mind . . . oh, never mind."

"Wouldn't mind what?"

"I'm not telling, so don't bother to ask and I'm not jealous. I've told you before I don't want to be your

242

girlfriend, just friends, so what do I care? Go ahead and date them. Date all of them at once if you like."

"For just friends, you don't look or sound very happy." He stared at her as if he'd just discovered a lizard person living under her skin. "Let me get this straight—you don't want anyone thinking you're my girlfriend. You don't want me touching you, even holding hands, because you figure I'll turn into some kind of werewolf if I do, but you don't like any one else touching me, either. I'm sort of off-limits to the world, like some kind of global quarantine."

She'd had enough. If he thought he was confused, he should try looking at the world through her eyes. Without warning, she stormed out of the room.

She heard him call her name, but she didn't stop until she was outside. There, she breathed out hard like a deer trying to clear human scent from her lungs.

Uncle Jeremiah was sitting on the bench ten feet from the exit. "How's the—"

Raising her hand, she shouted, "I don't want to talk about him."

Jeremiah stood slowly and nodded. "Fine."

He drove Noah's truck back to the ranch and passed the house as he pulled the old piece of junk straight into his museum of a barn.

"What are you doing?" she asked.

"I'm going to clean up this engine before it sputters so hard the damn thing falls out in protest."

"Why? It's not your problem."

Jeremiah stepped out of the cab. "I know. When he's driving, I don't much care, but I don't want him having any trouble when you're riding with him."

"Why?" She decided she had no knowledge of men from sixteen to eighty-six.

"Because," he said without looking at her, "you're the only niece I got, and I don't want to lose you in a wreck."

Reagan's heart took his words like the kick of a bull. For a few seconds she couldn't breathe. He'd claimed her. Uncle Jeremiah had claimed her as his kin with no one else around, and she hadn't even asked or begged.

She climbed out of the cab and walked around to where he'd lifted the hood. "I'm staying," she said. "I just want you to know, I'm staying here forever, so stop waking up every morning thinking I'm leaving."

"Good," he said in his usual bland tone. "Hand me that wrench."

Chapter 34

HANK LIFTED SARALYNN ONTO HIS SHOULDER and moved through the Tuesday morning crowd at the Blue Moon. His tiny niece waved at everyone as if she were riding on a float, then giggled when

244

they waved back. Most, from the three-piece suits to the overalled farmers, smiled at her. The few who didn't, Hank mentally marked down on his waste-of-flesh list.

"What are we today?" Edith asked as she wiggled past them with four plates of food.

"She can't talk, Edith," Hank whispered. "She's a mermaid, and everyone knows they can't talk around humans. All she can do is wave and look beautiful."

The waitress nodded, as if he made perfect sense. "I'm guessing she'll want the usual with a little seaweed on the side."

He winked and moved on. As he watched the people, mostly men this early in the morning, he couldn't help but wonder if the arsonist was among them. Could a man who looked so much like every one of them be thinking of destroying not just their land, but their way of life? Hank had heard of small communities in the Texas panhandle that faced a disaster and never recovered. The buildings left standing simply marked the boundaries of ghost towns.

Hank pushed the dark thoughts aside and headed toward the only empty booth. He noticed Willie and Trooper Davis at one table, but even if they'd invited him to sit down, he didn't want to talk about fires in front of Saralynn. The young man and the old trooper made a strange pair, but because they were both named Davis, Hank guessed they were somehow related. In this town, it would be hard to find a jury made up of people who didn't know or weren't related to just about anyone who committed a crime.

Last year he'd had to take Aunt Pat in for double parking in two handicap spots and she'd known every person in court, even served as a character witness of one and paid another kid's fine because she swore he came from good people and should know better than to run a red light.

Hank looked around and thought what he always thought. His town. His people.

He lowered Saralynn slowly, as always taking care not to bump her leg braces on anything, then sat beside her. "How about I order for you today?"

She nodded and folded her hands, fingers outstretched, over her chest.

"Morning," Tyler Wright said as he slid into the other side of the booth. "Mind if I join you?"

Hank had to admire the man; he always asked, even though they'd been eating meals across from one another once a week for probably ten years. "Morning, Tyler. How's business?"

"If it gets any slower, I may take the day off and go for a drive. Nobody wants to die in good weather, but wait for the first cold spell with snow flurries and we'll have the hearse heated up and running all day." He grinned as if the lack of work didn't bother him in the least. Hank had to admit the chubby little undertaker seemed happier lately than he'd ever seen him.

Hank thought of asking Tyler to watch for fires, but he held back. Trooper Davis had planted a seed of doubt about the funeral director. Hank told himself he didn't believe a word of it, but he still hesitated inviting Wright into the inner circle.

"What do you do on these drives?" He tried to make the question casual.

"Mostly I just like to get out in the fresh air and think. Sometimes I look for signs of the past. Every man or animal who ever crossed this land, and believe me most just crossed without thinking of staying, left a footprint somewhere, and I like thinking once in a while I'll find a sign of that passing."

Hank told himself there was nothing odd about that. "Tyler, do you know of anyone who might want to harm our town?"

"Sure, every tourist who eats at the truck stop just south of the hospital."

Hank smiled. No locals had eaten at the gas station/curio shop/restaurant since a month after it opened, when the meatloaf sent a dozen people to the hospital. After that, everyone thought it lucky the two buildings were so close together.

After Edith brought their coffee and juice, Tyler fished in his vest pocket and found a quarter. "It's not a new one, darling," he said to the mermaid next to Hank, "but I've heard it's waterproof and that's very important to you these days."

Saralynn laughed.

Tyler tugged a tiny felt bag from his pocket and passed it over. "I found this. You might want to keep it safe in here."

When Saralynn opened the bag a tiny glass bead, like the ones Hank had seen in fake flower arrangements at the funeral home, fell out.

Tyler's eyebrows shot up as if he were surprised. "Oh no, I must have left a dragon's tear in that bag so long it turned to clear stone."

Saralynn beamed. "A dragon's tear. May I have it?"

Tyler nodded. "It's magic, you see. If a mermaid holds it, she can talk."

Hank fought down a groan. He played along with Saralynn's fantasies, but Tyler was adding to them. Pretty soon Hank would be having breakfast with a wood nymph and a troll.

Tyler chuckled at Hank's frown as if he'd read his mind.

Hank knew beyond all doubt that he wasn't looking at an arsonist.

When Edith plopped down the plates, the mermaid's pancakes were circled in seaweed that looked a lot like parsley.

His niece began planting each tiny branch on top of her pancakes and watering her garden with syrup.

Knowing Saralynn had lost interest in the conversation, Tyler asked Hank, "How's the painter in your family doing? I hear she'll have a show soon."

Hank spread jelly on his dry toast. "She's very creative, I'll give her that. Her latest is called *More Coffee, Dear*. It's a man floating in a huge coffee cup, facedown."

Tyler had his cup halfway to his lips. He reconsidered and sat the coffee down.

Hank smiled. "Hey, it beats the one she did of a guy impaled on a wall by a remote control. It was called *Last Change*."

"Sorry I asked," Tyler said as he concentrated on his oatmeal.

After breakfast, Hank took his mermaid to school, then dropped by the station. He had tons of work to do at the ranch, but he still couldn't believe the firebug hadn't started another grass fire. It didn't make sense. Why would he go three-fourths of the way around Harmony and stop?

When Hank pulled up, Alex was getting out of her car across the street.

"Mind if we talk a minute?" he called to her.

She shrugged with a frown.

Just once Hank wished that she'd look glad to see him, but he guessed it would be too much to ask in this lifetime.

He knew that Alexandra wasn't a morning

person, but where he was concerned, she wasn't Miss Sunshine in the afternoon or evening, either. Hank held out little hope for the night.

They walked to the handicap ramp beside the entrance to the city offices, seeking the shade of the old oak. Legend was that the oak had been brought to West Texas by Harmon Ely himself when he hoped to settle here and then send for his family. But his family had all been killed in a raid near the border, leaving Harmon alone and bitter. The three men who worked for him—Truman, Matheson, and McAllen—all sent for their wives, and as the years passed, Harmon watched their children grow and play beneath the tree he'd brought for his children. Some in town thought that was why he willed all he had to the men who worked for him.

"Something's bothering me," Hank began. "I've been reading up on arsonists, and they don't just stop. Maybe they're frightened off, or maybe something makes them stop, like a car wreck or something else happening that's more exciting and draws them to the action. But we've had no one to close in on and make nervous enough he might stop, and nothing's happening of any interest around here."

Alex crossed her arms as she leaned against the railing. "So now you're upset because our little terrorist hasn't come out to play?"

"Something like that." He realized how odd he

must sound. "Maybe he's just laying low. Hell, maybe he just ran out of matches and has to wait until payday."

"You'll drive yourself crazy guessing," she offered. "The only thing exciting that happened in the past few days was my little brother almost dying at the rodeo. I swear everyone in town has been by to see him. Half of them bring cookies. Add to that, my dad's still here fretting over Noah worse than Mother does."

Hank didn't want to talk about the three-ring circus that was usually going on at the McAllen house when Adam came back. He'd heard about Adam and Fran enough from Warren when they were younger. "The rodeo and the fires couldn't be connected."

She met his eyes. "Or could they? Half the town was at the rodeo. Maybe our arsonist was there, or was working one of the booths. Maybe he watched the whole thing."

"Or maybe he was pulled in to handle the crowd, or drive the ambulance, or take a shift at the hospital?" Hank tried to think like an arsonist. "If the guy sets fires for the excitement, he just might have found his fix that night at the rodeo, or afterward at the hospital."

An hour later they were sitting in Alex's office making a list of everyone they'd noticed in the waiting room at the hospital. Most were relatives and friends, but Hank remembered seeing a few he didn't know, and when he described them, Alex couldn't think of anyone she knew fitting the description.

Alex stood and grabbed two juices from the tiny refrigerator under her desk. She handed Hank one and sat back down across from him. "Now, we list everyone we know who's been around for the fires. If one person keeps popping up, maybe we've got our man."

"Someone besides me and you and Kenny from the paper?" Hank grinned.

"No. We list everyone *including* me, you, and Kenny." She picked up her pen and pointed it at him. "And for now, we keep this between the two of us. No one else. If we're wrong and this list gets out, it would hurt someone innocent. If we're right, we can keep an eye on any suspects without them being aware of it."

It was almost noon by the time they'd made lists of everyone involved in every fire. Alex had run checks of arson arrests over the past twenty years, and Hank had gone over his notes of every fire that had happened near Harmony in a year. Two firemen, besides himself, had responded to all the fires. Willie Davis, who never missed anything that happened at the fire station, and Andy Daily, who was sleeping at the station every night he wasn't working dispatch for the sheriff's office. Kenny, the newspaper's only reporter not using a walker, came to take pictures of the fires, but the flames were usually out by the time he made it to the scene.

Neither Alex nor he realized how long they'd worked until Alex's secretary poked her head in asking if the sheriff wanted lunch.

Alex hesitated, while Hank answered, "No, we're heading out to one of the burn sites. We'll pick something up on our way."

When the secretary backed away, Hank lowered his voice. "If I'm reading Willie's notes right, three of the early fires were called in by the same person. His name is Zackery Hunter and he owns a gas station out where two county roads cross. This was early, before we thought the fires were connected, so we didn't ask as many questions as we should have."

Alex smiled. "So now we should go out there and talk to him. Did he see the fires, hear about them and call in, or set them?"

"Exactly."

By the time they'd made it to Alex's cruiser, Trooper Davis pulled up beside them and decided to tag along. Hank had been around the man a few times. He seemed like a by-the-book officer, but there was something about him Hank didn't care much for. He jumped too fast. Rushed in when he should hesitate. Hank also had the feeling that Davis considered himself an expert on just about any subject. If this had been a hundred years earlier, Davis would have been a bounty hunter, Hank figured.

He felt, more than knew, that Alex didn't care for the man, either. Maybe it had something to do with Warren three years ago. Hank couldn't be sure, but he thought he remembered seeing Davis the night Alex's brother died, but there were so many highway patrolmen around that night, he couldn't be sure.

From the way Davis said the word *Sheriff* every time he addressed Alex, Hank sensed the trooper felt the same way about her as she did about him.

On the way over, with Alex driving, Hank found himself staring at the place just below her ear. If he leaned over and put his mouth exactly there, he might feel her pulse pounding in her throat and smell her hair at the same time.

And that time would be one second before she slammed his head into the windshield. He groaned. He was just guessing here, but he doubted she wanted him nibbling on her neck while she drove out to question a witness.

"What are you thinking?" she asked as she made the last turn and headed for the country store at the crossroads.

What he was thinking was, how do women know just the right time to ask that question? Can they sense when a man's thoughts step over the line, or are they just guessing that something is up because he gets some kind of strange glaze over his eyes? Or maybe men are so often thinking about things they won't talk about that it's a good question to ask anytime.

He answered with the first plausible response that came to mind. "I was thinking it's not going to be this easy."

They pulled into the crumbling parking lot of the little store. Country Corner had been there for fifty or more years and didn't look like it had been upgraded since the grand opening. It sold gas and snacks mostly, along with beer. The only thing that kept it going was the fact that it was halfway to anywhere from this point. For those who wanted to travel the back roads, it was the only restroom stop, ice cream break, or pay telephone around.

"I can't believe he has that old thing." Hank looked at the phone booth. "Who doesn't have a cell these days?"

"Cell service is iffy out here."

Hank checked his phone just to make sure he could be reached if needed. Between the fires and Saralynn's medical problems, he was never without the phone on his belt.

Trooper Davis joined them as they went into the store. Hank didn't miss the fact that Davis checked his gun as if expecting Bonnie and Clyde to be waiting just beyond the door.

The place was empty except for the owner.

Zackery Hunter sat on a stool behind the counter reading a magazine he quickly shoved out of sight. "Hi, folks. Just taking a drive, are you?" When he smiled, his teeth were so yellow Hank swore he must color them.

Alex, as always, was all business. She flipped open her notepad and began asking questions. Davis tossed in a few, but Hank just watched. Zackery was a talker and stretched out every answer as much as he could. He hadn't seen the fires; they'd only been reported by folks coming by. He was left of one, right of the other. The third, he heard about from a farmer who saw the smoke from his place, but Zackery called it in anyway.

Alex made a list of each of the people who'd stopped by to even talk about the fires.

Zackery scratched his stubble. "The funeral director from Harmony stopped by for an ice cream, but he always takes the back roads and I seem to be his ice cream stop. Sometimes I see him twice, three times a week. I remember on the third fire, he was so interested in where it was he forgot to eat the Nutty Buddy and it started dripping on my floor."

Hank looked down, thinking that from the looks of the floor, the remains of the ice cream were still there.

"You think Tyler Wright might have expressed an unnatural interest?" Davis asked.

"I don't know," Zachery said. "I guess so, or maybe he was just making conversation. He's a nice guy, and last I heard loving ice cream ain't no crime."

Hank didn't miss the look Davis gave Alex. Davis hung back and motioned for Alex to do the same as they left a few minutes later. Hank walked on toward the car. He couldn't hear, but he sensed they were arguing.

A moment later Alex stormed past him. She'd climbed in and slammed her door even before he reached the passenger side.

When Hank climbed into her cruiser, Alex was gripping the stirring wheel so hard her knuckles were white. "He wants to bring Tyler in for questioning." There was no need for her to explain more.

"Tyler is not our man," Hank said.

"I don't think so, either, but I've got to go along with Davis. It's a lousy lead, but it's the only thread we have."

Hank pulled a Nutty Buddy ice cream out of the bag. "Lunch?" he asked.

Alex's smile didn't make it up to her eyes. "Thanks."

Chapter 35

TYLER WRIGHT TALKED WITH A COUPLE WHO wanted to do pre-need arrangements. He was a retired professor from over at Clifton College, and she'd been an accountant for a small oil-drilling company. They'd bought a place out on Twisted

Creek years ago and were finally settling down to becoming one of the nesters who stayed at the creek year-round. Neither fished. He was a bird watcher and she quilted, but they both loved sitting out in the evening and watching the water.

Since they were about an equal distance from Bailee, Texas, and Harmony, they picked Harmony to be their last resting place. Tyler often expressed pride in the town's cemetery. Early on, his grandfather had suggested that everyone who wanted to could plant a tree in memory of their loved one who had died. Wright Funeral Home would even order the tree and see to its planting—which not only brought in extra profit, it also made Harmony's Cemetery stand out as a place of beauty among so many of the dried-up, tumbleweed-collecting cemeteries in the area. There were a few cemeteries on the plains where the ground was so dry and hard it was impossible to dig a six-foot hole.

Tyler smiled at the old couple as he tried to remember what they'd said their names were a half hour ago. He had it written in the pages of notes somewhere. He really had to make an effort to remember details.

As they looked at caskets, he fought down a laugh as he thought of something funny that Kate had said last night. He wished he could hear her words and not just read them. She'd had a nice voice the one time they'd met. A solid voice, not whiny or too high. The kind of voice a man doesn't mind listening to.

Tyler remembered every detail about what she'd told him in her e-mails. Last night she'd said that sometimes she was so tired she'd just toss off her clothes and crawl into bed without even thinking about her pajamas.

After they'd said good night, he'd tried it—though he couldn't toss off his clothes, he had to hang them up, and he did leave his underwear and socks on when he went to bed. He had a wonderful night feeling free and thinking of Katherine.

The professor picked a wooden casket, his wife a metal one that sealed. Tyler did all he was supposed to do. He said all the right things, but he also counted the minutes until they left.

He wanted to go back and read through the e-mails from last night. Tonight was Tuesday, and for some reason they always talked about food on Tuesday. She said she loved to cook but never had enough time. He said he was learning, though unless sandwiches and cereal counted he'd never cooked anything.

The old couple left. Tyler stood on the steps smiling and waving as he thought that he might tell Katherine he collected coins. He might even tell her about his little friend, Saralynn. Thanks to Hank's bringing her to breakfast, Tyler felt like he'd watched her grow up. Sometimes, he thought he saw death's shadow standing just behind her, but she always made him smile, so it was easy to forget about the shadow.

Tyler had signed up to have each new quarter issued sent to him so he could give it to her. Last Christmas he'd given Saralynn a map of the United States with a spot for each quarter. She'd been delighted. She was a smart little four-year-old, and he wanted to tell Katherine all about her.

The sheriff's car pulled into the first slot in the funeral home parking lot. Alex McAllen and a highway patrolman got out. Tyler waited in the wind as they neared.

"Afternoon, Sheriff," Tyler smiled. "Trooper." Tyler thought his name was Davis. They'd talked a dozen times over the years. Or tried to, Tyler remembered with a frown. Davis wasn't a man who seemed to like small talk, unless it was about himself. There were very few people Tyler met that he didn't like, and this man was one. Strange, how he'd remember that name and not the names of hundreds of nice people he came across.

Alex didn't smile like she usually did as she climbed the steps to him. "We were wondering, Mr. Wright, if you might come down to the station and answer a few questions."

Tyler smiled. "I'd be happy to, Sheriff, just let me tell—"

Davis stepped forward and tugged his handcuffs off his belt. "You're going with us right now, Wright."

"That won't be necessary," Alex snapped.

Davis looked like he might argue, then stepped back.

Tyler's first thought was that this trooper didn't like Alex. Maybe because she was a woman, maybe because she outranked him. Tyler had no idea how it worked, but the man obviously wasn't a gentleman if Alex felt she had to order him around.

The next thought slammed like a shovel between his eyes. Davis was arresting him. Handcuffs! He'd never had handcuffs on in his life. His parents would not only roll over, but climb out of their graves in anger at the disgrace of their only child being handcuffed and dragged off the steps of Wright Funeral Home.

"I don't understand." Tyler focused on Alex, wishing he could see her eyes through the dark glasses she wore.

"We just need you to answer a few questions, Tyler. It's nothing, really." She touched her hand inside his elbow. "Please come with us."

He'd seen enough cop shows to know it was *not* nothing. "Do I need an attorney?"

"I don't think so," she said, "but I'll call one if you'd be more comfortable. There is nothing wrong or unusual about having an attorney with you."

"What is this all about?" Tyler's only crime for his entire life had been speeding. For a second it crossed his mind that maybe talking about sleeping with nothing on might be some kind of Internet crime. If he were arrested for that, it would be even more embarrassing then speeding down the back roads.

He looked back at the house, then toward his car, not knowing what to do. Hide. Run. Go with them. The sheriff tugged off her glasses as if she understood.

Alex's eyes softened as if she saw his fear and didn't want to shame an innocent man. He felt overwhelmingly grateful to her for that.

She tugged his arm gently with her hand. "We just want to see what you know about the fires, Tyler. We need your help. Please, come with us."

"Oh." He calmed. He could handle help. He was good at helping. "Then I'll do all I can, Sheriff." He took a breath, wondering: If he'd almost panicked as an innocent man, what would he do if he were ever charged with a crime he'd actually committed? He'd die of a heart attack on the steps. His only chance of living a long life was to follow every law. That did it, he reasoned. His speeding days were over.

Davis frowned when Alex opened the front door of her cruiser and waved Tyler in.

Tyler had sat in police cars many times. Once in a while families took a long time between the funeral and the procession to the cemetery. When he'd been a boy he'd often gone with his dad and loved asking all kind of questions about what everything did in the car. But today, he just sat next to Alex for the two-block drive to the station and wondered why Trooper Davis was so upset.

This would definitely *not* be on his list of subjects to talk about with Katherine tonight.

Chapter 36

REAGAN AND UNCLE JEREMIAH TOOK NOAH'S pickup back after school Tuesday. The old guy had it running like new. Jeremiah might move slowly, but he knew his way around an engine. He'd also let her help, explaining every step even if she didn't understand most of what he'd said.

She wanted just to park the pickup in front of the McAllen house and leave, but Jeremiah told her to go in and hand over the keys while he drove to the parts store for oil.

Walking up to the door, she tried to remember exactly why she was mad at Noah. Not because he got hurt. Not because he'd asked her to give him a hug. He probably didn't even remember the night of the accident and how she'd curled up next to him and slept until the nurse had tugged her away about midnight and told her to go home.

Reagan really couldn't be mad at him for hugging the cheerleaders; after all, he was hurt and tied to a bed. If anything, they took advantage of him. However, he could have protested a little harder.

It was the sheriff who answered the door, and for a moment Reagan tensed. Then she remembered that Alex McAllen was Noah's big sister and had already been nice to her several times.

Alex invited her in. Reagan had sat in the truck a few times when Noah had driven by his house to pick things up, but she'd never gone inside. The first thing that surprised her was that everything had an order about it. The house was one of the smaller old homes in what she was sure had once been the nicest part of town. Noah said that his mother bought it with a small inheritance from her grandmother, and his dad paid the bills.

Reagan couldn't help but think he'd done a fine job of keeping his family in style even if he didn't live with them. The place had that maid-twice-a-week look she'd seen a few times. Only problem was she was the maid when she'd seen houses like this, or rather one of her foster mothers had been. Her mom-of-the-month would bring a few of her foster kids along to help out. Reagan had never minded the work. It was easy and she could pretend that she lived in a house where the plants were all real and nothing was broken.

"Noah's in his room," Alex said. "First door on the right up the stairs. I'll bring you two some root beers before I leave. Try to cheer him up, Rea. He's been down for two days."

"Is he hurt bad?" Maybe she'd missed something at the hospital.

"No, just his ribs, and they'll heal. He was lucky."

Reagan climbed the stairs. The first door was open, a big airy room with floor-to-ceiling windows along one wall. Noah sat on the side of his bed picking at a scab across his elbow. He wore a pair of cutoffs that showed off hairy legs. A bandage circled his chest and another covered the top half of one arm, but the rest of him looked lean and tanned, but not as thin as she thought he might have been.

"Don't do that," she scolded. "It'll leave a scar."

"What'd you care? In rodeo no one minds a few scars." He glared at her. "I haven't seen you in days."

"Two days," she corrected as she dropped her backpack. "And I brought you something."

"What?" Curiosity overtook anger.

"Homework," she said, and he groaned.

Laughing, she moved to his side. She couldn't resist patting his unruly hair, which looked like it hadn't been combed or washed since he danced with the bull.

"I'm sorry," she whispered. It was the first time she'd ever said those two words and meant them.

He didn't pretend they were talking about the homework. "So am I, even though I still don't know what I did to make you so mad. Probably nothing," he reasoned. "I've always heard red-heads are like that, firing up for no reason. It's probably something I'll have to get used to if you decide to hang around."

"It had nothing to do with my red hair, you idiot."

He frowned and shook his head slowly. "See what I mean?"

"It wasn't my hair. It was something you did, I just can't think of what it was exactly."

"Well, when you think of it and get all mad again, warn me that temper of yours is coming, would you, Rea? I'm injured, you know; I might need a little more time than usual to get out of range."

She giggled and fought the urge to hit him.

The sheriff came into the room and handed Reagan two drinks and then ordered Noah back into his bed. "Mom says you're to stay in bed until tomorrow morning."

"I'm all right, Alex. I swear. I can't stand all this resting. It's driving me nuts."

Reagan saw the pain in his movements as he followed his sister's orders even as he protested.

"Now stay there." The sheriff pointed her finger at him. "I have to get back to my office and talk to someone. I don't have time to nurse you and referee for Mom and Dad, so don't call me like it's some kind of great emergency again." She pulled a chair from the desk and put it beside the bed.

"Your friend can stay ten minutes, no more." Alex looked at Reagan. "He needs rest."

Reagan nodded. "Ten minutes."

Alex left, and they listened to her bounding down the stairs and out the door. Whatever or whoever was in her office, she couldn't wait to get back to it.

"Where does it hurt?" Reagan asked.

"Everywhere," he admitted. "And if that's not bad enough, my mom and dad have been taking turns yelling at me. My mom tells me what I'm not going to do, and my dad tells me how I'm going to do it next time. They're downstairs in the kitchen now having coffee and talking about me. If you hear yelling, run. I called Alex and begged her to drop by just to check on them. Once in a while when it gets quiet like this, I worry that one of them has finally choked the other into silence."

Reagan laughed. "It couldn't be that bad."

"You don't know. They're both hardheaded and stubborn. Mom thinks she knows all about raising kids and takes every injury we get personally. Dad just thinks he knows everything, period."

"But they both love you."

Noah shrugged. "I guess, but lying around the house is more of a pain than being bruised." He settled his arm over a pillow and studied her. "We friends again, Rea?"

"Yes." She smiled. "But I'm not here to listen to you complain. If you climb on those bulls, you got

267

to figure sometime one of them is going to stomp on you. I've calculated that with no more brains than you have, you won't suffer much damage to the head, and the rest will probably heal. But if you're going to complain, stop riding bulls."

"Thanks for coming just to cheer me up." Noah rubbed the spot between his eyebrows. "You're not thinking of going into nursing, are you? A fellow could die real easy with your bedside manner."

She giggled. "Anytime, and no, I'm not thinking of going that direction, but with you for a friend I'd probably get lots of practice in. Want to hear what's happening at school?"

"Sure." He leaned back and closed his eyes. "And don't leave out any conversations you heard about me."

She told him everything she could think of that had happened in the two days of school he'd missed. When she got to what the cafeteria was serving, she noticed his long slow breaths and knew he was asleep.

She glanced at the door and saw the tall, thin man who'd saved Noah from the bull standing in the doorway. Part of her felt like she was looking at Noah thirty years from now. Same blue eyes, same unruly hair, same long frame.

"You're my son's friend," the stranger said in a low voice that rumbled like faraway thunder. "The one he calls Rea."

Reagan nodded.

"You want me to try to talk him out of riding?" he asked.

It was a strange but honest question, and she answered directly. "No."

"Why not?" He leaned against the frame of the door as if he had all the time in the world to talk to her.

"He loves it. It's in his blood. It's all he thinks about. Maybe it's not fair to shatter a dream, even one that knocks him around now and then."

"So, Rea." He said her name slowly like Noah did when he was talking and thinking at the same time. "What should I do? His mother wants me to tell him rodeoing is finished."

Reagan stood. "Teach him to ride. All he's ever had was a weeklong camp last summer in San Angelo. You could teach him more. I know you probably think he'll stop if you don't show much interest, but he'll never stop. He wants to go all the way to the top."

Adam McAllen looked at her a moment, then nodded. "I'll give it a try, kid, but you got to promise me you'll be there for him when he falls. No matter what I teach him, if he rides, he'll tumble."

She had the feeling they were making a pact. "I'll try."

He straightened. "That's all any of us can do. Try. Sometimes I think it's not the winning or the losing, or even the right and wrong of things, it's the trying that makes us keep on living and hoping."

She heard the toot of Uncle Jeremiah's horn. "I have to go; my uncle is back."

"Tell Truman that Adam McAllen said thanks. He'll know what I mean."

"All right." She ran down the stairs. "I'll come back tomorrow."

"You do that," he said from the landing.

When she climbed in beside Jeremiah, she told him what Adam McAllen had said.

"What'd you do that he thanked you for?"

"Don't remember," Jeremiah answered, and Reagan knew he was lying.

That meant she'd probably never know. Not that it mattered. She was glad to know that sometime, somehow, Jeremiah had helped Adam out and that Adam was grateful. In a strange way, she admired both men for keeping it to themselves.

Someday, she decided, she'd do a kindness for someone like that and never tell anyone about it. Never even expect a thank-you.

Chapter 37

HANK STOOD ACROSS THE STREET AND watched Tyler being led into the sheriff's office. The funeral director's shoulders were rounded, his head down. He was so nervous, he stumbled over one of the steps.

Thank God Alex hadn't handcuffed him. Hank had tried to talk her out of letting Davis bring Tyler in, but at least she hadn't embarrassed the man in front of the entire town.

Trooper Davis was grasping at straws. He claimed Tyler fit the profile. No close family around. No solid relationships. If anyone stood to benefit from a fire, he might.

Hank didn't buy any of it. Tyler once had family here. His roots ran deep in this town. He did have solid relationships. True, he wasn't married or dating anyone, but then neither was Hank, and no one was arresting him. And last, after Hank had seen the careful way Tyler closed the body bags of burn victims over the years, he found it impossible to believe the man would start a fire just in the hopes of getting a few more bodies for funerals.

Hank was halfway across the street when Alex shot out of the building, heading toward her car.

"What's up?" he asked, as if he had a right to know.

"I put Tyler in my office. Davis is checking in with his supervisor. He thinks the Texas Rangers need to be called in to talk to Tyler because the fires cover more than one county. He's working his way through proper command now. I have to run home and check on Noah, then I'll be right back."

"What can I do?"

She hesitated. "Off the record, you can go sit in

271

my office and make sure Davis doesn't question or harass Tyler while I'm gone. Irene will stand her ground, but Davis might try to pull rank and bully her. I don't want him talking to Tyler about anything before I get back."

She was gone before he could ask how he could stop Davis. Tying up an officer of the law wouldn't work. Slugging had some appeal, but it would only bring more trouble. Davis was the kind of man who wore on people. If he decided to deck the guy, he'd probably have to get in line.

Hank ran up the steps, deciding he'd stop Davis even if he had to start shouting that there was a green alien in Harmon Ely's old tree out front. If Davis had to lock him up for being nuts, it would give Alex time to get back.

When he walked into the secretary's office, Irene surprised Hank by handing him a tray. "Would you take this in to Mr. Wright? I'm on guard, but I thought he might enjoy a cup of coffee and some of my banana bread. The poor dear looks upset about something."

Hank had been in this office every day for more than a week, and Irene had never offered him banana bread. "Any way I might have a cup of coffee, too?" He smiled but knew it was wasted. Irene Lewis wasn't a woman easily charmed out of her banana bread.

"I'll bring you one when I have time." She pointed him toward Alex's office.

Hank found Tyler sitting at the round table by the window, looking like a man waiting for his last meal.

He frowned when he saw Hank. "They brought you in, too?"

Hank shrugged, playing along with Tyler's assumption. "I was told to wait in here until the sheriff got back." He hated seeing his friend so upset and tried to cheer him up. "Should we start planning our escape? I'm not sure what we did, but I hear the Rangers are riding in after us."

Tyler smiled and let his hands uncoil from the arms of his chair. "I'm sure they just want to ask us questions." He seemed to be talking more to himself than Hank. "Everything will be settled in no time and we'll be home for dinner."

Hank played along as he passed Tyler the cup. "I am worried. Trooper Davis isn't friendly on a good day, and today must be one of his worst."

"I know what you mean." Tyler took a piece of Irene's bread from the little plate. "I swear I thought he was going to handcuff me. Imagine that." He took a bite and seemed to breathe in the bread. "I always love Irene's banana bread."

Hank grabbed a slice and downed it whole before he added, "Me, too."

Irene hurried in with a cup of coffee for him, then hurried out, closing the door behind her. Hank thought he heard Davis's voice just as the door closed.

"What do you think they got the couple of us for?" Hank asked.

Tyler was back to his pleasant self. "I have little idea. Sometimes on the back roads I drive seventy-five."

"Most of the time I go about eighty. When I get a ticket, I always consider it supporting the highway system."

Tyler relaxed in his chair. "Alex said something about asking me questions, though I can't see how I could help her with anything she's working on."

Hank's mind finally put the pieces together. "You know the back roads, Tyler. You study maps. Maybe she needs your expert skill." As he said the words, something else became perfectly clear: Tyler drove the back roads following maps, not setting fires. If he crisscrossed this part of the country, it was only logical he'd be seen near the fires.

"I'm not an expert. Half the time I get lost and spend an hour trying to find my way back to a road sign." He took another slice of bread and leaned back. "I do find some interesting trails, though. For example, the other day I found the markings of an old wagon road across the back of your place. It might have been used to haul off all the buffalo bones left lying around after the buffalo hunters came through. Back behind your house is a ravine that could have trapped hundreds of buffalo. Hunters could have shot them, stripped their hides, and left their carcasses rotting. By the time this land was settled, there would have been nothing but bleached bones left."

Hank also took another piece of bread. "I think I remember my grandfather telling me about when he was a boy, how his father had hauled away bones to buy supplies the first winter after he inherited the land from old Ely. I'll never look at my back door again and just see the sunset."

Tyler laughed. "I heard Ely left the three families land, but no money. Some say he gambled the last of his cash away the week before he died, and the gambler who won it left town the morning of Ely's funeral."

"That's probably right. They say the Trumans came from Virginia and brought some valuables with them, but the Mathesons and the McAllens were dirt poor, working for what the old man paid them. Ely had land, but they say he spent most of what he had had trying to build a town around his trading business." Hank knew they were talking about something they both had heard every detail of, but sometimes it's calming just to talk.

Tyler seemed to feel the same way.

Hank was relieved to hear Alex in the outer office yelling at Davis. She was back, and she'd straighten out this mess.

Tyler was telling Hank about trails he'd found where old Model Ts had hauled dynamite out of a few sites where men had drilled for oil in the thirties when Hank felt his cell phone vibrate. He flipped open the cover and put it to his ear.

"Chief!" There was no mistaking Willie's excited voice. "Derwood spotted smoke in the canyon."

"How long ago?" Hank stood, shouting so loud Willie could probably hear him from across the street. He wouldn't need the phone.

The kid rattled on about how fire would climb the walls of the canyon. It could come out anywhere. They were fighting a monster now.

"Breathe, damn it, Willie," Hank shouted. "Get your gear on and make sure the call goes out to every volunteer. We'll need every man. Do you understand, every man!" For this fire, they'd need the dozen who always showed up and the thirty who never managed to make it.

He realized he was firing orders far too fast for Willie.

"I'll be right there." Hank closed the phone, tossed it on a pile of maps and papers, and stared out at the cloudless sky. Hank couldn't see a hint of smoke, but he could feel trouble moving in fast.

Tyler joined him at the window. "Fire?"

Hank nodded. "I've got to go." He hated the thought of leaving Tyler. On impulse, he turned and grabbed his friend's arm. "I'll be back. This will all get straightened out."

Tyler nodded. "Don't worry about me. You be safe."

When Hank exited through the outer office, everyone already knew there was fire in the canyon, and they were darting around and yelling. Andy was on dispatch, but he tossed a radio at Hank as he passed.

"I'll be there as soon as I can, Chief," Andy shouted. "I've got to help clear the calls first."

Hank nodded. Andy was always at fires; he'd be there as soon as he could pass the dispatcher duties along.

Hank brushed Alex's side with his hand, and she turned into him close. One look told him he didn't need to tell her how serious this might be.

"Let Tyler go," Hank whispered.

She shook her head. "Davis wants him locked up immediately. The best I can do is insist he stay in my office."

"Why? He couldn't have set this fire." Without turning loose of her, he began moving toward the door.

"Maybe not this one, but the others." Alex's voice was tight, as if she hated saying the words. "The state crime team found a quarter at three of the sites, and we both know he always carries quarters in his pockets."

"Pretty flimsy evidence." They were at the windy front door. Hank filled his lungs, swearing he could now smell trouble rolling in over the dry air. "Every man has change in his pockets."

"Not change. Only quarters."

"It's not enough to hold a man for arson."

"I know, but Davis thinks it's enough for a long talk."

"Then lock him up in your office." He tugged her closer for a fraction of a second before he let go and stepped out into the sun.

"I'll meet you at the canyon," she said.

He ran across the street, through the dry heat and dirt-filled wind whirling around him.

Chapter 38

REAGAN TURNED HER CHAIR TOWARD Jeremiah's and handed the old man one of the ice creams she'd bought when she'd done the shopping.

"What's this?" he grumbled.

"Ice cream on a stick," she answered. "Don't tell me you've never had it."

"Never thought to ask for it." He stared at the treat as if he were about to accuse her of poisoning him. "Why'd you buy it?" He took a bite.

Reagan thought for a moment, then said, "Where I've lived before, there were never enough of these to go around. There would always be a few of these good kind and lots of flavored frozen water. By the time the box got passed to me, all that was ever left was frozen water."

"Do you like frozen water?"

"No."

"What did you hate most about those places you lived?" He looked at her as if truly listening for once.

"I hated having to say thank you for everything given me. New clothes, used clothes, even the food on my plate. I was supposed to be grateful. And I was," she rushed on, "but sometimes they weren't giving it to me, they were just giving stuff away and I was handy."

He was silent for so long, she wondered if he'd dozed off, and then he said, "Buy more of these ice creams when you go to the store. In fact, keep the freezer stocked with them until you get good and tired of them."

"All right." She giggled.

"And get some of that frozen pizza I've seen. We need to keep it on stock for that boy who keeps coming around. I've heard it's fattening, and he could use some meat on his bones."

"All right." In all the weeks he'd never told her what to buy. He'd always said to buy the supplies she thought they needed. Now he was turning in an order for junk food.

Noah's pickup rattled down the lane at about half the speed he normally drove.

Reagan stood in alarm.

She watched as Noah pulled up close to their chairs and slowly climbed out of the truck. He didn't look any better than he had when she'd seen him after school.

"What are you doing here?" Reagan ran and pulled the old green wicker rocker off the porch. It was all they had with pillows in it.

He slowly folded into the chair. "I needed to talk to you, and you two don't have a phone between you."

Jeremiah looked up at her as if he hadn't noticed the bandaged, bruised boy sitting next to him. "Add that to the list. Order a phone. I have no idea how to do it, so figure it out. But I don't want any calls unless it's an emergency, so you might want to get one of those cell phones I see stuck to half the drivers' ears nowadays. You can use it and not give the home number to anyone, and I mean anyone." He pointed with his head toward the green rocker.

"It *is* an emergency," Noah said, "or it might be soon. There's fire down in the canyon on the other side of the Matheson place. If it reaches the grass, we could have trouble moving fast across dry land. Since I've been helping out at the fire station, they put me on the list to call, even knowing that I probably wouldn't be able to suit up and fight."

"You're hurt," Jeremiah said. "Only reason I can think of they'd put you near a fire is for kindling."

Noah shook his head. "It's mostly just a few bruises. Nothing really. We've got the fire to deal with now."

Jeremiah stood. "I'm not worrying about any fire till I know it's coming. My momma always said never waste worry, you never know when you'll need a bucket load of it and only have a thimbleful left." He headed toward the house, then turned and yelled as if Noah's injuries might have left him deaf. "You take care of yourself, boy."

"I'll try, sir," Noah yelled back. "You and Rea might think about moving out for a few days until this is over."

"I'm not leaving." The old man shifted to Reagan. "You might want to give him a couple of those ice-creams-on-a-stick of yours."

"Please, don't feed me," Noah protested.

Jeremiah glared at the boy as if Noah had just proven he was some kind of rodent and they might want to put out traps, then headed on toward the house.

Noah leaned over and said quietly, "Does he ever say anything nice like hello or good-bye?"

"Nope," she answered honestly, "but now and then if you listen real close, he does say something nice."

Noah leaned back and closed his eyes.

"You shouldn't have come," she whispered. "You're supposed to be in bed. The doctor told you to rest for a week."

"I had to get out of the house. I've got to clear my head." He scrubbed his scalp, sending hair flopping across his forehead. "I don't care what the doctor said or how it hurts. I couldn't stay there, and this was the only peaceful place I could think of to come."

"I'm glad you did," she said, "but your house is great."

Noah leaned forward. "It's not the house. It's what I just saw there. Rea, it was horrible."

She couldn't imagine what could be so bad that he'd leave. Violence, murder, and a few hundred other terrible sights came to mind. "Tell me," she said, wishing she didn't have to hear what he saw. She had enough of her own nightmares haunting her dreams.

Noah put his head in his hands and began, "I thought I'd go down the back stairs and sneak into the den without anyone noticing. I thought I'd play a few video games before Mom found me and sent me back to bed."

He pressed his palms against his eyes, as if trying to push out an image. "The sun was streaming in the kitchen windows. The hallway was in shadows, but I could see to move past my mom's bedroom to the den. When I heard little noises."

"What kind of noises?"

"Strange kinds of noises. Kind of like someone is hurting and laughing at the same time. Like they were being tickled to death, or something."

Reagan waited.

"Then I took a step and saw in my mom's room . . ."

"And," Reagan whispered, afraid of what he would say.

He looked up at her, horror in his eyes. "I saw my parents having sex. I'm scarred for life."

Reagan laughed. "Did they see you?"

He shook his head. "They were too busy at the time. All I can figure out is when the doc said for me to go home and go to bed, my parents must have been listening. It wasn't even dark, Rea, and they were rolling in the sheets."

Reagan giggled. "Preacher, sometimes you're downright adorable."

Chapter 39

AS THE FIRE ENGINES PULLED OUT OF THE STA-tion, Hank climbed into his Dodge and followed. If the fire was running the canyon's length, he'd need to put the trucks at the two ends, and then he'd need his pickup, loaded down with supplies and equipment, to get from one end to the other. No proper roads ran to where a canyon dropped down like a giant crack in the flat earth, but with the prairie so dry the Dodge would be in no danger of getting stuck.

While he drove, dispatch patched him through to Wild Derwood, still in the air.

"Right now all I see is smoke, low in the canyon." Derwood's words bounced through the phone. "Left wall. Little movement."

Hank swore he heard the man giggle before he

asked, "Does this make me a full-fledged fire-fighter?"

"Yes, but we're not finished." Hank wouldn't have been surprised if Derwood took off to tell his mother. The guy had been crazy so long no one even talked about it anymore. In Texas, being nuts was a more dominant character trait than any illness and Derwood was a prime example.

"Give me the orders, Chief," Derwood shouted through the radio. "I'm ready to do my duty."

"You've got an hour before dark!" Hank shouted. "Keep watching until you get low on fuel. There's a chance the rock along the wall will stop the burn. We'll be up top if it climbs. What I need you to tell me is which way it moves."

North, it could break out near McAllen land. South, it would hit his spread and then Jeremiah Truman's place. East or west, the burn would run itself out in the canyon.

Closing his eyes, Hank surveyed the land in his mind. His property would be fine. He kept fire-breaks plowed and all growth away from the buildings. If the fire reached the rim, he'd call and make sure his ranch hands moved any cattle. If it reached his house, the most he'd lose would be the far barn. Of course, the smoke would scare all the women he lived with to death. He'd make sure he called, giving them plenty of time to get out. They didn't even need to see the smoke getting closer. Aunt Pat and Aunt Fat would worry. At the speed they moved, he'd better call early. Claire would panic about her art collection, and Liz would probably explode in anger over why someone didn't do something about the smoke. The only calm one in his family was his mother. He wasn't sure she lived in reality most of the time, but he'd never seen her overreact. Maybe she'd gotten that all out of her system when his dad died. Since then, she'd been a rock.

Hank shook his head. Sometimes he thought fire was easier to deal with than all the women in his house, but right now, all he had time to think about was the fire.

The McAllen ranch wouldn't be so lucky if the fire came out of the canyon onto their land. Noah had been keeping an eye on the old place, but he was far more interested in horses than keeping breaks cut, and the couple he had living there didn't have time to do much. Alexandra's cabin on the rim would burn if the fire climbed out near her.

Then there was the old Truman place. A house built of sticks with old half-dead trees around. The orchard was irrigated, but if fire came, the trees would burn. If fire reached Jeremiah's land, it would destroy everything: the house, the orchard, the barns. If he managed to get fire trucks in before the fire reached Jeremiah, they could be trapped inside thanks to all the dead trees lining the only way out.

Logic told Hank to pray the fire came out on his

land. McAllen's was unprotected and Truman's would burn, but if it hit his place, Hank would take a loss. He'd have his best chance to fight and win if he fought on home ground.

Hank was driving eighty when he passed Lone Oak Road. He almost smiled, remembering Tyler's confession. If the sheriff arrested every farmer or rancher who broke the speed limit, they'd all be in jail except Bob McNabb. Stella would never let him speed, not even when he'd been called in to assist the volunteers. Half the time when McNabb showed up on a call, Stella had packed him a lunch.

Turning off the road, Hank headed across open range vowing he'd fight and beat this one, no matter what it took.

An hour later Hank and all his men were in full gear watching the sun set. Smoke drifted up from the canyon, but nothing climbed. The men were starting to celebrate, thinking maybe this wasn't going to be so bad, just another story they'd have to tell.

Hank didn't say anything. He stood at the edge, a foot away from a hundred-foot drop into the canyon, and watched.

Brad Rister stood beside him. "It's not out, Chief. I can smell it burning."

Hank had a strong feeling he was right, even if Brad was more drunk than sober. He'd been a fireman for a year in Oklahoma City. He was the only man in the department who'd walked in the door trained. Hank had a feeling Brad would be moving on after his divorce was final. Right now Brad and his wife were in hell, trying to hurt each other as much as possible. Like most couples, they couldn't let the marriage die quietly; they both had to beat it to death. Word was Brad's wife had started dating again, which probably explained why Brad had doubled his drinking.

Hank would be sorry to see Brad go, even though the Oklahoman rarely trained and skipped most of the meetings. Sober, he was one of the best Hank had. Drunk, he was as helpful as a flat hose.

"There's enough juniper and mesquite in the canyon to burn for two days and no way we can get down to it to put it out." Brad fought not to slur his words.

"I know." Hank had climbed down these walls near his ranch. He knew that there were places ten feet deep with dried tumbleweeds. "We'll leave five men and both trucks where they are to keep watch. Why don't you ride along with me to check things out?" Hank would rather keep the drunk with him than leave him with the team. The last thing Hank needed was a drunk working a fire line. Maybe a drive across open range would sober him up.

Brad nodded. "Sure, I'll ride with you, Chief."

They both knew that the trucks were so far apart all the ground couldn't be covered. There was a good chance if the fire came, it would have a good hold on the grass before they would even see it.

Derwood called again to say he was heading in. "I can see the trucks," he shouted over the noise of the plane. "Looks like the smoke is concentrated right between them, but the way the wind is kicking up, it's hard to tell."

Hank motioned for Brad to get into the pickup. By the time he'd bumped across uneven ground for ten minutes, Brad was already complaining that he wished he'd stayed behind.

They reached the spot between the fire trucks. Neither truck was in sight, but Hank could see wisps of smoke coming from down in the canyon.

Brad jumped out and made it several feet before he threw up. When he walked back, he looked pale, but steady.

"Get the ropes." Hank nodded toward the back of his truck. "I'm going down to have a look."

Hank kicked off his gear, not listening to a word Brad was mumbling. The only way to find out how bad the fire was would be to rappel down the wall, and he couldn't do that in gear. He clipped his radio to a carabiner on his belt. If his cell didn't work in the canyon, maybe the police radio would.

While Brad tied one end of the rope to the winch on the back of the Dodge, Hank strapped on his harness. The canyon wasn't deep here, a hundred feet if he was lucky. He and Warren had made it down sliding on their butts many times, but if there was fire this time, Hank would need to get down and back fast. He knew he could get down, even in the shadows, but the ropes would be a great help when he turned to climb.

"You know how to work the winch to pull me up?" Hank checked the tie-on. "Slow speed or you'll drag me. Got it, Brad? Slow speed."

"I know. I'll remember." Brad looked like he might vomit again. "I'll be ready to bring you up as soon as you send the signal, but Hank, this is a bad idea. If the fire doesn't get to you, the smoke could. It's too dangerous."

Hank wanted to say, *Compared to what? To waiting?* If the fire was growing, there was still time to call in every agency they could. If it had played itself out, he could get a few men in good enough shape to rappel down, and with backpacks they could take down enough fire retardant to contain it. With the wind shear along the rim, a plane could never make a good drop of retardant to reach the fire.

Hank tugged on his gloves and began working his way down, trudging backward when he could, jumping from rock to rock, using the ropes like a vine in the jungle when he needed to and rappelling when he had to. He'd taken a few classes on how to do it safely, but like most, he hadn't practiced.

"I'm getting too old for this." He swore as the muscles in his legs burned.

At sixty feet down he saw fire beneath all the smoke.

Another twenty feet lower he could make out the blackened burn crawling across the canyon.

It was a full burn, building as it inched across sagebrush and buffalo grass. A monster growing, eating away the ground growth and belching dark smoke. Because of the wind, the smoke had blown down the canyon and not up. The danger was far greater than he'd feared.

There was no way to get closer to the fire except on horseback, and before men could saddle up, the fire would spread the width of the canyon. It was already climbing the walls in spots, spreading through the scrub trees and dead cottonwoods along the dried-up creek bed. Before long it would break free of its confinement of canyon walls.

Hank felt every muscle tighten, preparing to fight.

He couldn't send men down. Much too high a chance they'd end up trapped. They'd have no choice but to wait.

Hank let the ropes take his weight as he reached for his cell. The case clipped to his belt was empty. He grabbed the radio, trying to remember where he'd left the phone that never left his side.

As soon as Andy at dispatch picked up, Hank began rattling off orders. "Call in the parks department. They'll need to find a place in both directions of the fire where they can stop it in the canyon." He remembered a water crossing a few miles up where the canyon widened enough to get trucks in. To the east, the canyon narrowed. If the parks service could get a water dump from the base at Altus, that would stop the fire from crawling along.

"And, Andy . . ."

"Yes, Chief?"

"Call in all the help you can get from towns around. This is big and it *will* climb the walls." Hank stared down, swearing that the burn had grown even in those few seconds. "It'll probably break out of the canyon in more than one place. We're going to need more men than we've got now to control this one."

"I'll call." Andy's voice vibrated with excitement. "And don't worry, Chief, as soon as I can get off this desk, I'll be out there with you."

Hank could feel the heat now as he began to climb, pulling his weight up a few feet at a time. His hands were sweaty inside the gloves. His muscles strained. Smoke climbed with him, robbing him of oxygen.

He jerked the rope, the signal for Brad to start the winch, then waited.

Nothing.

Night had settled in and, with the smoke, Hank couldn't see the edge of the canyon wall clearly. He felt his way, climbing. Jerking the rope to signal. Climbing.

He had no idea if he was twenty feet from the ledge or forty. He tugged the rope hard, sending the message to Brad for the fifth time.

"Brad better be dead," he said with his teeth clenched, "or I'm going to kill him when I get out of here."

His shirt turned wet with sweat, but he couldn't stop. He tried yelling for Brad, but the wind whipped his call away, circling it down the canyon.

Then finally, the rope jerked and pulled. Hank relaxed for a moment as he started rising, than realized he was moving too fast. Brad must have pushed the winch full throttle. He wasn't climbing now, but bracing his legs, trying to swing away from the walls before the edges pounded him. He felt like a boxer who couldn't get his footing before another punch sent him spinning.

Hank cleared the top, scraping his knee before he could roll over on his back. He yelled as the rope dragged him across solid ground, with flying dirt and weeds scratching his arms and face.

Halfway between the ledge and the Dodge, he finally stopped.

"Damn it, Brad!" he yelled as he released his harness from the rope. "You trying to kill me?"

He closed his eyes, took a deep breath of fresh air, and looked into the stormy blue eyes of the sheriff. For once in her life, she looked like she was too angry to speak. She stood above him, fists on her hips, glaring at him as if it were all his fault for almost getting himself killed.

Over by Alex's cruiser Hank heard Trooper Davis shouting on the phone, "We found him. Damn fool almost got himself cooked."

Alex offered Hank a hand up. He clasped her arm while she grabbed his and tugged him to his feet. They were so close he could feel her brush his chest when she breathed, building anger like steam.

Before she started cussing he smiled and asked, "Worried about me?"

"Yes," she said without moving back. "If you die, there will be all kinds of forms to fill out. How could you have been so dumb to go down alone? Who did you think would winch you up, a jackrabbit? Another five minutes swinging above that fire, you would have been a marshmallow in full burn."

He didn't try to defend himself. It was almost worth all the scrapes and bruising he got to see how much she cared, even though she'd probably clobber him if he suggested that caring might be at the bottom of all her anger.

Hank spotted Brad coming out of the shadows. "Sorry, Chief, I had to throw up again."

Hank would have let Brad have it, but right now he had something else on his mind and far too close to his body. Alexandra.

Like a dozen times before, all she had to do was

step away, but she didn't. Despite all her complaining, she was drawn to him.

He fought the urge to kiss her. She wanted him, needed him, just as dearly as he needed her. No matter what she said, she'd been worried about him.

"Right now, Alex, we've got a fire to fight, but when this is over," he whispered as Trooper Davis started toward them, "we've got unfinished business." He took a deep breath, loving the way she smelled. "And believe me, we will have time one day."

She didn't say a word, but her body brushing his was enough to make him hotter than the fire ever had.

Brad flipped on the bar of lights on top of the Dodge. Hank moved away from her and began folding up the ropes.

"Thanks for pulling me up," he said. "Remind me to teach you to use the slower speed."

She stared at Brad, figuring out where the problem must have been in Hank's plan. "How about I shoot one of your volunteers?"

"No need. He knows he's now an ex-volunteer." Hank tossed gear in the bed of the pickup. "How'd you know I was here?"

"Andy patched me through when the state parks service started asking questions. He told me about where he thought you were, and I headed this way while I talked." She looked at the rim of the canyon, glowing now as if dawn were just beginning to break. "What did you find?"

"It's growing, feeding off dried trees and brush. I'm guessing, but I think it'll break the rim before dawn, and then we'll have a full fight on our hands."

"Worst ever?"

He met her eyes. "Worst ever. You up for it?"

She nodded, and he realized he loved this wild, wonderful, brave woman.

Chapter 40

TYLER WRIGHT SAT IN THE SHERIFF'S OFFICE. He'd already tried the door. It was locked. At first he'd heard yelling and phones ringing, but then it grew quiet. The thought crossed his mind that everyone had left him behind, but he knew that would be too much to hope for.

He'd been worried for the first hour, eaten all the old candy in the sheriff's candy bowl the second hour, and finally slept a while in her chair with his feet on her desk. Which wasn't comfortable at all.

Tyler thought of trying to contact Katherine on Alex's computer, but doubted he could get logged on, and if he did he wasn't sure he wanted to leave a trace to Katherine on the sheriff's files. If he was in trouble, he might somehow pull Katherine in, and Tyler would face a firing squad before he'd tell them about his hazel-eyed friend. They had this private world no one else would ever know about.

He groaned at his own imagination. He had no idea why the law was keeping him, but he doubted he'd be shot for speeding. Hank had said they needed his help, but something didn't feel right about that. The sheriff, or rather that angry highway patrolman, wouldn't lock him up if they wanted his help. Davis had given him a look that said he'd already convicted him of something terrible and was just waiting around until some judge pronounced sentence.

Bored and nervous, Tyler began walking around the sheriff's office, examining everything. He discovered a closed vent over the door that when opened allowed him to hear conversations going on at the dispatch office across the hall.

He could hear the dispatcher calling in firemen for duty and giving directions to a meet-up spot a few miles north of the Matheson ranch.

Tyler moved a cell phone aside and unfolded a map sitting on the round table. He had no trouble finding the spot where the dispatcher was sending people.

The markings on the map interested him far more than the dispatcher's conversations. He pulled up a chair and tried to figure out what all the Xs and circles meant on the state map.

With his knowledge, it didn't take him long, and the meaning frightened him more than Trooper Davis ever could.

The *X*s were burn sites . . . fires . . . each marked with a date. And—he held his breath—they were moving in a circle around Harmony.

The fires must have been set. Nature would never play such a game.

Another hour passed as Tyler read the details of every report as if it were the world's best mystery novel. He guessed the sheriff hadn't left it for any outsider's eyes, but Tyler considered it like magazines in a doctor's office. If it was there, he could read it.

Hard fear settled in his stomach. Whoever was setting the fires wasn't some kid playing with matches. He reminded Tyler of a hunter circling his prey. Two, maybe three more fires and the circle would be complete. What would the madman with his weapon of fire do then?

Tyler knew the roads, even ones not marked on any map. He could see the arsonist's pattern. Finally, he stood and moved to stare out into the midnight sky. His eyes burned from reading, but he still smiled. He knew why they must have called him in. He could help. He could show them the back roads the man setting the fires would have most likely taken. Maybe from them the police could find a clue, like tire tracks or maybe even footprints.

Tyler wished he'd watched more of those detective shows and fewer dancing shows.

Some of the fire points of origin were close to

roads, but others were well off even the known unpaved roads. Whoever was setting them knew the area well. Maybe he'd grown up around here, or maybe he'd studied detailed maps like only the police and fire departments usually saw.

"Or maybe," Tyler said out loud, "he was like me. Collecting maps, studying roads, exploring."

Tyler didn't like the idea that any part of him could be like someone who would cause damage for no reason, but he felt he might be able to see inside a tiny part of the arsonist's mind and, in so doing, help in the capture of such a man.

The cell phone on the table began to vibrate. Tyler hesitated. He knew it was Hank's phone. He also knew the chief had forgotten it.

Slowly, he picked it up, deciding it was probably Hank on the line wondering where he'd left his phone. In all the excitement of the fire, he might not have had time to notice it was gone until now.

"Hello," Tyler answered.

"Uncle Hank?" came a small voice.

"No, dear, this is Tyler Wright." The caller had to be Saralynn. "Your uncle left his phone with me."

"Sir Knight," she whispered, sounding like she might cry. "I'm afraid."

Tyler forgot all about his problems. The little princess needed him. "What's frightened you, dear?" He glanced up at the clock and noticed it was almost two in the morning. Far too late for a four-year-old to be up.

"A man called and told my gram that we all have to leave our house by dawn. He said there may be a fire coming our way."

Tyler looked at the map. He wished he could lie and tell her everything was going to be all right, but if the wind was out of the north, it looked like the fire might just blow straight over the Matheson ranch.

"Is that true?" she whispered.

"It could be, child. But don't you worry, your mom and grandmother and aunts will get you out, and you will all be safe." Tyler knew Hank was out on the rim of the canyon right now with more than twenty men watching, waiting, ready. "If the fire does come, it will go around your house, but the smoke will make your eyes water and a princess's eyes should never water, so they'll take you somewhere to wait until everything is all right."

He heard a sniffle.

"Mom told me to go to bed, she'd come get me when it's time to leave, but I can't sleep. I can hear them all moving around the house." She sounded as if she might cry again. "Will you talk to me, Sir Knight? I don't want to be alone."

Tyler moved to a chair. "For as long as you like, Princess."

Suddenly Tyler wasn't tired and there was nowhere he wanted to go. He was right where he needed to be.

Chapter 41

ALEXANDRA WATCHED THE STATE TEAMS storm her office just before dawn. Cars and vans full of them. The county offices of Harmony were beginning to sound like a crowd at the state fair.

Highway patrol cars to handle traffic if smoke from the fires blocked the roads.

The state parks service officers, whose only worry was state lands already on fire.

A high-powered arson specialist from federal named Major Cummings, who worked out of Austin. She'd flown into Amarillo, rented a car, and driven to Harmony just to make sure she'd be in place before dawn.

Alex couldn't even count the endless reporters asking questions and wanting to be allowed at the site to take pictures.

The main office was packed with people, and Alex knew these were nothing compared to the numbers at the site near the canyon. She tried to make room for all of them and offer office space and chairs for all federal and state people. The place was a working beehive. Irene had come in early to pass out cups of coffee and pencils provided by the chamber of commerce.

Andy, who'd spent the predawn hours watching for fire, was back in his chair at the phones. He jumped up from the dispatch desk and rushed toward her. Some men look good with a few days of stubble on their face. Andy Daily wasn't one of them. He also looked like he could use one of those washers he owned. Maybe he could find a big one and just climb in, washing clothes and body at the same time.

She backed into a corner, away from the others as Andy Daily reached her. She hoped for a little privacy, fearing what he was about to say. "You need to get some sleep," she said, knowing she'd need to pull all the part-time people in if she could get him to surrender his headset.

He leaned in, ignoring her comment. He was too excited to whisper. "Fire's climbed the walls in three places. It's into tall grass on the north side and short in two places on the south wall. We've got a full crisis on our hands. It's going to take a lot more than our fire department to handle this one."

Alex raised her eyes to the crowd, who all seemed to breathe in at the same time. For a second the room was silent. She saw a world of different emotions in their eyes. Some frightened. Some nervous. Some excited. For the firemen, it would be a fight. For the reporters, it would be a great story.

One woman—middle-aged, slightly overweight, with intelligent hazel eyes—caught her gaze. Alex saw wisdom in those eyes and, more important, experience that had taught her not to overreact in times like these.

Alex nodded slightly, and the woman walked toward her. She'd been told that Major Cummings, the military's top arson expert in the area, was good, but this lady hadn't made a grand entrance, she'd simply walked in and gone to work on one of the break room tables. If Alex had to trust someone, this one woman would be it.

"Can we talk in my office, Major?" Alex motioned toward her door.

The woman picked up her briefcase. She was letting Alex take the lead, not trying to run over her authority simply because she was older. Just by the way she followed a few steps behind told Alex that she was there to help.

Alex forgot she'd locked Tyler in hours ago. She'd unlocked the door and stepped in before she remembered.

The major walked past her as Alex looked everywhere for the undertaker. He seemed to have vanished. Trooper Davis couldn't have taken him to lockup. First, he didn't have a key to her office, and second, Davis was at the site. Tyler Wright didn't seem the type who could pick a lock, but then, he was gone.

"I'm here to help," Major Cummings announced. "I'll never leak information and I'll never sugarcoat the truth. In return, all I ask is honesty and the opportunity to help when I can."

Alex accepted the woman's hand. She had bigger things to worry about than how Tyler got out of her office, plus she had a feeling that if he'd escaped, he'd probably gone home. "Thank you." Alex met the woman's honest stare. "I'll do the same, Major Cummings."

The major smiled. "Then let's go to work."

Alex quickly spread out Hank's marked map and showed her the area.

The major needed only a quick look to see the problem.

As Alex closed the open window, Major Cummings stuffed the map in her case and marched toward the door, "Call me Katherine, Sheriff, and I think it's time we head toward this fire."

"I'm Alex."

There was no more time for introductions. They had a fire to fight.

Chapter 42

HANK HADN'T SLEPT FOR TWENTY-FOUR hours, but he was pumped on coffee and adrenaline. The fire came over the edge of the canyon like a warrior charging into battle. Dry grass and wind were its allies as smoke breathed out a war cry.

He'd had word that other trucks from surrounding areas were coming in, but the fire came first. He hardly noticed the dawn as he fought through smoke and dust. His men, even those he feared would never stand in trouble, fought beside him. What they lacked in training, they made up for in spirit.

Hank yelled orders and the men moved in with every weapon they had.

And still, the fire spread. Twisting along the uneven edge of the canyon where they couldn't get water. Jumping in the wind. Flames three and four feet high in the tall grass. The heat made it seem like the hottest day of the year, and the smoke seeped through the equipment.

Half the team circled to the north to fight on the opposite rim, leaving Hank with less than half the men he needed. Trooper Davis kept yelling into the radio that more fire trucks were coming, but the fire was crawling sideways across the battle line, growing, raging, every minute.

By the time Hank saw the first truck bouncing across the field, he already needed two more. To his horror, vans from the TV stations nearby bumped along behind the fire truck.

"I thought I said no press!" Hank yelled at Davis.

Davis shrugged, as if he had no control over free press.

"Well, at least make them stay out of the way and far back." When this was over, Hank promised himself he would have a very long, very private talk with Davis. The trooper thought he knew everything, even ordering the firemen around. In truth, he couldn't handle his own job. He was a man who talked a good story, but didn't walk it.

Davis gave a mock salute as Hank cussed the man's incompetence. The highway patrolman directed the camera crew over to Willie, the only one of the volunteers not black and sweaty.

Closing his eyes, Hank swore under his breath, putting the pieces together. He'd already guessed that the trooper and Willie were probably related, and now he knew that Davis had brought the press in to take Willie's picture.

Hank had made the boy stay back for safety's sake. He had the least training and judgment, but now it looked like he'd be the hero on the news tonight. Hank couldn't help but wonder if Davis hadn't planned it that way to highlight his kin. In the past few days he'd seen the two men talking several times.

It didn't matter. Nothing mattered but the fire.

As the sun rose, Hank ordered his men to pull back a hundred yards and try again to make a stand. With shovels on shoulders, they all moved back. They were on land owned by a corporation. It had never been farmed and probably not grazed for years. There had also been no fire breaks cut . . . ever.

While they waited for the fire to crawl toward them, they all gulped down water and rested aching muscles. Hank took inventory. They'd been fighting the fire for three hours. Two men were hurt. Three looked like they couldn't go much longer. The fire was burning hotter, moving faster than he'd ever seen grass fires move.

He glanced at Bob McNabb manning the radio and first-aid station. There was no need for him to yell the same questions he'd asked a dozen times. No need for Bob to report the fire still raging across the canyon. Bob just shook his head, and Hank nodded once in thanks.

As soon as he got reinforcements, he'd order his men to rest at least two hours. If he didn't, Hank knew he'd be dealing with more injuries than a few burns. The EMTs from the hospital were about half a mile back, working as hard as the firemen.

Alex pulled up behind the fire truck and stepped out with a squatty woman at her side. They both marched right toward him.

Alex did a quick introduction of the major, then asked what they could do. He didn't miss the fact that Alexandra's gaze never left his face. She seemed to be reassuring herself that he was all right.

Hank described everything that had happened, but he noticed that Major Cummings was barely listening. She began walking the grass, bending now and then as if smelling invisible flowers.

"What's with her?" Hank asked, too tired to be polite.

"Federal government," Alex answered, as if that explained everything. "Where's this heading?"

"Unless the wind changes, right toward my ranch. The good news is we've got a great deal of open range to fight it first. No houses or herds to have to deal with. The bad news is we have open range. No roads, no breaks." He didn't sound upset. His mind had already thought every option through. He'd have to wait until the cards were dealt before he could play the hand.

Alex stared out at the black cloud on the ground crawling toward them. She looked like she wanted to empty her Colt into the wall of black smoke.

"One thing you don't have to worry about." He fought the urge to touch her. "Looks like it'll miss your place."

"What about your mother, the aunts—"

He didn't give her time to make the list of women at his ranch. "They're all out, and I've got the house protected. If it gets all the way to me, I'll probably lose the old barn my father built, but other than smoke damage, we'll survive. I knew the women would panic if they saw the wall of smoke coming, so I told them to get out before dawn. They've been in town for over an hour."

"Your stock?"

"I've got men moving cattle onto your land as we speak. Figured you wouldn't mind." He grinned.

"They'll eat all my grass."

"At least you got grass." He would have bet that

she'd complain. He also bet she wouldn't care if his cattle ate every blade of her grass.

Alex reached out and almost touched him. "You all right?"

"I'm fine. My biggest worry right now is Jeremiah's place, just beyond mine." He didn't say more. He couldn't. Hank might lose grassland for a season and fence posts, but Jeremiah stood to lose everything. The old man didn't have enough life left to rebuild.

"What can I do?" she asked, meaning every word.

"Keep Trooper Davis out of my hair. The guy gets on my nerves."

"Done."

The middle-aged major interrupted. "Gas," she announced from about five feet away. "Someone's seeded the grass here and there with gas. That's why it's flaring in spots. That's why it's moving so fast."

"But how?"

"I understand this land is owned by a company in Dallas. I assume no one patrols it." She didn't give Alex or Hank time to comment. "An arsonist would have had no problem crossing this land on a jeep or ATV, or even a pickup. He could have spread gas for a mile if he had barrels of it in the back of a truck. But he couldn't have crossed onto Matheson land," she said as she looked at Hank. "You have a working ranch, I understand. A stranger would be noticed." She made a face. "What I can't figure out is how he could get out here with a load of gasoline. Looks like someone would have noticed."

Hank had been so busy lately, he might not have noticed someone on *his* land, but the highway patrol had been watching the roads. "How'd you know all this?" he asked the major.

"I do my homework. You may have been up all night watching this fire, but I've been up learning all I could." She winked at him boldly. "If it matters, Mr. Matheson, I figured out the circle about three this morning. I'm glad to see that you did also. It's always good to know there is a logical man in charge."

"What do you think the gas means?" He found himself admiring the major. She might be short and built like an apartment refrigerator, but she had the most interesting eyes and a razor-sharp mind.

"I think"—she raised one eyebrow as if pleased to be asked—"that he's getting restless. He's tired of waiting for his big fire. If this one doesn't burn bright enough, I think he'll set another soon."

Hank agreed. "So, what do you know for sure, Major?"

"First, we know this was set. That's a matter for law enforcement. We let them do their job. Second, get your people back and let it burn. If one of your men is standing in a puddle of gasoline when the fire line reaches him, we could have a casualty. I'm thinking he wouldn't have had time to make more than one run spreading the gas. The chances he'd get caught were too great."

When Hank started to argue, she continued, "If we act fast and move back, we can form a break; the tanks can water it down before the fire line gets to it. Those folks in Dallas won't be happy that we let their land burn, but it's our best chance of stopping the fire."

"How far back?"

She pointed past his fence line. "Three, maybe four hundred yards that way."

Hank agreed. It was a hard course to take, but it might be their only chance.

Like an army of ants, they all began to move. Hank drove his truck, loaded down with men, to the fence. By the time the others reached his land, he'd pulled out enough fence poles to let them pass.

Alex banished the reporters to Lone Oak Road and Trooper Davis to the roadblock. The highway patrolman looked like he might argue, but in the end he didn't. Two more volunteer fire departments joined the fight. There should have been a half dozen more by now, but Hank would take what he got.

For the first time in hours, Hank thought they might have a chance.

While they waited for trackers to plow a row and trucks to water the barrier down, Hank picked up the radio and asked Andy to patch him through to his mother. He needed to know she was safe. He didn't want her to know that they were fighting a fire on his land.

"Mom," he said when he heard her voice.

"Yes, dear," she answered. "Are you all right?"

"Fine, and you?"

"Pat, Fat, and I are at the bed-and-breakfast. We didn't get any sleep packing up last night, so we've checked in and are having breakfast before we take a morning nap. You're not going to believe what colors they've painted this place. I've already decided to suggest a better color scheme for a house this age."

"Good." Hank hated listening to his mother talk about colors. It crossed his mind that maybe she should have spent more time talking to his sister Claire, who only painted in black, white, and red.

She continued, oblivious to the fact that Hank hadn't commented. "Claire packed her paintings in the pickup and is going to drive them on to Fort Worth before something else threatens to harm them. Liz and Saralynn went over to Liz's friend's house who has a pool. They plan on swimming a few hours if it gets warm enough today and then joining us here."

Hank didn't like the idea of Saralynn swimming with Liz. His younger sister might be smart, but she'd never been able to keep a goldfish alive. If he didn't have his hands full, he'd go get the little princess right now. "Mom," he said. "Do me a favor and call Liz. Tell her not to let Saralynn in the water unless she's right there."

"All right, but you should give her some credit. She's not ten years old, she's twenty-seven."

"Promise," he insisted.

"All right. I promise. When I finish breakfast, I'll call."

"Good." He clicked the radio off, but he couldn't shake his anxiety.

Chapter 43

TYLER LET HIMSELF IN THE BASEMENT DOOR of the funeral home, slipped out of his shoes, and rushed up the back stairs to his bedroom. He could hear Willamina in the kitchen making breakfast with CNN blaring away on the kitchen TV. His housekeeper had insisted on the TV ten years ago and, to Tyler's knowledge, she never watched anything but the news and *Oprah*.

He crossed to his bathroom and stripped off his bloody shirt. Crawling out the window in the sheriff's office hadn't been easy. Halfway through he'd gotten stuck and decided he'd probably be there until he lost ten pounds, but after finally wiggling out of his suit jacket and vest, he'd dropped to the rosebushes below the office window.

There, he'd been bloodied and unfortunately several of the rosebushes died in the battle for him to break free.

Like a thief in an old film, he darted through the darkened streets, constantly on the move and completely out of breath by the time he'd gone the two blocks to the funeral home.

Now he didn't bother with treating his wounds; he simply slipped on another white T-shirt and then pulled on an old sweatshirt he hadn't worn in years and a pair of even older tennis shoes. Sometime over the past twenty years he'd begun dressing the same way every day. Always a starched dress shirt. Always a suit or sports jacket if it was the weekend. Always polished shoes.

He glanced in the mirror and decided he looked like a pumpkin in his orange UT shirt, but he had no time to worry about it. He was on a quest.

Running back down the stairs, he slipped out the basement door and climbed into the old van they used for moving flowers from the home to the grave. The seats smelled like dusty potpourri and damp cardboard, but Tyler hoped the van wouldn't be missed or noticed.

Saralynn called just as he reached the city limit sign. "Are you still coming, Sir Knight?" she whispered.

"I'm coming, Princess. Did you walk around the house one more time like I told you?" He'd hoped someone was still there packing and thought the kid was sleeping. He couldn't believe she was really alone.

"I did. I even called up to Momma's studio. I can't climb the stairs." She took a breath and continued, "No one is in the house but me. Momma told me to ride with Aunt Liz, but by the time I got out to her car she said it was too full and I'd have to ride with Momma and the aunts in the van. When I got all the way back to the garage, the van was gone."

He could hear her crying, and it broke his heart. He'd seen her walk using crutches a few times. Each step looked like it was slow and painful. The Matheson house was big, and she'd had to walk the length of it from the front steps to the back.

"They left me," she said between gulps for air. "They all forgot about me."

"No they didn't, Princess. You're the most important person of all. They just each thought that you were with someone else."

He heard her sobbing and wished he had more knowledge of kids. "I'm coming," he said. "I promise. I'm on my way." His foot shoved the gas pedal harder. "I'll be there soon. Can you get your bag of medicine ready?"

"I saw it on the counter. Someone must have packed it."

"Good. Get it and meet me at the front door."

"Can I call you back? Uncle Hank's phone number is the only one I remember. He got it special because of me. When I spell out my name on any phone, I get him. I can even leave off the last *N* and still get him."

"You bet you can call back. I'll keep your uncle Hank's phone in my hand until I get there." Tyler smiled at the interesting way Hank had taught her not only to spell her name, but to call him. "You get all your things together and then call me right back."

"What things?"

"Well . . ." He had no idea what little girls would think were important. "Things a princess should always have with her."

"Oh," she said. "I'll pack."

When she hung up, he closed the phone, hoping he'd be within sight of the ranch house by the time she collected her things.

He turned onto Lone Oak Road and saw the roadblock just past the Truman gate. To get to Saralynn, he'd have to pass Jeremiah's place and, from the number of cars, there was no way. After all, he'd escaped from a locked office. Somehow that couldn't be a plus. He was now a man on the run. The last thing he needed to happen was to be caught before he reached Saralynn.

Laughing to himself, he could hardly wait to e-mail Katherine tonight and tell her of his adventure. Of course, he'd have to leave out a few details.

Tyler pulled off the road and tried to think. He

had no map with him, but he could see every back road in his mind. He'd even mentioned one to Hank yesterday.

Turning around, Tyler headed for a back road that would run into a trail that would lead to wagon ruts still marking a path where buffalo bones had been hauled off Matheson land a hundred years ago.

It was full daylight by the time he reached where the path would have been, and to his delight, he could see slight impressions in the earth now and then, marking the way. As he drove, he also saw something else. Smoke, moving like a long rolling cloud toward him. It was still miles away, but it looked to be on a direct path to the ranch house.

Tyler gunned the engine, not caring that he was probably sending the old van to the junk heap. He had to get to Saralynn.

The house was dark when he pulled up at the front door. Leaving the van running, he jumped out and bounded up the steps.

"Saralynn!" he yelled.

She was nowhere in sight.

He tried the door.

Locked.

Panic jolted through his entire body. He tried pounding on the door, then listening. Nothing. Out of his mind with worry and smelling the fire growing closer, he started around the house, stomping on flowers and knocking over pots as he tried every window, every door.

All were locked. How could five women leave the house, locking every door, and forget to take Saralynn?

He took a tumble in the mud where someone had left a garden hose dripping in what looked like a newly planted garden. Getting to his feet, he tugged off the orange shirt, now soaked and dirty, and kept circling the house.

"Saralynn!" He wouldn't leave, couldn't leave until he found her. He tripped again, watching only the windows and not his footing. A branch caught his shoulder and bloodied the skin as it ripped the cotton of his shirt.

He'd made a complete circle and started another when he felt the phone in his pocket shaking.

"Saralynn!" He tried to sound calm. "I'm here."

"Sir Knight," she said. "I can't carry my things and walk with the crutches. Will you help me?"

"Where are you?" He could smell the fire now and knew it was getting closer. They had no time to waste. If she'd been another child, he would have yelled for her to run, but his little princess could barely walk and, if she hurried, she might fall and hurt herself.

"I'm in my bedroom next to the kitchen."

Tyler looked over at what looked like it might be a kitchen door. A few feet away, on a bench, he saw the gardening tools. Without hesitation, he committed a crime. He grabbed the hoe, raised it like a bat, and smashed the window in the door.

A moment later, he was in and moving toward the first room off the kitchen. "Princess?" he yelled.

He opened the door to the laundry room and almost swore aloud. "Princess," he called again as he moved to another doorway

"Yes," she answered just as he opened the next door.

She was sitting on her bed, her toys all around her. Relief washed over him.

She smiled up at him. "You are a mess, Sir Knight."

He caught a glimpse of himself in her dresser mirror—his shirt bloody in spots, mud on his face and hands, and not even a hat to cover hair he didn't remember combing since yesterday. "I've been fighting my share of dragons today."

Taking a step toward her, he bowed as politely as he knew how. "Are you ready to go, Princess?"

She stuffed the toys into what looked like a laundry bag. "I'm ready."

Tyler strapped her medical bag over one shoulder and a bag of toys over the other, then lifted her up as carefully as he'd seen Hank do in the diner.

She put her thin little arms around his neck and held on tightly as he moved though the house to the front door. He didn't want her to see the broken glass or the smoke moving toward the back of her home.

"I'm very tired," she whispered and rested her cheek against his shoulder.

"You sleep now, little one; I'll get you to town. It shouldn't be hard to find your aunt's sports car or your grandmother's old van. In no time you'll be tucked into a blanket and down for a morning nap."

"Okay." She sounded almost asleep.

Tyler smiled. He'd gotten her in time.

At the front door, he turned the knob and stepped out into chaos.

Chapter 44

ALEX HEARD THE REPORT OF A BREAK-IN AT the Matheson home on her radio. Hank was one of the few ranchers who'd installed alarms, to satisfy the fears of the women in his household. Hank's house wasn't anything fancy, but between his mother's pots and his sister's art, someone might have decided to take advantage of the fire to do a little looting.

Katherine caught her attention. "Go," she'd said. "Check out that alarm. There's not much you can do here."

Alex nodded and climbed into her car. She had to cross over open ground to get to the road and then go back almost to Lone Oak Road to enter the Matheson ranch entrance.

It took her five minutes and, by the time she pulled up, Trooper Davis was already there, his gun pulled and waiting.

"He's in there," Davis snapped. "He left his van running so he could make a fast getaway. Let me handle this, McAllen."

Just then, the door opened and a mud-and-blood-covered man pushed his way out. He had bags on both shoulders and a child in his arms.

Saralynn!

Alex started to move, but Davis shoved her back with one hand as he yelled. "Take another step and you're dead, Wright."

Tyler Wright? She hadn't even recognized him. This was impossible. Some kind of sick dream. She'd never seen Tyler with even a smudge on his suit, and why would he be taking Saralynn?

Alex glanced at the van. It was the one usually parked at the back of the funeral home.

"Put the kid down and step away from the door," Davis ordered.

"No," Tyler answered. "I'm not putting her down."

Davis raised his service weapon at Tyler's head.

Alex reacted. No matter what it looked like, Hank's words came back to her. *Tyler isn't guilty.*

"Hold your fire, Davis!" she ordered as she stepped out in front of the trooper and moved toward Hank's friend. If Hank believed in the man so completely, she could believe in him a little.

320

"What's going on here, Tyler?" Alex snapped.

He looked at her with fear in his eyes.

"Get out of the way, McAllen. You're blocking my shot!" Davis yelled. "There's only one thing to do with a pervert who kidnaps a child."

Alex didn't move, and she heard Davis mumble "Bitch" under his breath.

Tyler lowered his head slightly and spoke softly. "They accidentally left Saralynn, and I had to break out of your office to come get her. I'll replace the roses I fell on and the window I broke here, but I'm not putting her on the hard ground."

Alex looked down at the little girl. "Are you all right, honey?"

"I'm a princess," she whispered in a sleepy little voice, "and Sir Knight came to rescue me."

Alex smiled at Tyler. "You've had a rough time of it, even for a knight."

He managed a smile. "Just part of the job."

Alex extended her arms and lifted Saralynn. "How about you ride with me? There's a blanket in my car and I'll drive you around until we find your grandmother."

When she stepped away from the porch, Trooper Davis slammed Tyler Wright to the ground. His head made a thud like a melon as it hit the stones steps. Alex twisted to block Saralynn's view as Davis jerked Tyler's hands behind him and began reading him his rights.

"That was not necessary, Davis," Alex said.

He smiled as he pulled Tyler to his feet. "Oh, yeah, you know right from wrong, don't you, Sheriff? Sleeping your way into the job teach you all you needed to know about being a cop?"

Alex headed toward her car. She'd deal with Davis as soon as she'd made sure Saralynn was safe. He'd had something against her from the day she'd been sworn in, and now hatred was boiling to the surface. Davis wasn't mad about the crime he thought Tyler had committed or frustrated about the fires. He was furious at her. She could hear it in his words, feel it in his stares. Maybe it had always been there, boiling deep inside, but she knew without doubt that he wished it had been her head that hit the walk.

Hank's Dodge came flying across the pasture at a speed that looked as if he were about to become airborne. He slammed on his brakes just in time to slide into the flower beds. A moment later he was out of the car.

"We caught the burglar!" Davis yelled with pride. "Making off with two bags of plunder and your niece."

Hank stormed up the path and stopped in front of Alex. He placed his dirty, smoke-covered hand on the back of Saralynn's head. "Are you all right?"

She nodded. "Sir Knight came for me when I called your phone."

That seemed to be all Hank needed to know. He moved toward Davis as Alex hurried Saralynn to the car. She had no idea what was about to happen, but she guessed the language wouldn't be for children. Flipping on the radio, she made the little girl promise to stay in the car for a few minutes.

Saralynn leaned against the armrest, looking too tired to answer.

Alex covered her with a jacket and closed the door, then noticed Major Cummings sitting in Hank's Dodge. As always, the woman seemed to be studying everything around her.

Alex marched back to the men. Whatever Trooper Davis's problem, they'd deal with it here and now. Whether he hated her being a woman in what most thought of as a man's job, or loathed the whole county, she knew she could ignore his attitude no longer.

Hank was nose to nose with Davis, demanding he take the handcuffs off Tyler Wright.

Tyler stood, feet wide apart, head down as if it was taking all his effort to keep from falling over. Blood dripped from somewhere on his forehead into a puddle between his feet.

"So you want me to just let him go after he tried to steal you blind and do God knows what with your niece?" Davis looked angry enough to shoot Hank for getting in the way. "You're about as brain-dead as this sheriff who slept her way to—"

Hank's fists slammed into Davis so hard the man toppled backward, almost taking Tyler with him.

"That's it!" Davis said as soon as he could get to

one knee. "I'm arresting you for assaulting an officer of the law. Turn around, Matheson, and lock your hands behind your head."

Hank didn't move except to harden his hand into a fist. "Get off my land," he said in a low, angry tone.

Alex knew she had to do something. "Wait!" She pushed her way between the two men. "This is ridiculous."

Davis turned on her, but his words were for Hank. "I can't believe anyone in this town even speaks to this woman, especially you. Don't you know she's the reason your best friend died? I should know, I worked with both Warren and his partner. I heard him talk about you, and after Warren died, I heard his partner talk about what he'd done that night with Alex while her brother was out on a back road getting killed."

Hank pulled back as if he'd been slapped. "You're insane."

Davis smiled, sensing that his words hurt more than any punch could have. "Am I? Why don't you ask her what she was doing when her brother was shot? Or better yet, who she was with. If she hadn't begged Warren's partner to stay behind and play, Warren would have had backup that night. He wouldn't have been shot."

Davis pulled Tyler forward, no longer interested in dealing with the sheriff or the fire chief. He knew his words had wounded them both. "I've waited three years to file a formal complaint against you, Sheriff." He said the last word as if it tasted dirty in his mouth. "I'll have your badge, McAllen, and there'll be an arrest warrant waiting for you, Matheson, when you finish with this fire. I wouldn't be surprised if the folks in Harmony don't run you both out of town."

Pushing Tyler down two steps, Trooper Davis froze as the major stepped forward and dumped the bag of toys out on the ground. "Interesting things for a man to steal," she said in her calm way. "Toys and a small bag of medicine."

Alex watched confusion cloud Davis's face. For the first time, he seemed to question his logic.

"You're arresting a man for saving a child's life." Major Cummings straightened to all of five feet two. "If you don't remove those handcuffs, I'll see that you not only are fired, but are also sued for every dime you have in retirement."

Alex swore the major smiled before she gave Davis his only out. "Now, Trooper, I suggest you get back to the roadblock and stay there. Sheriff McAllen will handle everything here without your assistance."

Davis growled. He could fight one of them, maybe two, but apparently they had decided to gang up on him. He jerked the handcuffs off Tyler. "You're right. We've got bigger problems than petty theft to deal with."

He was gone before Alex could think of anything

to say. She'd always thought she was a good sheriff, able to handle anything, but she'd just witnessed a master at work. She had a feeling Katherine Cummings could stand down an army and win.

Major Cummings picked up the toys as Hank helped Tyler to the cruiser. When she finished her simple task, she said as calmly as a den mother, "Now, we get back to the crisis at hand. Sheriff, if you'll take that poor man to the hospital, then drop the child off somewhere safe, I'll go back to the fire with the chief and keep you posted."

"Chief," the major said to Hank, "we've got a fire to put out. Set all else aside."

He nodded once and stormed back to his truck without looking at Alex.

Katherine hurried to climb in before he drove back to the cloud of smoke at the same speed at which he'd driven home only minutes before.

Chapter 45

REAGAN WOKE TO SOMEONE POUNDING ON the front door. She slipped on her jeans, tucked in the T-shirt she'd been sleeping in, and ran down the stairs.

Uncle Jeremiah was already there and fully dressed.

Noah stood on the porch, looking only slightly

better than he had the day before. He still had bandages and bruises everywhere.

"This ain't the hospital, son," Jeremiah said. "I think you came to the wrong place."

Reagan moved around her uncle, who seemed to think at eighty-six he should start his comedy career. "What is it, Preacher? Noah wouldn't be here if it weren't something very important."

"The fire is spreading this way," he said. "I came to warn you. You need to get out."

"I'm not leaving my land," Jeremiah said, and turned back toward the kitchen.

"That's why I'm here," Noah said. "I knew you wouldn't listen to anyone."

Jeremiah turned back. "And you thought I'd listen to you, kid?"

Noah shook his head. "No. I came to get Rea out. I can't stop you from staying, but she needs to be somewhere safe."

She looked from Noah to Jeremiah. "I'm staying with my uncle."

"No, you're not," said both men at the same time.

"I'm not leaving this land." She widened her stance, as though she were willing to fight them both. "I stay and fight. Tell me what to do."

Jeremiah almost smiled. "That's right. Trumans stay and fight, no matter what comes." He'd never tried to tell her what to do and he wouldn't start now.

Noah took a long breath. "Then it's settled. When the fires come, I'll be standing right here beside the two most stubborn people in the world."

Jeremiah shook his head. "We're not much of an army. An old man, a busted-up kid, and a girl. If I was the fire, I'd be real scared about now." He reached for his hat and stepped around Noah.

"Where are you going?" Reagan finally found her voice.

"I'm going to the orchard and turn on the water. I saw the smoke at dawn and got both windmills pumping. If the fire makes it this far, it'll try to burn down the orchard first. The irrigation system will have the ground good and wet in a few hours and if the fire comes too close, I'll pull the water tank down and flood the place for a hundred yards around."

They watched the old man climb into his little cart. The old dog hopped into the passenger seat and they started off down the path to the orchard.

Reagan looked at Noah. "What do we do, Preacher? There's got to be ways we can help besides just waiting."

"Turn on the water hoses. Wet down everything you can." Noah stared at her. "Rea, if fire comes, it'll hit those old evergreens and tall brush between here and the road. If we stay too long, we may not be able to get out."

"I'm staying," she said. "What do we do next?"

He shook his head. "I don't know much. I only

had a few days of training, and most of it was on when to get out."

They moved outside. "I guess we round up buckets," he said, "anything that will hold water, and old blankets. If we place them around the house and barn, maybe we can fight back when the grass catches."

Reagan looked around. "What about the trees?" The house was surrounded. Old elms dry from winter, brown vines of all kinds twisting around every pole and pipe, bushes years past needing to be trimmed. "If one of the trees falls on the house, it'll burn. With the trees blocking us in, not even the fire truck can get to us."

Noah stared at the farm, not seeing the peace of now, but the horror that might come. "We got to make a wider circle. Not just the house, but all these trees around here."

She looked at the hundred-year-old elms circling the house with sheds and barns underneath them. Uncle Jeremiah hadn't hauled off a piece of wood in thirty years. Even the new chicken coop had been built in front of the old one. "What do we do?" she whispered, realizing she was standing in the center of what had the makings of a huge bonfire.

"I'm in no shape to hoe and we don't have a tractor. I'm still thinking we leave."

"We do have a tractor, several. Can you drive one?"

He nodded. "Easier than I can hoe or fight grass fires."

She helped him back into his truck and they drove behind the house, where Jeremiah kept his prized collection hidden away in a barn. Reagan didn't have time to think about how the old man was going to react. "The keys are in the few that take keys. Pick which one you think will do the job and I'll help you guide it through the doors."

Noah moved around them. "These are beautiful."

"Pick one!"

Minutes later, they were turning over dirt in a wide row around the barn and house. Reagan rode with him, helping him with the gears as he drove one-handed and held his side with the other. If he was in pain, he never commented on it.

One by one they circled the groupings of trees that had been planted by Trumans years ago. The dirt row they made scarred the earth. Reagan fought back tears, realizing that tomorrow morning, if there was a tomorrow morning at this place, Uncle Jeremiah wouldn't be able to look out at this land and see it wild and untamed as his grandfather had. But, she reasoned, he'd have a porch to sit on.

When the grounds around the house had five feet of dirt around it, Noah used another tractor to dig a trench and Reagan began filling it with water. The place was starting to look like a fortress surrounded by a tiny moat.

"Should we go check on Uncle Jeremiah?" She could see the line of trees that ran along the boundary of Truman land and Matheson land. He might not care about anything but the orchard, but Reagan loved it all. Every inch. "Do you think he's all right?"

Noah shook his head. "He's where he wants to be. I don't think anything has ever mattered to him besides that orchard. He's got the cart. If fire takes the trees, he'll make it back here."

Chapter 46

HANK FELT NOTHING BUT THE DULL ACHE OF numbness as he worked. He told himself to keep his thoughts on the fire and what to do next and not let any emotions about anything else surface.

His land was burning as he watched. His niece could have died if she'd gone much longer without her medicine. Tyler almost got killed trying to save her, and at some point Trooper Davis would probably return the punch Hank had given him, plus some, even if he didn't carry through on arresting Hank for assaulting an officer of the law.

Hank couldn't, wouldn't think of any of that. He had a fire to fight. He planned to stay on point until he collapsed with exhaustion and they had to carry him off. Maybe then, he could sleep and forget the ugly things Davis had said about Alex. Maybe he could get the hurt in her eyes out of his mind.

As Hank worked, the memories of his best friend came back. He could not remember a time when he hadn't known Warren McAllen. They must have been in the church nursery together, probably fighting over the same toy. Hank remembered the summers spent riding horses and swimming. And then the college days when they roomed together and fought over almost every girl either of them dated. The hours they'd spent talking about their dreams and the problems at home. Warren had been the only person he'd ever totally trusted. Hank's father was dead; his mother was always preoccupied with her work. Warren's parents fought, and his dad spent most of his life on the road. As boys, they'd had each other to depend on. As men, neither ever doubted the other would be there when needed. Sometimes Hank swore he could still see Warren standing in his doorway holding two longnecks and asking if Hank had time to talk. Problems with work, or women, or family were shared, if not solved.

He'd never had a better friend than Warren. Letting him go was the hardest thing Hank had ever had to do. If he could have traded his life for Warren's that night on the bloody road, he would have.

Don't think, Hank almost screamed. *Just fight the fire. Don't think.*

He was barely aware of a hand patting him on the arm.

"Hank," Bob McNabb yelled over all the noise. "The major wants to see you."

Hank nodded and moved back away from the fire. He felt stiff, as if he'd turned into a tin man from the hours spent in the heat. He hurt in so many places they'd all blended together in a dull throbbing he barely noticed.

He grabbed a bottle of water and moved to where she'd set up a table out of everyone's way.

Major Katherine Cummings looked up from a chart she'd been studying. "Chief," she said.

"Major," he answered. "Don't try telling me to stop."

She smiled. "I won't waste my time. I just wanted to tell you that it looks like we're finally winning. Unless the wind kicks up before three, we may have this fire under control by then. I've been in touch with the National Weather Bureau, and they predict a relatively calm day with a slight chance of rain. That may be the break we need."

Hank tried to relax the knots in his shoulders. "How much of my place will we lose by then?"

"Half the grass and fences. One barn. All the trees along the breaks to the north. But we saved the house and grounds, thanks to your foresight."

"Half," he said, thinking that he was barely keeping the place going when he had all his land. He'd have to buy feed to cover the grass he lost.

With the price of cattle, he'd be lucky if he could hold out the winter.

Any other time the news would have buckled his legs, but now it hardly registered.

"You've been up and fighting thirty hours, Hank," she said.

He didn't want to be told to quit. That word had never worked for him. "How's Tyler Wright?"

"Tyler?"

"The man who saved Saralynn. Alex should have reported in by now. Is he all right?"

Katherine frowned. "I haven't heard."

"You know him?" Hank asked.

"No." She hesitated, as if trying to put a puzzle together but the pieces wouldn't fit. "I know a different Tyler. A shy gentleman."

She looked down, and he was surprised to see her cheeks reddening as if she'd said more than she'd intended.

Hank shrugged. "Beneath all that mud and blood was a knight, Major Cummings. A true knight. He very well may have saved my niece's life."

"If you say so," she answered. "All I saw was the mud and blood and . . ." She smiled and added, "The way your niece held on to that filthy man's neck. I knew the minute I looked at her that she was not being kidnapped."

Two more trucks from counties fifty miles away pulled up, and men moved in to relieve exhausted fighters.

"I can take over here for one hour. You've already sent the original teams home to rest." She glanced at his house in the distance. "Go take a shower and eat something; you'll feel better. We're holding the line here."

Hank had finally reached the point where he was too tired to argue. She was right; with the new men, she could hold the line. He tossed his gloves in the back of his truck and drove across dried grass toward home.

Five minutes later, he climbed the outside stairs to his rooms, stripping off clothes as he climbed. By the time he reached his bathroom, all he had left to pull off was his jeans, and then without hesitating, he stepped into a cool shower.

The steady stream of water had washed away all thought when he heard someone call his name. For a moment, he just stood beneath the water, unwilling to step out. Then he flipped the shower off and grabbed a towel as he opened the shower door.

Alex was standing at his bathroom door staring at him.

Hank didn't bother to cover up. She'd seen all of him anyway. "What do you want?"

"The major said you wanted to know about Tyler."

Hank dried off, waiting for her to speak or leave. He didn't much care which. "What about him?"

"The hospital put three stitches along his hairline where Davis slammed him into the concrete, and then they doctored a dozen deep scratches that will heal without stitches. He's going to be fine."

"Good. I'm glad you got there in time to stop Davis. If I'd been alone he probably would have shot me." Hank couldn't believe he was talking to her as if nothing had happened. Maybe they were just both pretending Davis hadn't made the comment about it being her fault Warren died.

He pulled on his underwear, ending her peep show.

"Katherine deserves the credit for saving you. It was funny . . . all the way to the hospital, Saralynn slept and Tyler didn't say a word until we were checking in at the desk. At that point, he asked me what the hazel-eyed lady's name was. When I said Katherine, he looked so sad, like something had just died."

"Did he know her?" Hank pulled on a pair of clean jeans and pushed Alex out of the way so he could grab a shirt from a drawer.

She followed. "I asked him that, and he said no."

That was it, they'd both run out of anything to say. He stood holding his shirt. She stood fighting back tears, her arms crossed as if holding the world at bay.

He swore and tossed his shirt on the bed. "Come here," he ordered.

"Why? So you can hit me? So you can tell me how much you hate me?"

"Come over here." Hank felt like yelling, but he kept his voice low. "I've been trying to get close to you for years, but this time, Alexandra, you're going to have to make a move in my direction."

She took a step, and he saw a touch of fear blended with uncertainty in her eyes. She'd always drawn off his strength, even when they wouldn't talk about it. Now, he needed to draw off her.

Like he knew she would, she stood so close to him he could feel her breathe. The nearness of her made all the tension in his body slip away. When had it happened? When had he stopped being her rock and she had become his?

He slowly raised his hands and moved them along her arms, tightly folded across her chest. He took her wrists in his hands and pulled them until she gave way and her arms fell to her sides.

Then he wrapped his arms around her and drew her against him the way he'd always wanted to hold her.

She fought for a moment, stiffened as if to rebel, but she'd come to him. She'd crossed the room and he wasn't going to let her push away this time.

"Relax. I'm not going to hurt you and you know it." He kissed her hair. "Relax, baby."

She slowly melted against him, raising her arms to rest them on his shoulders. When she

337

swayed against him, he released his hold and moved his hands to cup her face, forcing her to look at him, hating the tears he saw in her blue eyes.

"Let's get one thing straight right now, McAllen," he started, and felt her try to tug away. He didn't let go. This time he wasn't letting go.

"I don't give a damn what Davis said. I know you would never hurt your brother intentionally." He kissed her forehead. "And you should know that I'd know that."

He kissed her full on the mouth, hard and completely like he'd wanted to for years. He felt passion shatter in his arms and flood over them both.

When he broke the kiss, she whispered, "It was my fault . . . I should have . . ."

He kissed her until she gave up trying to talk, then whispered in her ear while she caught her breath. "I don't want to talk, baby. I just want to be with you."

She wrapped her arms around him so tight he could barely breathe as he lifted her up and walked toward the bed. "We've only got a little while. I don't need sleep or food. I just need to hold you."

And then his wild and strong Alex did something he'd never seen her do, not even when she was a child.

She cried and he held her tight.

Chapter 47

TYLER WRIGHT WAITED IN THE HOSPITAL room for Willamina to bring him some clothes. He refused to walk out of the hospital looking like he'd been in a bar fight with a mud monster.

He also refused to stand up, knowing full well that the hospital gown he had on did not meet in the back. The nurse had come in twice to tell him that he could go, but he'd wait for his clothes.

He tried to piece together everything that had happened this morning from the time he escaped out of the sheriff's office. It all seemed like one of those late-night movies people watch but can never remember the name of at dawn. He'd never done anything wild in his life . . . until this morning. His rap sheet was probably a full page by now. Breaking and entering. Speeding. Resisting arrest.

And in the mix of everything, he'd seen a woman with hazel eyes. Alex said her name was Katherine, but Tyler decided he'd misunderstood. Maybe at that low point in his life he just wanted his Katherine to be there. A woman he talked with on the Internet would not simply appear in his world at a low point. His Kate couldn't be that Katherine.

The nurse brought him in a hanging clothes bag

and announced that the woman who delivered them said she didn't have time to wait, this was her shopping day. Tyler wasn't surprised. He'd bought Willamina the little Saturn five years ago and she'd yet to let him ride in it.

Tyler called one of the men who worked for him to come over and pick him up, then hurried to the bathroom to dress.

A few minutes later when he walked out to the black Cadillac, he looked and felt almost back to normal, even though he hadn't had a proper bath and a huge Band-Aid covered his forehead.

He stopped off for two double-meat cheeseburgers and fries before going home and straight to his study. He pulled up his e-mails. None from Katherine.

He typed a hello to her and ate one of the burgers while he waited. He checked again. No answer. He ate the other burger and all the fries and tried one more time.

When she didn't respond, he climbed the stairs to his room, locked the door, turned off the phone, and went to bed.

Eight hours later, after he'd taken a bath and redressed, he came back downstairs. His supper was cold, but waiting for him. Every lock was locked. Every light out.

Tyler discovered something. The world hadn't fallen apart when he took himself off call for a day. It had functioned just fine without him. Even the flower van had looked like it had been brought back from Hank's ranch, washed, and put back in place at the back door.

After checking his e-mail and finding nothing, Tyler did something he'd never done at night. He went for a walk.

Chapter 48

HANK LEFT ALEXANDRA ASLEEP ON HIS BED AS he slipped from his room and went back to the fire. An hour hadn't been long enough to hold her, but it was a start.

He could feel change in the air even before he reached the fire trucks. The wind was still. The air not quite so dry and smoky. It was over, he thought. Finally, it was over.

Most of the firemen were still working, but a few were standing back, watching the monster die.

Hank stepped up beside the major. "You were right."

"I usually am, about work anyway." She smiled. "That's why they pay me the big bucks. Are you ready to go back to work?"

"Yes." He pulled on his gloves and winked at her. "The hour's rest did wonders."

She smiled as if she understood. "I hoped it might. Now you're back, I'm moving to the sheriff's office. I've decided to camp there until this is over." She looked like she felt sorry for him. "This isn't over. You know that, don't you, Hank? Our troublesome arsonist will strike again. We've got to be ready. Twenty years in this business has taught me a few things. One is, when he hits again it will be harder and faster. My guess is he's getting frustrated, and that will make him careless. Likely he's taking this personal. We killed his plan and now he's out for revenge."

Hank wanted to say he didn't know if his team could take a stronger hit, but he'd worry about that when the time came. She'd been right about everything so far. He knew she was right about this, too. "Revenge on who?"

"Who knows. You, the sheriff, the town. We stopped his beautiful burn and he's probably mad. He'll use his weapon of choice to hit back. Our job now is to guess where, and maybe when, if we can."

"I'll meet you at the office as soon as I know this fire is out."

"I'll be waiting."

Hank turned back to the battleground. Black earth seemed to be everywhere. Fire still sparked in patches, but teams were moving across the land, putting them out one by one. Willie Davis was like a pup who'd been kept penned during the hunt and now could run free. He led the charge across the hot spots, yelling and running circles around the tired men.

Hank worked with them for an hour, then returned to the fire truck. "How's the fire on the north rim?"

Bob poked his head around the door. "They've got it contained, but it burned a few thousand acres of beautiful natural grasslands."

Hank shook his head. "You have to be born in Texas to see miles of nothing but grass as beautiful."

"Good news is when we get rain, it'll grow back."

"When," Hank echoed. "It's been so long since this county has seen rain, we'll probably all go outside and just stand in it once it comes. I think the rubber on my windshield wipers has fossilized."

Bob laughed. "My Stella says it's coming, she can feel it. She says it's a few days off, but it's coming."

Hank leaned against the truck, needing to talk to someone. "When this fire is over, we need to get the trucks serviced and ready to roll as fast as possible."

"I figured that," Bob said. "The last few fires have looked set. I'd be willing to bet a dollar that when we climb down in the canyon we'll find this one was, too. I don't know much about firebugs, but I watch a lot of shows and it seems to me they're kind of like serial killers; they keep going until they're caught."

Nodding agreement, Hank turned south and

stared at the orchard a few feet beyond his fence line. He could barely make out the old man standing in the shade of the trees, watching.

Hank raised his hand in greeting. Jeremiah didn't return the wave. Hank didn't know whether Jeremiah didn't see him or still held a grudge against all Mathesons. Grinning, he thought of how his aunt still called the old man Dimples when she mentioned him.

As Hank walked back to help with the cleanup, he saw the circle around Harmony in his mind's eye. It was close to complete. The only spot left between here and the first fire would be either old Truman's place or a run-down trailer park built in the cottonwoods along a dried-up creek bed. The aluminum homes were scattered to within sight of town. If fire started in the brush and trees around the creek bed, it would move fast, burning homes and wood until it hit town.

On a hot day, in hot clothes, Hank felt the chill. If the arsonist wanted to make a big fire, maybe one that would do more damage than the canyon burn, he'd hit Truman's place next. Truman's people had never been much for ranching or farming, but they'd planted trees. Evergreens from the road to within a hundred yards of the house, apple trees along the fence line, pine and oak in groupings around barns and storage buildings. And hundred-year-old elms around the house. Hank had no idea what all Jeremiah stored out on his land, but he surrounded it with trees. A big burn there could take the fire right into town in one direction and take out the rest of Hank's grass in the other direction.

If the arsonist hit Truman's place, it could turn into a nightmare.

The sky was midnight blue and free of smoke by the time he made it to the sheriff's office.

At first, it seemed everything was back to normal. Dallas Logan stood in front of the counter complaining about her streetlight. The smell of burned coffee drifted from the break room. Andy manned the calls and looked like he might have gotten a few hours' sleep.

Then Hank saw the changes. Major Cummings had put two desks together at a right angle in a corner and appeared to be working on two computer systems at once. A highway patrolman sat in Irene's office, looking like he was fresh out of school. Trooper Davis's replacement, probably.

Hank thought for the hundredth time how hard it must be for Alex to deal with these men who wore the same uniform as her brother, but she'd done it if for no other reason than it was part of her job. He wondered if she had any idea how proud Warren would be of her.

A few reporters were still hanging around, waiting for the wrap-up story. It would be on the news at ten, which he planned to miss.

Alex crossed the room to greet him. When he

met her eyes, he saw something he'd never seen before: a peace in her stare. No anger or worry or frustration, only peace. She was in the middle of the worst crisis to hit Harmony on her watch, but inside she'd changed. Without Davis, Hank might never have known the guilt she carried. If she'd said something about it, he could have told her three years ago that no one, including Warren, would have ever blamed her.

"How long did you sleep?" he asked as they walked toward the coffeepot in the break room. His hand brushed over hers when they reached for cups. The need to touch her was an ache he feared he'd never cure.

"Too long." She smiled. "Your bed's comfortable to sleep on."

"So am I."

She tilted her cup up to hide her smile. "I might test that theory one day, but right now we have a major staring at us."

He glanced around. Sure enough, Katherine Cummings was waiting at Alex's door with a load of printouts.

As they moved toward her, Andy Daily left the dispatcher desk and hurried across the room, his pockets jingling with change. "Doesn't it feel good to have it all over, Chief?"

"Yeah," Hank answered, slowing down to talk to Andy.

"That was really exciting." Andy almost danced

with energy. "I wish I could have been out fighting the fire more, but I was needed in here. I heard we got coverage of the fire all the way down to the Dallas stations. I thought about driving down one night just to buy a paper or two with *Harmony Fires* on the cover. The fire really put us on the map."

Andy drove the oldest Toyota pickup Hank had ever seen. He was surprised the piece of junk, which usually had one or two of Andy's broken washers or dryers rattling about in it, could make it ten miles out of town. He'd give it no chance of making the trip to Dallas.

Hank motioned for Alex and the major to go on in. "Thanks for all your help, Andy. We couldn't have done it without you." In truth, Andy was far better at talking than working, now being an example, but Hank figured the guy needed a pat on the back. Volunteers ask for nothing. A thank-you seemed little reward.

"I never saw anything like that fire." Andy shook as if with real fear. "It was like doomsday riding in on a cloud of black smoke and we were no more than toothpicks standing against the wind."

"You're not going to become a poet on me, Andy, are you?"

"No." He seemed to realize he might have gotten carried away a little. "I better get back to work. I got another hour before my shift is over."

Hank raised his cup in salute and watched the lonely man take his chair at the dispatcher desk.

Andy was the kind of guy everyone knew, but few would call him a friend. The kind who joined the campus cleanup team in college, not to help but so he'd have an almost-gang of friends to hang out with.

Hank stepped in Alex's office and noticed that the sheriff and the major already had their heads together, talking. It had been his experience that when two women do such a thing, it's never good for the only man in the room.

Before they could outline all their plans to keep watch, Hank's phone rang. He saw his sister Liz's number and wondered if it was too late to tell Tyler to keep the phone.

"Excuse me," he said as he stepped out and flipped his cell on.

"Hank," Liz said, without waiting to hear him say hello. "Mother and Claire are both mad at me. It wasn't my fault Saralynn got left behind. My car was already full; what was I supposed to do, unpack? There was plenty of room with Mom and the aunts. I had no idea they were planning to leave so early, and Claire is her mother, she should have put her in a car before she drove off with the stupid paintings."

"Liz." Hank cut her off. "I'm mad at you, too. In fact I'm furious. So add me to your don't-call list." He hung up, remembering how it had felt to answer the radio at the fire site and hear his mother say they couldn't find Saralynn.

He wasn't surprised when Liz hit redial immediately. Hank let it ring. Liz was the youngest. When they'd been growing up, they'd always stopped when she needed to, eaten where she would eat the food, gone on vacation where she wanted to go. She'd been running the family since she'd been born, with no thought of anyone but herself. It was no wonder her husband divorced her. Hank wanted to divorce her and he was blood.

He wondered if the family could get together and all vote her off the ranch.

"Stop plotting the murder of your sister and get back in here." Alex's voice and hand pulled him through the office door.

"You overheard."

"Liz didn't mean to leave Saralynn. It was an accident. She just wasn't thinking."

Hank shook his head. "She doesn't want to work, or go to school, or help out around the house, or do anything. I think she's campaigning to be the family pet. She wants us to do everything for her, including taking her to get trimmed and bathed for ticks. I've had enough. I'm thinking of calling that bum of a husband she left and demanding he take her back."

"For a man who lives with so many women, you don't understand much. She's just looking for a hero to save her. Her husband must have refused to do that."

"Well, we'd better look in lockup for her next match, because any free man will run as soon as he talks to Liz for ten minutes."

"You'll see. One of these days she'll find a man who has problems bigger than what she thinks hers are. He'll save her by having her worry more about him than herself."

"Maybe." Hank shook his head. "But he'd have to be on trial for murder, find out he had cancer and a brain tumor the same day he was struck by lightning, and bankrupted to top her daily list of problems."

Alex laughed and tugged him back to the round table. They began going over every theory they could reason out about what might happen next. Two hours later, Hank walked across the street to the fire station and crashed.

Just before he closed his eyes, he looked out the window and saw the sheriff's office light burning bright. Alex and the major were still working.

HIS PHONE WOKE HIM THE NEXT MORNING AT dawn. He rolled out of bed and picked it up, mumbling that if it was Liz he would personally sign her up for the Coast Guard. They were a thousand miles from any ocean. That should be far enough away for her to live.

"Uncle Hank?"

"Yes, dear," he answered, trying to sound awake.

"Gram says I have to eat breakfast with them

350

here at the bed-and-breakfast, but if I do I'll be late to school."

"I'll be there in ten minutes."

When he walked out of the fire station to his truck, he noticed both the major's rental car and Alex's Jeep still parked in the same spots they'd been in last night. Either they'd worked all night, or they were early risers. As soon as he got Saralynn to school, he'd drop by with a dozen doughnuts and see if they'd made any progress.

Thank goodness Andy Daily's Toyota, with broken washers in the back, was gone. It always junked up the parking lot, plus if Andy was still there, he would eat half of any box of doughnuts Hank took in. The man had no life other than the firehouse and the desk in dispatch. Most of his meals were passed to him from the drive-up windows in town.

Saralynn was waiting for Hank when he pulled up at the B&B. His mother and aunts might love sleeping in the old home decorated in antiques and plastic flowers, but one look told him Saralynn hated it.

"When can we go back home?" was her first question.

"A few days." Hank didn't want to admit that he felt safer with them in town. "I thought you girls might like a little holiday."

"You're kidding, Uncle Hank. There's a wall of old hats in that place, and last night the aunts kept me up laughing as they tried on every one, twice. Can I sleep with you at the station?"

"I wish you could, Princess. We need someone who can cook around there."

They pulled into the diner parking lot and he lifted her out.

"Will Sir Knight be here?"

"I don't think so," he said as he scanned the windows and saw Tyler, wearing a hat, sitting alone at a booth. "Correction, he's here."

Saralynn was all smiles. When they reached Tyler's table she insisted on giving him a kiss. When his hat fell off, she had to kiss the Band-Aid over his stitches. She told Edith that she planned to be a nurse whose kisses could cure.

After she finally settled into eating her breakfast, Hank asked Tyler, "How are you?"

Tyler smiled, but his eyes looked tired and sad. "I'm fine. Lost contact with a friend yesterday, and that hurt more than my stitches."

"Anyone I'd know?"

Tyler just shook his head. "Just someone I was corresponding with. It's nothing. Any clues on who's setting the fires? Besides me, of course."

"Davis was a fool. He wasted good time going after you. He disappeared after the roadblock broke up. Word is he was called down to Austin to do some explaining. Alex said if he goes after me for slugging him, you can go after him for false arrest."

"I wouldn't do that," Tyler said. "I just want to forget the whole thing."

"I figured that, but he doesn't know it."

Tyler nodded. "Alex understands what really happened. Is she the one who turned him in?"

Hank shook his head. "The major did, and it wouldn't surprise me if she has the ear of all the top people down at the capital. She's quite a lady."

"I'm sorry I didn't get a chance to meet her." Tyler's eyes were sad again. "I would have liked to talk to her."

Hank tried to cheer him up. "Good news about Willie; our youngest firefighter is becoming a star. He's now conducting interviews on grass fires, and one of the stations wants him to come in to do a series of shorts on fire safety. The kid's eating it up. They say he's got a face the camera loves. Who knows, he may give up firefighting and join the news team." Hank didn't add that the kid might be better at it. Willie tried hard and had all the excitement and enthusiasm in the world, but he lacked judgment.

Conversation stopped when the food arrived. With half his plate empty, Tyler finally broke the silence. "I want to thank you for standing solid behind me. The sheriff told me you fought to stop Davis even before I knew he was after me."

"That's what friends do," Hank said simply.

"Just like you dropping everything and rushing to save Saralynn."

Tyler smiled. "You're right. That's what friends do."

Chapter 49

~~~

TWO DAYS AFTER THE FIRES WERE OUT, NOAH showed back up on Truman land. Most of the bandages and bruising from his bull ride were gone, but his movements were still slow.

Reagan feared that when he came over Uncle Jeremiah planned to let him have it for driving one of his tractors and plowing up good grassland when the fire never reached them. The old man had been complaining about the scarred earth for two days. When she saw Noah climb out of his truck, she knew Jeremiah was about to cause a great deal of trouble. By the time he got finished yelling at Noah, it would probably be another fifty years before the McAllens and Trumans would speak to one another.

Her uncle moved to the porch, widened his stance, and prepared to yell at the only friend she had.

She knew she had to do something or the two would say things they could never take back. Bonds and battles in this town went on for lifetimes.

Reagan picked up the hot chocolate pie she'd just made and ran out the side door. Just as Noah stepped on the first step of the porch, she threw the pie, plate and all, at his face.

It smacked flat in the middle of his smile and slid down his shirt.

Both men were so stunned, neither could say a word.

Reagan saw her chance. "Get off Truman land, Preacher. We don't want you here. You plowed up good land and almost ruined a tractor that belongs in a museum. My uncle and I hate you for what you did. We hate you!"

Jeremiah was so stunned by her outrage, he felt sorry for Noah. "Now settle down, Reagan," he yelled, as if they weren't standing five feet apart. "The boy was just doing what he thought was right. The grass will grow back, and I can fix the tractor good as new. I think you're way out of line here, kid."

Noah used one long finger to push a slice of pie off his cheek and into his mouth. "Fiery, isn't she, Mr. Truman. I've got a theory that it's because of all that red hair. Somehow it clogs up her brain."

Jeremiah stared at her. "I've been complaining for two days. I guess she took up the cause. As for red hair, mine was red until the day most of it fell out. Then, I swear what was left turned white with mourning that same day."

Noah laughed and stepped on the porch. "You

got a towel I can borrow"—he ate another bite—"or a plate I can scrape this onto so I can finish eating?"

Reagan didn't like being ignored. "I thought I told you to get off my land."

Noah sat down in the green rocker. "I didn't come to see you, Rea. I came to see your uncle."

Reagan turned to Jeremiah. "Are you going to let him stay?"

"Of course. In fact, boy, you're welcome to stay for supper."

Noah smiled without giving Rea a glance. "Might as well. I've already had dessert, though. To tell the truth, things are crazy around my house. Mom's cooking and Dad is fixing things. I saw her give him a list of chores this morning, and he smiled. Can you imagine that?"

"Kicked once too often in the head during his rodeo days would be my guess." Jeremiah sat down beside Noah. "Is he acting loco? Bumping into walls. Talking to himself. Sleeping more than normal."

"He and Mom both are. They've been acting so strange, so often, I can't sleep at night."

Jeremiah, who had no knowledge of relationships, nodded as if he understood.

Reagan slipped into the house and grinned. She was brilliant. The two men were talking.

She could hear them as she checked on supper. Noah said he'd stopped by to tell Jeremiah that he saw Andy Daily pull off Lone Oak Road at the opening to Truman land when he was driving past.

Reagan moved to the window.

Noah saw her, winked, then continued talking to Jeremiah, "I slowed to a stop just past your turnoff and waited a minute, then turned on the dirt road just because I thought it odd that a guy hauling old laundry machines would be heading your way. It's not like there's anything else along the turnoff to your place."

Jeremiah leaned forward in his chair. "Is odd. Never seen Andy Daily on my land. Know who he is, though. I nodded at him a few times in town. He's the fellow with those two laundry places. There was an article about him in the paper a few years back. Something about making his living a quarter at a time."

"That's him." Preacher leaned closer. "I think he may be dumping old broken washers and dryers in that brush between the trees at the turnoff. He was acting real strange. When I turned in a few hundred feet behind him, he drove into the ditch like he was trying to hide from me. He got so far off that dirt you call a road, he almost disappeared in the trees. If he'd been coming to see you, he would have moved on. If he'd accidentally turned onto your road, he would have turned around and waved."

Jeremiah hollered for Reagan to wait on dinner a while. By the time she got out of the house,

Preacher and Jeremiah were in the cart and heading toward Lone Oak Road.

She'd told Jeremiah the trees needed work for weeks. Old evergreens with dead branches on the ground caught every tumbleweed that blew close. Even Noah had mentioned that it was a real fire hazard. Now Andy Daily thought he could dump his trash in the pile of dead wood and brown branches.

The old dog whined beside her.

"Hate being left behind, do you, boy? So do I."

On a whim, she walked to Noah's truck, found the keys still in the ignition, and hopped in. The old dog barked and jumped in the back. They made it to the edge of the trees when she heard shouting.

Reagan jumped out and saw Jeremiah standing beside the cart, yelling, "Get off my land! This ain't the city dump, you fool."

The roar of an engine being pushed to the limit sounded, and she spotted Daily's Toyota parked in a ditch halfway between the road and the clearing. The man driving gunned it again, trying to get up the embankment. Something sloshed out of the washing machines in his truck bed, splashing over the ground.

Jeremiah yelled again as he backed toward the cart.

Reagan felt her blood chill. She couldn't see Jeremiah's features clearly, but she knew something was horribly wrong.

Suddenly, the old Toyota rolled backward and then shot forward in an all-out effort to make it up the embankment. Over the noise, Andy Daily yelled something that sounded like a curse.

She heard the roar of the engine, then saw a washing machine tumble out the back as the truck almost reached the chalky dirt road. The front of the truck bucked like a bronco and rolled, crashing back into the ditch along with the load of washing machines. Whatever liquid he carried inside the machines splashed out around the truck.

The smell of gasoline flavored the dry, warm air.

One blink later, fire shot from the ground, engulfing the truck in a ball as bright as fireworks.

Jeremiah jumped into the cart and pulled forward, but smoke and flames shot across the road before he disappeared.

Reagan thought she heard a cry, like a wild bird, then only the sound of a raging fire sweeping up the dried trees.

She started toward them, but fire seemed to be swinging in the branches. She could no longer see the cart, and she knew she couldn't drive into the black smoke that blocked the road. She was trapped.

Crying so hard she could barely see, Reagan turned the truck around and raced for the house. She ran to the water and turned it on, knowing that she only had minutes before the flames would reach her. The fire would take the trees, crawl across the prairie grass, and be at the plowed ground before help could get here from town.

Pulling the cell phone she'd bought yesterday from her pocket, Reagan dialed, then froze. The road was on fire. No one would get to her.

She was alone. If fire jumped the barrier Noah had plowed, she would have to fight it alone.

"Noah," she cried. Oh God, where was Noah? Had he been in the cart? He had to be still in the cart. He was hurt. He wouldn't have gotten out. Pushing tears away, she whispered, "He's in the cart with Jeremiah and they're on the other side of the ball of fire." They had to be. She wouldn't think of any other possibility.

She ran around trying to wet everything she could as the sound of the raging flames grew louder. Forcing herself not to look toward the road, she filled the buckets still scattered about the yard. She soaked all the blankets she could find as she tried to remember what else Noah had told her to do.

The fire crackled and roared. The air grew thick with smoke, making her eyes water. Or maybe she was still crying. She no longer knew or cared.

The air grew warmer and wind whipped heat, like the first breath from a hot oven, in her face.

She checked the trench where the garden hose was running. It would never be full in time. She ran to the water tank. With fumbling fingers, she tied a hoe to a long rope and swung it over the top of the tank.

One. Two. Three times. No luck. The hoe clanked against the side of the tank and fell to the ground.

How could she pull the tank down if she couldn't get a handle on the top? Something Preacher had said one night at the rodeo echoed in her mind. *Failure is not an option.* She tried again and again. The heat of the fire now radiated through her clothes. Pulling one of Jeremiah's old bandannas from the clothesline, she wet it and wrapped it around her head. She picked up the hoe and tried again.

On the sixth try, the hoe caught on something and she pulled.

Nothing happened. She pulled so hard she was airborne, but her weight wouldn't take the tank down. It was old and rusty and used only to irrigate the garden and water the trees around. But it was still stronger than she was.

Reagan looked down the lane to the road. The trees were all on fire, shooting flames into the sky that looked miles high. She could feel the heat of it blistering her face already. The black cloud on the ground that Noah had described was crawling toward her like hungry fingers. He'd said that from a distance, you couldn't see the flames on grass, all you see is a black cloud smoking its way across the ground.

"NO!" she screamed. "You can't have my home! I'm not giving it up."

Reagan pulled the rope once more, then swore. "Hopeless," she mumbled just as she saw the dog, still sitting in the pickup as if he wanted out of this place. Reagan ran for Noah's truck. She tied the end of the rope to the bumper and jumped in. When she gunned the engine and threw it into gear, the truck shot straight into the chicken coop, sending boards and chickens flying. It also tumbled the tank behind her.

The tank tilted in slow motion for a few seconds, and then a waterfall flowed down. Water hit the ground like a tidal wave, flooding everything.

Reagan lowered her head against the steering wheel. If the water didn't work, she'd lost. She'd lost everything.

Chapter 50

HANK HEARD THE ALARM SOUND A MOMENT before he saw a ball of fire shoot into the air from a couple of miles away.

They'd gone over what to do a dozen times, and he'd prepared every one of his men to respond quickly. The trucks were headed toward the fire before the siren stopped screaming, and he was dressed in his gear and running.

When Hank jumped in his truck to follow, Alex climbed in the other side.

He hit eighty before he glanced over and asked, "Why not your cruiser?"

"This thing can go more places faster and I'm going with you. The major will take care of setting up roadblocks, and we've already started calling in surrounding help if needed."

"But—"

Before he could say more, she added, "Noah called in the alarm. He was screaming so loud I could have probably heard him if I'd opened the window of my office. I could also hear the fire. He hung up before I could tell him to get away."

"He knows to get back. I drilled that in his head the first day he came to train."

They didn't say another word as they raced down Lone Oak Road. Smoke thickened like fog, and Hank slowed as he moved toward the bright lights of the fire trucks flashing like beacons.

When he pulled up beside the trucks, he saw that the old trees lining the lane to the Truman place were all ablaze. His men were everywhere, letting the trees burn, but putting out any sparks that flew off and threatened the grass on the other side of the road.

Alex saw only the little cart Truman always drove around his place and her brother standing beside it. She jumped from the truck and ran toward him.

Hugging him wildly, she heard him groan. "You're killing me, Alex. I'm going to have bruises on top of bruises."

She pulled away as Hank reached them. "What happened, Noah?"

"We caught Andy Daily dumping a truckload of old washers in the ditch along Truman's lane. They must have been filled with gas or something, because when his truck turned over trying to get out of the ditch, flames shot up like fireworks."

He looked at his sister. "The old man and I started toward Daily, but there was no way we could get to him. Jeremiah must have known we wouldn't have time to turn the cart around. He raced through the smoke to the road. Those trees shot up like huge matches. I swear, there was nothing we could have done for Andy."

Hank yelled over his shoulder as he moved toward his men. "Andy wasn't tossing old junk, he was setting a fire. He's our arsonist."

Alex had figured that out, too. Early this morning Major Cummings had reported that several of the closest fire departments didn't get the emergency signal until hours after the canyon fire started. Andy Daily had manned the phones that morning. He hadn't made the calls, even though he'd told the other dispatcher he would.

Alex radioed the major, filling in details as she patted her little brother. When she clicked off, Alex looked at Noah.

"Where's Truman?"

"He's over there yelling that the men should forget about the trees and go in to get Rea. She's at the house. Every fireman here has already told him it's impossible."

"Will the fire reach her?"

He shook his head. "I don't think so. She's got a plan. Truman even said he told her a story about how his grandmother survived a prairie fire once by climbing in the root cellar and putting wet blankets over her. I just hope the old guy remembered to show Rea where the root cellar is."

Alex made Noah sit down, then checked in again with the major. In what seemed like minutes they heard other sirens coming in. This time the calls went in immediately. Clifton Creek and Bailee were already sending men with police escorts.

She walked beside Hank when he passed. He went to his truck to get extra gloves. She didn't speak; she just watched him. She needed to be near him.

Then he looked up at her, and for one moment she knew he was remembering their time together. "When this is over . . ."

"I'll be waiting," she answered, and then he was gone to do what had to be done and she stepped back into the role of sheriff.

By the time the fire began to crawl from the trees to the grass, a hundred men and six fire trucks stood by to fight. In an hour, there was nothing but smoke and ashes.

Hank loaded Alex, Noah, and Jeremiah into his truck and drove past the orchard, still standing. He crossed onto his land and stopped long enough to cut fence before he pulled around the apple trees and headed down the path toward Jeremiah's house. No one said anything, but they all let out a long breath when they made out the shadow of the house in the distance.

"Better fix that fence before fall," Jeremiah grumbled. "I don't want your cattle crossing onto my land and eating apples."

"I'll do that," Hank promised as he bumped his way over a plowed row and splattered mud for twenty feet when he pulled into the yard.

"Looks like it flooded," Noah said. "Where'd all this water come from?"

"She downed the tank." Jeremiah grinned. "That niece of mine is a smart girl."

Reagan stepped out of the house just as they reached the steps, and she was smothered in hugs.

Everyone talked at once. No one was listening, but Hank didn't think it mattered. He could feel a weight rising off his shoulders. It was over.

Jeremiah invited them in for supper, a slightly burned pot roast, but Hank and Alex begged off, knowing they still had a great deal of work to do.

As he circled Noah's truck, half buried in what looked like the remains of a chicken coop, Hank saw the boy lean down to hold Reagan, and he noticed her pull away. A strange reaction from a friend, he thought, but they were just kids; they'd have years to figure it out. Hell, he was still working on it.

Alex must have noticed it, too, because she slid across the seat until their bodies touched from knee to shoulder. "I'm not an easy person to get along with," she whispered, "and I suspect I won't be easy to love."

"You're not telling me a thing I don't already know. I've loved you for years and I can testify it's not easy."

She kissed his neck, almost making him drive off the path. "My place when this is over?" she whispered.

"It may be late, but I'll be there. And this time, baby, we're not rushing anything. I'm taking all the time I need to show you how I feel about you."

The fire this woman was starting in him was a slow burn that would take days to put out . . . maybe even a lifetime.

He didn't touch her when they got out on Lone Oak Road. He didn't dare. He wasn't sure he could let her walk away if he did.

Chapter 51

~~~

W HEN A LEX GOT BACK TO HER OFFICE, THE major was packing up. "We got him," Alex said.

"The fire got him," the major corrected. "I'd been watching him for two days. I couldn't put my finger on it, but something wasn't right. I even ran a background check and only came up with one fact: He was bankrupt. But that wasn't enough."

"Why do you think he did it?" Alex asked.

"We'll probably never know. I had my eye on Brad Rister first, thinking with the divorce and getting kicked off the fire department team, he had nothing to lose." She shrugged, silently admitting her first hunch was wrong. "Hank called in to say Brad was out with the others fighting tonight, and from the looks of it he was sober. Willie Davis loved the excitement too much and went a little crazy during the fires, so I watched him, too. Once I met his uncle, Trooper Davis, I figured crazy ran in his family."

Alex smiled. "You read people so well, you should move to Harmony."

"I've got my twenty years in, I just might. But to be honest, I'm not a great judge of people when they're not suspects at the scene. I can't seem to tell the good ones from the bad ones when it comes

368

to me. All my life I keep finding a prince that turns into a toad when I kiss him. Several years ago I gave up and decided to just do my job. Know of any knights in shining armor?"

"Nope, but I'll keep my eyes open." Alex liked the major. She helped Katherine load all her computers into her rental car. "Where next?"

"I have to go to Washington for hearings, and no one knows how long those will take. I'd far rather be out in the field working than talking about it. Maybe I'll take some time off when I get back to Texas."

"Good idea." Alex hugged her, hoping that if the arson specialist were ever again to come to town it would be for a different reason.

After the major left, Alex looked over at the fire station and noticed that the trucks were still out. Which meant Hank was still at the site, probably waiting for everything to cool down so they could retrieve Andy's body or what was left of it.

She remembered something Andy had said one night as he manned the emergency calls. He'd said, "Life without thrills and danger isn't worth living. It's oxygen in my blood. I have to have it or I'll die."

Alex wished he'd found another way to get those thrills. In the end, he probably didn't want to hurt anyone. He was just after the buzz.

She stretched, realizing it was Saturday night and all she wanted to do was go home. The air was still tonight, and she thought she could smell rain in the wind.

Climbing into her Jeep, she took the long way home, wanting to avoid the mess on Lone Oak Road. She drove slowly, watching big white clouds roll across the evening sky. The country was so beautiful, it took her breath away sometimes. The openness of it. The way you felt everything around you was untouched.

A half hour later, she was in the shower when she heard someone call her name. Grabbing a towel, she stepped out, and there was Hank standing in her doorway making no attempt not to look.

Chapter 52

MONDAY MORNING NOAH, STILL PATCHED AND bruised, came back to school.

Reagan tried to act like she hadn't missed him terribly. Everyone wanted to talk to him. They wanted to relive his accident at the rodeo and hear all about how he saved the old Truman place from fire.

Noah "Preacher" McAllen was surrounded, and he loved every minute of it. She could almost see him famous, fighting off reporters and girls. Some people are born to ride fame. Whether he liked it or not, Noah would follow in his father's footsteps. He'd be a legend one day. The only question in her mind was, would she still be his friend?

The only time all morning she thought he noticed her was once in history class when he looked over his shoulder and winked at her. Other than that, he was in a crowd, and Reagan hated crowds.

At lunch, she thought she'd have time to talk to him, but when he walked out without his usual sandwich in one hand and drink in the other, she knew he was just stopping by to say hello before joining his friends.

"Busy?" he asked, propping up one long leg on her bench.

"Not very," she answered, telling herself she didn't care one way or the other if he stayed.

"Have time to come along with me? I got a strange text message from my sister this morning. She wants me to pick up food she ordered at the grocery and drive it all the way out to her place."

"She sick?"

"I don't know. I think maybe so. No one's seen or heard from her since Saturday night. She told me to leave the bags on the porch and don't bother to knock."

"She must be really sick."

"That's what I'm afraid of. My folks took off for parts unknown yesterday. If Alex is dying, I'm all she's got."

Reagan stood. "I'll help."

Fifteen minutes later, they had picked up the

groceries and were pulling up in front of Alex's cabin. They eyed the huge black Dodge parked beside her little house.

"Good," Noah said. "Hank's here to help. He'll drag her to the doctor if she's bad off."

Noah climbed out of the pickup. "You better wait here in case she's got something contagious."

Reagan nodded. The last thing she wanted was to get sick. She'd spent all day yesterday talking Uncle Jeremiah into making some improvements around the place. He'd even said he'd paint the house. She noticed the boxes of spring flowers on the sheriff's porch and decided she'd talk her uncle into flowers as well.

Noah carried the bags of groceries to the door and walked into the cabin without bothering to knock. Two minutes later, he stormed back to the pickup and got in. Banged his head against the steering wheel several times, putting swear words together in such a mixed-up order they made no sense.

Reagan panicked. "What's wrong? Is she dying? Oh, no, she's not dead already. Oh, God."

"No," Noah looked up at her. "She's fine. So is the fire chief. But me, I'm double scarred for life. First I see my parents in bed and now I walk in on my sister and Hank Matheson. I'll probably be in therapy for years." He hit his head one more time for good measure. "I swear, I'm living in a porno movie."

Reagan laughed. "Did you give them the food?"

"Yeah, but they didn't look too interested. Both of them yelled at me, then forgot I was there by the time I reached the door. My sister makes those funny little sounds my mother does, and that is way more information than I need to know."

He started the truck and backed out to the road.

Reagan talked about everything she could think of except Alex and Hank, but Noah remained silent until he reached the parking lot. When she climbed out, he stayed in the pickup. "Tell everyone I'm too tired or that my side is hurting. I'm heading home."

Reagan thought he looked pitiful, but she couldn't tell if he was sick, tired, or hurt from banging his head. "Preacher, I won't tell anyone."

"I know, Rea. You're the one person I know that I can trust with just about any secret that comes along."

He drove off before she could respond. She felt sorry for him. They were within six months of the same age, but sometimes she swore she was a hundred years older than him. Reagan had a feeling she always would be.

That night after supper, she did her homework, then tried to call Noah on her cell. There was no answer. She thought of calling Alex and telling her to check up on him—after all, she was his sister—but Reagan figured Noah would get mad if she did anything like that. He'd probably gone home and gone to bed in a quiet house.

Uncle Jeremiah came in from working on the tractor they'd used to plow up his grassland before the fires. He claimed Noah must have poured dirt into the engine.

He stopped in the kitchen for a drink of water and watched as she picked up her books. "You ever consider all McAllens could be nuts?"

Reagan was tired of him complaining to her about Noah. "Nope. It never crossed my mind." She thought of adding that she knew so few men who seemed sane that it was hard to gauge normal.

"Well, you should think about it some, since you got one hanging around here all the time."

Reagan was tired. She'd spent all morning worrying about Noah not speaking to her and all afternoon thinking about how he trusted her with his secrets. Worrying about him could turn into a full-time job if she didn't watch it. "All right, Uncle, I'll consider whether all McAllens are nuts tomorrow."

He frowned. "Might want to do it sooner than that. There's one tied up out in the drive."

"What?" The old man was making no sense.

"When I came in from the shed, he was sitting in the bed of his pickup. He asked me to tie him up tight, and since I owed him a favor, I did."

"Thanks," she said as her uncle poured out the rest of his water and put the glass back in the cabinet, a practice Reagan hated. "I'll go see what he wants."

She walked out the back door. It took a minute for her eyes to adjust to the darkness, and then she moved to Noah's truck and leaned over to look in the bed. "You want to tell me what you think you're doing?"

He tugged on the ropes. "The old man did a great job of tying me up."

"Preacher, tell me."

He stared up at the full moon and said, "I think I got us figured out."

"There *is* no *us*."

"I know, and I think I know why. You keep thinking I'm going to turn into a werewolf or something and attack you. Every time I get within a foot of you, you jump. Well, I'm tied up, I can't hurt you, and I'm staying here all night to prove I won't change."

"Look"—Reagan climbed up and sat on the side—"maybe I just don't like being touched. Not by anyone."

"You didn't seem to mind it after the fire when Alex hugged you, and Jeremiah, and even Hank. It was only when *I* tried that you stepped away. Rea, do you have any idea how that makes me feel?"

"Why don't you go hug on one of the cheerleaders? They're all rounded and soft and I don't think they'd mind a bit."

Noah pulled against his ropes. "I don't want to go hug on anyone, Rea. I just don't want you to be afraid of me. What do I have to do to convince you that I'm never going to hurt you?"

She smiled. "You know, Preacher, I think you're doing it right now. You mind if I hang around and make sure no werewolf shows up?"

He didn't move. She slipped into the bed of the truck and stretched out a few inches from him. Not touching, but closer than she usually got to him.

"This blanket smells like a horse," she complained.

"That's who I borrowed it from. Put your head on my shoulder and I'll be your pillow."

She hesitated, than rolled closer and lowered her head against his shoulder. "Doesn't smell much better," she whispered.

He ignored her comment.

They lay watching the stars for a while before he whispered, "Any chance you'd kiss me?"

"No," she answered. "But, I might snuggle a little. It's getting cold and I guess if you're tied, you'll be safe enough."

"I hadn't noticed the cold," he answered as she moved against him. After a while, he added, "You know, Rea, we're almost hugging."

She didn't answer.

"Rea?" He pushed at her head with his jaw.

She shifted, moving closer and turning her face up.

"Rea? Are you asleep?"

When she didn't move, he leaned over and

kissed her lightly on the mouth. Then he tugged one hand free of the rope and pulled his jacket over them both.

He put his hand back inside the loop and turned his face toward hers. "You know, I lied, I do want something. I want you next to me." He kissed the top of her head. "I wish I could tell you how much I love your hair. I think it's really something."

She didn't move as she felt his breathing slow, and then she spread her hand out lightly over his chest and felt his heart. He was proving he could be trusted, and in a few years she'd tell him how much that meant to her.

Chapter 53

RAIN

REAGAN WAS ALMOST ASLEEP WHEN A PLOP OF water hit her arm. Then another and another. All falling from hundreds of feet to land and splattering into tiny beads.

At first, she tried to ignore the drops, but Noah jerked awake beside her.

"Untie me, Rea, it's raining." He kicked at his bindings.

She laughed and shouted above the thunder. "What do you care if you get wet? You won't shrink."

"I might. Haven't seen rain in so long, I don't know what will happen." He lay flat as she untied his arms. "We might both shrink. I'd end up your size and you'd be about leprechaun height."

Scrambling, she pulled the ropes free, and they jumped from the truck, laughing. The downpour hit just as they reached the house. Sheets of rain blocked out everything beyond the porch.

He wrapped his arm around her shoulders and they watched the heavens open as they breathed in the fresh smell of a spring rain.

When it slowed, he tugged her a bit closer and lowered until their noses almost touched. "You okay with this?"

She was shaking, but she nodded and he closed the distance between them with a light kiss. He let her go and stared down at her. "Still okay?"

"Yes." His kiss hadn't brought back the night-mares she thought it would.

"Friends?"

"Friends," she answered.

He jumped off the porch and ran for his truck. "See you tomorrow, Truman."

"See you tomorrow, McAllen."

A FEW MILES DOWN THE ROAD, HANK LIFTED Alex from the bed and walked out of the cabin and into the rain.

She came awake squealing, then laughing when she realized they were standing nude in a downpour.

"Want to dance?" he asked.

"In the rain?" She laughed.

"No, not just the rain, forever." He offered his hand as if they were on the dance floor at Buffalo's.

She accepted his hand and his proposal and they danced.

HOURS EAST OF HARMONY, THE RAIN POUNDED down on the roof of Quartz Mountain Lodge beside a lake in southwest Oklahoma. The bar was empty except for one man who'd been there for a long while, holding a glass of wine he hadn't tasted.

Lightning flashed now and then across the lake, but Tyler Wright didn't turn and watch nature's show. He was busy tonight waiting.

In his imagination, he pictured Major Katherine Cummings walking up to his table and asking, "Is this seat taken?"

He'd move his wine aside and stand. "No," he'd say. "I was saving it in case you came." Then he'd stare into her hazel eyes and offer his hand just as he'd done the first rainy night they'd met. "I'm Tyler Wright. I'm a funeral director in a small town called Harmony. I'd be very happy if you could join me."

He imagined her responding, "I'm Katherine Cummings, but you can call me Kate."

"Kate," he'd say, as if the word were a cherished gift. "Please, Kate, call me Ty, if you like."

He'd pull out her chair and she'd smile, teasing him. "Thank you, Sir Knight."

He'd act surprised. "I thought I'd scared you off forever that day after seeing me all muddy and bloody."

He couldn't think what would happen next. Maybe he'd kiss her? Maybe he'd suggest they step into the restaurant and have dinner. Then maybe they would walk along the covered paths outside and watch the rain sparkle across the water . . .

The waitress passed by his table again. She no longer asked if he wanted to order dinner. She just looked at him as if she felt sorry for him. She didn't know how lucky he was.

He was waiting for someone. He was waiting for Kate.

The storm grew louder and the only other guest in the bar called it a night.

When the manager circled by to tell him they were closing, Tyler stood, leaving his wine untouched. He hardly noticed the rain as he walked across the parking lot to his Cadillac.

The first Monday of next month he'd be back, and he'd wait again.

Chapter 54

REAGAN TRUMAN CLICKED ON HER FLASH-light and walked out of her bedroom. The storm had knocked the electricity out again. She giggled. This place was spooky when there were no lights. Hell, she thought, it was spooky even in broad daylight. At least the rain was washing away the burned smells.

The faces of dead Trumans in the pictures along the walls were watchful as she moved downstairs.

Reagan flashed her light on each as she passed. The beam of the flashlight caught on something peeping out just behind one of the frames. She stopped and tugged a large yellowed envelope free and continued on down the hallway to the kitchen.

Uncle Jeremiah was already there, making coffee before he headed out to watch the dawn. He'd had to light a fire in an old potbellied stove that had probably sat in the corner since the house was built.

"It's raining," Reagan announced. "We can't go outside."

"I noticed," he said.

She grabbed a warm Coke and crawled into her chair. "Whose turn is it to make breakfast? I can't even remember."

"Then it's yours," he answered and sat across from her.

She shoved the envelope toward him. "I found this."

He turned his flashlight toward it but didn't reach for the envelope.

Reagan noticed the calendar on the wall. Ugly black Xs crossed out each day of the month that had passed. "You're marking off the days until I leave, aren't you?" It was a statement, not a question.

"Everybody leaves. I reckon you will, too."

She'd had enough. She stood, collected the cereal bowls, milk, and two boxes of cereal, then returned to the table. Without looking at him, she set breakfast down and reached for the calendar.

He didn't say a word as she rolled it up and tossed it on the fire inside the old stove. "I'm not leaving."

He filled his bowl and said without emotion, "Then I guess I'll quit counting."

She considered kissing his cheek and telling him she loved him, but he didn't need to hear the words any more than she needed to say them. They both knew. She was finally home and she wasn't going anywhere.

Halfway through her breakfast, she asked, "What's in the envelope?"

Jeremiah flipped it over. "My mom used to collect bonds. Put them behind every picture in the house during the war."

"You never cashed them in?"

He frowned. "Figured I would if I ever needed them. I even cashed one or two in a few years ago, but didn't see much fun in it."

"What did you use the money for?" she asked. Knowing him, the cash was stuffed somewhere.

"Built the shop."

She thought about it through the rest of the meal, then stated simply, "When it stops raining, we're going into town and putting all your collections of bonds in a safe-deposit box." If he'd built the shop for his collection with one or two bonds, no telling what a handful would be worth.

To her surprise, he didn't argue.

She waited a minute and then added, "Any questions?"

He raised an eyebrow. "How big is the box?"

THEY SPENT THE DAY CLEANING UP THE DRIVE between the house and the main road. People Reagan didn't even know came to help.

That night she was so tired, she tumbled into bed, but she couldn't stop smiling.

For a moment she thought of all the money from the bonds might buy, and then she realized she had everything she'd ever needed or wanted right here, right now.

"Home," she whispered, liking the sound of the word. She was finally home.

Center Point Publishing
600 Brooks Road ● PO Box 1
Thorndike ME 04986-0001 USA

(207) 568-3717

US & Canada:
1 800 929-9108
www.centerpointlargeprint.com